MONSTER

KEITH FERRARIO

Gabriel's Horn Press

This book is a work of fiction. The names, characters, places, and incidents are products of the writer's imagination or have been used fictitiously and are not to be construed as real. Any resemblance to persons, living or dead, actual events, locale or organizations is entirely coincidental.

Second Print Edition 2017 Gabriel's Horn Press, LLC.
Minneapolis, Minnesota
www.gabrielshornpress.com
First Print Edition 2015 Samhain Publishing, Ltd.
Edited by Don D'Auria

ISBN-13: 978-1-938990-29-8
ISBN-10: 1-938990-29-3

ACKNOWLEDGMENTS

I would like to thank Jim Thom, Heidi Wright and Louis Wright for their time and support. You guys believed this story was worth writing and you kept me going. Thank you for your comments and honest criticism. In addition, I would like to thank my editor, Don D'Auria, for giving *Monster* its first home at Samhain Publishing, and Laura Vosika for its new home at Gabriel's Horn Press.

PART ONE

CHAPTER ONE

JANUARY 23, 1991

Outside with clear skies, the temperature had barely reached thirty degrees Fahrenheit—an average high for summertime at McMurdo Station, Antarctica.

Inside his heated hangar, Adam Hayes popped the cap and checked the level of antifreeze in his DeHavilland DHC-6 Twin Otter. Special wheel attachments helped to get the plane in and out of the hangar, but for taking off and landing on the snow, large skis had replaced the wheels of the landing gear. The only other change Adam had made to the craft was to arrange the insides to carry more cargo and fewer passengers—a tradeoff he found acceptable and more profitable.

After twisting the cap back on, Adam grabbed a nearby rag and wiped his callused hands clean. He remembered how his wife teased him about the contrast between his hard, rough hands and his soft baby-blue eyes. He joked back that she would probably leave him for a young surgeon or pianist, instead of staying with a thirty-two-year-old pilot. "Not even when that gorgeous brown hair of yours turns a mousy gray," she would tell him.

Adam's wife died seven years ago. Shortly after that, he relocated his cargo business to Antarctica. He needed a clean start and the cold had a strange appeal for him at the time. As it turned out, over the past two years, the climate and his work kept his mind, body and soul strong.

He gave the plane one last spot inspection. By the engine block, Adam rubbed off a black smudge and felt a rough edge. A cracked hose clamp. Replacing the part would take less than ten minutes, and it would be far worth the time rather than taking the chance of it snapping off in mid-flight. He grabbed a replacement clamp and screwdriver from his toolbox.

While Adam was up to his shoulders in plane, a gruff voice came from behind him. "I'm looking for a Mr. Hayes," the man said.

His work being top priority, Adam didn't even bother to raise his head. "This is a restricted zone," he responded instead, tightening the new clamp before removing the old. "Please return to the office area."

"Listen, I'm looking for the pilot. I don't need back talk from a mechanic."

"Wait in the office."

"Do you know who I—"

"In the office," Adam repeated. By the lack of a response, he assumed that the man had finally listened and obeyed.

Ten minutes and a double check of his work satisfied Adam that the craft was in top shape for flight. Retreating to a back room of the hangar, he cleaned up and changed into his flight suit. There wasn't a shower, but the room had a sink with plenty of hot water and a mirror. He pushed his spare shaving kit to one side and grabbed a clean towel from a side shelf. For those times when rushed, this setup was more convenient than having to go back to his quarters to get ready. A final splash of water on his face, a quick comb through his hair, and he was ready to meet his passengers.

Going through the doors leading to the office, Adam spotted two men and a woman waiting—all wearing heavy parkas. They turned his way as he entered. The woman had plain features and her dark hair had been pulled back tight and tied off. At her side, she carried a square black camera bag. The two men were in stark contrast to each other. A younger, taller man standing at least 6′4″, easily weighing 225 towered next to an older, stockier man of fifty-plus years with thinning black hair. Where the younger man had the bearing of a bodyguard, the other was definitely a pencil pusher.

"Not you again," the stocky man said on Adam's approach. "I'm looking for the pilot—a Mister…"

"Hayes, Adam Hayes." He recognized the man's voice—the idiot bugging him back in the hangar. Adam extended his hand. "At your service."

The man did nothing to return or even acknowledge Adam's gesture. "Why didn't you say something?" he complained instead. His furled eyes moved up and down as if trying to size Adam up.

"Too busy working on the plane. There's a storm coming this way in less than four hours. You want to get to Station 7 before it hits, don't you? Of course you do," Adam said, not giving the rude man time to respond. "Then I didn't have time for jawing."

"I...well, I..." The man cleared his throat. "In that case, I'll keep the introductions short. I'm Richard Baines." The man gestured over to the woman. "This is Margaret Walker."

"Hello, ma'am," Adam said.

"Actually, it's Dr. Walker," the woman said with a smile. "But Margaret will do." She shook Adam's hand.

"Yes, doctor," Baines said, sounding irritated about the correction. "And this is Bruce Manning—Lieutenant Manning," he added, giving the doctor an inexplicable stare.

"Lieutenant?" Adam asked.

"Naturally," Baines said, "the station is partially sponsored by the military."

"Richard," Margaret said, "you requested an officer?"

"Wasn't my idea," he told her.

"I volunteered for this assignment, ma'am," Manning said. He stood relaxed, yet still at attention—he towered over the woman.

"Well, if you're all ready," Adam said, not caring who asked for this or volunteered for that.

"We're still waiting for one more," Richard said, "my personal assistant. She should be here shortly."

On the man's last word, the door opened. A fur-lined hood hid the person's appearance, but by the fit of the tight jacket, the gender was obvious.

"It's about time," Richard said. The woman pulled down her hood revealing a very attractive face surrounded by long red hair. Richard Baines' eyes widened, but quickly changed to two furled slits. "Who the devil are you?"

"I'm Carol Chambers, Mr. Baines. I've been assigned to you."

"Where the hell is Debbie?"

Shock washed over the woman. "Oh, I assumed that you had already been told."

"Told what?"

"There's been an accident. Debbie's in the hospital. I understand someone ignored a stop sign and ran her off the road into an embankment."

"Oh my," Margaret Walker said.

"It sounds far worse than it is," Carol said. "Fortunately, Debbie suffered only whiplash, but I'm afraid she can't assist you on this trip. That's where I come in—I'm her replacement."

"You any good?" Richard asked.

The woman smiled. "I'd like to think so."

Interrupting the useless banter, Adam insisted that they take off now. With that the group walked to the runway and loaded into the plane. Except for a red, one-foot-wide stripe running from nose to tail, the plane was all white. The only other markings on the body, in black stencil, were designation numbers on the tail and the words: "Snow Bound Cargo" on the fuselage, eight inches below the wings.

The engine roared to life. The propellers began to turn.

"Buckle up," Adam said.

It was a smooth takeoff and the plane climbed to flying altitude.

"Pardon me," Carol said, calling up to the pilot. "Do you think we will arrive at the research station before dark?"

"I certainly hope so. Where we're going 'dark' isn't for another five months."

"Oh," she said.

Adam smiled. People new to the continent always seemed surprised by the months-long "day." Even if they knew to expect it, experiencing it was a different matter. It took a bit to get used to—constant light, even in the nighttime hours. And the closer you got to the pole the longer the day became. At McMurdo Station the daylight lasted a constant four months—at the pole, six months. What a difference twelve degrees made in this part of the world. Though, total darkness at the South Pole only lasted about three months. The remaining weeks were tinted by ever increasing or decreasing shades of twilight, depending on the time of year.

Today the clear blue skies spread out seemingly forever and Adam loved to fly on days like this. The storm in the forecast was still some time away and would be behind him the entire flight down. Below him, the sunshine beamed back off the perfect white landscape of snow and ice. He enjoyed the ventures far south, though he couldn't deny his slight apprehension. According to his math, he had just enough fuel to get to Station 7 and back, with a thirty-minute margin for error during head winds. He didn't like cutting it that close, but the money was good. And since his small cargo service was the best in the territory, he got a lot of business.

Supplies and, in this case, people came down from New Zealand on LC-130 Hercules transport planes. Those larger aircraft could make the longer eight-hour flight to McMurdo, but they needed a long runway to land and take off, something that research stations in the barren plains of Antarctica don't have. That's where his plane came in handy. With its mounted skis, he needed only a tenth of the distance and any flat piece of land would do. Shipping supplies to regions inaccessible by the much larger LC-130 was his bread and butter.

Still, he couldn't help but wonder what prompted this special trip to fly a crew to the station on such short notice. Usually he dropped off mail and supplies, and once in a while brought a package or two back on the return trip. He hadn't had to fly a man out in the last seven months. They must be anxious to get down to that frozen wilderness if they couldn't wait ten days for his next regularly scheduled monthly run. But considering he was getting double pay for this extra trip, he didn't mind one bit.

Adam glanced back at his passengers. The lieutenant was fast asleep, meaning the man could probably sleep through anything—he had most likely been on so many flights, for him it must all be so routine. The others appeared comfortable enough, which was good, since the cabin heater had already been turned three-fourths to maximum. He saved some heat in reserve. The closer they traveled towards the South Pole, the colder it would become. The temperature could differ about forty-five degrees between McMurdo Station and the pole.

"Mr. Hayes," Carol said. "I'm afraid air travel doesn't quite agree with me. Will we be landing soon?"

"Another forty-five minutes, easy," Adam said. Seeing that the lady did have a pale tint to her cheeks, he reached under his seat, pulled out a small white bag, and handed it to her.

"What's that for?" Richard asked.

"For just-in-case," Adam replied, not being fond of cleaning frozen vomit off the floor of his plane.

The snow plane proceeded on its flight for another forty minutes. No one spoke, which was fine with Adam. He wanted to enjoy the view.

"There it is," Carol said, a definite sound of relief permeating her voice.

"That's our stop sure enough," Adam replied, "but it will still be a little while. It's easy to spot the compound. It's the only thing on this chunk of ice. Still another five minutes or so." He saw the woman squeeze the vomit bag with a tight grip. She hadn't had to use it yet. Adam wasn't sure if that was a good sign or not. It had been his experience that the last five minutes of a flight were the hardest with troubled passengers—being so close to the end of the trip.

The plane started its approach on the straight flat path he always used. Adam had made many trips to the station within the last year, and the runway didn't ever change much. The plane touched down on the snow and at the end turned with a graceful glide.

He taxied the plane as close as he could to the largest building. Next to the structure stood a tall metal tower with a cluster of antennas grafted to its top. Snowdrifts had formed between the tower and the building but there were paths cut through the high mounds.

Richard Baines nudged Lieutenant Manning out of his sleep. "We're here," he told the slumbering man. The big man's eyes shot open. He was set to go.

The plane slowly slid to a stop by a plowed walkway in front of the building. But between the high banks rested about three inches of blown snow. Obviously, not enough to plow, or enough to be a real annoyance.

"No footprints," Bruce commented.

"Lieutenant?" Carol said.

"In the snow—no footprints."

"Is that important?" she asked.

"It means no one has left the compound in several days."

"Don't be paranoid," Richard Baines told the soldier. "That only means they hadn't had a chance to plow yet."

"The lieutenant's right," Adam said. "That snow is a few days old. Even if they didn't bother to plow, there should be some footprints—some sign of movement."

"What are you trying to say?" Carol asked.

"I don't know," Adam told her. "What *am* I trying to say, Mr. Baines?"

"I wouldn't know," Richard replied.

"Tell them," Margaret Walker said bluntly. That was the first time the woman spoke the entire plane trip—what a way to start.

"You forget who's in charge here, Doctor."

"Tell them—they have the right to know."

"Know what?" Carol asked. Her face went blank and her voice trembled slightly.

"We've lost contact with the station," Richard said. "They're supposed to check in twice a day via radio."

"And how long has it been?" Adam asked.

"Seven days," Richard answered.

"You didn't send a reconnaissance team?" Adam asked.

"We're it," Lieutenant Manning told him. He slapped the ammunition clip into his automatic pistol.

"Is that really necessary?" Margaret asked, staring at the loaded gun.

Manning said nothing, but his piercing eyes told her he certainly thought so.

"Maybe they just lost their radio," Carol said. "Electronics are always breaking down."

"Not likely," Manning told her. "Their radio man is top notch. He could fix it with chicken wire if he had to."

"Really," Margaret said sarcastically.

"Ever since we were kids." Manning smiled. "The radio man's name is Eric Manning—my brother. And like I said, he's the best."

"I'm happy for you both," Margaret said. "Can we get going?"

"Bundle up people," Adam said, wrapping his wool muffler tight around his neck, then zipping his parka up to his chin, "it's plenty cold out there." Behind him, he could hear the chorus of zippers as the others followed his lead. "Make sure to wear your sun goggles—you don't want to get a case of snow blindness."

"Blindness?" Carol said.

"Mr. Hayes is exaggerating," Margaret said. "Our exposure won't nearly be long enough."

"Maybe," Adam told the doctor, "but at this altitude, the sunlight is very intense. With all the reflected light coming from the snow it's a whole lot safer not to go outside without some eye protection—there's always risk of snow blindness. And here there are some things you want to become habit. Wearing goggles is one of them. I have a spare pair if anyone forgot theirs." No one spoke up. "Okay people, let's go."

Opening the door to the plane, Adam was slapped by a blast of cold air —brisk winds were already moving into the region. He stepped out and waited for the others. The women came first. He took Carol by the arm and helped her down. He tried to do the same for the doctor, but she waved him off. Richard Baines came out next, followed by Bruce Manning.

His coat may have hid the fact that he was carrying a gun, but the man's hard expression told Adam that the soldier was ready, willing and able to use it. Adam wasn't sure if he should stay close to the lieutenant or far away.

"Is it always this cold, Mr. Hayes?" Carol asked.

"Wind's picking up," he said. He took off his muffler and wrapped it around the woman's neck and chin. "It's better if you try not to talk. Save your energy until we get inside." He motioned to the others. "That goes for the rest of you."

They all nodded.

Luckily, the snow wasn't too heavy. Even three inches of a heavy coating would make the walking tough going—the hundred yards would have felt like a mile. This snow was light fluff resting on the packed crust below.

Hayes marched his passengers towards the main building, kicking up tracks and sending white puffs of powder into the wind, which drove it up several more feet. On their way, they passed two smaller huts. Snowdrifts had formed along the wall of the closest hut and rose up to the windowsill. No one noticed the eyes staring at them through the frosted glass while they passed the arched metal structure.

Adam had no notion of what the other huts were for, so he figured bringing the group to the main building would be his best bet. Since there were no objections, he figured he must be on the right track. With the exception of the one night he had been snowed in, he had never spent a lot of time at the station on his monthly runs—at least no more than it took to drop off the mail and a few supplies, not to mention the time it took to down a beer or two along with a plate of grub.

The group approached the prefab structure and the first thing they saw was a sign: UNITED STATES RESEARCH INSTITUTE, STATION 7. Surrounded by a thousand miles of nothing but snow and ice, Adam always thought it amusing that they bothered to designate it "Station 7." Like someone might confuse this place with another.

He didn't understand a lot of the work done here, but he liked the group of thirteen: nine men and four women, most of them being "Beakers" (Antarctic slang for Scientist)—and they always seemed glad to see him too. But then again, you don't want to piss off the guy who, except for a radio, was your only connection with the outside world.

Once, over a beer, John Blackwood, a Ph.D. in some such thing, tried to explain his work in ice core research. How they would drill out three-inch-diameter samples from the ice sheet and examine the different layers. The man's voice actually bubbled with excitement when he began saying something about dating the fragments by analyzing the concentration of oxygen atoms in the ice. Adam nodded his head a lot, trying to be polite, but he didn't understand much of what the man said, and the part he did understand, he thought rather dull. But John had always struck Adam to be a good guy, so he did his best not to show any lack of interest.

John's wasn't the only research done at Station 7. Susan Dawson's work dealt with the hole forming in the ozone layer, and Mathew Perlman studied the weather and different atmospheric conditions. These scientists really believed that they could help the world, but from this giant piece of ice, Adam couldn't imagine how. Now, as Richard Baines had revealed, the crew hadn't reported in for the past week. Adam would agree that it was pretty strange. The guys here loved their routine, maybe because it's all they really had to keep themselves from going stir-crazy.

Reaching the entrance to the building, Adam pulled on the handle, but the door didn't give. "Terrific. You got a key?"

"Shouldn't need one," Richard said. "The first section inside is designated a warm room." White vapors followed the man's words from under his parka hood. "With the changing weather and frigid temps, locks might freeze up, leaving some poor unfortunate stranded outside. Couldn't take a chance on the scientists freezing to death. Besides, there's nothing inside of any value."

"You're all heart," Margaret said.

Bruce Manning pulled down his hood. "It must be frozen shut," he said. "Should be easy enough to deal with." The lieutenant walked to the front of the group. "Stand back."

Adam followed the man's instructions—no point in arguing. He couldn't get them in any quicker and he was curious to what the soldier had in mind.

Manning eyeballed the distance, lifted his big boot and with the bottom of his foot kicked the door.

"Wasted effort," Richard said. "This exit was designated an emergency exit. That door opens out, you're kicking against a steel frame."

"He's right," Adam said. "It's the same way at McMurdo. Only non-emergency doors open inward. That's what you get when you follow 'the Code'. I've always thought it was a stupid rule."

Manning ignored the men and kicked once more. Then he signaled to

Adam to help him grip the handle. Both the pilot and soldier heaved. Nothing.

"Again," Manning said.

Both men yanked a second time. It worked. The door burst open. Adam lost his balance when the door popped, but Manning managed to grab his jacket sleeve before he fell backwards.

"Impressive," Margaret said, glancing over to Richard. Even with his face partially covered, it was clear that the man didn't appreciate the woman's sharp tone. Adam figured they must have worked together for quite a while for such a simple statement to piss him off.

"Not really," Manning said, replying to Margaret's praise. "When these types of doors aren't opened regularly, condensation forms and freezes along the metal frame. It's simply a matter of cracking the ice."

"Enough talk," Richard said, "let's get inside."

They all stood for a moment peering into the blackness.

"Go ahead," Margaret taunted Richard.

"Please, someone go in," Carol said. The woman was bouncing on her heels trying to stay warm.

Adam stepped up to the entryway. He uttered something, but no one could make out his words. Then without another second's pause, he disappeared into the darkness.

"Wait!" Richard said. "The power might be off."

But Adam either didn't hear his words or he chose to ignore them. Moments later, the lights snapped on. Then Adam stuck his head outside. "Come on in. It's a little warmer in here."

Carol pushed past Margaret, practically sprinting through the door. Wasting very little time, Margaret and Richard followed the impatient woman, with Lieutenant Manning taking up the rear. The interior couldn't be described as balmy, but with no wind and the small amount of heat coming from the ceiling vent, the temperature was comfortable enough for the group to pull down their hoods.

Adam waved his hand high up by the heating vent. "Must be clogged with something," he said. "We should be getting more heat."

"I'll take whatever it will give," Carol said, standing directly under the vent. She pulled off one glove and raised her bare hand to the warmth.

"You took a big chance," Richard told Adam. "The power might have been off. And if there is trouble here, you could have walked right into it."

"Some men are just braver than others," Margaret said.

Adam smiled. "I can't take the mantle of bravery. When we walked up,

I could hear the generator was still running. It's around back. And I've been here enough to know where the light switch is located."

"So much for knighthood," Richard said.

"He still took action, unlike somebody who will remain nameless —Richard."

"You know I hate when you do that."

"What's with you two?" Adam said, having enough of their bickering. "You fight like you're married."

"Not since the divorce," Margaret snapped.

"It wasn't my choice to bring you down here," Richard said. "I'm sorry you were pulled away from your precious research. If it had been up to me..." The man simply shook his head.

"For the sake of our wits and your own," Adam said, "you two are going to have to try to get along." He pulled off his gloves and shoved them into the pockets of his parka.

Manning had made his way to the interior door. Something there definitely caught his eye. "This damage is new," he said.

"What damage?" Adam asked. He and the others darted over to the soldier.

"How'd this happen?" Richard said, astounded by the deep cut marks in the metal door.

"Someone wanted in pretty bad," Manning said, gently touching the gashes, being careful not to cut his fingers on the sharp edges.

"In this cold," Carol said, "who could blame them."

Without saying another word, Richard Baines shifted his attention to the number pad next to the door. He pressed out six digits. A small red light blinked on and off. He mumbled something and reentered the numeric sequence. Again, a red light came on then went off. "We have a small problem," he said. "I think the access code has been changed."

"Maybe the panel got damaged when whoever it was tried to break in," Carol said.

"No," Richard replied, shaking his head, trying the access code once more. The red blinking light returned. "It's been changed."

Manning examined the small panel. "If I could get this faceplate off, I may be able to jump the wires. I don't suppose anyone has a screwdriver."

"In my toolbox on the plane," Adam said. He started for the door.

Manning stopped him. "I'll get it," he said, turning a quick glimpse towards the bickering couple. "I could use the fresh air."

"Thanks a lot," Adam commented, wanting his own break from the pair.

"I'm trained in survival tactics," the man joked, hurrying out the door. A cold breeze shot in. Carol pulled her coat tight and stepped back several feet, taking shelter behind some crates.

"I was thinking," Margaret Walker said, examining the gashes in the metal door. "Whoever did this—where is he?"

"Or her?" Richard interrupted. "Never underestimate the female of the species."

Margaret just rolled her eyes and continued as if her ex-husband had said nothing. "The lieutenant pointed it out when we first landed—there were no tracks outside."

"That doesn't mean anything," Richard said. "We have no idea how old this damage is—could be days—a week maybe. Our John Doe could have tried to bash the door down, failed, then left. The slightest breeze would be enough to wipe out his tracks."

"Then that brings up another point," she countered. "If you're right, where did he go?"

"One of the other buildings," Richard said, stating it as obvious.

"We are making a rash assumption," Margaret said. "We are thinking that there was only one person trying to break down the door. Could have been two, maybe even three. Who can say?"

"How dreadful," Carol said. "To freeze to death."

"How do you figure that?" Richard asked, giving the woman a hard stare. "There's absolutely not one shred of evidence anyone froze here."

"But if they were still alive," she said, "wouldn't they have come out when we landed? Come out to ask for help?"

"Unless…" Margaret began.

"Unless, they don't want to be found," Richard finished.

"We should know more when Manning returns and he gets that door open," Adam told the group, but he could tell his words did nothing to ease the rising tension.

"Where *is* the lieutenant?" Carol said. "He's been gone quite a while now."

Adam tried to reassure the woman with a smile. "Don't worry. It'll take him a little time to walk to the plane, find the toolbox and walk back."

"Yeah," Richard said, "the man's tough—he can take it."

Margaret opened her mouth to say something, but at the last moment held her tongue.

"Let's all relax until he gets back," Adam said.

"I'm for that," Carol confessed, and dragged a small wooden crate away from the wall. She sat and sighed with relief. The others followed her lead.

Being a man used to waiting the weather out, Adam plopped himself down, and leaned back against the nearest crate. This wasn't a cozy campfire—he didn't feel the need to move any closer to these people. They were an odd lot. A doctor, a soldier, he could understand, but those other two—especially this Richard fellow. He had to ask. "What's your story, Baines? You don't look the explorer type."

"No, Richard is a great believer in doing things himself," Margaret said, clutching herself to stay warm. "He couldn't possibly trust this excursion to anyone else."

From his own crate, Richard said, "And why should I? If you want something done right... Besides, I placed several of the personnel on this station myself and I've studied the files of all the rest. I feel it's my responsibility."

"Still," Adam said, "you could've sent someone."

"You sound like my predecessor—a desk jockey if ever there was one. When I became director of this little project I intended to be hands-on all the way."

"Even if it meant coming all the way down to Antarctica?" Adam asked.

With a very straight and serious face, the man answered, "Obviously."

"I certainly hope we can get inside soon," Carol said.

"It shouldn't be too much longer," Adam told her, folding his arms in front of his chest as if getting ready to take a nap.

"And I think once we do," Richard said, "we should initiate a room by room search. Whoever was trying to get in was trying for a reason."

Carol shivered. "Maybe they just wanted out of the cold."

"Where are the others?" Margaret said. With that, the group turned towards her. "The other scientists," she continued. "Someone had to change the access code, and clearly from inside the complex. You would think they would come out by now."

"Not if they think there's a mad man at the door wielding an ax," Richard said.

"They must have heard the plane land. Wouldn't you think?"

Adam said nothing. The whole situation had a real bad feel to it.

"He doesn't have the ax with him anymore," Carol said softly.

"And how would you possibly know that?" Richard asked.

She pointed to a far corner. Next to a red gas can was a previously unnoticed bundle of rags. In the middle of the heap, partially concealed by the tattered cloth, was a heavy blade. Adam and Richard stood up and cautiously approached the pile. Margaret and Carol followed close behind.

"Do you think that's what was used on the door?" Carol asked, her shoulder brushing up against Adam's arm.

"It's a good bet," Richard said.

"More than good, I would say," Adam told them. "The blade...it's all marred up." Adam gingerly pushed back the rags to expose more of the cutting edge. "That type of damage can only come from metal striking metal." Adam took the ax by its neck, being careful not to catch his hand on the jagged head. He pulled the entire ax from the pile.

Suddenly, Carol screamed!

Richard and Margaret gasped.

Adam dropped the ax.

On the end of the wooden handle, obviously in its final grip, was a hand. Even when the ax hit the floor, the detached extremity refused to release its hold.

Carol gave out another short whine, clenching her fist in front of her mouth.

The other three knelt down to examine the hand, when the outer door burst open. Manning stormed in—toolbox in one hand—pistol at the ready in the other. "Hold it right there," he shouted. He hadn't wasted any time bothering to re-zip his parka after retrieving his gun. As a result, his front was draped with freshly blown snow. His eyes moved from face to face to face. "I thought I heard someone scream."

"You did," Carol moused out, staring at the barrel of the gun.

"Put that thing away," Richard ordered. "We have other problems."

"I'm afraid we found something quite gruesome," Margaret told the soldier.

Manning returned his gun to its holster, set the toolbox down, and joined the others, except for Carol, around the ax and hand. If he was surprised or shocked, he didn't show it. "Any clue who our friend here is?"

"Not a one," Adam said.

"We could take his...its fingerprints," Richard said.

"You always had a real sick sense of humor, Richard," Margaret sneered.

"Who's joking?" he replied. "All the scientists had their fingerprints taken before they were allowed to start work. It was all part of their background checks."

"You are serious," Margaret said. "I hope you don't expect me to…I'm not touching it."

"Just wrap it in those rags," Richard told her.

"These aren't rags," Adam said, pulling up a shirt—all its buttons were still threaded in the matching holes. "They're someone's clothes." Tucked up and inside the shirt Adam found a cotton T-shirt—both articles had been resting on top of a pair of pants. Stranger still, like the T-shirt, a pair of white-cotton long underwear were inside the pants with both legs running completely down the empty length.

"This is all very odd," Margaret said.

"It is," Manning acknowledged, "but it may also be useful. Check for a wallet, or some other ID."

"You just can't go through someone's things," Carol said, returning to the group.

"Watch me," Richard said. The man went quickly and deliberately through each pocket. "Nothing," he said.

"It was worth a try, I suppose," Adam said, thinking Richard didn't need a lot of coaxing to go through what could be a dead man's clothing.

"Look at the hand," Manning said.

"I'd rather not," Carol told him, turning away.

Manning ignored the woman. "You notice anything funny about the wound?"

"I don't see," Richard said, but was interrupted by his ex-wife.

"Very good, Lieutenant!" Margaret said, rotating the ax handle to get a better view of the hand.

"You two want to share," Richard said, "and illuminate us all?"

"Go ahead," Margaret told Manning, "you saw it first."

"Can we stop with the games?" Richard snapped. "I don't give a nickel who saw what first—just tell us."

"I'm no expert, mind you…" Manning started. By the frustration on Richard's round face, one would think Manning was trying to purposely aggravate the man. Adam couldn't hold back his smirk. "…but most detachment injuries are either ragged or smooth cut."

"Great," Richard said, "the man has a fetish for body wounds."

"Richard, don't be morbid," Margaret said, "and let him speak."

"He's not making any sense. Ragged cuts—smooth cuts—what's the difference?"

"I've seen enough injuries to *know* the difference," Manning explained.

"Fine, fine, can you get to the point?"

"Open your eyes, will you," Margaret told Richard.

"It's a hand—so what."

"This wound's different," Manning said. "The injured flesh is tapered. It almost appears melted."

"God," Richard said, "can you get serious? It's not made of wax, even I can tell the difference."

"It's horrible," Carol said from her corner. The others, again, ignored her useless remark.

"What would cause something like that?" Adam questioned, first of Manning, then of Dr. Walker.

"Acid," Manning said.

"I knew letting the soldier boy talk would be a waste of time," Richard scoffed.

Adam wanted to get out from between the two, figuring Manning was ready to deck the guy—he sure would have. He was surprised when the lieutenant let the dig slide.

"He's right," Margaret said, which removed the smirk from Richard Baines' lips. Apparently, no matter what he felt for the woman personally, he did respect her opinion.

Seconds later though, Richard shook his head. "I still don't buy it. And the condition of the clothes don't back you up either—especially the shirt." The limb was a right hand, so Richard picked up the right sleeve and held out the cuff. "If it was acid, why aren't there any burns on the sleeve?"

There were a few moments of silence.

"I don't know," Margaret finally said.

"That's right, you don't."

"Maybe somebody put that...that thing there," Carol said.

"Sure, that's it," Richard snapped. "Some sicko burns a guy's hand off with acid—carries it out here—wraps the fingers around the ax handle—holds it in place until rigor mortis sets in—then finally hides the whole mess in a bundle of old clothes—a complete set of clothes at that—right down to the underwear. Not bloody likely."

"Not a complete set," Adam observed, clearing away the pant legs. "Where are the shoes?"

"What?" Margaret said.

"The shoes. As Mr. Baines so elegantly pointed out—'down to the underwear'. But the shoes and socks are missing."

"This is getting us nowhere," Richard said.

"I'm afraid I have to agree," Margaret told the others. "I think we'll only find answers inside the complex."

"I'll get to work on the door," Manning said, picking up the toolbox before proceeding on to the access panel.

"What do we do about our friend?" Adam asked.

"Nothing. Leave it. It certainly isn't going anyplace."

"The proper thing would be to cover it," Margaret told her ex-husband.

"When did you get so squeamish?" he asked.

"It has nothing to do with being squeamish. It's a matter of respect for the dead."

"Who said the guy's dead?"

Margaret hated to admit it, but again she had to agree with Richard. It was possible that the owner of the hand was still alive, just terribly injured. She really hated him sometimes. "Please, cover it," she said.

"Have it your way." Richard took the shirt and spread it across the hand. "We may have to retrieve it before we leave."

"Heavens, why?" Carol asked.

"Evidence," he said to the woman. "If there is something funny going on here, it may be the only proof we have. We'll start the search after Manning gets that bloody door open. I'd like to be out of here as soon as possible."

"That would be tomorrow," Manning said, pulling out a red wire. "I forgot to mention, it's blowing pretty hard out there."

Adam remembered that the soldier had returned coated with snow, but at the time, he was too caught up with the hand to pay it any mind. He scrambled to the door leading outside. Opening it, he saw Manning was right. This storm wasn't supposed to get here for several more hours. So much for weather forecasts, he thought.

"A little snow won't keep us here," Richard said. "Tell him, Hayes."

"I wish I could, but I can't. The lieutenant is right. Even if I could take off, we wouldn't get very far. We're here until it clears up."

"For the night?" Carol whined.

The term night really didn't apply, but Adam didn't bother to correct the woman. "At least," he said instead, studying the blowing snow. "But by the way it's whipping up out there, it might not let up 'til sometime early tomorrow."

"Should we radio someone?" Margaret asked. "Let them know we won't be coming back as scheduled."

Adam pondered the heavy white blanket blowing past the door. "I wouldn't want to try going back to the plane in this stuff. Too easy to get lost." He closed the door.

"Lost?" Richard complained. "It's not that far to the plane."

"It would be stupid to try," Manning said. "A person could get turned around out there—be three feet from a building and never even know it."

Before Richard could spew another word, Margaret spoke up. "Use your head, Richard. If he gets killed, we will be stuck out here for more than just a night. Maybe you would like to try instead?" she added, gesturing towards the door.

Richard said nothing.

"Too bad," Margaret said, "I'm sure we could all use the peace and quiet."

Adam wasn't too sure he liked the woman referring to his early demise in such a casual manner, but he understood her point. She was scared. She did well to hide her fear, but he could still spot it in her eyes. "Don't be too concerned. My crew back at the strip knows I wouldn't try to fly in these conditions. They'll assume we'd be staying here."

"I hate to bring this up," Carol said, "but is anyone else hungry?"

"How could you bring up food at a time like this," Richard said, "especially after…?" He stared back to the outstretched shirt.

"It's actually not a bad plan to get some food in our bellies," Adam said. "It's important to keep our strength up. It takes a lot of energy to maneuver around out there…and we might have to dig the plane out if this storm gets any worse."

A hush washed over the group as they contemplated their current predicament—a snowstorm behind them, a locked door in front. "I could use a bite," Margaret was the first to admit.

"I'm sure we'll find something in the galley," Adam said with a smile.

"If we ever get inside," Richard mocked, watching the soldier still pulling wire.

At that moment, Manning touched two exposed ends together, which produced a small spark. The metal door slid open, but not more than three inches.

"That's not going to cut it," Richard said.

Manning said nothing and tried again, but this time the door closed back tight.

"That's worse."

"Sorry," Manning said, "wrong wire. That lurch was set off by a short. I've found the right one." With another touch, the door slid along its track and opened wide.

"Good job," Richard said, patting the man on the back while passing him to enter the complex.

"You might not want to rush in so fast," Manning warned Richard. "We don't know..." His words fell on deaf ears. Shaking his head in disbelief, Manning added, "We better keep up with him."

After the others had passed through the open doorway, Carol snuck back to the disembodied hand and drew back the cloth. She had only seconds to take it all in. Then returning the shirt to its original position, she joined the rest of the group in the long hallway.

CHAPTER TWO

"Will you hold up?" Lieutenant Manning called out to Richard Baines, following the stocky man into the complex before he could get too far ahead.

"Don't sweat it, soldier boy. I have no intention of going off by myself."

"I think it's a good idea," Adam said, "if we all stay together until we learn a little more about what we're dealing with here."

"Speaking of sticking together," Margaret said, "where is that assistant of yours, Richard?"

"Temporary assistant and I don't have the slightest clue."

"I'm right here," Carol said, coming through the door. "I had to stop a moment to catch my breath. This whole thing is so unnerving."

In front of the group stretched a long, slightly curved hallway. The white tiles along the floor had many black scuffmarks from heavy foot traffic. On the ceiling there were double sets of fluorescent lights spaced every four feet. The long line of white tubes shined down farther than they could see.

"I'd hate to be the one paying the electric bill for this place," Margaret said, a slight echo followed her voice.

"Hello-o-o," Richard shouted. "Can anybody hear me?"

Everyone stood perfectly still listening for any trace of a response—any indication of life. Even after a full minute, they heard nothing.

"This can't be right," Richard said. "There has to be someone here."

"It's spooky, if you ask me," Carol volunteered. She crossed her arms in front of her body, grabbing hold of her own elbows.

"Let's not lose our heads people," Adam said. "This is a good sized structure."

"He's right," Manning told the group. "You could shout up a storm and not be heard on the other end even if all the doors between here and there were open. And some of the compartments are airtight and soundproof. Inside one of those rooms, you're as quiet as the dead to the outside world."

"Could you not use that term: 'dead'," Carol said.

"Sorry, I only meant..."

"We know what you meant," Richard said, interrupting the man's apology. "And I'm sure Miss...Miss..."

"Chambers," Carol said, glancing down to the floor.

"...I'm sure Miss Chambers appreciates your sensitivities, but we can't get all caught up on each word we say."

"That's Richard Baines," Margaret said, "Mr. Politically Correct."

Richard glared at his ex-wife. "Can we get on with it?" he said.

"What do you suggest?" Manning asked.

"I thought you being a soldier, it would be quite obvious. A search, Lieutenant, a search of this facility. Maybe we can find someone or something that will shed a little more light on the situation."

"I'd say we already found something," Adam said, "or by a strange point of view, someone back in the entryway—and we've already been told enough."

"And what would that be?" Richard asked with a snip.

"Someone's dead."

There was a heavy stillness. No one would admit it earlier, but now it was appearing more and more to be the truth.

Then Richard said, "Let's all stick together." He looked over to Bruce, then to Margaret, then to Carol and back to Adam. "It makes no sense putting this off any longer." He marched up to the first door.

"That's just a storage closet," Adam told him.

Richard ignored the man and pulled the door open anyway. He found three shovels and a large metal garbage can containing a sand and salt mixture with a red plastic scoop. On the layered shelves, Richard found two spare flashlights, a pair of heavy gloves and a pair of jumper cables.

"Like I said, a storage closet."

"I heard you. But you can never be too careful. We have to search everywhere. No matter how stupid it may seem."

Adam let it go without another word. The man had a point, but it was his attitude Adam didn't like.

The group came up to a second door.

"What's this?" Richard said. After a moment, he turned to Adam. "Well?"

"Cold storage. It's full of freezers and liquid nitrogen canisters."

"Freezers?" Carol said. "Now I know you're joking. It must be fifteen below zero outside."

"No," Richard said, "he's right. They're special units to store samples." He opened the door. The back wall had three large stainless steel hatches. Along the side of the room were a dozen or so steel canisters with a large red N2 stenciled on their front. On the wall hung arm-length gloves and long metal tongs. "The units are accurate to a half-degree and all three have their own regulating controls."

"With all that cold outside?" Carol asked.

"That's the point," Margaret told her. "It's *too* cold outside. The research team extracts and collects samples from the ice sheet. The cores they pull up have to stay frozen to make studying them possible and studying them outside wouldn't be practical. They have to keep them at a controlled temperature. A researcher can take them out for short periods of time, but they have to be careful to keep them frozen enough so they remain viable."

"That's why this room is so close to the main entrance," Adam volunteered. "So the beakers can get the samples into a controlled environment before they deteriorate."

"Very good, Mr. Hayes," Margaret said, with a smile. Adam hadn't noticed until that smile that she could be attractive, if she wanted to.

"No big deal. You share a drink with the guys, they tell you stuff."

"It shows you listen," she said. "You don't know how important that can be." Margaret glanced over at Richard. "Anyway, these three freezers are for short-term storage. I'm sure you noticed the other buildings as we landed. Three of them have long-term storage lockers, all with their own backup generators. The reason being, to paraphrase the old adage, not to put all the samples in one basket. These lockers are for the most recent samples at different phases of examination. After all the data is collected, they too will be transferred to another building."

"How is it you're so familiar with this setup?" Carol asked.

"It was her concept and design," Richard said, taking it upon himself to answer the woman's question. "One thing you can say about Margaret is that when it comes to research procedures, she's on the ball."

"A compliment, Richard? You must still care."

"Let's not get all mushy about it."

"I do believe you're blushing," Margaret said, obviously trying to get a rise out of the man.

"Knock it off," Richard grumbled, and stomped his way towards the cold room. "We have important things to get done. Let's find out what they've been working on."

It was going to be a little tight, so Margaret left her bag outside the door before following Richard in. Adam followed her, then the lieutenant, and lastly came Carol, who didn't fancy being in such close quarters.

Bruce Manning found the liquid nitrogen canisters interesting. He tapped one with the toe of his boot. It produced a dull thud. The casing must have been heavily insulated to make that type of sound.

"Be careful around those canisters, Lieutenant," Margaret warned. "They'll freeze your metals off."

"Sure thing," he said. "Doctor, you don't think this stuff would have the same effect on tissue as..."

"Acid? No, Lieutenant, I don't. After any frozen piece thawed, its edges would be rough, not smooth. Nice try though."

"It was just a thought," he added, then said, "I'll check out the freezers."

While the soldier made his way to the first steel door, Richard moved over to a small metal table, pulling out the built-in drawer. It was empty. He slammed it shut.

"What did you expect to find?" Margaret asked.

"Notes, research papers, something, anything."

"This isn't the lab," Margaret said. "Strictly storage."

"Don't you think I know that?" he snapped. "But it wouldn't hurt to try, would it? I was hoping maybe..." He scratched his head slightly above his right ear and whispered, "This is so damn peculiar." Richard turned his attention to the door as if he expected someone to miraculously pop up out of the blue. "The whole crew couldn't have simply vanished." He turned back to his ex-wife. "Could they?"

"Highly unlikely," she said, "I'm sure there's..."

"Mr. Baines, Dr. Walker," Manning suddenly called out from the farthest locker, "I think you need to see this."

"What is it?" Richard asked.

"I'd rather you look for yourself."

"All right, all right."

"Have Mr. Hayes stay with Miss Chambers," Manning added.

Adam responded with a tight and baffled expression upon hearing those words. "I think I should..."

Margaret glanced briefly over to Carol. Then she spoke to Adam, but in a mild tone. "I'm sure the lieutenant's concern is for my ex's assistant. I don't think any disrespect was directed towards you. For now, stay with her."

Adam agreed—reluctantly, but he agreed. He made his way over to Carol, who hadn't stepped more than a foot past the door.

"I really don't mean to be such a burden," she said.

Adam shook his head and said in a kind and gentle voice, "You're not a burden. I bet it's some security thing—this being a government facility and all."

"I'm Mr. Baines' assistant, remember. I may be temporary, but I have all the clearances."

"Maybe it's me then. You have to guard me. Make sure I don't steal any secrets. Hey, snow is big spy stuff."

Carol laughed. "I really doubt that. But thank you." She touched his hand. "Thank you for your concern for my feelings. I'm sure Lieutenant Manning feels he's doing what's best, considering my previous behavior—not exactly a pillar of courage."

"Hey, don't be so hard on yourself. This can't be what you signed up for, stranded in a deserted research station with a blinding snow storm outside."

"You couldn't be more right about that. I took this job because I needed the money."

Lieutenant Manning came out of the cold locker. The soldier forced a smile. "You can go in now," he told Adam. "Dr. Walker would like to speak with you for a moment."

"What's with all the cloak-and-dagger?" Adam asked.

"I'm sure she will explain."

"I'll keep your place in line," Carol joked. She looked up at her new bodyguard—he towered over her. "I don't want to know, do I?"

Manning answered only with another forced grin.

After walking to the freezer door, Adam turned, peering back once before entering. He gave Carol a reassuring wink.

"Manning said you wanted to talk with me."

Richard and Margaret stared at each other, trying to decide who would speak.

"We need to show you something," Margaret said at last.

Richard took a short step to the side. It wasn't until then that Adam noticed a blue plastic tarp about three feet long lying across the lowest of the six slide-out racks.

"Brace yourself," the woman added, taking hold of one end of the tarp. She gently pulled it back.

"My God," Adam said. No words could have possibly prepared him for what he saw.

Before him, in the chilly air and on the cold steel rack was a corpse—but not a whole corpse. On the right side, its ribs were sticking out of the dark ruptured flesh. That was the largest remaining part of the body. The left side had been completely dissolved up to what would have been the armpit except there was no arm. And the left side of the man's face was nothing more than smooth white bone.

"I know it must be difficult, but do you recognize him?" Margaret asked.

"Yes, I do. His name is...was Emmanuel Phillips." Adam pulled his eyes away.

"Are you sure?" Richard said. "He's pretty bad."

"I'm sure. I'm sure. And if you paid as close attention to those personnel files as you claim, you wouldn't have needed to ask me."

"How so?" he asked.

"Emmanuel's the only black man assigned here. Now that I've answered your question, could you cover him up?"

Without a word, Margaret gently and carefully returned the blue tarp to its position over the dead man.

"What could cause this amount of destruction?" Adam asked, trying to compose himself. He couldn't shake the image of that half-missing face. This wasn't a stranger lying on a rack—he knew the man, he had talked with him, drank and ate with him. Maybe Emmanuel was just another name on a list to the other two, but to him he was a friend.

"We were discussing that before you arrived," Richard said, glancing towards the body.

"You must have some suspicion."

"It's possible," Margaret said, "that it could be some strain of virus."

"You can't be serious," Richard said, staring at the woman. "No virus could do that."

"Ebola," she simply said.

"Ebola!" Richard bolted back almost crashing into the wall of the freezer. He gasped as though his newly formed words died right there in his throat. After a half-cough, he managed to speak. "If you thought it was Ebola, why for God sakes didn't you tell me?" Tiny beads of sweat formed on his temples.

"I didn't say it *was* Ebola."

"Yes, you did!" Richard raved. "Yes, you did!"

"Will you hold it down?" Adam said, grabbing Richard by the arm. "Your assistant is terrified enough now."

"I don't give a rat's ass!" He pulled free of Adam and stepped closer to his ex-wife. "Now," he said, taking a deep breath to calm himself. "I want you to tell me, is it or is it not Ebola?"

"I don't know, but I doubt it."

"I guess that's something anyway," Richard said. His shoulders eased back and he set free another heavy breath.

"There's too much damage. The cellular breakdown is way beyond Ebola."

"I really hate when you do that," Richard said. "Can you give me a simple answer without the dramatic pause?"

"Answer. You want a simple answer. Okay, try this one. A man's dead. Over half his body has been dissolved by some unknown agent—possibly virally induced."

"Possibly," Richard snapped, "you said possibly. You don't know."

"Of course I don't know absolutely, but all the signs are there."

"Okay, Doc," Adam said, "for the sake of argument, let's say it is a virus of some kind. Then where would it come from? Something this terrible would most surely have shown up before now."

"They must have dug it up with one of their core samples. A virus trapped down within the ice—maybe, if they went deep enough, from under the ice."

"You can't be right," Adam said. "Nothing could live in, or even under, all that ice—within all that cold and pressure."

"Don't be so sure," she said. "We really know so little about our planet. That's why this facility is here. To explore the unknown and learn some of its secrets."

"Yeah, yeah, yeah," Richard said, "space, the final frontier. Now can we talk about something a little more serious? Like how to avoid being exposed to this virus or whatever this thing is."

"If it is a virus, we all were exposed the moment we entered the front door. Remember the hand. It had the same pattern of tissue damage. And if we weren't exposed then, we surely have been exposed now."

"Great," Richard said, "just great." He threw up his hands.

"Relax," she said. "Exposed doesn't necessarily mean infected. Whatever it is may not even be airborne. It may only be spread through an exchange of bodily fluids. Like AIDS, blood being passed between two people, etc. It's also possible that the virus has a very short life after the host dies. We could all be perfectly safe."

"But you don't know," Richard said.

"If you're asking for a guarantee, I can't give you one. But I can tell you, it's fast acting. Emmanuel, here, has been dead for about a week. And since that's about the time radio contact was broken with the station, he was probably the first to die."

"First?"

"No one has come out to meet us," Margaret said matter-of-factly.

"Granted," Richard replied, "but I don't see any other bodies. Do you?"

"You keep forgetting about the hand," Adam said.

"The hand, the hand. Sounds like the title of a bad horror movie. I'm merely saying that someone carried this poor devil in here. If others died, wouldn't they be brought here too? With a crew of thirteen, including the cook, and minus our friend at the door—that still leaves eleven people. It only makes sense that the remaining crew would have kept any bodies together."

"They could have used a cold locker in another building," Adam said.

"Use your head, man. There's five other racks, why would they bother to bring the bodies to another building, but leave this one here?"

"I hate to admit it," Margaret said to Richard, "but you have a good point."

"You bet I do. Besides, who says that hand doesn't belong to this man here—he's missing an entire arm."

Both Adam and Margaret were dumbfounded by Richard's total lack of observation. It didn't take long for him to realize his mistake. The hand in its death grip around the ax handle had obviously come from a Caucasian.

"You should have quit while you were ahead," Margaret said.

"Do you have your camera?" Richard asked her, ignoring the comment.

"Left it in the hall."

"Make sure you snap off a few shots for the report. I'm sure the boys back at the office will be interested in all this when we get back home."

"We can't leave here," Margaret said.

Richard's eyes widened. "What are you talking about?"

"If it does turn out to be some unknown virus, we can't take the chance on bringing it back with us. We could spread it among the general population. There's no telling how many people could die."

He nodded. "We can't chance letting this thing out."

"I'm glad we agree."

"You're the doctor." Richard took a glimpse of the shrouded corpse. "And facts are facts. What a way to go..."

"Don't get ahead of yourself. It might be nothing."

"But it could be something," Richard said.

"How long until we know for sure?" Adam asked.

"I would say twenty-four hours without any symptoms and we'll be clear of any immediate hazard. I suppose we could leave then, but when we get back to McMurdo, we'll have to spend time in isolation and get full blood workups."

"What kind of symptoms?" Adam added.

Margaret's face became very stern as she looked Adam square in the eye. "Do you really want me to describe what I think?"

"No, not by the tone in your voice."

"That's probably for the best, considering I'm sure you want to sleep tonight. Let me say any symptoms will become obvious."

"Twenty-four hours, huh?" Adam said. "That storm outside could easily last that long. Which means, we can't go anywhere until tomorrow anyway." His eyes returned to the tarp lying across the body of Emmanuel Phillips. "What will we tell the others?"

"The truth," Richard said. "I would want to know. Wouldn't you?"

Both pilot and doctor agreed. The others would be told.

"What should we do about Emmanuel?" Adam asked. It was an odd thought, but the last joke told to him by Emmanuel Phillips ran through his head. The man's jokes were never that funny, but Adam wouldn't mind hearing him tell one right now.

"Leave him," Richard said bluntly.

Adam didn't appreciate the man's callous attitude, but before he could object Margaret spoke up. "I'm sure Richard meant that there's nothing to do for him. It would be best to keep the body here—safe and sound."

"When we get back," Richard said, "I'll send another team equipped to handle things like this. They will secure the body and bring it back for burial. Is that sufficient?"

"*If* we get back," Adam said. "The odds on that have fallen some."

"It's the best I can do!" Richard snapped and bolted from the room.

"He's a hard man to figure out," Adam told Margaret.

"You're telling me? Most of the time he means well, but right now, he's scared. He'll never admit it, but we were together long enough—I can read him pretty well. We'd better follow him out. I think the explanation to the others will need a gentle tongue."

"I agree, but I have to tell you, I'm scared too."

"The line forms behind me," Margaret said. "Let's get with the others."

"Why did you say that!" Carol shouted. "Why can't we leave here!" That was the first thing Adam and Margaret heard reentering the hall. Margaret dashed over to the woman on the verge of hysterics.

"I'll handle this," she told Richard, pushing him aside. Margaret gently but firmly took hold of Carol. "Listen, it won't be for long."

"It's true," Carol said. "You mean it's true! He wasn't lying. Tell me he's lying."

"I'm afraid I can't do that." Margaret released her hold, then said, "You have to be strong. We found something—it's probably nothing. But to be certain, we need to stay here a while."

"How long?"

"Just a day," Adam assured her.

"A day," Carol said, letting out a small laugh. "A day? Mr. Baines made it sound so serious. A day isn't very long."

"No, it's not," Margaret assured her. "You still hungry?"

Carol nodded.

"I'm sure all of us could use a bite," Adam said. "I flew in a huge load of supplies less than three weeks ago. Plenty of food. We'll find something in the galley."

"I'm hungry too," Lieutenant Manning told the group, "but I suggest we continue our search before we indulge ourselves."

"I agree," Richard said.

"The kitchen and galley are in the center of the complex," Adam volunteered. "If we do continue searching, it would be a while until we get there."

"I can wait a bit," Carol said, realizing that the decision was being left up to her.

Margaret smiled at the woman. "Then it's agreed. Besides, I haven't totally given up on the notion of finding someone quite yet."

"What's that supposed to mean?" Carol asked. "There are people here. There has to be."

"And you're probably right," Margaret said. "Lieutenant, would you be so kind as to take the lead?"

"You got it." He reached beneath his jacket and pulled out his gun.

"I don't think that will be necessary," Margaret added, troubled by the weapon. "Not yet, anyway."

"Well, I don't know about you," Carol said, "but in this situation, a man with a gun is plenty welcome by me." She scurried up towards the soldier.

"Okay," Richard said, "let's get on with it." The group started off again, but he stayed back by his ex-wife. "What was all that about telling them the truth?"

"Did I lie?" she asked.

"No, but you left out one little detail. I doubt something like a virus—or whatever it is—would simply slip your mind."

"Sue me. I didn't want a hysterical woman on my hands. Did you? She's almost on the brink now. When I get the chance I'll have a quick talk with Lieutenant Manning."

"What makes you think he can handle it any better?"

"You did," Margaret said.

"I'm not so convinced of that." Richard began a pace to catch up with the others. "But remember one thing…"

"And that is?"

He smirked. "When you told me…I wasn't carrying a gun."

CHAPTER THREE

Walking down the long corridor, an uneasy silence accompanied the group. No one spoke a word. It had been a good thirty-foot stretch of nothing before they came to another door. Margaret happened to catch the hard glance thrown her way by Adam. With the glare of contempt in his eyes, it wasn't difficult to figure out what he was thinking. How did that quote go, she thought—truth is the first casualty of war. This wasn't war, but she couldn't help feeling those words somehow fit in this case.

"What's in here?" Richard asked, stopping at the door. His voice tore into the dead air, the words bouncing off the bare walls with an echo.

All eyes fell on Adam. "Cook's quarters," he answered.

"An Italian named Sebastiano Giovannelli," Richard added. "I hired him myself. Best cook I could find. I figured being posted on this frozen waste was bad enough—the crew should at least eat well."

"The crew called him Sam," Adam said. "Easier on the tongue. His English wasn't the best, but, like you said, he was great with the chow. Never left on a return trip without first filling my stomach with his linguine."

Considering the tension and the peculiar circumstances, such a casual comment drew stares from the others.

"What can I say? He was a good cook."

"Let's check it out," Richard told the soldier. He was the one with the gun after all.

Lieutenant Manning signaled the others to step back a little, before trying the door. The knob turned but the door wouldn't budge.

"Must be locked," he said. Trying once more and again failing, he added, "I'll have to force it in."

"Do it," Richard said.

With a single hard hit of his big shoulder, the lock gave way. A ping rang out along the floor when the metal strike plate rolled back into the hall. It stopped at Carol's feet. The woman jumped back as if the small piece of steel would cause her great pain.

The others peered inside. They were stunned to find the room in shambles. Books thrown across the floor, a reading lamp knocked over and next to the door, a small nightstand lay smashed to pieces. Even a heavy writing desk hadn't escaped the mayhem, being shoved at an angle towards the center of the room. But the strangest thing of all was a small heap of clothing off in a far corner.

Manning moved in for a closer view. He started to reach out for what appeared to be a shirt.

"Don't touch it with your bare hands," Margaret called out, stopping him.

He nodded and rummaged around for something to use as a probe. Finding nothing useful at arm's length, he stood up, opened the top desk drawer and pulled out a long newly sharpened pencil. Returning to the corner and the strange pile of clothes, the soldier spotted a framed picture of a very lovely girl with long black hair, nailed to the wall. Below it he saw another, and still another. By the careful arrangement of these photos, they had to be of someone very special. The makeshift shrine had Bruce Manning wondering about his brother—would they find him…would he be alive?

"Lieutenant…Lieutenant Manning," a voice called out. "You okay?" Margaret asked.

"Yeah, sure, fine." Without another word, Manning returned to his previous position in front of the bundled mound. The others watched while he used the pencil tip to poke and prod the fabric. Identical to what they had found in the main entryway, the shirt and pants had underwear —T-shirt and briefs—tucked away inside. But that wasn't the only unusual thing about the outer shirt—its right sleeve now hung on entirely by a few unbroken threads.

"What so interesting?" Carol asked. "Besides, the obvious, I mean."

"I'm not sure," Manning said, "it might be nothing."

"Don't keep us in the dark," Richard told him.

"These clothes are damaged...like they'd been worn during a struggle—a fight maybe. The tear to the sleeve indicates that the wearer was being grabbed at or maybe pulling himself away from..."

"An attack?" Richard interrupted. "By who?"

"Or what, for that matter," Adam said. He didn't know what possessed him to say that. It was just that ever since they entered the complex, he had a strange feeling—he could almost sense an unknown presence.

Manning shook his head. "Sorry, no clue."

"I think I would like to leave this room now," Carol said. Her eyes nervously shifted back and forth, seemingly afraid someone or something would pounce on them, even though the compartment was much too small to conceal an attacker. "Please, can't we go?"

Margaret nodded. "We've seen enough here."

With those words, Carol ran from the room.

"One of you two," Margaret told Adam and Richard, "stay with her. I need to speak with the lieutenant for a moment."

Out in the hall, the rest of the group stood waiting while the doctor spoke with the soldier.

"You must think me a big baby," Carol said to Adam.

"No," he told her. "No, I don't. This is hard on everyone here."

"I'm usually not so on edge. I've never realized how easily I can be pushed over. It's somewhat disheartening. I wish I could be stronger like you." She brushed the tips of her fingers down the back of Adam's hand.

"Truth be known," Adam said, "I'm petrified."

"You're only saying that to make me feel better." She drew in closer to kiss his cheek, but stopped when she saw Richard Baines watching them. "Thank you," she whispered instead.

Lieutenant Manning and Dr. Walker came from the room. The man was clearly unsettled about something, but drawing nearer to the others, he put on a different face.

They searched the rest of the living quarters—all were deserted of personnel. Most were tidy, a couple were obviously lived-in, but clean. Three were in the same disturbing condition as the cook's room—things thrown around, toppled over and broken into pieces. And in two of those rooms were more weird sets of empty clothing. The weirdest being the room with shoes and socks dropped off the end of the bunk, but the pants and shirt were flat across the top in such a way that it looked like someone had taken the time to carefully lay them out.

Besides the sleeping quarters, the group found a couple more closets, a small combination storage and laundry room and a full bathroom with shower.

"Thank God," Margaret said, relief accompanied her words. "I didn't think I could hold it much longer, and I really didn't know how to bring the subject up."

"Still modest after all these years," Richard commented.

"Some things are just private," she said. "And if you all will excuse me."

"Maybe she should have an escort," he added.

"I think I can manage this one alone, Richard."

"Hey, I wasn't volunteering. Manning's the one with the hardware."

"It may be best if I check inside before you go in," Manning said.

"Fine, but make it quick." The thought of being able to relieve herself made the need all that much greater—in a moment she'd be bouncing on her heels. "Make it quick," she repeated.

Manning held the door open and surveyed the enclosed area. "It's okay, but..."

"That's good enough for me," she said, rushing past the soldier. She hurried to close the door and get to the toilet praying and telling herself she could make it. She started to unzip her winter pants, but in her rush snagged the zipper.

"Not now," she groaned. With a sharp snap of her wrist she pulled the slide back up the plastic teeth about an inch. Using much more care, she brought it down again—all the while the pressure inside her body increased. The thought of walking out of this bathroom with a large wet spot on her pants flashed through her mind. The idea did not sit well. She could practically hear Richard laughing.

Finally, she got the zipper down enough to remove her pants and sit. She couldn't describe the ecstasy as her bladder emptied. It wasn't until several moments later that she noticed how cold the seat felt against her bare skin.

Finishing up, she reached for several sheets of toilet paper. It was then when she noticed the three small holes in the wall—bullet holes. A second later, she spotted a fourth. She stuck her pinkie finger in the closest one. The angle indicated that the shots were fired from across the room. But there was nothing there except the shower stall with its light green curtain —its *closed* green curtain.

Staring carefully at the shower, she thought she saw small puncture marks in the hanging plastic. She leaned forward and nearly fell off the seat. Instead of breaking her neck that way, she finished her business, brought her pants up and walked to the stall. Margaret couldn't resist sticking her finger in one of these holes as well. She eyed the path back to the wall. Both sets of holes lined up perfectly.

Whoever fired the gun did so from the shower. But why would anyone fire a gun from behind the curtain and then bother to close it after leaving?

Then it struck her. Maybe she wasn't alone.

Margaret raised a slow hand towards the shower curtain. She lightly touched the plastic trim with her fingertips. It felt dry, rough and even a bit cold. She trembled.

She pulled her hand away and let out a short, nervous laugh. Right, someone was skulking in the shower, she amused herself with the thought. Like someone would be hiding there listening to her pee.

Margaret was about to turn, leave and rejoin the others. But instead she stopped. She stared back at the closed green shower curtain—that plastic green curtain.

Quickly she seized hold and pulled it open. She couldn't stop herself—she had to know.

Despite Richard's objections, the door closed behind Margaret. "She could be a while," Richard said. "She was always making me wait." The others ignored the man's comment.

"Carol, are you still hungry?" Adam asked, glancing over to the woman.

"Starving," she replied immediately.

Adam caught her tiny smile. It was both pleasant and uncomfortable.

"The galley's just up ahead another ten feet," he added, pointing to the next door in the hallway.

"Great, let's go," Richard said. He didn't need any more convincing.

"Shouldn't we wait for Dr. Walker?" Carol asked.

"Aren't you the one who's starving? Besides, like the man said, it's only ten feet away."

"I don't know," she told him.

Richard raised a hand into the air as if conceding some great point. "Okay, okay, let the soldier here stand guard while we go round up some chow. He's the one with all that military training. You have any problems taking that duty, Manning? When Margaret reemerges refreshed and all, you two can join us."

"Fine by me," the lieutenant said.

"Then it's settled. Let's go get something to eat." With that, the three went off.

Adam stopped to say something to Manning, but the soldier nodded him on instead. Adam nodded in return.

After pausing in front of the door to the galley, Richard had second thoughts about being first inside. He backed away. That left Adam staring at the handle.

"Get on with it," Richard ordered.

Adam had always thought he found the man's tone of voice irritating, but now he was sure of it. Though, instead of bothering to say anything that would make matters worse, he pushed the door open and stepped through. Richard was right on his heels, followed by Carol.

Inside, they found three round tables surrounded by four chairs each. On the walls were a few posters of tropical settings and a bulletin board with neatly arranged notes situated just right of a serving window. Close by was a steel, two-tier table with stacks of white porcelain plates on top and gray plastic trays below. The space appeared very clean considering the circumstances. Something puzzling happened here. The crew had vanished, but still someone had taken the time to clean up.

"So much for food," Richard quipped.

"This is the dining area," Adam replied, understanding why Margaret would divorce the man, but not why she would even marry him in the first place. "They store the food in the kitchen. Makes it a little more convenient when cooking." Adam pointed to a doorless entryway. "It should be well stocked, just made a run about three weeks ago."

"You mentioned that already," Richard said, pushing past Adam.

"I'm sure he doesn't mean to be rude," Carol whispered.

Adam simply shrugged his indifference, then he and Carol began their own trek to the food. When they got to the kitchen, Richard had what could best be described as a hunger-lust in his eye.

"Hayes, I certainly hope you're not prone to exaggeration," the round man said, reaching up for the first of many cupboard doors. He pulled it open and something rolled out. It barely missed him and crashed to the floor. Another two inches to the left and Richard would have been hit square in the kisser.

The sudden banging against the hard floor made Carol jump. She grabbed Adam by the arm. After a few seconds, she seemed embarrassed by her actions. "Oh, I'm sorry," she said, releasing her hold.

"Don't mention it," he replied. He smiled at her. She blushed.

"Green beans," Richard told them.

"Excuse me?" Carol said.

"Green beans." Richard picked up the slightly dented can. "A rather freakish way to die, wouldn't you say? Having your skull crushed by a can of green beans." He laughed.

Neither Adam nor Carol found humor in the man's comment.

"Lighten up," Richard said. "I like green beans," he added. "I wonder what other goodies we can find." The next cupboard he opened with greater care, while Carol and Adam began their own hunt for food.

True to Adam's word, the kitchen was well stocked. The cupboards were full of both canned and dried box goods—flour, sugar, all sorts of baking ingredients. There were many different herbs and spices. The refrigerator had milk, eggs, butter, water and beer, among other things.

"There's a bigger fridge, next to the meat locker," Adam said, glancing past a large stainless steel sink and over to a pair of swinging doors leading to a small pantry towards the back of the kitchen.

"Meat locker?" Richard said, following Adam's line of vision. And a split second later he was on the go in search of this new treasure.

Adam and Carol had to hurry to keep up.

When Richard lifted the door to the freezer box, he smiled. There were over three dozen packages wrapped in white butcher's paper. "The mother load," he said, reading the labels. "Steak, chicken, veal, lamb. We certainly won't starve." He pulled a package marked PORTERHOUSE from the corner. He tapped on it, producing a hard click. "Frozen solid, but nothing a little warm air won't cure."

"Those will take forever to thaw," Carol said.

"Several hours, but not forever," Richard assured her.

"And when would you expect to eat them?" Adam said.

"Hey, we have to spend the night. I think they would make a great steak-and-egg breakfast."

"I just had a thought," Carol said. She stared down at the white wrapped packages, then back into the kitchen at the teeming shelves. "Do you think this food is okay to eat?"

"Would you mind explaining, 'okay'?" Richard asked.

"I don't mean to be a worrywart," she said, sheepishly meeting the man's gaze, "but we don't know why all the people here disappeared. Maybe it was something in the food."

"We don't know that *all* the staff has disappeared," Richard said. "And we have to eat."

Adam looked at Carol. "He's right, on both counts." His face gave away his distaste in agreeing with the man. "But still, we should play it safe. Until we know more, we should stick to canned food and leave the rest alone."

Richard's eyes almost doubled in size. "Canned food only?"

"Hey, you said you liked green beans."

Richard opened his mouth to speak, but he was cut off by the sound of Margaret calling out from the bathroom. The sound of urgency filled her voice and the others wasted no time vacating the galley.

By the time the three arrived Manning had already entered the bathroom. He and Margaret were staring in the shower stall—the curtain had been pushed aside.

"Please, don't tell me she saw a mouse?" Richard said, beating the others through the door. "My mouse killing days are over."

"I'm touched by your concern," Margaret said sarcastically.

"Dr. Walker has made a grim discovery," Manning told him, his eyes not budging from the spot.

Adam and Carol came in behind Richard, curious to know what provoked such turmoil.

In the stall was a full set of clothes. They were empty, lying flat, but intact and complete—shoes filled with black socks, pants with a belt and a tucked in shirt. But most disturbing of all, on the stall floor at the end of the flattened right sleeve was a revolver.

Manning knelt down and reached for the weapon, then pulled his hand back at the last moment. He glanced up at Margaret.

"Go ahead," she said, "being this far into the complex, it's a good bet we've already been exposed."

"Exposed?" Carol said.

Manning picked up the gun and checked it. "No surprises here," he said. With a hard flick, he opened the gun. He cupped his hand and caught the spent shells. "It's been fired." He put the barrel to his nose. "A couple of days ago maybe. Hard to tell for sure."

"What's that on the back wall?" Adam asked, pointing to a stain of dark reddish brown. There was one large splatter and many, many, smaller specks spread out in a pattern that stretched towards the ceiling. Mixed in the dark material were some small grainy bumps.

"My guess...blood and tissue," Margaret told him.

"You don't mean..." Carol started.

"That the guy blew his brains out," Richard finished. "I'm afraid she does."

"This may sound like a really stupid question," Carol said, "but where's the rest of him?"

"Tell her," Adam said, firmly meeting Margaret's eyes with his. She had no doubt now why he seemed upset earlier. "She has the right to know," he continued.

"Tell me what?"

"We think," Margaret said, "that there may be an unknown strain of virus here."

"Virus?" Carol released a tiny laugh. "You're joking. A virus can't do that. There's nothing left of the man."

"Almost nothing," Richard said, which spawned many angry stares. "Sorry."

"To be honest with you," Margaret told her, "I really don't understand much of this myself. We found a body earlier, but there was also some tissue...missing."

"A body?" Carol asked. Her head turned to Adam.

"Yes," he admitted. "A body."

"Why didn't you tell me?"

"I..."

"It was my decision to keep it from you," Margaret said. "I thought it better if..."

"Better!? Better!? Better that I didn't know something here could kill me? That's why we can't leave, isn't it?"

"That and the storm," Adam said.

The woman turned away from him. "If there's anything else you feel you can't tell me—tell me anyway. I want to know."

"Dr. Walker?" Manning said, standing up. While the others talked, he took it upon himself to make a closer examination of the abandoned clothing. "Have you considered that maybe someone simply took the body?"

"And what?" Richard asked. "Strip down the corpse then position the clothing back on the floor exactly the way they were if still being worn. A pretty sick joke, not to mention the time and patience it would take."

"I hate to say this," the soldier said, "but there's not a lot to do here. It's easy enough to go stir-crazy."

"You think someone snapped?" Adam asked. "And he or she is stealing bodies out of the need for a new hobby?" Adam always liked to keep an open mind, but the lieutenant's explanation was a little hard to swallow.

"Not just stealing bodies. Our friend here fired all five shells. And with the direction of the bullet holes in the curtain and over on the wall, he was definitely shooting at someone. That is, before he did himself with the last bullet."

"He could have been delirious," Margaret said. "Maybe even out of his mind by the virus."

"If you must have a conspiracy," Richard snidely told the soldier, "try this one? He didn't kill himself at all. Someone else blew his brains out then shot the other bullets to make it appear he had fired the gun. But that of course, doesn't explain the missing body."

"What's your point, Richard?" Margaret asked, her irritation clearly marked in the question.

"My point is that we don't know. All we can do is guess. And until we get more information, we can suppose a vast number of scenarios. Which invariably leads me to the statement: this is getting us nowhere. I suggest we return to the galley for a bite to eat. After a good meal, this whole thing won't seem so bleak. We'll all think clearer with a full stomach."

"Food?" Margaret said, as though a light snapped on. "I don't know if that would be such a prudent course of action. It could be the source of infection."

"I've already suggested that we only eat the canned goods for now," Adam told her.

"That was very sensible of you," she said. "When we find the lab, I'll take some food samples and check them for any trace of contamination. Who knows, we might get some answers."

"Or waste perfectly good food," Richard said.

"Does...that have to stay there?" Carol said, pointing to the empty clothes.

"I'll take care of it," Manning said, about to grasp the pant leg.

"Don't move anything," Margaret said. "Just close the curtain. We'll deal with it after we learn more. Let's not disturb the area any more than we already have."

Carol's eyes widened. "This is the only facility we've seen since we've been here. I don't know if I can—you know, with that in the shower."

"Try not to think about it," Margaret said. "With the curtain closed we'll never know it's there."

"I'm not sure I can," Carol said, "but if you think it's best not to move it, I understand."

"Okay," Richard said, "if that's all settled, back to the galley."

Adam noticed Manning tucking the newly found revolver in his waistband. "You keeping that gun?"

"You've got that right. I'm sure we'll find ammo somewhere. I can't shake the feeling that we're going to need some extra protection."

Adam nodded, but he really wasn't too happy about it—he felt the same way.

The group made their way to the kitchen and continued the quest for food. They made a meal out of those items they felt would be free from any foreign impurity—canned peaches, soup, baked beans, and Adam couldn't stop himself from serving up a big old bowl of green beans. He used two cans. For drink, they decided on the cans of 7 Up and the bottled beer. The bottled water had been opened and those containers still sealed were warm.

They spoke very little while they ate. None of them really had much in common. If it weren't for the strange set of circumstances that had thrown them together, they would pass each other on the street without so much as a word. Though, Adam did want to say something to Carol. He had felt bad that the others had decided to keep her in the dark about the virus and its potential danger. He wanted her to know, that from the very start, he thought she should have been told everything they knew—about finding Emmanuel—about the virus—all of it. There should have been no secrets. He wanted to tell her, but he didn't—instead he sat quietly and ate his soup.

CHAPTER FOUR

After the makeshift meal, the group decided to continue the search. A brief discussion ensued about the women staying in the galley, but Margaret objected. After a lively exchange, they made the decision that it would be wiser if they all stuck together for now.

The first door they came to was locked.

"What's behind this?" Richard asked Adam.

"Rec room. TV, Ping-Pong table, pool table, dart board, the usual stuff."

"Why would it be locked?" Carol asked.

"That's the number one question," Richard said. "Lieutenant, if you don't mind." He held his hand out, gesturing for Bruce to break down the door. It didn't give the big man much of a challenge—the sole of his boot against wood produced a large crack. Though besides the bolt keeping it closed, something else blocked the way in. After forcing the door a few inches, they all saw someone had pulled the Ping-Pong table across to use as a barricade.

Manning shoved the door and table enough for them to enter. What they discovered didn't make them feel a whole lot better. The room had been torn up—chairs knocked over, books and magazines scattered across the floor, pool cues snapped in half. And worse yet, on the floor, three more sets of clothing—one right smack in the middle of the room, a second a few feet away from the back wall, and a third set only about two feet left of that, but partially covered by an upside-down overstuffed chair.

"Interesting," Margaret said, deciding to inspect the half-concealed clothing. The pants had been pinned by the heavy weight, but the shirt remained unencumbered. She carefully turned back the collar revealing the white T-shirt underneath. Standing up, the woman removed her camera from its bag and took two shots from slightly different angles. Then she replaced the shirt to the exact position it had been before.

The rest of the group spread out, hoping to uncover any clue to what could have possibly transpired here. Richard followed Manning towards the center of the room. Carol stayed with Adam.

"Has all the signs of a brawl," Manning said. "Except..."

"Except, no bodies," Richard added.

"No bodies." Then the soldier spotted something odd. He knelt down to lift the shirt, when Margaret called out to him.

"Be very careful. These...piles are the only evidence we have so far. Try to keep contact to a minimum."

Manning nodded and gently lifted the sleeve. His suspicions had been right. The bulge he spotted under the shirt was unmistakable. "Another gun," he called out.

"Any splatter marks?" Richard asked loudly, taking a step closer.

"Do you mind?" Adam said, from the other side of the room. "I knew these people. They were on the brainy side, but they were good people nevertheless."

Richard didn't respond to Adam's objection. Instead, he said, "Any indications that he used the gun on himself?"

"No," Manning said, "I don't think so."

"That fits," Margaret said, standing up. She had already proceeded on to the next bundle of clothing. By the undergarments, a bra and panties, she confirmed the first female victim. She walked over to Manning and took the gun from the floor. She opened it and four empty cartridges fell out, followed by one live round.

"What fits?" Richard asked.

"The others...those clothes over there," she said. "They each have two bullet holes." Margaret took a breath and reached down for the unspent shell. "I'm afraid it appears that this person shot those other poor souls."

"What are you saying?" Carol asked, her head turning towards the female apparel.

"Just that. Whoever this was, gunned down the others. The only question is why?"

"Now we know who the guy in the shower was shooting at," Richard said.

"We do?" Margaret asked.

"It's pretty obvious," Richard stated in his typical overly confident tone. "Our shooter here, goes after the guy in the shower, then turns his gun on these two."

"I wouldn't be so certain of that," she told him. "We have no proof that the two events are related. In fact, the signs indicate nothing like what you suggest."

"What signs?"

"The bullet count for one. Four bullets shot, four empty casings."

"So, he reloaded."

"No, she's right," Adam said. "There were no bullet holes in or near the stall. All the shots were fired away from the shower. Also the Ping-Pong table next to the door was put there to keep someone out."

"You don't know that for sure," Richard said. "This place is a disaster area... There's a terrible struggle over the gun, things are knocked over and broken, while others are pushed and shoved aside—including the Ping-Pong table. The gun goes off...and that's that."

"I don't think so," Manning said. "At least one person was killed before any struggle."

Richard stared at the soldier. "And you figured this because..."

Manning simply pointed. "Because that chair was tipped over onto the clothing—obviously after the shooting. And if you take away the chair both sets of clothes are in the open, directly in front of the shooter. If someone fired a gun at a person next to you, what would you do?"

"I'd duck for cover," Richard said.

"Exactly," Manning told him. "So, shouldn't they be several feet apart?"

"Then he held them still at gun point," Richard simply stated. "You're trying to add to a mystery that's not there."

"But the shooter fired twice," Margaret added. "That would give the other person more than enough time to run. Even if they didn't make cover, the bullet holes wouldn't be so close together and more than likely be in the back, not the chest."

Margaret glanced at Lieutenant Manning. His slight grin and raised eyebrow told her he was truly impressed by her observation.

"Then you're saying," Richard said in disbelief, "that these people allowed themselves to be shot. What the hell for?"

"Why did the man in the shower kill himself?" Carol asked. Up to this point, she hadn't said much and such an obvious question surprised the others. One which none of them thought to address.

"Why does anyone commit suicide?" Margaret said. "He couldn't bear some tragic event. Or he didn't want to face something unimaginable—some terror."

That word: "terror" forced a stillness over the room. No one spoke for several moments. They looked around at each other, then at the mess and the abandoned clothing.

"I wonder if we have our answer," Margaret said. "That the group met with something so horrifying that they would have rather died than succumb to it."

"Now you're way over the top," Richard said. "As tragic as this whole situation is, call it what it is—murder. Why do you have to complicate things?"

"Murder or suicide," Adam said, "whatever happened here finally happened to the shooter as well. Am I the only one bothered by the missing bodies?"

"It bothers me too," Carol said, "a lot."

"I think we've all seen enough here," Richard told the group. "We still have a lot of area to search. Let's not get tied down in one room. We'll put the pieces together when we have them all."

"That's assuming we get all the pieces," Adam said. That drew a harsh sneer from Richard. And that didn't surprise Adam in the least. The more time he spent with the man the more he found him to be pompous, arrogant and egotistical. Normally, Adam's tolerance was greater, but they had been at this for hours. It wouldn't be long until he could use some shuteye. He wondered if any of the others felt the same. Then again, they all had the chance to sleep in the plane on the way up.

His plane. He wondered how it was faring out in the storm. Normally he would have preferred to protect the engines and propellers with a tarp, but he figured it should be fine for one bad night.

"You okay?" Carol asked Adam.

"Sure."

"You seemed lost in thought."

"Well, not exactly lost."

Carol softly touched Adam's arm. "Let's catch up with the others."

The next closed door had a small black lacquered metal COMMUNI-

CATIONS ROOM sign. Manning took hold of the handle and turned. The door swung open freely.

"That should save on the shoulder," Richard snickered.

The soldier ignored the man and said nothing—something was obviously bothering him. He entered the room. His expression was not that of surprise, though it should have been.

In the far corner of the room, the insides of the radio were sprawled out across the tabletop. The gray metal casing had a fire ax straight down its center. Some wires and bits of electrical board had spilled off the table onto the floor. What made this so odd was that unlike the rec room, this destruction was not random and was confined strictly to the equipment. The full racks of shelving, a storage locker, even a padded metal chair, though tossed to one side—all were intact and had been left alone.

"Not too hard to explain the loss in communications," Adam said.

"Who would do this?" Richard asked. "Do you realize how expensive this equipment is?"

"I'm sure the thought made them cry while they smashed it to Hades with that ax," Margaret said.

Richard scowled. "You never understood the value of money."

Letting the two bicker, Manning began a careful search of the floor. The room didn't have that many places to hide anything of size, but he searched under and around the table, by the metal locker—he even lifted the chair out of the way to get an unobstructed view.

"What are you expecting to find?" Margaret asked, motioning Richard to shut up for a moment. When Bruce Manning raised his head, the hardness of the soldier's eyes startled her. They were so cold.

"My brother's clothes," he said.

Canvassing the entire room, neither Manning nor the others found the slightest sign of those strange piles—not even as much as a loose thread.

"Have you given it any thought," Margaret said gently, "that your brother might be one of those we've already come across?"

"That had occurred to me, but—but I would know. And nothing we've seen so far feels right to me."

"I found something," Adam said, walking back to the group and stacking the two small boxes down on the table. "Ammunition."

"Finally something we can use," Richard said, seizing the top box. He slid it open and found it was two-thirds empty. He did the same to the second. That one was full. "It's good to know we can defend ourselves."

"Like those poor people in the rec room?" Carol said. That single statement brought with it the unsettling realization that they were as defenseless against whatever took the station crew as the crew were themselves.

"Where did you find these?" Manning asked.

Adam pointed over to the small storage locker. The padlock hung open in the metal loop.

Manning said nothing else and stepped over to the bin. He raised the lid, then pulled out another much smaller locked metal box. He brought it back to the table and pulled the ax from the busted radio. The metal blade easily came free, followed by a flume of sparks from the equipment. Carol let out a squeal and Adam jumped down to the floor and pulled the plug from the wall.

"Sorry," Manning said, holding the ax with both hands.

Carol simply smiled at him. Then she smiled at Adam as well.

Manning, with a sharp eye, used the ax blade to carefully pry the lock. When it opened, the others understood the reason for his gentle force. Inside there was another box of Ammo and two more handguns.

Adam reached for one of the weapons.

"Careful," Manning warned. "They're probably loaded."

Adam opened the cylinder. He found that the soldier was correct in his assumption. "Including the lieutenant's piece, that makes five," he said. "Under normal conditions I would be very nervous around so many guns. But if the truth be known, I don't know what makes me more nervous, having all this firepower, or knowing it didn't do the others any good."

"Let me have yours," Manning said to Margaret.

"Pardon me?" she replied.

"Your gun." He paused for a moment waiting on the woman. "The gun you picked up in the rec room. You never put it down…I saw you sneak it into your camera bag."

"I only thought," she started, then put her hand into her bag, "with the remaining bullet, I could use it for protection." She pulled out the gun and handed it to Manning.

"Not much protection there," Manning said. He opened the firearm, inserted four more bullets, snapped it shut, and handed it back to the doctor. "Now you can use it for protection."

"Try to use it, is more like it," Carol said.

"Great," Richard muttered. "That's all she needs is a gun."

Manning gave Richard one of the weapons from the metal box. The stocky man tested its weight in his hand. Then Manning took the first gun, the one from the shower, from his waistband. He loaded it and tried handing it to Carol.

She shook her head and eased the revolver back. "No. No, thank you. I'll do without. Besides I don't know how to use one of those things."

"Simple," Richard said, aiming the gun barrel towards a clipboard hanging on the far wall. "You point and pull the trigger. At close range you can't miss."

"Still, no thank you. I don't want one of those things. Please don't make me."

"Sure," Manning said, with an understanding tone, "I'll keep it with me along with the rest of the ammo. It's here if you change your mind."

"Little chance of that," she said, inching away from Manning and his guns. She positioned herself towards the door almost as if she planned to make a quick break for it.

"Okay, okay," Richard said, "if that's all settled, we should get moving. I don't think there is anything else here right now that would do us any good." He put the gun in his jacket pocket. "We don't have much more to go," he added. "The sooner we start again, the sooner we finish."

The next door they came to was another storage closet, but instead of cleaning supplies and the like, it was filled with lab equipment. Beakers, flasks, test tubes, glass tubing, rubber tubing, the whole bit. There was even an Apple Macintosh computer still in an unopened box. On the top shelves were heavy rubber gloves, a neat stack of strapped canvas bags and white lab coats still in clear plastic wrappings.

Finding nothing suspicious in glassware or electronics, they advanced to the next room. Its door sign simply read LAB. Obviously, no further explanation required.

Entering the room, one could easily forget that this research station was out on the ice floes of Antarctica—the laboratory would be the pride of any university. There were two more microscopes; one had a long box of glass slides next to it. There were centrifuges, Bunsen burners, crucibles, petri dishes. Racks and racks of test tubes, more beakers and flasks. The other pieces of equipment appeared strange to the group, except for Dr. Walker—she recognized almost all of them. Along the wall were several cabinets hanging high over white Formica counters that matched the floor. On a desk, near a bank of file cabinets, was a 40 MHz Macintosh IIfx computer setup with two extra hard drives and a case of floppy disks. At the far end of the room was a large steel door exactly like those in the cold room.

"I had no idea," Adam said. His gaze drifted through the room. "John

Blackwood would talk about their projects, but I never imagined the amount of work involved. I always figured they just dug up samples and shipped them back to the States in dry ice."

"To the contrary," Margaret said, "these men and women were some of the best minds in the field of Glaciology. They would analyze the samples themselves—testing and recording their findings on different levels of the ice sheet.

"Enough with the lecture," Richard said. "We need to search this lab. If we don't have any luck, then I suggest we…"

"I can think of one place to start right off the bat," Margaret suddenly said, and briskly marched to the computer. Tapping the power switch of the keyboard, she waited while the screen lit up. And after a few moments of a soft hum, she began probing the main hard drive. "There's a lot of files here," she said, shaking her head. "They'll take some time to go through." She took the mouse and clicked on the most recent file. A graphic image came up on the monitor. It was of two spirals linked together by short, straight lines. On each of these lines were a pair of letters made up of four possible choices: T, A, G or C.

"What's that?" Carol said, focusing on the screen.

"It's a model of Deoxyribonucleic Acid—DNA. Those lines represent the double helix connected by strands containing Thymine, Adenine, Guanine or Cytosine."

"DNA?" Richard asked. "What the blazes are they doing analyzing DNA?"

"You got me. This program was originally designed to model the breakdown of samples to the elemental level. Somebody's done a little code rewriting." She clicked the mouse again. The image rotated ninety degrees. The bond started to flash. "It could only have been Kevin Ferris. He helped design the programming, and in his day wrote a few lines of 'C' code."

"What do those letters mean?" Carol asked, pointing to the screen. The flashing shifted from one letter to the next.

"Genetic bonds," Adam replied.

"Very good," Margaret said, mouse-clicking on one of the bonds. "It's not every pilot who can spot a genetic code."

"I read a lot," he said.

The computer image changed. It zoomed in on the strips between the spirals. "You'll notice that the bonds are a combination of either A and T, or C and G." She used the mouse to zoom in on a different fragment of the

DNA strand. "What's this?" One of the pairs had an "X" instead of the usually expected character. She repositioned the cursor, clicking on another section of the double helix model and saw several other "X"'s. "Something's not right. According to this, there are new bonds—unknown bonds—in this model."

"Maybe it's a bug in the program," Adam said.

"That could be it, but…"

"Dr. Walker," Manning called out. "What are these for?" Across the room, he held up a small wire cage. The one in his hand was perfectly clean, but the others on the floor had wood-shaving bedding mixed with small brown pellets.

The man's question had Margaret doing a double take. "I'm sure you mean other than for holding mice and guinea pigs?"

"I was wondering more for the reason of their use," Manning said. "I didn't realize the research here dealt with animal testing."

"It's not in the mission plan. I don't even know how those cages got here. They were never part of the original manifest."

"I brought them," Adam said.

Surprised, the woman tilted her head to the side.

"On my last run. Dr. Blackwood radioed me to make a special order. He wanted a dozen lab rats. I hauled up four cages with three rats each. Nothing else extra—only rats."

"And you didn't think to mention this earlier," Richard snapped.

"It didn't seem important, considering…"

"Important? Important? At this stage, everything is important!"

"Easy on the man, Richard," Margaret said. "He can't be expected to convey all that has gone on here over any set period of time. He's not stationed here, remember."

"No," Adam said. "He's right. I should have said something. And thinking about it, John was acting a little strange the last time I talked to him. I dropped off my fuzzy little cargo and he wasn't quite right—almost distracted, nervous about something. He didn't even want to sit down for a drink and our usual chat. I chalked it up to work stress. He got that way sometimes. I never took it personally."

"But rats! What was he doing with rats?" Richard asked. "Running them through mazes?"

"No," Margaret answered. "Most likely he was using them for tissue testing. But then the question would be, testing what?"

"Does it have anything to do with all that DNA stuff on the computer?" Carol asked.

"I wouldn't know for sure until examining the tissue samples. And he'd probably put any test specimens in the freezer."

The group's attention shifted to the stainless steel door. No one said it, but they all thought the same thing, remembering the contents of the previous freezer they walked into.

After a moment, "Let's get this over with," Manning said. He walked up to the steel handle and gave it a tug. They all watched as the freezer opened.

"Oh, my God," Carol shrieked. She turned her head away, burying it in Adam's chest. "I have to sit down," she said. Adam helped her to a nearby chair.

Inside, frozen eyes stared up at the group—the body propped up along the back of the freezer. The legs barely fit up to the door. In fact, one knee had frozen in a thirty-degree angle. Streamers of ice dripped down from the man's beard and mustache. His skin was a slight shade of blue.

"Who is it?" Richard asked. None of the personnel photographs he remembered seeing had any men with beards. The facial hair had been an addition over the last eighteen months.

"It's John Blackwood," Adam said, after making sure Carol would be all right. He took a step inside the locker—his breath produced a heavy white mist. Adam carefully knelt closer to his dead friend. First he examined the man's hands, then reached down and gently touched the man's pants at the ankle. Both legs were very cold, but intact. "Forgive me on how strange this may sound, but he's all here." Adam did not relish pawing over his friend, but it had to be done. He turned John and checked his back. "No bullet holes either."

"Frozen to death," Richard said. "Not a pleasant way to die."

"I don't think so," Manning told them. "This locker is airtight. He would have suffocated long before he froze."

"Still, not a way I'd like to shuffle off this mortal coil," Richard commented.

"Me neither," Manning said, studying the locker door. He pulled on the small inside lever. The latch popped right up with each try. "What I don't understand is why didn't he simply walk out."

"Maybe he struck his head," Margaret said, "knocking himself unconscious."

"No, he didn't," Adam said, standing up and coming out of the freezer.

"I checked. I didn't find any cuts or bumps. Even in the cold, there should be something apparent from getting bashed on the skull. He should have been able to walk out under his own power."

"Unless he didn't want to," Manning stated flatly. "Unless there was someone waiting for him out here."

"That doesn't make any sense," Richard said. "Why wouldn't that 'someone' simply open the door to get him? The freezer door wasn't locked—it can't be locked."

"I don't have an answer for you," Manning said, "except with all we've seen so far it's another piece to a very weird puzzle."

Adam turned his head back towards the open freezer door. "Someone help me with John."

"Help you do what?" Richard asked.

"We can't leave him all crouched up in there. He's not a load of garbage to be left and forgotten."

"Certainly, you're not talking about moving him," Richard said.

"I am."

Richard's mouth twitched. "Why would you bother doing that? He's fine right where he is—there's no reason to move him."

"I'll give you one," Margaret interrupted. "I'm not going to work in this lab knowing John Blackwood is dead in that freezer."

"He can't hurt you," Richard told her. "He can't hurt anyone."

The woman's face sharpened. "I may have to go into that freezer and I refuse to have to step over a dead man. The notion is not only morbid, but sick...even for you."

"Fine. Fine. I don't want to argue about it," the man said. He glared at Adam. "You started this, Mr. Hayes, now deal with it."

"We'll take the body to the other set of freezers where we found Emmanuel," Adam said.

"Who?" Carol asked.

"But that's all the way down on the other end of the complex," Richard replied. "I'm not sure if I can..."

"I'll help you," Manning volunteered. "No one should be left like that."

"Use something to cover the body when you carry him out," Carol said with a quivering voice. "Okay?"

Adam gave her an understanding smile. "Sure thing."

"I'll get one of those lab coats from the closet," Manning told the others. "That should do the job."

"And while you two do that," Margaret said, already halfway across the laboratory, "I want to get a peek at those file cabinets."

The metal drawers were completely full of paper-stuffed folders, all dated within the last few weeks. The accumulation of information bordered on impossible for the relatively short time span. Margaret skimmed through the first batch. It didn't take her long to conclude she had no grasp of what she was reading. The earliest dated sheets said something about a new site where the research team had been extracting samples, but besides that, none of it made any sense.

"It's going to take some time to go through all this," she said. "With all the paperwork and the computer files, I'm sure there will be some duplication of data between the two. But a lot of the notes are handwritten and I doubt he had time to transpose them all into the computer. Besides, those genetic models we saw take up quite a bit of disk space. I won't know what's here until I review each and every file." The woman stretched out her right arm, then pulled it back and rubbed her neck. "I don't know about the rest of you, but I could really use some sleep."

As Bruce Manning returned with the lab coat, the decision of sleep became the chief topic. He had to admit sleep wouldn't hurt right about now.

So they all agreed to return to the center of the complex and make use of the crew quarters. For Carol's sake, it was suggested waiting back a few minutes until after Adam and Bruce took care of the body of Dr. John Blackwood. Then returning from the freezers, they would meet up with the others to choose rooms.

With all agreeing to this course of action, Adam and Bruce set out on their delicate task. Carol diverted her eyes as the two men picked up the body and carried it from the room.

The cold Adam felt while he supported the weight of John's frozen remains triggered a memory of his first job in a meat packing plant. He hated that job, but this was so much worse. He knew this man enough to call him friend.

"You managing okay?" Manning asked him.

They had just passed the rec room.

"Sure, I..." Out of the corner of his eye, Adam thought he saw a shadow scurry past the open door. "Did you see that?" he said. "Something moved in there."

Both men stopped. "No, I didn't," Manning said. "What was it? A person maybe?"

"No, I don't think so, but I only got a glimpse. It was just a shape really. I..." Adam shook his head. "I'm not positive I saw anything at all."

"You want to stop and check it?"

Adam's eyes slipped down to the lab-coat shroud. "No, it was probably my brain screaming for sleep. Let's finish this up and get back with the others."

Inside the locker, Bruce and Adam put Dr. Blackwood's body on the rack below Emmanuel Phillips. Adam thought about saying a few words, but decided it would be more appropriate at a funeral, not in a meat locker. Besides, what could he possibly say?

The men left the freezer and headed back down the hall. Passing the rec room, Manning stopped at the entrance.

"I said it was nothing," Adam told him.

"I know, but what will it hurt to take a short gander." And that it was. The soldier didn't go in more than two feet. His eyes did a fast scan of the area.

"I told you," Adam said from the doorway. "Nothing but my imagination. Let's get back to the others."

Manning said nothing and followed Adam from the room. Behind them, a black thing disappeared up the air vent.

Moments later the group was reunited. They had picked out the five rooms closest to the bathroom, which Richard Baines was currently using.

Carol greeted the men with good news. "We had some luck. Several of the quarters are neat enough. And I found some clean bedding. If it wasn't for the weird things going on, this could almost be fun."

"You have a strange view of fun," Margaret said.

"This one's mine," Carol said ignoring her. "I only wish I knew who she was."

"She?" Adam said.

"There's a picture of a pretty blonde woman standing next to a rather attractive man. They're holding hands at Disney World. It must be her room, considering the clothes I found."

"Pretty and blonde? By your description it has to be Hannah Wyatt."

"Was she a nice person?" Carol asked. "I felt like a sneak thief going through her belongings."

"Very nice. And I'm sure she would understand. In fact if she was here, she probably would have offered you their use."

At that moment, Richard came out of the bathroom. "Next," he bellowed.

"That would be me," Carol said.

After the woman excused herself, Adam wandered over to the sleeping quarters directly across from those Lieutenant Manning had picked out for himself. He stared into the mess. It was the one room torn apart that they didn't find an empty pile of clothes in. Now he knew why.

"Something wrong?" Margaret asked him, reading his glum expression.

Adam shook his head. "It's nothing really. These were John's quarters. It's an eerie feeling having just carried his body to a storage freezer. If there's a reason for all this," Adam said, finally looking over to the woman, "I'd really appreciate you telling me."

"If only I could, Mr. Hayes," she admitted. "If only I could."

A minute later, Carol emerged from the bathroom.

"Now that we are all back together," Margaret said. "I know it may be difficult, but you all must try to get a good night's sleep. Tomorrow morning I want to give each of you a physical exam. Under such limited conditions, it would help if you were all well rested. If any of you find it impossible to sleep, wake me and I'll give you something to help. I found some tranquilizers in one of the medical kits."

Without much conversation, the group acknowledged the woman's offer.

"Now that that's settled," Richard said. "I suggest we all meet in the kitchen at eight-thirty. I don't know about your rooms, but mine has an alarm clock. If you're not up by then I'll wake you myself." That statement produced no complaints, which evidently pleased the man. "Goodnight," he added and disappeared inside his room. The others followed suit.

"Miss Chambers," Lieutenant Manning said before she had a chance to shut her door.

"Carol, please."

"If you insist, Carol." Manning pulled the loaded gun from his waistband. "Are you sure you don't want this?"

"We've already been over that."

"I know, but I thought having it would help you sleep better."

"Quite the opposite I think, but thanks anyway."

"If you're sure?"

"I am. Goodnight, Lieutenant."

"Bruce," he said.

"Goodnight, Bruce."

CHAPTER FIVE

Adam snapped off the small lamp on the nightstand next to his bed. Lying with one arm tucked between head and pillow, his eyes adjusted to the darkness. Strange and wonderful shapes merged and formed in the blackness. Within the last eighteen months, he had stayed overnight at the station only one other time. And under similar circumstances—an unexpected storm with tremendous winds. It grounded him.

Though back then, even at night the station was alive with activity. He could always hear one sound or another. People walking down the hall, the hum of machinery, even the faint sounds of music. In the morning, he asked some of the crew how they managed. One said earplugs. Another said it was simply a matter of getting used to it. Getting used to it? What a strange thought. Now there was nothing but dead silence and Adam knew he could never get used to it.

He had barely closed his eyes when a soft knock cut the nothingness. Adam lifted his head from the pillow and turned towards the sound. At the base of the door where the hall light crept under, he saw the dark spots unmistakably made by two human feet. He got out of bed and stumbled across the floor, scarcely managing to pull his pants on as the third soft knock sounded. Then the spots moved away. Adam opened the door to find Carol turning back around with a smile. She stood barefoot and had on a lavender cotton robe, which came down to her knees.

"Did I wake you? When you didn't answer I thought maybe you had already dropped off."

"No, not yet. I was just thinking."

She stepped up to his door. "About what?"

Adam grinned. "Nothing important." He studied her for a moment. "Are you okay? Do you need something?"

"For starters, may I come in?" she asked.

"Oh, of course. Let me get the lights." Then when they had a clear view of each other, he said, "That's better. So, what's on your mind?"

"I wanted to apologize for the way I behaved today. You must think me a silly woman."

"No, not at all."

Carol eased forward several inches. The bottom hem of her robe ruffled slightly. "And I very much appreciate that you had Dr. Walker tell me the truth about the virus."

"You had the right to know. But it may be nothing. None of us are showing any signs of being infected."

"Still, I'd rather be prepared for the worst. I could tell you were upset with Dr. Walker, but I have to admit, at the time I didn't understand why."

"I got over it," he said.

"You're a strong person Adam Hayes. I find this whole thing terribly frightening."

"Considering the circumstances, practically being trapped in a deserted station in Antarctica. The crew missing, except for the ones we found dead. That certainly justifies being frightened in my book."

"Like you said earlier today, it wasn't exactly what I signed up for," she said. "But there is a bright side."

"It can't be the food."

"No, not the food." She gently caressed his right cheek, then leaned closer and kissed him on the mouth. "That's a thank you," she said.

"You're very welcome."

She kissed him again.

"What's that one for?"

"Because I wanted to," she said. "Do you like your room?"

"It's fine."

"Only fine? I think it suits you. Masculine, but still gentle. To be honest, I picked my room because I found it to be very lovely. It has a cozy, almost homey feel to it. You can tell a lot about a person by how they pamper themselves. Take this robe, for instance. It's soft and warm." She put the sleeve to her nose. "It even smells good."

"And it fits you well."

"It does, but I never liked this color. It clashes with my red hair." She opened the robe and let it drop to the floor. She stood there naked.

"Yes, I see," Adam said.

On the bed, Adam reached up and touched Carol's breasts with both hands. She arched her back at the sensation, stopping her rhythm. She softly moaned, pulling his fingers tighter to her body. She cupped and squeezed the back of his hands to increase the pressure and her pleasure. Then she brought her head down to his neck and kissed him. Her hips returned to their motion of ecstasy.

She began to grind her hips down on him, harder and harder. Her force increased with each passing second. Her body began to tremble. Then from the hall came a loud crash.

"What?" Adam said, by instinct sitting up a bit.

"No," Carol said, pushing him back. He was surprised at her strength.

"Did you hear that?" he said.

"Nothing. It was nothing," she said breathlessly. She kissed his neck again. Her hot, deep breathing filled his ear.

Another loud crash came from the hall. "We should find out what that is," he said.

"It's probably one of the others stumbling around out there."

Then came the gun shots. Three of them. Blam. Blam. Blam.

This time there was no argument. Both Adam and Carol jumped off the bunk. The sexual excitement peaking mere moments ago had now been lost. Adam struggled with his pants. Carol took the robe from the floor and threw it on, making sure to tie it closed.

There was another shot and Richard began to shout from the hall. "Something's here! Something's here!"

Adam grabbed his own gun and along with Carol rushed out into the corridor where Richard stood holding his revolver with shaking hands. The tip of the gun wavered back and forth as he tried to take aim. The four bullet holes were easy to spot in the wall. Unless the wall was his intended target, the man had missed clean.

Manning had beat the couple into the hall and Margaret was just now coming from her room. No one seemed to notice the sweat on the hair around Carol's face, nor the few long strands of red hair on Adam's chest.

"Do you see it!" Richard yelled. Before Manning or anyone else could answer, the frightened man shot off another round, hitting a nearby door. The thunderous blast made Carol jump—she screamed. Manning bolted forward and wrestled the gun away from Richard.

"No," Richard shouted, "we have to shoot it."

"What?" Manning said. "Shoot what?"

"It was… It was black… I heard a noise. I came out of my room. That door, that door." The man fell against the wall and slid to the floor.

"What about the door?" Adam asked, trying to keep the tension out of his voice. "Richard, what about the door?"

"It was shaking…rattling…banging…like someone was fighting to get out." Richard had to stop briefly to catch his breath. "It rocked back and forth in its frame."

"That accounts for the loud crashes," Adam said.

"You heard them too?" Manning asked.

"Yeah." Adam glanced over at Carol. "I heard them too."

"How about you Miss Cham…Carol? Did you hear any noise?"

"Yes, I think so."

"Count me out," Margaret said. "I can sleep through a thunder storm." She shrugged. "And I have."

"So what came out?" Carol asked.

"What?" Richard said. "Came out?"

"Out of the room," Manning added. "You said someone or something opened the door and came from the room."

"No," Richard told them. "No, I didn't say that. It didn't open the door. It didn't have to." Richard pointed to the small grill at the bottom of the door used for circulation. "It came from there. It poured out…oozed out… it was horrible."

"You've been sleep walking again," Margaret said. "He did this all the time when we were married. Sadly, I could live with that." She fought back a yawn. "He gets in these waking dreams. It doesn't happen often, mostly when he's under a lot of stress."

"I would count today as one of those days," Adam said.

"I know what I saw," Richard insisted. "I know what I saw. I shot right at it. I hit it at least three times. Maybe more."

Manning pointed to the wall and door. "You fired five rounds and there are five bullet holes. If there was something, you missed clean."

"No, I hit it."

"There's no blood, Mr. Baines," the soldier informed him. "There's no blood."

"There has to be something," Richard said. "I hit it dead on."

"Check for yourself."

"Goddamn it, I'm not crazy! I saw it—I shot it! Case closed!"

"Please, excuse me, and know I'm not doubting you, but where did it go?" Carol asked.

"I'm not sure," Richard told her, "I turned away when I heard Manning coming out of his room. It was gone when I looked back." He used his robe sleeve to wipe his forehead. "Maybe it went back in its room."

"Its room?" Margaret asked.

"It did come from there." The man let out a labored breath. "And as far as I'm concerned, if it wants that room it can have it."

"What if he did see something?" Carol said. "I mean, if he really wasn't sleepwalking."

"I wasn't sleepwalking! How many times do I have to tell you all that? I wasn't sleepwalking."

"Then let's check it out," the soldier said. "Did you bring your gun?" he asked Adam.

"Yep, right here."

Manning took a step forward, then paused. "This room is too small if we have to start shooting. I think it best if the rest of you stay out here. We'll leave the door open in case we have to make a hasty retreat. It might be a good idea to stand clear."

The two men approached the entryway. "Remember when we passed the rec room?" Adam whispered to Manning. "I thought I saw something myself." He hoped the others couldn't hear him.

"I was just thinking about that."

"What were you thinking?"

"I was thinking we better be careful."

The men disappeared into the room. Almost immediately a light came on and poured back into the hall. Several moments passed. The others watched the doorway for their return. When it wasn't forthcoming, Carol called out, "You guys okay?" They did not answer. "Adam?"

Seconds later, Adam did come out followed by Lieutenant Manning.

The doctor spoke first. "Find anything?"

"Yes," Adam said, "an empty room. It's hard to tell—maybe there was something in there, maybe not. It's pretty messed up."

"It shouldn't be," Carol said. "It wasn't messed up before. I know—I'm the one who picked out the rooms. I thought it was lucky that we had an extra one to choose from."

"Lucky," Richard said. "For Christ's sake, how could it possibly be lucky?"

"I don't know. It just seemed…"

"You're back in your usual mood, Richard," Margaret said. "Snapping at the one person who believes you. The experience couldn't have been that traumatic."

"I believe him too," Adam said. Not more than five minutes ago, he and Carol were in his bed. He recalled her smell and the warmth of her body. He had half a mind to take her and continue where they had left off. But instead he said, "Okay, if there is something here, we should try to find it." He stared down at the gun in his hand, then at the bullet holes in the wall. He remembered how shaky Richard's hands were when he fired the gun. He must have missed. There's no other explanation. Or at least not one he wanted to think about.

"If what you say is true…there is something here," Margaret asked, "and we do find it, what then?"

"Good question," he admitted. "And I don't have a good answer for you, but I'd rather set out after it, then have it coming back for one of us. I'm not asking anyone to come with me."

"I'm certainly not staying here," Richard said. "Besides, I'm the only one who actually saw the thing."

"And you might need help," Carol said.

"I agree," Manning added. "This isn't the time to split up. We can watch each other's back."

"The safety-in-numbers bit," Adam said. "Works for me, if you're all up to it."

"You don't expect us to sleep now do you?" Margaret told him.

It turned out to be a simple decision—to stay together—searching the complex again as a group—searching for Richard's black monster. Except for returning to the rooms for more appropriate apparel, the small band remained close together. Even then, when one entered their borrowed quarters to change, the others waited in the hall making sure no one or no thing would catch them off guard.

Margaret was the last to dress, but when she came from her room, they were ready to begin. They worked their way down the hall looking in each room—the other sleeping quarters, the rec room and all storage closets. It was a repeat of the trip down, and although they were tired, they managed a complete and thorough inspection.

"I'm beginning to think this is pointless," Richard said, poking his head under the bunk. He was starting to doubt if he had indeed seen anything at all. But then the memory of the thing oozing through that door grate returned, and so did the terror. Okay, he thought, I saw it—I saw it. I only wish I hadn't.

"Hey, this is your monster hunt," Margaret said.

Richard stood up. "Believe me, you don't have to remind me." He hurried over to the door. "I sure wish we could open a window." He wiped his forehead. "God, it's stuffy in here."

Hearing a slight tremor in her ex-husband's gripe, Margaret turned a doctor's eye towards him. His color was a little off.

"Don't look at me like that. I'm fine. It's just this stale air." Richard stormed out, pushing past Adam and Carol.

"I suspect that means we're finished here," Margaret said. "I'd better make sure Richard really is okay." She disappeared through the door, followed by Lieutenant Manning.

A moment later Richard yelled from the hall. "I told you, I'm fine. I don't need you feeling my forehead."

Finally alone with Carol, Adam stepped closer to her. They hadn't had a chance to speak since Richard's shooting spree. For a half-second, he thought about walking past her, but forced himself to overcome his reluctance. He lightly touched her arm.

"Carol, I..."

She stood there watching him fight with his words.

"I'm sorry," he said, "I'm sorry about...about not..."

She stopped the man by tenderly placing her index finger against his lips. "There's nothing to be sorry about," she told him with a tiny hint of a smile. "There really wasn't anything either of us could do. When a man starts shooting bullets outside your bedroom door, it's bound to break the mood. Besides," she added with a gleam in her eye, "there'll be other times." She peeked over her shoulder making sure they were unobserved, then gave him a quick kiss. "Count on it."

"I will."

"You two done in there," Manning said from the threshold. "We have to move on."

"We're finishing up now," Adam said, gesturing to Carol for her to lead the way. He turned the light switch off.

The group continued on to the cook's quarters. Richard led the pack. Not because of a newfound bravery, not because he thought it the right thing to do, but because he was getting sick of Margaret poking and prodding him.

"You didn't touch me this much when we were married," he protested, tearing himself away. He told her over and over again that he felt fine—as fine as you could be in a place like this.

Richard entered the room, glancing back once, seeing the others came up fast. He groped along the wall for the light switch until his hand hit a picture frame, which he accidentally knocked to the floor. He heard the sound of glass shattering.

"Shit," he said, then thought, who's going to care? He continued fumbling his way through the dark. He inched his way farther inside; a piece of glass crunched beneath his shoe. Finally, he found the switch.

When the light came on, a hand landed on his shoulder. If there were a way to describe the shortest period of measurable time, it would be the moment between when the hand touched Richard and the time it took him to realize that the others were still down the hall. Richard's gun fired as he turned with a start. Without another thought, he pointed his gun. And again pulled the trigger. He thought his heart would burst when he heard the empty clicks. He had forgotten to reload his weapon and carelessly wasted his one remaining bullet.

"What happened?" Manning yelled, tearing through the opened door. "Why did you fire?" The others were right there behind him. "Did you see your monster?"

"No. No, monster," Richard said with a shaky voice, then pointed to the man on the floor next to the bunk. The sound of the single shot had been enough to terrify him. Curled up in a ball, he was sobbing while both hands tightly cupped his face.

Even with only the back of his head exposed, Bruce Manning recognized this man. It was his brother.

"Eric," Manning said. "Eric. It's me, Bruce." The man's sobbing didn't cease. "Eric, can you hear me? Can you speak?"

"Is he hurt?" Margaret asked.

"I don't know. I can't tell."

"Get him over to the bunk," Margaret said. "I can examine him there. But be careful not to get any blood on you."

"He doesn't appear to be bleeding," Manning said, taking his brother by the arm. "Come on, Eric. I need you to sit up."

Though he obeyed the order, the man was numb to his brother's voice. He sat with his eyes staring out into space. His lower lip quivered.

"How did you find him?" the soldier asked Richard, while at the same time holding his brother so he wouldn't tip to his side.

"I didn't. He found me. The fool snuck up on me. I nearly blew his head off. It's a good thing I'm out of ammo."

Bruce stared down at the gun in Richard's hand then shifted his eyes back to meet the portly man's gaze. "Yeah, he was lucky—too," was all he said.

Richard didn't like how that sounded. He didn't know why, but he knew he didn't like it one bit.

Dr. Walker knelt down and with delicate fingers pried open the man's eyelids to check his pupils, then she felt his neck for a pulse. The man's heartbeat seemed strong and regular enough.

"What's wrong with him?" Bruce asked.

"I'm not sure. Shock maybe." She observed the man closely. She had never seen anything like this—the man appeared to have regressed to the mental state of a child. What would cause such a severe reaction? Like his brother, the man was a trained soldier.

"Shock? From what?" Carol asked.

"Look around," Richard snapped. "Haven't you been paying attention!"

"There's no reason to yell at her," Adam said.

"This arguing is getting us nowhere," Margaret told them. "We are all bordering on exhaustion. We should all return to our rooms and try to get some sleep."

"First, we need to decide on what to do with him," Richard said, referring to Eric Manning. "He should be locked up in one of the spare quarters. I think we would all sleep easier."

"We're not locking him up," Bruce said bluntly.

"He could be dangerous," Richard complained.

"He can stay with me. I'll watch him."

"You will never get any sleep that way," Margaret said. "We all have to be at our peak."

"I told you I'm not locking him up."

"I'm not saying we have to. I have another suggestion."

"I'm listening."

"I can shoot him up with tranquilizers. That way you both can get some rest. And judging by his appearance, your brother is in desperate need of sleep."

"Aren't tranquilizers dangerous in his condition?" Carol asked.

"No. It shouldn't require much. Just enough to relax him and nature should do the rest."

Manning nodded. "If you think that's best."

"I'll move one of the other beds into your room," Adam said. "The floors here aren't too comfortable."

"Thanks," Manning said, putting his brother's arm over his shoulder and helping him up from the bunk. "Let's get going." Bruce guided his brother down the hall with Adam and Carol only a few paces back.

"What about…about the thing?" Richard asked.

"What about it?" Margaret said.

"Aren't we going to search anymore?"

"Search where? We've covered every place. If there was something, it's gone now. And I don't know about you, but I'm going back to bed."

"What about…?" he started again.

"If you're so worried, Richard, feel free to stand guard." Margaret followed the others down the hall. She didn't look back once.

Richard stood there alone, keeping open a sharp ear. He heard nothing but the eerie hum of the overhead lights. His eyes darted back and forth once, then twice. After a third, he hightailed it to catch up with his ever-distancing comrades.

CHAPTER SIX

In the dining area, the very next morning, Dr. Margaret Walker was almost finished with her examination of Carol Chambers. Carol sat very still in the hard chair while Margaret gently ran her fingertips along Carol's jaw line, checking for any swollen glands. "How do you feel?" the doctor asked.

"Fine. Maybe a little tired."

"After last night, I'm not surprised." Margaret gave Carol a reassuring smile. So far, everything fit well within the norms. Margaret eased her hands to the base of Carol's neck. "How's your throat? Are you having any trouble swallowing?"

Carol shook her head. "Not at all." She let out a small reflex cough when Margaret felt the sides of her windpipe. "How is Bruce's brother doing?" Carol asked.

"Still sleeping, thank God." Margaret took the woman's pulse, then placed the diaphragm of the stethoscope she had found in the medical kit to Carol's chest.

Carol finally asked the question foremost on her mind. "You don't think he's got that virus you talked about, do you?"

Margaret motioned the woman not to speak as she listened to her heartbeat. After a moment, she pulled the rubber tips from her ears, and said, "No, I don't think so. The fact that he's still alive and in one piece is a sure sign."

"I'm so glad the lieutenant found his brother. I love happy endings."

The doctor jotted down a few notes on her clipboard. "Hold that good thought. This mess isn't over yet."

As the two women spoke, Adam entered the kitchen wearing his boots and parka. He smiled at Carol when she turned his way and she immediately returned the gesture. That simple act made Adam feel so much better. He was afraid that maybe she was upset with him for last night. He had thought it best if they went back to their own rooms. When he told her so, she agreed, but he thought he heard some subtle irritation in her voice. He didn't want to hurt her. She was special—it was rare these days to find someone so caring. She showed true concern last night for Lieutenant Manning's brother, a man she had never set eyes on before. And now while coming into the room, he overheard her asking about Eric's well-being.

"I'm glad you're here," Dr. Walker told Adam on his approach. "I'm almost ready for you."

"I thought you might be, so I came to let you know it will have to wait. If we want to get out of here, I'd better check on the plane. That storm came through pretty hard last night."

"Those words sound wonderful," Carol said, *"get out of here."*

"Apparently you're not giving me a choice, so all right," Margaret said, taking the stethoscope from around her neck and laying it flat on the table. "I just have you and the lieutenant left. The rest of us have shown no negative signs. And considering the close proximity we've been to each other, I really doubt that only one or two of us would become infected by the same virulent strain that took the station crew."

"Great," Adam said. "I hate getting checkups."

"I didn't say you were off the hook. I only meant that your exam could wait. But be assured, it will happen." She gave him that stern look only doctors seem to produce. It must come with the bad handwriting.

"Okay," Adam said, "when I get back." He started out of the room.

"Be careful," Carol said.

Adam turned and once more smiled at the woman, then walked on.

He headed down the long hall—his heavy boots produced a soft echo with each step. Adam kept a sharp eye out for anything unusual and found himself glancing in every open doorway. He remembered thinking he saw some weird shape in the rec room—afterwards he convinced himself it had been a mischievous trick played on him by the light and dark. But what about Richard Baines' little target practice last night? The man said he was shooting at something horrible. The jury's out on that one, though it did make a guy pause for thought. Even with a second search, they unearthed nothing horrible—no monsters—no shadows and now, eyeing each room, he still didn't expect to find anything. So why did he feel so apprehensive?

On the way to the main door, Adam glared back towards the freezer room. The remains of two fine men were stored there like so much racked beef. "What in God's good name happened here?" Adam said to the empty air, almost as though he was asking his dead friends. Maybe Eric Manning knew something, he thought, but the man was in no shape to give out any information. Adam shook his head—this place was really starting to get to him. He would be glad to leave.

Adam pushed at the door, forcing back a small pile of blown snow. Several small drifts had formed between the building and the plane. The wind continued its constant build-up of white powder. If it blew much harder, he'd have to tell the others that their trip back to McMurdo Station would have to be postponed again, but he didn't see the need for that quite yet. Small particles of swirling snow hit his cheeks like tiny wet stinging kisses. He slipped on his goggles and pulled up his hood. He started his walk to the plane—his tunnel vision was almost of pure white. He would look up every ten seconds or so to keep on track.

Tromping through some of the higher drifts, Adam paced his steps so not to overtax himself. It was important not to get exhausted in this cold. These weren't the best conditions where one could stop to take a breather.

When he reached the plane, Adam gave the exterior a quick going over. All in all, the craft appeared to have weathered the storm with little difficulty. The wings would need to be brushed off, but on the bright side, with the snow there would be no ice. He also saw that the props would need a bit of brushing too.

Adam moved back to the door and began brushing away the snow, clearing off the window. The handle turned easily and with a single tug the door swung open. The sunlight poured in. Stepping up, he made his way through the interior of the craft.

"What the fuck," Adam said. His eyes opened wide and he stared blankly into the cockpit.

"That doesn't sound encouraging," Manning said from behind him.

Adam jumped. "Jesus Christ! Do you have to sneak up on a guy like that?"

"Sorry, I thought I could lend a hand."

"It's much too late for that, I'm afraid," Adam said sharply. "It appears someone has already had a hand in it."

"I don't understand," Bruce said, though by Adam's tone, he could clearly hear that the man was upset about something.

"They're smashed," Adam added bluntly. "The controls are all smashed." He continued into the cockpit and threw himself down into the seat. His foot crushed several small pieces of broken glass. He yanked back his hood and tore off his goggles. Several more four-letter words filled the air.

Manning pulled down his own hood. "This isn't good."

"No, it's not." Adam flicked a sliver of glass from the tachometer. "Not at all." He ran his gloved finger over the shattered altimeter, then onto the fuel gauge. The damage was thorough—the compass, the air-speed indicator, the oil pressure gauge—all rendered useless; even the throttle control had been bent out of shape.

"And I assume repairs are out of the question."

"You assume right!" Adam slammed his fist against the control column. "Who could have done this?"

"A very good question," Bruce said. "Except for yours, I didn't see any other footprints."

"That's right you didn't. With all this blowing snow, ours will be gone too within twenty minutes or so. I hate to ask you this, but...but do you think your brother...?"

"No, he wouldn't. And physically, he couldn't. You've seen his condition. He can barely stand under his own power."

"Then," Adam said, but both men had the same thought, "it seems we're not as alone as we thought we were."

"How's the radio?" Manning asked.

The faceplate had been shattered, the wires had been pulled out from the back, and the microphone had been torn off and laid cracked open on the floor of the plane. "It's garbage," Adam said.

"How do we explain this to the others?" Manning asked.

The pilot shook his head. "I'm not sure. Very carefully, I guess. It's not going to come as good news that we're stuck here for a while."

Adam glanced out through the windshield and by chance looked over at the smaller storage building next to the main building. Even through the blowing snow, for a second he thought he saw a face staring back at him, but as abruptly it disappeared. He briefly turned away, then looked back. The face had reappeared. "Lieutenant," he said.

"I see it," Manning replied. "Seems you were right about us not being alone."

"Yeah, good for me. The question is what to do about it?"

Manning had put his hood up and was adjusting his goggles, when he said, "I suggest we circle around. Approach the entrance on its blind side."

"You think that's wise?"

"I do. Whoever it is, didn't stay put last night." He nodded down at the smashed controls.

"Point taken." Adam pulled his own hood forward. He stood up and left the cockpit, following Manning towards the plane's exit.

"It's only a matter of time," Manning said when they reached the hatchway, "until they decide to come into the station. If we expect to protect ourselves, we should go on the attack...the best defense being a good offense and all that."

"They. They? You think there's more than one?"

"Don't know, but we should anticipate the worst."

"I have to tell you, Lieutenant, your tone does not reassure me."

"Should it?"

"Probably not," Adam said, and then pushed the plane door open. A blast of cold air surged up and under his hood.

The two men headed back towards the main complex. But instead of entering, they moved along its perimeter. They waded through the heavy snow, making their way to the back of the storage building.

Adam pointed to the side out of the wind. Manning nodded his agreement and waved him forward. The only window on that side was midway along the outer wall. If they kept close to the structure, they would stay out of sight.

They crouched down to pass under the window, then finally crept around to the front door. Adam, with his back to the wall, firmly grasped the handle. He looked over at Manning, who signaled his readiness. Adam tore open the door and both men rushed inside.

In a small entryway they were met by three more doors, one directly across from the main entrance and one on either side.

"Pick one," Adam said, easing up his goggles. They were out of the wind, but it was still too cold to remove their hoods.

"I would say to the right or straight ahead."

"Agreed." Whoever had been watching them did so from a window on the right side of the building, allowing the men to disregard the left door.

Though not knowing the layout behind the remaining doors, either could hide their quarry. "That still leaves two," Adam added.

"First things first—or in this case first door first." Manning chose the one to the right. His reason? It was the closest to him. The room was very small. Bigger than a closet, but too small to be used for an office or living quarters. Then he noticed the piece of oil pipe, the exhaust tubing and the dark stains on the floor. At one time, the small chamber must have been a generator room. "That leaves door number two," he said.

Cautiously proceeding through the next section of building, they discovered several large wooden crates and over two dozen smaller boxes. The area was warm enough for them to drop their hoods, which restored the use of their peripheral vision. Taking only a few more steps, Adam's foot hit something. It clattered during its roll along the floor. Bruce picked it up—an empty can of Van Camps Pork and Beans. But it hadn't been opened by normal means. It had been hacked open—possibly with an ax or hatchet.

"So much for stealth," Adam said. Then he spotted another can. He knelt down to retrieve it and found it in the exact same condition as the first. A little farther down the floor he saw still another empty can and another and another.

"Someone sure likes beans. I..." Before Adam could finish his sentence, there was a loud scream followed by a shotgun blast. Luckily, he managed to jump for cover. The crate next to him suffered a large hole, the contents of which dripped down on his head.

"Lieutenant," Adam called out. "You okay?" He heard nothing. "Lieutenant? Bruce, answer me." The soldier did not respond. Then from behind came another scream and another blast. Adam kept low. This time the screams didn't stop, but fused with another voice.

"Over here!" It was Lieutenant Manning. He had snuck around, getting behind the shooter, and was now in a struggle. Adam jumped to his feet, pushed past the crates and grabbed their attacker in a bear hug. The struggle became a tug-of-war with a slide-action shotgun standing in for the rope. The person also wore a parka, but had the hood up. Manning took his best guess to the location of their chin and struck a blow. The unknown person crumbled to their knees. Adam let go and the body fell, while Manning kept hold of the weapon.

"You hurt?" Manning asked.

"No."

"You're bleeding."

"I don't think so." Adam felt his forehead. It surprised him to find red on his fingertips. He smelled the dark smear, then tasted it. "Ketchup," he said. "The shotgun blew into a crate of the stuff. It went everywhere—including on me, it appears. Now let's see who killed the condiment." Adam bent down and pushed the parka hood back. To his and Manning's astonishment, their attacker was a woman. She had short brown hair and a tiny button nose. Her lips were chapped and her nose, cheeks and forehead were smudged with dirt.

"Susan Dawson," Adam said. "She's stationed here with the others."

"I didn't know," Manning explained, putting the gun down and kneeling beside her. "If I knew I wouldn't have hit her. I don't hit women." And to make things worse, now that she lay unconscious, Manning saw that she was a small woman, though he would never have guessed by the way she fought. She had the speed and strength of some wild creature.

"In this case I don't think you had much of a choice."

Susan's eyes began to flutter open, then widened with terror. She tried to force herself up to run, but Adam held her down.

"It's me, Susan, Adam Hayes."

Her eyes focused on his face. She timidly extended a hand to touch him, but pulled back.

"I don't think she recognizes you," Manning told him. "She's too frightened."

"Susan," Adam said, "are there others here with you?"

She answered him with only a blank, far-off stare.

"You're not getting through to her. We should bring her back with us."

"No," Susan finally said. "No. I ran before it got me. It killed the others."

"What? What killed the others?"

"The ice. The ice. Deep in the ice." The woman began to weep.

"I think Dr. Walker should examine her," Manning said. "And the sooner, the better."

"I'm open to suggestions, but I don't think it's going to be easy with her in this state. She might not care for the idea of being taken from here. And I don't think we could manage with her kicking and screaming all the way back. If she runs off, we could easily lose her in the blowing snow. It wouldn't take long before she freezes to death." The image of his plane's smashed control panel popped back into Adam's head. If his crew back at the airport didn't send help soon, that could be a fate they all shared. The station's oil tanks had to be getting pretty low by now.

"We can't leave her," Manning said, "and she can't stay here by herself." Manning eased towards the woman. "Hi, Susan. My name's Bruce. I'm Eric's brother. You remember Eric—Eric Manning."

She nodded her head.

"We found him and he's safe. You can be safe with him—with us. He's your friend. I want to be your friend too. We won't let anything hurt you… I won't let anything hurt you. Come back with us."

She peered up at him with fawn eyes.

"Susan, will you come with us? It will be all right—you'll see."

She nodded again and asked softly, "Eric is okay?"

"Yes, he's okay. And now, so are you." Bruce helped the woman to her feet. She stood shaking. Then Bruce picked up the shotgun.

"You want to let me in on what you're planning to do with that?" Adam asked.

"I'm bringing it back with us. There's a box of shells on that crate to your left. We should bring them both."

"Why?" Adam asked. "I think we have enough guns."

"If there is something back in the main complex, we can never have enough guns. Besides, if we don't need it, we won't use it. Simple."

"Sure simple. But it still scares the crap out of me. If I hadn't ducked when I did, this red stuff would have been more than ketchup."

Margaret Walker decided to return to the lab and begin gathering up some of the notes and files. Space would be limited for the return flight home, so she thought it best to go over the data and bring back the most pertinent information at hand.

Richard had told her that Bruce decided to join Adam with the inspection of the plane, which meant *two* examinations she still had left to perform. She couldn't help but think that both men were using the plane as a convenient excuse. What was it about men that had them disliking being examined by a female doctor?

Even though she, Richard and Carol exhibited no signs of any abnormality, she wanted to be thorough. The exams had been quite routine, even boring, except for the surprise of Richard's blood pressure. It was down—in fact, it was normal. When she commented that he must be taking better care of himself, Richard mumbled something about doctors always making a big deal out of nothing.

Now with the time she had, she thought it best to get to work. Where to begin was the only question. There were so many notes, books and files. She hadn't even gone through the desk yet, which in a way made it the perfect place to start.

The desk was locked, but turned out easy enough to jimmy. She opened the top drawer. It contained pens, pencils, paperclips and other things extremely ordinary. In the second drawer, she found a neat stack of notebooks. And lying on the very bottom of the third drawer, atop a half-used ream of paper, she found an unlabeled cassette tape. She scanned the room for a recorder, but saw none. It couldn't be all that important, she thought, why else would it be discarded so haphazardly in the bottom of the lowest drawer? She put it in her sweater pocket—she'd listen to it later.

Not finding anything else of value in the desk, Margaret picked up the first few notebooks. She decided to start with only those volumes from a week before the station lost contact with the outside world. She could always go back further, if she needed to.

Opening the notebook dated January 16, 1991, she thumbed through the pages. They were all in the handwriting of John Blackwood. A shiver went through her body remembering the man frozen to death. Why would a man allow himself to die that way? Manning said the freezer wasn't locked—he could've come out anytime he wanted. Then why didn't he? She hoped the answers would be somewhere in all these notes.

The more she read, the more perplexed she became. She expected a simple log of core samples. Instead, she found pages and pages of precise hand-drawn models of recombinant DNA and nucleotides, the extent of which confused and amazed her. The detailed sketches of DNA sequences contained the four bases of Adenine, Cytosine, Guanine and Thymine together in the accepted bonds. And some sketches had those strange extra-unknown bonds, the same ones displayed on the computer screen.

These notes would make more sense being in a lab performing experiments in genetic engineering rather than a lab studying core samples dug up from the Antarctic ice sheet. The rewrite of the analysis software spoke volumes that there was something specific to be examined—some genetic material. But where would the material have come from? Then it hit her. Of course, how obvious, where else? From under the ice. The crew must have dug up some specimen, probably partially fossilized, and were trying to analyze it.

What do DNA, a fossilized sample and a group of missing scientists have in common? She sat back in the chair and rubbed her temples. None of this made any sense. And adding Eric Manning's condition into the equation, it only got more and more difficult.

Before she could give the whole situation another thought, Carol burst into the lab. "Dr. Walker, come quick," she said. "Adam and the lieutenant have returned. They found someone."

Margaret couldn't hold back her surprise on hearing the news. "Where? Who?"

"I don't know. They said she's one of the researchers."

"She?"

"Please, hurry! They're asking for you."

Margaret threw the open notebook down on the desktop. "Is she hurt?"

"I don't know."

Both women ran down the long hallway to the main entrance. Adam and Bruce had already removed their parkas and were trying to convince Susan to do the same. When Carol and Margaret drew closer, the woman pulled away from the men and bolted for the door. With lightning-like reflexes, Bruce grabbed Susan by the arm. "It's okay. No one will harm you." His voice succeeded in calming her.

"Who is she?" Margaret asked.

"Susan Dawson," Adam said. "We found her in the next building. She must've been living out there for days."

It took Margaret a moment to remember the name. "Dawson? Yes, she's the station's metallurgist." The doctor took a step towards the woman, who immediately hid behind Lieutenant Manning. "I won't hurt you," Margaret tried to assure her.

"Careful, Doc," Adam said. "She's a little unpredictable."

"What's the matter with her?" Carol asked.

"By her appearance and mannerisms," Margaret said, "extreme shock. Along with a heavy dose of paranoia." Cautious not to make any sudden movements, she approached the frightened woman. "Everything's going to be fine. I only want to check you for injuries." Margaret gently and slowly raised her hand towards the woman. Susan flinched back a bit. "Easy now." The doctor carefully lifted the woman's eyelids. "Her pupils respond normally. I don't think she has a concussion. Except for being a tad bit emaciated, she seems healthy enough."

"I think all she's been eating," Manning said, "were cold cans of pork and beans."

"We should get her something from the kitchen," Margaret said.

"Will we have enough room in the plane to take her back with us?" Carol asked.

"About that," Adam said, "we have a problem." His voice trailed off for a moment, then, "Where's Richard? He needs to hear this too."

"He's sitting with Eric," Margaret said.

"Is there something wrong with my brother? I mean something new?"

"No, I just thought it best, in case he wakes up. Actually, Richard volunteered. Though I think it's because he wants to be the first to ask the questions—him being the great leader and all."

"Did I hear my name taken in vain?" Richard said, suddenly appearing from behind.

Without warning, Susan Dawson screamed out. She snatched up a nearby shovel and began to swing it wildly.

"Look out!" Adam shouted. He was the closest and took the first blow against his arm. He shifted his body nimbly enough to avoid being hit a second time.

Bruce attempted to seize Susan's weapon in midair, but had to sidestep to dodge the steel edge. On the back swing, the scoop-side struck Richard on the upper arm, knocking him to the floor.

The woman continued to scream and charged towards the fallen man. From behind, Adam managed to snag her around the waist. Quickly, Bruce stepped forward and took hold of the shovel. Like some wild animal, she kicked and clawed at the soldier, leaving red scrape marks on the side of his neck. Susan gave out one final shrill and passed out in Adam's arms.

"She's not…?" Carol asked.

"No, she's not dead," Margaret said, touching the woman's throat, checking for a pulse.

"What made her go so berserk?" Adam said. "She saw Richard and went nuts."

"Maybe she was trying to save time," Margaret said. That brought out a cold response from the group. "I'm joking." She looked down at her ex-husband. "It's all over, Richard. You can get up now." He didn't stir. "Richard, stop milking it."

The man didn't budge an inch. Carol leaned down to check him, then stared up at the others. "He must've struck his head," she said. "He's out cold."

CHAPTER SEVEN

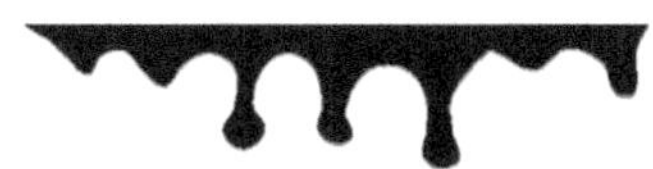

Richard Baines moaned as he returned to consciousness. In his dream, he had been relaxing aboard his sailboat on a clear sunny day. But the skies had darkened with the storm rolling in. The rain began to pour and he and his small boat were being rocked back and forth, back and forth. He held tight to the mast, afraid he would be thrown overboard by the rough motion—back and forth, back and forth. His eyes opened. Someone stood above him, shaking him back to the real world.

The fuzziness began to clear and the blur above him solidified into Margaret Walker. He didn't recognize his surroundings at first. It took him a few moments to realize that he was back in his temporary accommodations located within the United States Research Institute, Station 7. He tried to sit up in the small bed, but instead allowed himself another moan and plopped back down.

"Easy, Richard," Margaret told him. "You took a nasty blow to the head."

"Reminds me of your divorce lawyer," he said, "but it doesn't hurt as bad."

"Funny man. You'll live."

He tried to sit up again and this time he painfully succeeded. "You really do know how to hurt a guy." He became very dizzy—he thought his head would explode. "You got any aspirin? Be a doll and say you do."

Margaret handed him two white tablets and the water she had already prepared for him. "Drink slowly."

It took Richard two swallows to down the pills. "Thanks," he said, handing back the glass. "How long?" Richard turned towards the nightstand and tried but failed to focus on the clock face.

"Were you out?" Margaret added. "Three hours."

He nodded, winced, then decided not to move his head for a while. "And you've been here with me all that time."

"Sorry to disappoint you, but no. I've checked in on you from time to time—nothing more."

"Admit it. You were worried."

She shook her head, then shrugged and said, "Maybe a little—like any good doctor should. I didn't think that a knock to the head would have affected you for so long."

"You old softy," Richard needled her. His haze continued to lift and the memory of recent events began to return. "Would you mind telling me what's going on? Who was that crazy woman?"

"I don't like the word crazy, but in this case…"

"I hope you tied her up," Richard said, with a tiny cough.

"Nothing so dramatic, but she's been taken care of for the moment." Margaret studied her ex-husband carefully. He may be arrogant, pompous and a general pain in the ass, but Richard wasn't one to fake for sympathy. She felt concern for him. Or could it be guilt for the way she yelled at him when he was down? "Are you feeling well enough to meet with the others?"

"That's why you woke me?"

"I have some information and I think I should explain it to everyone all together."

"Can you give me a few minutes to clear out the cobwebs? I still feel a little dizzy."

"Sure," she said. "We'll be in the lab. Can you make it there okay?"

"Not a problem. It's not like I can't walk. I'm fine now. I just need to catch my breath a bit."

"Come when you're ready."

Richard watched Margaret leave the room, shutting the door behind her. The moment the door clicked into place, he slid his feet to the floor. He felt a sharp pain shoot through his entire body and a sudden wetness under his nose. He lightly touched the edge of his upper lip. When he pulled back his fingers, he found them tipped in blood.

"Damn," he said aloud, grabbing a tissue from a nearby box. Quickly rolling one end to a dull point, he unceremoniously stuffed it up his bleeding nostril. Then trying to stand, Richard felt a wave of nausea wash over him. He reached over to the water glass and took another sip. It helped some. By chance, he caught his own reflection in the small wall mirror next to the bed. He looked terrible. Richard ran his fingers through his thinning hair—he had been sweating.

Pulling the tissue from his nose, he found that the bleeding had stopped. After sipping more water, Richard forced himself to stand up straight. If he had to meet with the others, he didn't want them to see him in such a weakened state.

~

Margaret closed the black notebook, then turned towards the lab door. "He said he'd be here. Let's wait a few more minutes."

"No need," Richard said, entering the room. He walked to the table and took a seat. "Let's get this over with." The man appeared somewhat pale, but no one mentioned it.

"I spent the last few hours going through some of Dr. Blackwood's notes," Margaret told the group. "I haven't finished completely but I've learned something startling. It seems that two weeks ago there was a minor earthquake, and though that event was nothing special, its effects were. A deep fissure opened. And it was wide enough to get equipment to the bottom."

"Is that your big find?" Richard snapped. This was more than his usual, annoying banter. He was overtly harsh.

"As you all are aware," Margaret continued, ignoring his tone, "one of the purposes of this station is to drill into the ice and pull up samples for study. The deeper they go, the older the sample. With this break in the ice, a new depth was achieved. One never hoped, or even dreamed of. From this depth the ice-cores extracted were as old as 35 million years—the very first layers of the Antarctic ice sheet."

"That's incredible," Adam said.

"What's more incredible is that on the fourth day of pulling up samples, the team found something." Margaret ran the tip of her index finger along the black plastic binder. *Here comes the hard part,* she thought; it was tough enough for her to believe what she was about to say—how were the others going to react?

"Isn't that the point?" Richard said. "To find something?"

"What they found was alive," she added bluntly.

All of them began to speak at once. They darted questions at Margaret faster than she could possibly respond. And with the melding of voices, the words became almost gibberish. "One at a time," she said, "this isn't getting us anywhere."

They stopped talking, except for Manning, who asked the one question they all must be thinking. "How could it be alive? It was frozen in the ice." He glanced over to Adam, who returned the look, both men recalling Susan Dawson's words about something being "deep in the ice."

"I don't know. At first, they thought they pulled up a fragment of some frozen animal. But the sample was part of a living organism. And after failing to identify it, the crew used a larger bore head to dig up a bigger specimen."

"And why wouldn't they have failed?" Richard said. "This team…this station was never equipped for such research."

"Lack of equipment wasn't necessarily their problem," Margaret told him. "We all witnessed the DNA modeling on the computer. The organism didn't conform to the normal base pairs. Or I should say some of its base pairs were incomplete. It could take several years and a full blown research study to understand this life form."

"I don't know much about all this science stuff," Carol said, "but life can't exist with incomplete pairs of DNA."

"Life as we know it," Margaret said. "Strands of DNA slip, the bonds break during the reproductive phase and recombine to form new cells. That's how we are all created and grow. But this life seems to have permanent breaks in its DNA chain."

"Do you honestly grasp what you're saying?" Richard scoffed, using a handkerchief to wipe away the small beads of sweat forming on his forehead.

"I do. That this life form is fundamentally different than anything else seen before on this planet."

"Maybe it's from outer space," Carol said. That caught everyone's attention. It left them all speechless.

"An interesting idea," Margaret said, "but I don't think so. The odds of a meteor carrying something alive through space and crashing on this planet are truly astronomical. Besides, the DNA it does have is common enough. It's those gaps in the genetic bonds that make it so unique. No, I think that this discovery came from good old mother Earth. And I do mean old."

"Will you get to the point," Richard complained, "and stop beating around the bush? If you have something to say—say it." It was becoming more and more apparent to the others that something was not quite right with the man. And Richard could tell by the silence and stares how the others felt. "Sorry," he said, wiping his forehead again. "I'm still not quite myself yet. Please continue, Margaret. Please continue."

"According to his notes, John Blackwood believed that this life form could have developed on Earth 50 million years ago, perhaps even earlier."

"Is that possible?" Adam asked. "How could life like that develop in the Antarctic?"

"Blackwood didn't believe it did—well, not directly anyway. And as strange as his hypothesis may be, it's the only thing that makes any sense."

"And that is?" Richard asked, a restrained hint of impatience in his voice.

"Pangea," Margaret said.

"What?" Carol said. Her eyes opened very wide.

"Pangea, the super continent. Antarctica was once part of a greater landmass. At that time the climate was much more temperate. It was then, when this life form developed."

"Isn't the super continent rather...ahmmm...hypothetical?" Carol asked. "I'm no authority, but there's been no real evidence."

"Not so," Margaret said. "Less than ten years ago, a fossilized marsupial was discovered on Seymour Island. It belonged to the family of Polydolopidae, which was previously known only from South America. It proved Antarctica and South America were connected some 40 million years ago—the period classified as the Eocene Epoch of the Cenozoic Era." By the blank expressions, Margaret realized that her scientific exactness was not helping the situation. She needed to keep her explanation simple. "During the continental drift, the organism became trapped on this section of land. Over time it became encrusted by more and more snow and ice. Eventually entombed until the day a small amount was released by the crew of this station."

"35 million, 40, 50 million," Richard said. "Can't you narrow it down a little more?"

"That is narrowed down," Margaret told him.

"And this organism survived all those millions of years?" Carol asked, showing a little impatience of her own.

"It appears so. Remember, it's not an animal in the sense we think of. The cells are very simple. And if it is a viral type of organism, it would be a colony made up of millions of cells and still barely be seen by the human eye. It could resemble common bathroom scum. Possibly even a mold of some kind."

"What I saw last night," Richard objected, "wasn't a virus or mold. It was big…fast…black. And it didn't have a shape of its own."

"And Emmanuel Phillips?" Adam said. "By the condition of his body, it would take something a lot bigger than a spot of mold to do that."

"Agreed," Margaret said, "and I'm not ruling anything out."

"I think we're all forgetting something," Adam said. "I knew these men. If they dug up some new virus, mold, or whatever this organism turns out to be, they would've certainly told someone. John Blackwood was a scientist. That was his entire life—doing research and sharing his findings with the rest of the world."

"He did," she said, picking up the black book. "This is one of his private journals—one of many. He kept them separate from the sanctioned research notes. He recorded all his communications—both times and dates."

"All his communications?" Manning looked over to Richard. "You knew what Blackwood was up to and you did nothing about it?" The soldier's eyes cut through the man as if he wanted to stand up, walk over and rearrange some body parts—for starters. "You could have stopped this whole mess from happening. My brother would be fine now if…"

"That can't be right," Richard interrupted. "We lost contact with the station. They stopped transmitting. And considering the smashed radio and lack of personnel, that's one part of the mystery solved."

"And before that?" Adam asked. "Did they ever mention anything in past transmissions?"

"You're the top man, Baines," Manning said. "Let's have it. And no doubletalk this time—give us a straight answer."

"As far as I'm concerned, things here were proceeding uneventfully. I'm sure I would have been told if there was something happening outside normal operations."

"Told?" Manning questioned. "You'd have to be told?"

"I do have responsibilities other than this winter wonderland."

"So much for being hands-on," Adam said under his breath.

Richard ignored the comment and switched his focus to Margaret. "Who did Blackwood contact?"

"He only wrote down initials: C.F."

"C.F.," Richard said. "Who the devil is that? All transmissions are required to pass through my office for logging. And I don't know any C.F."

"Come on, Baines," Adam said, "level with us."

"I'm telling you," Richard kept insisting, "I don't know any more than you do."

"He's telling the truth," Margaret said. "Anything Richard would know, I would know too. It may be hard to believe, but he's not holding anything back."

"Thanks a lot," Richard responded in a halftone.

"Nothing against you, lady," Adam said, "but I don't know you. You both could be lying."

"This is getting us nowhere," Richard said. "You'll simply have to take my word that I know nothing more than you. I can't give you any more assurances than that."

There was a moment of silence. "All right," Adam said, "I'll give you the benefit of the doubt." Carol and Bruce hesitantly agreed.

"Now you're coming to your senses. We have to approach this in a logical manner. For starters, let me have that notebook." Margaret didn't see the harm and handed him the binder. Richard stared down at the very first page. "What are these numbers?" he asked, pointing to the right uppermost corner.

"I don't know," Margaret said. "Could be anything."

Adam glanced at the page. "Looks like a radio frequency."

"Sure does," Manning concurred, "but on a weird setting. It's not a government band."

"Meaning?" Richard said.

Adam looked Richard square in the eye. "That Dr. Blackwood had a contact outside your office and was covertly passing on information."

"Why would he do that? Give me one reason?"

"Money," Margaret said. "Turn to the back of the notebook. There are also what appears to be bank account numbers with dollar amounts next to them. The oldest reason known to man—greed."

"Why would he sell his findings?" Richard asked, his forced patience slipping fast. "What good are they to anyone? Next you'll be saying the entire station crew was in on it."

"No, it's possible John Blackwood tried to keep the whole thing under wraps, thinking he could control whatever it was. But something went terribly wrong."

"Keep it from the other scientists?" Carol asked. "Why?"

"Who knows," Margaret told her, "germ warfare, genetic research? The sample would most definitely have some very unusual properties. Introduced into the human body, who can say what would result."

"Did anyone else just become very afraid?" Carol said. "When do you think your crew will send a rescue plane?" she asked, her eyes shifting over to Adam.

"Rescue plane? Someone want to fill me in?" Richard asked. He quickly turned to each of them, but no one gave him an answer. "Anyone?"

"You didn't tell him," Adam said to Margaret.

She shook her head. "No, in his condition, I thought it best to wait."

"My condition be damned. What's wrong with the plane we came up in?"

"It's...ahmmm... It's..."

"Trashed," Adam blurted out. "Radio, controls—all of it—destroyed."

"How? When?"

"When..." Adam said. "Best guess, last night. How? Does it matter? We're trapped here until help comes." Having no desire to throw Susan Dawson to the wolves, he decided to keep his speculations to himself. She probably trashed the plane and radio without even realizing it. In her state of mind, she wouldn't have known what she was doing. Her actions teetered on the brink of insanity.

"I hate to burst your bubble," Richard said, "but we are the help. Remember?" Before anyone could say another word. "Who destroyed the plane? It was that crazy woman, wasn't it? We should question her."

So much for keeping it to himself, Adam thought, but he didn't get a chance to utter an objection—Dr. Walker beat him to it.

"I can't in good conscience recommend that," she said. "The poor woman's very unstable."

"Tell me about it." Richard rubbed the back of his head. "But that doesn't change a thing. She wrecked our only means of getting out of here."

"We don't know that she did anything," Manning said. "And I'm sure Adam's people will send another plane up in a few days."

"Yes," Adam said, trying to reassure Richard and the others, including himself, "a few days." He only hoped it would be soon enough. "If they don't hear from me, they'll assume I had trouble."

"And in this case they'd be right, wouldn't they," Richard snapped.

"Relax," Margaret said. "We have plenty of food. It's only a matter of time, before others come. Let's make the best of it."

"Best of it? Best of it? You can't be serious. There's some kind of thing prowling around this place. And after me shooting at it, I wouldn't be the least bit surprised if it was pretty pissed off by now."

"Do you think what Mr. Baines saw last night was the organism?" Carol asked.

"No way of knowing," Manning said. "And I think we should not jump to conclusions. Or we'll be chasing down every little sound or end up shooting each other by mistake."

For the next few moments, the small band glanced back and forth at each other.

Finally breaking the awkward lull, Margaret said, "Well, that's all I have. If anyone has anything else to say now is the time."

No one spoke up.

"Then I suggest, Lieutenant, you check on your brother," Margaret added.

"I'll make sure Susan is still sleeping," Carol said.

The group rose from the table. Richard was the last to stand, but when he did, Margaret said, "Richard, I'd like to show you something. Could you stay a moment?" She smiled at him.

"If I must," he said, hiding his clenched fist behind his back, fighting the pain seeping down his legs.

The others left the room. When Margaret returned to her chair, her smile disappeared. "Okay, spill it," she said. "Why wasn't I told?"

"About what?"

"You know damn well what? Why wasn't I told the real reason for this trip?"

"You were. My god, it's like playing a broken record. We lost contact with the station." Richard's expression changed. "You're scared." A tiny smile formed on his lips. "I never thought I'd see the day."

"You bet your ass I'm scared. I'd be a fool not to be."

"I know this won't change anything, but I'm sorry you had to come all this way and deal with this mess. And if the truth be told, you weren't my first choice to bring up here. However, you being a medical doctor and your familiarity with most of the personnel and their mission in this god-awful place, you were the best we had."

"Stop slinging the bull. You knew about the organism or virus or whatever it was Blackwood dug up. You knew all the time."

"What was all that about you saying 'anything I would know, you would know too' and 'Richard isn't holding anything back'? Have you already forgotten those grand words of ringing confidence?"

"That was so the others wouldn't tear you apart. Now, I'm asking you point-blank, did you know?"

"And I'm telling you—no. I've been square with you." Richard glanced back at the closed door. "With all of you. Besides, consider this little fact, if there was something here, and I knew it, would I really come myself?"

Margaret's face eased. She shrugged. "There is that. I'm sure I'm going to regret this, but I believe you."

~

Carol Chambers made her way to the crew quarters directly across from the galley where they had put Susan Dawson down to rest. Margaret had given the woman a sedative by the same means she had for Eric Manning—through injection. Carol hated needles. When she was a little girl, she skewered her thumbnail with the bobbing needle of her mother's sewing machine. Ever since that day, the mere thought of having a piece of metal stuck anywhere in her body turned her stomach.

She gently knocked once before entering. She didn't expect an answer nor did she wait for one. Pushing open the door, her eyes immediately fell to an empty bunk. She rushed over and pulled down the covers. There was nothing there—absolutely nothing. In an odd way, it was a good thing—she expected to find an empty pile of clothes like all the others. Here she found only empty sheets and blankets.

A short creak came from behind her. Turning, she saw the door had moved. She stood still for a moment and again the door shifted under its own weight. Carol snickered. There was nothing sinister about an out-of-balanced door and she had more to worry about than creepy noises. The missing woman could be the key to the events going on here. She might have the answers they were searching for.

Leaving the room, Carol spotted Richard Baines coming towards her. The man didn't look at all well.

"Can I get you something, sir?" she asked when he passed. She closed the door to Susan Dawson's room.

He simply shook his head and continued on his way. Seconds later, he entered his own room, then slammed the door shut.

Deciding to head off on her own, Carol intended to find Susan without telling the others. She chose to concentrate her search on this half of the station. Since they held their meeting in the lab, their voices would clearly resonate from that end of the complex. Being confused and frightened, Susan was more apt to avoid an area full of people.

So starting at the rec room door, she tried the knob. It turned effortlessly in her hand. The door swung freely, making only the slightest squeak. Carol called out in a clear voice, "Susan, are you in here?" Eyeing the vacant space, she saw the small mounds of clothing still on the floor. She walked over to the bundle of women's clothes and nudged the fabric with the tip of her shoe. How bizarre, she thought, empty clothes right down to the bra and panties—and the woman obviously had boring taste in underwear.

Finding nothing else of interest, Carol moved from the rec room back to the long empty hallway of white tiles and black scuffmarks. Not far down the corridor, she realized how eerily quiet this part of the complex could be with only the slightly humming lights overhead for company. Above her, the hum of one light changed to a buzz, then to a crackle. The light flickered, then faded, flickered once more, and went out. She stared up at the long white glass tube. It snapped on with a pop. She jumped.

Carol couldn't lie to herself—she was a little scared. And as she had overheard Margaret say to Richard—she'd be a fool not to be, though the doctor had no real idea of why. But Carol knew if she stayed in the light, she should be safe enough. Though last night, the light didn't help Richard. That's what disturbed her—the hall was lit up when he wasted the ammunition.

She told herself to stop thinking about last night. If the information she had been given was incorrect she would just have to improvise—thinking on her feet had always been a strength. Her number one task at the moment was to locate Susan Dawson. After stopping and standing perfectly still, she listened very carefully for any sound.

"Susan?" Carol called out. "Susan, where are you?"

A sudden thud echoed from up ahead, though it was so short, she couldn't tell exactly where it came from. She proceeded cautiously, keeping a sharp ear out for anything, but had gone a ways without hearing another sound. She was beginning to think that maybe the thud had been made by Richard Baines banging around in his room. When she heard it, the noise seemed to come from farther down the hall, but the way sound bounced off these bare walls that may have been an illusion.

She had almost walked passed the section of sleeping quarters, when a second thud came from the room she had just passed. Carol stopped and backtracked to that door.

Then carefully, gently, she opened it—"Susan?" she said, entering. Besides the overturned dresser and pulled mattress, the room was empty. Carol was about to leave, when a faint bump came from the closet. She inched up to the folding door and slid it open.

Trembling in the corner of the small space was Susan Dawson. The woman, confronted by an intruder, shrieked like a trapped animal and tried to bury herself farther back into the closet.

"It's okay—I'm here to help you," Carol told her. "I won't let it get you." Carol wasn't sure if it was her words or the remnants of sedative in Susan's system, but the woman began to ease some. Taking a step forward, Carol saw that Susan had hold of something. In a tight grip, close to her chest, she protected an exquisitely framed photograph.

Carol crouched down, hoping not to appear at all threatening. "What do you have there?" she asked.

The woman didn't respond. Her eyes showed no emotion—her fingers gently stroked the smooth glass of her captive treasure. Susan Dawson, being such a tiny woman, could easily be picked up and carried back to her bed—Carol only hoped it wouldn't come to that.

"Are you hurt? Can you come with me?"

Susan's expression changed from vacant to afraid. A dark tall shadow engulfed both women. Carol gasped and spun around.

"Sorry," Adam said, "I didn't mean to startle you."

"That's okay," she said with a nervous giggle. "It's this place. It's pretty spooky." Carol turned back to Susan, who was still shaky from Adam's unexpected appearance. "She wandered from her room."

"No, she didn't." Adam knelt down to meet the woman eye to eye. "Susan, you remember me, don't you? Remember how you always beat me at pool?" Like Carol, he also saw her gripping the photo, but he also knew it might be the key to gaining the woman's trust. "Can I see?" he said, holding out his hand.

Susan whimpered and clutched the cherished keepsake even tighter.

"I would very much like to see your picture. I won't hurt it." He slowly guided his hand to the frame and gently took hold. "I promise."

Finally, she released her grip.

The photo was of a tall man proudly displaying a largemouth bass. "I remember this. You showed it to me once. His name is Michael, isn't it?" He smiled at the picture. "You said he loves to fish. Do you remember telling me that? Do you?"

The woman stared up at Adam, and then nodded her head. "I remember," she whispered.

"Good," he said. "That's very good. Now Susan, I need you to leave here with me.

"No," she cowered, "must stay here."

"We need you to stay with us. We need your help." Again, he reached towards the woman with an open hand. "Please, Susan, you can trust me."

Finally, Susan took hold of Adam and he helped her out of the closet. Adam glanced over to Carol.

"How did you know she'd be here?" Carol asked him.

"Simple. This is her room. The picture is of her husband." Adam handed the photo back to Susan. She took it, and pressing it to her body, slowly moved towards Adam and Carol.

"We'll bring you someplace safe," Adam told her, but deep down wondered if anywhere on this station really fit that description.

Susan took only three steps, then fainted. Adam grabbed her before she hit the floor.

"Put her down here," Carol said, pulling the mattress back onto its frame.

Adam lifted the woman to the bed. It amazed him how even while unconscious she managed a tight hold of the photo. He eased her down. "I'll go find Dr. Walker," Adam said. "You stay here with her." He turned to leave, but Carol took hold of his arm.

"No," she said. "I mean, don't leave me alone." Before they had a chance to argue about it, Susan moaned. "I think she's coming to."

CHAPTER EIGHT

"How are you feeling?" Bruce asked softly, sitting at his brother's side in the most uncomfortable folding chair ever stamped out by a metal press. Only seconds earlier had Eric Manning's eyes opened and he looked up in a drowsy gaze—the drugs in his system still keeping a strong hold.

"I thought I dreamed you," Eric wheezed, his dry lips on the verge of cracking with each word. Bruce took a glass of water from the nightstand and held it to his brother's mouth. After a few sips, Eric signaled he had had enough. Bruce took the water away and returned the glass to its spot on the nightstand.

Fighting against the sedative, Eric spoke again with a very weak voice. "What the hell is my big brother doing here?"

Bruce smiled. "Watching your ass—as usual."

Eric let out a coughing laugh. "How's my boy?" he managed to ask.

"Getting bigger everyday. He'll be like his old man. Nancy sends her love. She included a kiss with the message, but I told her that would have to wait until you get home and she could give it to you herself."

"Thank you for that small favor." Eric coughed once more, then passed out again.

Bruce watched his brother sleeping so peacefully. Last night the man had been babbling like a baby. But now…but now he seemed his old self—tired, but his old self. Bruce would never pretend to be a doctor, and didn't understand exactly how the human mind worked, but he had seen battle fatigue before. One minute its victim appears fine—acts, walks, talks normal, then the next moment they're screaming, running, fighting. He would keep a close eye on his brother—and the activities going on at this station. Something tragic occurred here—something traumatic—something that broke the man's will to reason and function. And that certainly would be no easy task. Between the two of them, Eric had always been the strongest mentally and Bruce would be the first to admit to that fact. It was nothing to be ashamed of—no man had ever been prouder of his brother.

Although the youngest, Eric had been the most outgoing, daring and even a little foolhardy. Boys being boys, they fashioned a parachute out of old sheets, and Eric was the one to try it out by jumping off the roof of their garage. The doctor used a metal pin to set his broken arm. Eric would charge his friends a quarter to see the scar.

And another time during a fishing trip, young Eric accidentally cut the back of his hand up to the wrist. He used a dull knife to scale his catch and the blade slipped. He joked while watching the doctor sew him up, saying he wondered how much to charge his friends to see this one.

With the thought of Eric's antics, Bruce smiled and glanced down at his brother's hand. His surprise forced him to look twice. He even raised Eric's arm off the bed for a better view. The scar was gone. There wasn't a trace of it at all.

He gently pulled up Eric's left shirtsleeve. He couldn't believe his eyes. The four-inch scar that had earned a seven-year-old boy five dollars and seventy-five cents had also vanished. The flesh on his upper arm was perfect and smooth. It was like the incision had healed cleanly and completely. But it hadn't—not during the time they were boys—not as an adult—and not before coming to this station.

In the lab, Doctor Margaret Walker sat alone, pouring over the many notebooks scribed in the very hand of Jonathan Blackwood. She thought the man had a peculiar habit of mixing strict scientific notes with personal thoughts and commentary, which made for some very long reading. She sat almost wishing she still smoked, but instead retrieved her Styrofoam cup from the desktop and took another sip of the strong black coffee. She had been at this for hours, nevertheless she had made up her mind to find out the truth to the events that had brought her and the others to this dreary place, even if it meant going over each and every word in all the books and files. Besides, it's not as if she had anything better to do or had anyplace to go instead. And exhausting as the work may be, it was a distraction.

She closed one notebook, then leaned forward and grabbed the next in line. Setting the book down on the desk, she sighed heavily, then rubbed her temples with her free hand. Could she have overlooked something, she wondered. Or was the answer staring right at her, but she was simply too tired to recognize it.

Margaret opened the notebook and began reading. Her eyes widened with the words: *This morning we found what was left of Emmanuel. I don't know if there is a connection between his behavior and the missing organism.* Margaret stopped reading and looked up at the computer screen displaying the weird DNA sequences.

"Missing?" she said aloud. She continued reading: *I have not ruled out that one of the crew has stolen the organism. It was a small sample and is easily concealed. It has been several days since my last contact with C.F. and it's possible he has negotiated a better deal with another of my staff. The only question is with whom. At this point, I don't trust any of them—I can't trust anyone.*

Several days, she thought, that can't be right. She examined the pages and found to her surprise that it was indeed correct. A large gap spanned the dates between this book and the last. There must be at least one more notebook somewhere. She checked the others. Luckily, the missing book was the *only* missing book. But where was it? Had it been misplaced, deliberately hidden or possibly stolen?

Margaret put the lost notebook out of her mind and would consider it later, when she had more time. Her best chance to figure this whole thing out was to concentrate on those notes she already had in front of her. She continued her work.

The body appeared partially dissolved by some type of acid, the book went on to say. Though the amount needed to do that much damage would be tremendous and not easily contained nor handled.

The entry, Margaret thought, was cold—emotionless. It mentioned nothing for the dead man, or the crew's reaction to the loss. It was just flat clinical observation and a selfish concern about someone else stealing his pie.

The next few days worth of notes were theories based on the data generated by the rewritten sampling program. Margaret could only guess that the foundation for John Blackwood's research had been in the missing notebook. Without knowing its contents, scientifically speaking, his line of reasoning seemed flawed—being nothing more than conjecture lacking any substance to back it up.

Then Margaret came upon a second disturbing entry: *Another crewman has vanished—Rob Hutter. The only thing we could find of him were his empty clothes. Several of the others believe the same madness that possessed Emmanuel has taken hold of Rob as well. That he stripped off his clothes and in his delirium ran outside to his death. Eric Manning and I went out after him, but came back with nothing. Naked and exposed to the sub-zero temperatures he couldn't have strayed very far. Nevertheless, we found no body. One strange note: the clothes—they were all intact—down to briefs inside of pants—socks neatly tucked within shoes. Another symptom of the madness—I wonder.*

Margaret scanned the notebook for other disappearances. She skipped over any technical jargon, theory, supposition, hypothesis or conjecture. It didn't take her long to find what she was looking for, but wished she hadn't.

Two more of the personnel have disappeared, bringing our numbers down to nine. The remaining crew wanted to radio for help—to call for an airlift. I managed to talk them out of it, telling them we can find the cause for the disappearances ourselves. I managed to convince them—for now. I suspect these events are an elaborate ploy by whoever has my sample. A ploy to get the organism off the station. I can't let that happen. No one else is going to get credit for my work...my discovery. I've spent years in the shadow of others—but not this time.

The next day's notes had nothing to do with science—far from it.

I destroyed the radio. Last night going into the kitchen I found Sam's empty clothes, right down to his cooking apron still tied in place. I knew such a thing would cause the others to want to call for help and this time I would not be able to sway them against it. But I also couldn't allow a call to go out. I destroyed the radio and focused the blame on Sam—blamed it on his madness. No one even questioned it, especially after finding Mathew's empty clothes in Sam's torn-up quarters.

The following pages of script, like the previous day's, read not of a dispassionate scientist, but a man bordering on insanity.

I don't know what to think anymore. The few others that remain have locked themselves in the rec room. I haven't decided if I should join them. If I keep by myself, the real killer will have to reveal himself—or herself—to me. I don't trust any of them. I won't be caught off guard—not like Emmanuel, Rob or even Sam.

Margaret turned the page. It was blank. She thumbed through the rest of the book and found only other blank pages. It was very peculiar that a man who bothered to put his sins down on paper would stop so abruptly. One would think he would have left some final word.

"Maybe he did," she said to the empty room.

Margaret remembered the tape she had found earlier that day. With all the recent events, she had almost forgotten about it. She pulled the cassette out of her pocket. Staring at the plastic case, she wondered if it held any answers. After returning the tape to the safety of her sweater, she began to scour the lab for a recorder. She searched in the storage cupboards, the desk drawers, the file cabinets, but there was no player to be found.

Then it hit her. Who said the tape had been recorded in the lab? She thought back. Which room did Adam say belonged to Blackwood? She had to think. Were they the quarters Bruce had picked out? No, it was the room directly across the hall. Margaret ran from the lab and down to the sleeping area.

She was confident that Dr. Blackwood left the cassette where it would be found. Who else could have secured it in the bottom drawer of his desk? But then why not leave the means to play it? She considered the text of his notes and then the reason became clear. They were enough to destroy the man's career. Realizing this, he had taken steps to ensure that if he was found alive, he could still conceal his involvement. And if not, he would make sure to warn others of the danger. Definitely a conflict of conscience. All this led Margaret to believe that a recorder may be found in John's private quarters.

The woman opened the door to the dead man's room and stood peering at the mess, hoping that the cassette player wasn't lying smashed under a shirt or blanket. She began her hunt, not even knowing the best place to start. She lifted any item of enough size to hide a player. Though it would have been easier if she knew exactly what type of equipment made the tape—it could have been as small as a Walkman or as big as a boom box.

After a few minutes, she finally found a desktop model cassette player under the bed. By the position, she could tell it had been placed there on purpose. While popping the tape in, Margaret mumbled a short prayer that the batteries weren't dead. She didn't see a power cord anywhere and didn't have the slightest clue where to get one.

Margaret hit the play button. There was a small amount of tape hiss followed by a voice she recognized immediately—John Blackwood. His words were frantic—almost raving.

"If you're listening to this tape, you must leave this place, though it may already be too late for you. I can't tell you more—only that I was wrong—I was so very wrong." In the background there was a loud crash. "It's coming for me! I must hide where it can't get me! I give you this warning and tell you to abandon the station. It's much bigger now..." There was a pause. "Oh my god! Oh my god!" The tape ended.

She rewound the cassette and played it again. The answers Margaret hoped for weren't on this tape, only more questions. He said he would hide where "it" couldn't get to him. They had found his body in the laboratory freezer. "It" couldn't get to him there—why? What had Blackwood gotten himself—and the others—into? Could "it" be the organism? And the word "bigger" didn't make her feel all that good either. All this led to one unmistakable conclusion—there was something here with them—something—something not human.

~

Richard Baines had returned to his quarters after a short walk he hoped would break up some of the stiffness in his joints, but the more he walked around the complex the worse he felt. And that damn headache—what could he do to stop the intense pounding?—nothing helped. Instead of going to Margaret with his pain, he had snuck four more aspirins from the medical kit. He downed the white pills with a large glass of cool water that felt good running down the back of his throat. He plopped down on top of the bunk, not even bothering to crawl under the covers, thinking maybe the medication would help him sleep. He was wrong.

There were times when Richard would almost nod off, but short stabs snapped him back over the threshold. He was sure that the pills should have kicked in by now, but by his continued agony knew they had failed. He took in a breath, but a seizure in his chest made him cough it out.

Several times he thought about going to the lab under the pretense of checking on Margaret's progress with all the notes and files. He sure wasn't going to ask for her help outright. She would see his suffering and try to do something for him—maybe give him something stronger than aspirin. But each time he would start to rise, immediately he fell back to the bed. A dizziness would wash over him and the pain got worse.

His eyes moved around the room, to the walls, to the ceiling—his mind tried to find something else to focus on besides the pain. Wild thoughts began to flow through his head. If he let his mind go blank and thought of nothing, the images would play out in front of him like a motion picture of disjointed scenes. Images of people running and cowering. Of people screaming with no voice. The faces were always distorted—like looking at them through a clear Mason jar filled with water—and always from an abnormal point of view—from either above or from below.

Though, not all the faces were screaming. Some were still—calm—resting motionless in a deep sleep. Then in his mind Richard saw himself sleeping—propped up in a steel-folding chair—his arms crossed in front of his chest—his head sloped down in slumber. And the oddest feeling accompanied all these images—an overwhelming hunger.

The floating images left him as suddenly as they began and in their place came another puzzling sensation. It was the feeling that he was no longer alone. It was like the feeling you get when you discover someone watching you. He lifted his head and looked towards the door. He truly thought that Margaret had entered his room to check up on him. But she was not there. No one was there. Still the feeling didn't go away. Someone was in the room with him.

Then without warning, Richard's left leg began to ache. At first it was a dull throb, but quickly sharpened. It grew past a slow thrusting, twisting of a knife blade tearing at his skin to a fierce flame causing his flesh to boil and blister. The burning jumped to his right leg. It caused his body to buck with a jolt like being struck by an electric prod. Totally out of his control, the muscles in both legs began to spasm at once.

His teeth snapped tight in a hard clench. Richard barely managed enough strength to lift his head to look down at the end of his bunk. He wanted to scream out, but his throat closed off. His eyes strained at what they saw.

The man tried once more to cry out, but the terror left him utterly speechless as his socks collapsed and lay empty on the bunk. His pant legs up to his knee thrashed back and forth like two giant snakes fighting for the same rat. The motion continued up his thighs, up to his waist. He could not control the wild movements of his own flesh.

The pain left his legs and traveled up to his hips and waist. He could not take his eyes off his belt—it collapsed down and his trousers drooped to one side. He tried to fight it and sit up. His arms flung wildly knocking over the table lamp. The bulb shattered on the floor plunging the room into darkness. He fell back to the bunk, no longer having the bone or muscle to stay up. Richard Baines opened his mouth in one final attempt to make a sound—any sound, but with his chest cavity emptied of his heart and lungs, it was much, much too late.

~

"Who are you people?" Susan asked. The petite woman glared up at the couple from the bed where she sat still clutching her husband's photo close to her chest. "Why are you here?" Her eyes were full of fear and her voice trembled somewhat. She looked directly at Adam, then said, "I know you."

"Yes, Susan," he said. "I'm Adam...Adam Hayes. I bring up the supplies. I fly them in."

The woman's face became more and more relaxed—her mind slowly emerged from its prison. "Adam. I do remember you. I do know you. I thought it was all a dream. I didn't think I would ever see another living human again."

"Why is she remembering now?" Carol asked.

"I think it's this room," Adam told her. "Being back around familiar things has helped to snap her out of whatever dark place her mind had thrown her into. She must have been witness to some pretty horrible things for her mind to try to shut it out so."

Adam knelt down to meet the woman's gaze, though at the moment, her eyes were fixed on the photo. He had only seen the picture once, but it was when he saw it again that he noticed the strong resemblance between Susan Dawson's husband and Lieutenant Bruce Manning. It explained why Bruce had such a calming effect on the woman earlier today. He wouldn't say the men would be mistaken for brothers, but the hair color, the shape of his head, the sharp chin, even the eyes, in her dazed state Adam could understand how Susan might think Bruce was her husband.

"Susan," he said. "Can you tell me what happened here?"

She turned her head up towards him, but with a blank expression. For a moment, Adam thought she might be returning to her previous state. Her hold on reality was at best fragile.

"Susan? Stay with me Susan."

"The others—it got the others." Her eyes returned to her precious photo. "I miss Michael," she said.

"And I'm sure he misses you too," Adam said. "We'll all be leaving here soon. You'll be back with him."

She shook her head. "No," she whispered. "I don't think so." A single tear ran down her cheek and landed on the framed glass plate. "None of us will ever leave here. Like the others, they are all gone. It got them. There's no escape. All the others are gone."

"All the others?" Carol said. "No, not *all* the others. Eric Manning. He's with us."

Susan stared up at Carol with a hard disbelief.

"Yes, that's right," Adam told her. "Eric Manning. We found him—just like we found you. It didn't get him and it won't get you." He smiled at her. "Now, can you tell me what happened here?" He watched her very closely. "Please, Susan, tell us?"

"The ice," she finally said. "The ice. They dug it up out of the ice." She turned away as though merely saying the words caused her great pain.

"What was dug up? Was it something alive?"

Her eyes returned to him, but not with terror, but with surprise. "You know. How do you know?"

"We found some papers—in the lab. Dr. Blackwood had documented…"

"Yes, yes," she said frantically, "John, he knew, he knew. He figured it out."

"Figured what out?" Carol snapped. "What did Dr. Blackwood figure out?" The woman's tone was on the edge of being harsh, which surprised Adam. It was the first time he heard Carol lash out at anyone since they arrived at the station. The stress must be getting to her, he reasoned, though he marveled she had managed this well so far.

"Easy on her," Adam said, "she's been through a lot."

Carol nodded, then calmly asked her question again. "What did John Blackwood figure out?"

Neither Adam nor Carol were sure if Susan even heard the question. All she said was, "Did you see it? Did you see it?"

Margaret felt herself shaking while she rewound the tape. When it stopped and the machine automatically turned off, she jumped at the sound of the rewind button snapping up. She hit the eject button, popping the tape out of the machine. Then almost immediately she changed her mind. She replaced the cassette and picked up the entire player. The others would want to hear the same thing she had heard—the last words of Dr. John Blackwood and in his own voice. She hated to think so, but she wasn't sure if any of them would believe her. They would want to hear the terror in the man's voice for themselves. And she couldn't fault them—after all, the whole thing was a fantastic story—an unbelievable story—a terrifying story.

Standing at the threshold of the room, Margaret peered out into the vacant hallway. She figured Bruce was still sitting with his brother. She hadn't a clue to where Adam and Carol might be. Richard said he was returning to his room and she had no reason to believe any different. With tape and player in hand, Margaret stepped out into the quiet—that eerie quiet that makes you look back as you walk. And she did—all the way—with each step.

Before gathering up the others, she would talk with Richard first. It may be best if he were the one to tell them about the notebook entries and the tape. After all, he was the one to put this whole excursion together and like it or not, he was in charge. Also, she thought that if he was forthright with the information, they might trust him again. They would accept that he really wasn't hiding anything. And in the back of her mind, it would prove the same to her too. She could judge Richard's reaction to her findings. If he already knew, he couldn't fake his surprise well enough to fool her. Then there would be his willingness to share the information. If he refused to tell the group, she would know he had been lying about the mission and its real purpose.

She made her way down the hall. Once more, she couldn't help looking back the way she came. This place was starting to get to her. She was seeing moving shadows at every turn. At least she hoped they were only shadows. With what she uncovered, she could never be sure of anything again.

She walked up to Richard's door and lightly knocked. When they spoke earlier, she got the distinct feeling that something was bothering him. Of course, he would never tell her. It was the same while they were married. He always kept things inside. It was the topic of many arguments.

"Richard," she whispered, cracking the door slightly. The only light piercing the room came from behind her. "Richard," she repeated, while entering, not even sure if he was here. After three steps, her foot hit something. She barely made out the single boot kicked away from its mate. Well, that answered that, she thought, Richard would never walk around the complex in his stocking feet.

In the darkness, she thought she made out some movement on the bunk. She crossed the room. Running around last night, made for a long day—she could use a good rest herself. At times, Richard could be a very big pain in the ass, but right now, she did regret having to wake him.

Margaret leaned down to rouse him, but her hand hit nothing but the blanket and sheets. She tried reaching over for the table lamp, but found it missing. She took another step and a small piece of glass crackled under her foot. Rather than stumbling around, she headed back to the door and the light switch.

She turned towards the bed, when she heard a bang. "Richard, are you up?" She didn't wait for an answer. "I found something. I think we have to talk." With a flick of the switch, the overhead light came on.

"I know this may be..." Her words died off when she turned. Richard wasn't there. Margaret approached the bunk. The shock stopped all motion. She stared down at the empty set of clothes—Richard's clothes.

"Oh my God," she said. Before she could say anything else, something crept from under the bunk. It started towards her.

CHAPTER NINE

A piercing scream echoed down the long hall. Shocked by the sharp sound, Carol and Adam stared at each other for what seemed like several seconds.

"Dr. Walker," Adam said. He had never heard the woman scream before, but unless there was another female hidden somewhere in this station, she was the most likely candidate.

"She should be in the lab," Carol told him.

"Come on," Adam said, moving towards the door.

"What about her?" Carol asked about Susan.

"Bring her with. I don't want her roaming around alone." He gazed at the door to the hall and then back to the two women. "Can you manage if I go on ahead?"

"I think so."

And with that, he was off. He tore down the hall. It seemed a lot longer when you were in a desperate hurry. His heart began to pound as he ran full bore. About halfway to the lab, Bruce Manning stepped out of his room. The two men almost collided, but Adam managed to stop before impact.

"What's going on?" Bruce asked. "I thought I heard a scream." Bruce was ashamed to admit he had fallen asleep while watching his brother. He did the best he could to hide the tiredness in his voice.

"You did hear a scream?" Adam said. "It was Margaret. I think it came from the lab." Adam regained his speed down the hall. He assumed the lieutenant was right behind him.

At the open lab door, Adam rushed in, only to find an empty room. The computer was still on, but Dr. Walker was nowhere to be found. For a second he considered the freezer, but with it being airtight, it was also soundproof. He wouldn't have heard her screams if they came from there.

Adam turned towards the door expecting to find the soldier. "She's not here…" His voice trailed off when he saw he was still alone.

Then he heard Bruce's voice coming from back the way he came. "Down here," the lieutenant yelled. "She's down here."

Adam backtracked and spotted Carol helping Susan down the hall.

"Is she okay?" Carol asked.

"I don't know…"

"In here," Bruce called out. They all approached the door to the room used by Richard Baines. Inside, Bruce was kneeling over the body of Margaret Walker.

"Is she…?" Carol asked, not able to bring herself to say the final word.

"No, she's not," Manning said. "She's only fainted." He gently rocked her. After a second, she came to and sat up. Her eyes looked from side to side.

"Richard," she said. "Richard—he's gone."

"Gone?" Adam asked.

"Like the others," Susan said. "It's happening again." She pointed to the bunk and the clothing. "We have to get out of here." The woman started to cry. "Why did you bring me back here? Why? I was safe." She started to pull away from Carol.

"Where are you going?" Carol said, barely holding onto Susan's wrist. "You have to stay with us."

"No, I'm leaving. Going back to the other building." She started to hit Carol's hand. "Let me go. Let me go!"

Adam hurried over to the frantic woman. He took her by the upper arms. "We all have to stay together until we know what we're dealing with."

"No. No, let me go."

Adam shook the woman. "Listen to me," he said, "listen to me. You'll be okay with us. You have to stay with us. We'll protect you. I'll…I'll protect you."

Those words must have meant something to Susan Dawson or maybe it was just exhaustion due to the whole affair, but she collapsed in his arms crying.

"It will be okay," he said. "It will be okay."

"Would someone mind getting me a chair?" Margaret asked. "I don't fancy being on the floor."

Carol grabbed the chair next to the closet and pushed it across the tiles, producing a sharp screech. "What did you see?" Carol asked Margaret, who pulled herself up, then sat. "Was it the organism? Did it get Mr. Baines?"

"I don't know," Margaret said, "and that's about the only answer I can give to all your questions."

"Can't you tell us anything?"

"There was something in here," she started. "I'm not sure, but with the quick look I got, it had to be the same thing Richard saw last night."

"Then he wasn't sleepwalking," Manning said. "What he described sounded so incredible, I really didn't believe him. Call me naive, but I wasn't really convinced about a lot of this stuff."

"Do believe it," Margaret told him. "It was exactly how Richard described."

"It's obviously not here now," Carol said. "How did it escape?"

Margaret said nothing. Instead, she pointed to the ceiling and the grate of the air vent.

"Why didn't it attack you?" Manning asked. The others gave him strange stares. "I only meant if it killed Richard why did it leave you alone?"

"Good question," Margaret said. "It could've jumped me anytime after I entered the room, but it didn't. And as soon as I turned on the light it took off up the wall and through the grate." The edges of her mouth turned up in a slight grin, the same way it always did when she caught Richard in one of his little white lies. "That's it. That's why we haven't seen it until now. It doesn't like the light."

"But Mr. Baines saw it last night," Carol reminded her. "And the hall was pretty lit up."

"Yes, but it came out of and retreated back into a dark room. It might be able to stand bright lights for only short periods of time. Though, at this point I have to admit I'm only guessing."

"Where is it now?" Carol said. "Where could it have gone?" No one said a word. Those had been questions that no one else wanted to ask. Then a soft bang coming from the ceiling gave them the answer.

"It's still in the air vents," Manning said. They all looked up. "This is our chance," he added.

"Chance?" Adam said. "Chance to do what?"

"Kill it," he said blankly.

"You can't be serious," Margaret said. "That's insane."

"When will we have a better opportunity?" Manning asked. "For the first time we know where it is."

"And how do you suggest we go after it?" Margaret said. "Go climbing around in the air ducts? It would be quite a fit."

"You said it hates the light."

"I would say dislikes light—hate is a little strong."

"Whatever the case. If we turn on all the lights in all the rooms except for one, that thing would be drawn there."

"Except the air ducts are dark enough for its liking. What makes you think it will leave them?"

"Because we'll force it out."

"How?"

"Flares. We'll use flares. Light them up and stick them in the vents with the thing right between them. That should draw it out."

"And burn the place down while we're at it," Adam said.

"No, I don't think so. The metal of the vents is thick enough to contain the heat and flames."

"He's right," Margaret said. "But then what?"

"I say we blow it back to your Cenozoic Era. We have a shotgun and several handguns. We should be able to blow enough holes in it to stop it." The banging started again. "Sounds like it's moving. We don't have any more time to talk. If we're going to do it, we have to decide now."

"Which room?" Adam asked.

"The rec room. It's the biggest. We'll have plenty of maneuvering room."

"And room to retreat if this plan of yours fails," Margaret told the group.

"That too," Manning said.

The group separated to carry out Lieutenant Manning's plan. The women moved from room to room switching on the lights. Manning set out to get the flares he remembered being stored away in the front storage closet. It was all the way by the main entrance and he knew he would have to hurry there and back. Adam loaded the shotgun and made sure all the handguns were full. Every so often, the creature in the upper air vent would let go with a bang. The sound served to keep track of its location as well as to remind the crew to hurry.

Manning came back down the hall with the red flares. He passed Susan on his way. "You okay?" he asked.

"I think so."

"You'll do fine." He continued on his way to Adam, who was handing the loaded weapons to Margaret and Carol.

"Bring them to the door of the rec room. We'll be along soon."

"Be careful," Carol said, smiling at Adam. "We still have some unfinished business."

Finally, all was ready.

"You have a watch?" Manning asked.

"No, I don't," Adam said.

"Here, take this," Margaret said, handing him a very expensive Rolex. "It was Richard's. I'm surprised he still wore it."

Adam didn't understand what she meant until he spotted the inscription on its back side. It read, "Happy First Anniversary. Love M."

She shrugged. "Who would have thought?" With her arms full of weapons, she headed down the hall. "Good luck," was her parting comment.

"Okay," Manning said, handing Adam a flare. "You ready?"

"Does it matter?"

"No, I guess it doesn't." Manning checked his watch. Adam did the same. "In exactly two minutes light your flare and throw it down the vent. I'll do the same at my end. You'll have to toss it so it rolls into the main junction over the hall—about six feet. Not a tough throw, if your aim is straight and you don't hit any of the vent walls."

"Sounds easy enough," Adam said. Then again, he thought, a lot of things sound easy.

"Keep in mind," Manning said, "if you're late, that thing, whatever it is, is going to back up this way. You might find yourself with some real nasty company. I'm sure I'm making myself clear on this point."

"Crystal," Adam said, "crystal clear." Nothing like a little pressure to really motive a guy, he thought.

Manning walked to the door of the room. "Let's roll." He checked his watch one more time.

Adam nodded.

"Two minutes. Go." Manning took off, running down the hall. The echo of his fast footfall became more distant by the second.

Adam slid the bunk under the grate and jumped on top. His foot kicked a wallet onto the floor. He wasted a few seconds staring at the black leather, the thought that Richard's fate would be his fate too if this failed. He reached up for the grate to pull it free. His finger slid in between the metal slats. He pulled. The right side snapped off cleanly. He pulled again to free the left side, but it would not release.

"Great, just great." Adam looked where the metal had bent and saw a small screw covered with the same enamel paint as the grate. From the floor, it was almost invisible, but up close, it loomed larger then life.

Adam glanced at his watch—a whole minute had passed. He had to hurry. He scanned the room for something to pry the grate off. There was nothing.

Forty-five seconds left.

He had no other choice. He grabbed hold of the grate and tugged with all his strength. It took some effort, but the metal began to bend. He forced it open wide enough to stick his head up. The path for the flare was clear.

He pulled his head from the opening and checked the time. Ten seconds. He yanked the igniter cap off the flare. He struck it on the white tip. It let go a spark, but it didn't catch.

Five seconds.

Again, he struck the cap against the flare. This time it burst to a red flame. Swiftly as he could, he tossed the flare past the grate. He cringed when he heard it bouncing against the metal walls of the air vent—the exact thing Manning had cautioned him about.

He returned his head to the vent opening. The mounting smoke made him cough. His eyes stung but he focused on the red glow cutting through the white bitter vapors. Had he thrown it far enough?

Adam adjusted to the smoke enough to verify that he had succeeded in his task. It hadn't been a great throw, but a good throw—it would suffice.

He jumped off the bunk, ran out into the hall, and hurried down towards the rec room. Within moments, he saw Manning coming back from the other way.

"I take it all went well," the soldier said.

"A piece of cake," Adam said, feeling his heart still beating hard.

"Now what?" Margaret asked, handing Manning the shotgun.

"We wait," he said.

The room before the group was in almost total darkness and the smell of burning sulfur permeated the air. Manning pulled the door all but closed. The thin spray of light entering the room was contained to about a two-inch spread—not enough to frighten the thing off.

"How will we know if it's working?" Carol asked Lieutenant Manning. She slipped closer to Adam. With her body blocking the view, she touched his hand.

"Be patient. It will work. Listen."

"Listen? Listen for what?" Margaret asked. "How can we hear anything with the door closed?"

Suddenly a bang came from right above them.

"There's your answer."

"Oh, my god," Susan said. "It's…it's that thing."

"You have to be brave," Manning said. "We have to do this. Stay behind us. But try to remain calm."

She nodded.

There was another bang. It sounded like something was being slapped along the metal—a wet rag or towel.

"Here it comes," Manning said in a sure tone. "I would think a couple more minutes."

"What if it goes to another room?" Margaret asked.

"It won't. You turned on all the lights, right?"

"I know, but…"

"When it realizes it's trapped on both sides by the flares, it will retreat back here. The only dark place." He pumped the shotgun once, loading its chamber. "The only place to go. When we get in," he told Adam, "start firing." Manning's finger set gently on the trigger. There was a loud bang inside the rec room. "Everyone ready?"

He didn't wait for an answer. Instead, he tore open the door and switched on the light. On the back wall, pouring down from the vent was a large black blob. The sudden light caused the thing to fall to the floor.

Susan couldn't hold back a short scream.

The thing pulsated, almost looking like some kind of onyx jellyfish highlighted with swirls of deep purple. But even a jellyfish had a stable shape, where this creature did not. It seemed impossible that such a shapeless form had the ability to move under its own power, but it did. It would flatten then swell up, pouring itself over in waves and ripples.

"Fire," Manning ordered.

Adam began pulling the trigger of his pistol. The creature drew back as the bullets passed through it. Adam could barely believe his eyes. The thing was like hot black tar, except where the bullets hit. From those spots, a bluish goo oozed out.

Margaret also took shots at the thing. "We're having no effect," she cried out.

"Stand clear," Manning yelled. He shoved his way to the front and with a thunderous blast fired the shotgun. A large hole formed in the middle of the black creature. The nose of the barrel kicked up, but Manning held tight. With a sharp pull to load another shell, he shot again. A second hole appeared. More blue goo poured from around the creature's wound.

Once more, Manning pumped and shot. This time several chunks of the creature tore off and splattered onto the wall and floor. A loud high-pitched squeal followed the devastating wounding. It was at such a pitch that it hurt human ears. Carol and Susan tried to shield themselves from the noise.

Adam winced but continue to fire. With the loud wail, he didn't immediately hear the clicks of his empty gun. He dropped the useless weapon and pulled a second from his waistband. Margaret tried to shoot, but the pain forced her to cover her ears with both hands.

"We're hurting it," Manning yelled, seemingly impervious to the sound.

Then a long black tentacle-like stem shot out of the creature and whipped wildly through the air. Manning took careful aim and shot again. The tentacle retracted, then dropped to the floor, and only twitched slightly. The sharp squeal also died down.

"We got it," Manning said.

The black thing, now covered with many blue oozing spots, quivered on the floor in the corner. It didn't try to get away. It seemed to be waiting for something.

"What's it doing?" Adam asked.

"It's over," Manning told him. He pulled the shotgun one final time and took careful aim down the sight.

Then without warning Adam bolted forward. "Stop," he shouted. "Don't shoot." He tried to grab the gun, but Manning fired before Adam got to it.

The blast hit the creature dead center. A large crater formed and pieces flew up into the air.

"Why did you do that?" Manning asked angrily.

"I just realized," Adam started.

"Look," Carol said, pointing to the creature. The smaller pieces were rolling back towards the larger mass and reattaching themselves. After the organism had completely reformed, the blue goo started to flow even faster coating the entire surface. It started out shiny, but quickly became dull. Then a dry hard crust formed, and it began to crack.

"Is it dead?" Susan asked.

"As a doornail," Manning replied with a big smile.

"I wouldn't be so certain of that," Adam said. He took the shotgun from Manning.

"What are you talking about—look at it. It's dead."

"Sorry, I'm not as sure as you," Adam said, then with the butt of the shotgun, he hit the encrusted creature. It shattered like a ball of dry clay—a hollow ball of dry clay. There was nothing under the crumbled mass except for a hole in the floorboard from the shotgun blast itself.

They all walked over to where Adam stood staring at his discovery. Even Susan came over. Like Adam, they all stared at the hole.

"How did you know?" Carol finally asked.

"I thought it strange that it could move so freely, so quickly, yet it didn't try to escape. Sure, it was hurt, but not dead. When the smaller pieces rejoined, and that blue stuff started to pool on top, I figured it out. I think that's how it survived in the ice. It cocoons itself in its own dead tissue, like a protective shell."

"But it's not in its shell now," Carol said.

"I know. I think it realized it had a way to escape and took it."

"Realized a way?" Manning said. "You talk like that thing is smart or something." Manning snorted a little laugh of disbelief. "What's your opinion Dr. Walker? Is the creature smart?"

"I don't know if I would call it an intelligence."

"Exactly," Manning said.

"But," she continued, "it must have a strong sense of self-preservation. Enough to trick you into giving it an escape route."

"You can't be serious," Manning said, staring at them both, almost doubting their sanity. "It tricked me? Then where is it now?"

"Under the complex," Adam said. "And we have no way of knowing where."

"And by now it must be pretty pissed off," Margaret said.

"And that's my fault," Manning said. "I thought I could destroy it."

"I think the others thought so too," Adam said. He glanced over at the piles of empty clothes still on the other side of the room. "They probably tried and got the same results. It explains a lot," he added, remembering the bullet holes. "Once they realized they couldn't kill that monster, they must have decided to destroy themselves rather than suffer such a death. Poor devils...they must have thought it was their only escape."

"But they didn't escape," Carol said, "did they. It still took their bodies. Why would it do that? For what reason?"

"There's only one reason that makes any sense, Miss Chambers," Margaret said. "For food."

Carol gasped.

"I want to take a sample of that dry crust," the doctor added. "Find me something to put it in."

The group searched around the room. Carol came back with a clear glass ashtray. "Will this do? It looks clean." She handed it to the doctor.

"That will do fine." With the edge of the ashtray she broke off several small pieces and scooped them up, being careful not to touch any with her bare hands. She wasn't sure what effect it would have on human flesh. "This should do," she said. "Now if you'll excuse me, I'll be going back to the lab."

"Lab?" Susan yelled. "We have to find a way to defend ourselves."

"That's exactly what I had in mind."

The weary band started down the hallway to their quarters. No one spoke. It had been a while since their last meal, but the issue of food seemed a trivial matter at the moment. Carol and Adam kept Susan between them—the woman was still shaking from their encounter with the very thing that had forced her self-imposed exile to the storage building.

Out of nowhere, the silence was shattered by a loud scream rising up and tearing through the corridor. More than just a cry of pain, it was also a cry of terror. Bruce Manning took off running—there was only one person down in that part of the complex.

Being a soldier, Bruce made good time, leaving the others several seconds behind. He stormed into the room and found his brother on the bed having a seizure. The way his body arched up, it reminded Bruce of someone getting electric shock treatments. It was as if his feet and arms were bound by some invisible straps while the current drove mercilessly through his body. Bruce remembered that the attending physicians would use a small rubber gag to prevent their patients from biting off their tongues.

Bruce wasn't afraid Eric had lost his tongue, but rather that he had lost his mind. Eric began shouting wildly, "I couldn't stop it. It came back. It's here. It's here." His words changed to sobs and whimpers. If Bruce didn't know better, he would have thought that his brother had the mind of a very small child.

Though, ever so often Eric's eyes would appear normal and his mouth tried to form words, but then the nonsensical babble would begin again.

Eric started to swing his arms wildly, trying to strike anything within reach. Bruce grabbed his wrists and pinned them down to his side, not to avoid getting hit, but to stop his brother from hurting himself.

The others finally arrived at the doorway. They witnessed for themselves the struggle between brothers.

"Get me the medical kit!" Margaret told Adam. "It's in the lab." Next to the lieutenant, he was the fastest person there. They didn't have time to waste having her run at half the pace to retrieve the kit.

Adam nodded, then bolted down the hall.

"Hold on," Carol said. "Help's on the way." She turned to Margaret. "Should we help him?"

"We would only be in the way. He can manage."

"I hope you're right," Bruce said, holding down his brother's arms. He had always thought that old wives' tale about a madman having the strength of ten men was a load of shit—until now. Suddenly, one of Eric's arms broke free. It caught Bruce on the side of the head. After dodging the blow enough to make it ineffective, Bruce regained his balance and once more took hold of the flailing limb. "What's keeping Adam?"

"He's coming now," Carol shouted. "Hold on for a moment more."

"That's easy to say."

Just then, Adam returned and gave Margaret the medical kit. She opened it and removed a hypodermic and a small vial. After handing the case back to Adam, she filled the syringe, and swiftly moved to the bunk. Pulling up Eric's left sleeve, she wiped a spot with an alcohol-drenched cotton ball.

"Is that really necessary?" Bruce asked, struggling to keep his brother under control. "Give him the shot already."

She did.

Within moments, Eric's body eased and he stopped fighting.

"I gave him a double dose," she said. "He should be out for quite a while."

"Thanks Doc," Bruce said, looking down at his sedated brother.

Without telling the others, Margaret had returned to the cold room. She opened the first freezer and walked over to the body of Emmanuel Phillips. After putting on a pair of rubber gloves and pulling back the blue tarp, she scraped off a few samples of tissue from various parts of what remained of his body. She then took a scalpel and made a large incision over the man's remaining lung. She wanted to know if there was any dry material that would visibly match the residue she had picked up in the rec room.

She pulled back the layers of skin and muscle. There appeared to be nothing unusual in the tissue. Then she removed several of the partially dissolved ribs. Besides the obvious, something about them wasn't quite right—they were more porous than expected, making them very brittle. She took a piece for closer examination.

Then past the ribs, she cut into the lung. There she found something that resembled what she was searching for. But instead of blue powder, she found small blue crystals lining the lung membrane. She put one crystal in a glass petri dish and with the blade of the scalpel, she crushed it. It crumbled down to fine grains almost matching her sample. She would need to examine the two powders side by side to be sure.

Using a pair of long tweezers, Margaret pulled out several more crystals. Some were deep inside the air sacks of the lung wall. Pushing the tissue aside to gather her specimens, a sudden wave of bewilderment poured over her. What she was seeing made no sense. It almost appeared that all this destruction came from within and worked its way out or, by the damage, fought its way out.

After finishing with Emmanuel, she proceeded over to the body of John Blackwood. She turned down the lab coat being used for a makeshift death shroud. That frozen expression of horror was still etched on the man's face. She had forgotten the fear locked in his eyes.

"Was it worth it?" she said to the dead body.

She began by examining the corpse for any open wounds, sores or discoloration. Finding nothing, she took another scalpel—a clean scalpel—and collected several specimens from different parts of the body. When done, she unceremoniously replaced the coat.

Margaret sealed her tissue samples and put the instruments back on the tray. After leaving the freezer, she made sure the door closed tightly behind her. That last blast of cold air hit her square in the face. Margaret couldn't help wondering if all this could have been avoided, though she feared that the moment the organism was brought into the station, the answer was no. John Blackwood had set a course of events into play that she doubted could be altered.

About to leave the cold room, Margaret noticed the canisters of liquid nitrogen. And above the metal containers was a pair of heavy insulated gloves. She thought about taking one of the canisters back to the lab. If she found anything, she could preserve it for the trip home.

Home, she thought. It had been only two days, but with all that had been going on, it felt more like two weeks. When would Adam's crew send out another plane? He would only say, soon.

She stepped into the main hall where there was still a trace-odor of sulfur, even with the fans drawing in fresh air. She stopped and listened, though she really didn't know for what. For a brief moment, she questioned her own judgment about coming down here alone. That thing was still creeping around somewhere under the complex. Bruce tried to convince them that it had crawled away and died in some dark, black hole. As much as she would have liked to believe it, she had trouble doing so. And if it wasn't dead, she hoped it would stay in the darkness below the building. In an attempt to keep the thing at bay, they had decided to keep all the lights on. Though deep down, she didn't think the method was foolproof.

Then from behind her, a loud creak came from the door. A draft, she thought to herself. It creaked again. She had spent enough time here, she told herself, and began walking. She couldn't shake the feeling she was being watched.

Her pace picked up. She had to be careful not to lose any of her samples and still hurry down the hall. They had bounced once in the tray, but she stopped before losing any. She didn't plan to return to that freezer anytime soon, so these samples were it. She walked with a quick gait, but slow enough so the petri dishes and specimen bags stayed put in the metal tray.

Passing by the sleeping quarters, Margaret decided to check up on Bruce Manning. He had been sitting alone with his brother since she put him out.

"How's he doing?" she asked. She couldn't help but notice the man's head jerk. He had been nodding off and she felt a little guilty waking him. It had been a long day for everyone.

"Excuse me?" Bruce said.

"How's your brother doing?" she said in a soft voice.

"Fine, I suppose." His eyes turned down towards the bunk. "He's still out from the shot you gave him." He shook his head. "What's wrong with him? One moment he's normal, the other he acts like a madman." Bruce returned his gaze to Dr. Walker. "You have any ideas?"

"A guess—an educated guess. Shock, mostly, I would say. I only hope we can get him the help he needs. Or at least that the tranquilizers hold out."

Bruce rubbed his neck.

"How are your scratches?" Margaret asked. "Any signs of infection?"

"What, these things? I've cut myself worse than this while shaving."

"You know, Susan didn't mean anything by it. She was just very scared."

Bruce shrugged. "Is it any wonder? You should have seen her when we found her. I wouldn't be surprised if she thought we were that…that thing. A few little claw marks aren't enough to bother me."

"Let me know if anything changes," Margaret told him.

Bruce looked at the metal tray in the woman's hands. "You already seem busy enough without needing to worry about my scratches." He saw a shimmer of light reflecting off the small glass petri dishes.

"You know what they say, idle hands are the devil's plaything."

"How about," Bruce said, "all work and no play makes Jack a dull boy. Or in this case, the doctor a dull girl."

He looked at her with such a serious expression, she let out a small laugh. "Where are the others?"

"I think they've all turned in for the night," he said.

"Now, that's a real idea. You should consider doing the same."

"No, I'm fine."

"What was that a minute ago? The floor almost came up and hit you in the chin."

"You should talk. Here's the rest of us sitting on our butts and you're the one doing some real work. You're the one who needs the rest."

"Work? I'm just trying to satisfy my scientific curiosity. I have a 'need-to-know' complex. Besides, I'm used to burning the midnight oil. I'll be fine."

Before saying another word, Bruce let go with a tremendous yawn. "Oh, forgive me," he said, embarrassed by the display.

"You need sleep, Lieutenant. There's no shame in that. And if you ask me, you're the one person I would want well rested."

"Maybe you're right. I'm not much use to you all or my brother, if I'm half-dead on my feet." He stood up and walked towards the second bed. "I suppose a couple of hours of shuteye wouldn't hurt anything."

"Then I'll wish you goodnight." Margaret backed up to the door. "If anything happens, feel free to come get me." The woman smiled at the man then left him alone with his unconscious brother. The shot she gave Eric should last through the night. It would be close, but it should be enough for the lieutenant to get some rest himself.

Sleep did sound good, but the sooner the work started on these samples, the sooner she would learn something. Margaret headed down the long corridor. The hall had an eerie quiet to it—even more than usual. For a second she thought that maybe Lieutenant Manning had stepped into the hall, because again it felt like she was being watched. She stopped and turned but saw no one.

Convincing herself it was all in her overworked imagination, Margaret cleared the last ten feet and entered the lab. She put her tray down on the table. It took a few minutes to collect the other items she needed: microscope, glass slides, another pair of clean rubber gloves, even a jug of distilled water. Perfect, she thought, and arranged the equipment on the section of countertop next to the table with the Macintosh computer.

After setting up, she brought over her specimens. She decided to start with the blue crystals taken from Emmanuel Phillips' body.

Carefully she placed several crystals in a mortar and crushed them to a fine powder. She put a small amount on a slide. Then adding a drop of distilled water and sandwiching the mixture with a second slide, she placed the glass strips under the lens of the microscope. Switching on the small built-in light, she focused the eyepiece.

At first glance, she couldn't believe her eyes and pulled away. She looked again—this time moving the slide slightly to view a larger concentration of the blue particles. It confirmed her original observation. The crystals were made up of cells—animal cells. And instead of a normal structure, they had a double nucleus, as if they were about to split, but then abruptly stopped. It could have occurred during the solidification process, she thought, the crystallization halting the usual cell division.

Next, Margaret prepared a slide in the same manner with a small portion of the blue crust left behind in the rec room by the creature. Studying those cells, she found them irregular. They appeared to be incomplete—not fully formed—maybe even damaged. She considered if Manning's attack on the creature could have caused such abnormalities, but quickly dismissed the idea. A gunshot blast would definitely disrupt some cells, but not all of them. And these cells weren't broken nor torn which would be the result of that type of trauma.

She leaned back in her chair thinking that maybe she had reached a dead end. She knew that both sets of cells were connected in some way, but she didn't know how. They were very similar, but also very different. It seemed that the first sample of cells were missing something—some component—so they could divide and form completely. And she doubted that the second set of cells could ever divide at all.

Then she had a sudden thought—*if these were the same cells John Blackwood had been researching...* Margaret immediately booted up the Macintosh, and began the genetics program using the same file she had before. But this time she skipped on to the phase that simulated cell reproduction. After only a few seconds, the bonds broke down. Anywhere there was an "X", cohesion could not occur, causing full cellular decay. After running the simulation several times, she decided to check out some of the other files.

Using the mouse, she pointed to the open menu and brought up the next simulation. This one had two separate strands of DNA. Again, she began the reproduction phase.

The two strands of the first double helix separated and merged with the strands of the second, forming a new unique double helix. Then, because of those strange "X" bonds the process stopped. She ran it again.

Margaret shook her head. This view was interesting, but next to useless. She searched the program menus for something more useful.

"What do we have here?" she said, choosing the menu item labeled *Cell Mitosis*. The screen changed from the pair of double helixes to a pair of complete cells. She reran the sequence. The two cells began to merge, but within seconds stopped. Margaret's eyes widened. This new structure had a double nucleus, exactly like the cells from the crystals she had removed from Emmanuel's body. She repeated the simulation once more.

Then Margaret decided to switch back to the first file with the single strand, but she did not alter the view. The single cell, now in greater detail, seemed to match the sample from the rec room. When she ran the simulation, the cell quickly ruptured. But the cells she had found were intact, which only led to one conclusion—the computer model was wrong—its programming couldn't compensate correctly for the unknown bonds.

Though combined with other cells, the "X" bonds gained some stability. Was that what John Blackwood was looking for? A way to stabilize the DNA? Was that why he had the sampling program rewritten to test the creature's cell structure? To find a compatible combination of base pairs? And for what reason? She had gone through all his notes, but they mentioned nothing. If only she had the one missing book—the explanations must be there. She looked at the long list of computer files. He must have set up all these simulations to test whatever theory he had.

Without the notebook, she realized she had only one option—to run all the other DNA simulations. Though that could take hours to complete and she would need time to analyze the results. Then again, with the condition of the plane, time was one commodity she had plenty of.

Margaret watched over and over again as computer-generated events repeated themselves on the screen—pairs of double helixes breaking down and merging, only to stop halfway through completion. Boredom had her wanting to skip every other file, but she wouldn't. There was no way of knowing which one would have the answer she was searching for.

After two dozen or so simulations, she felt her eyes starting to drop. Her head bobbed once and she tried to shake away the sleep. Then she found something that snapped her wide-awake.

One of the simulations resulted in complete and stable cells. She ran it again to be certain of what she saw. Hurrying to switch the program back to the double helix view, she watched the models split and re-combine forming new and completely different DNA molecules. All the "X's" were replaced—filled in as it were—with nucleotides from the normal strand. The pattern had to be exact for the splitting and forming of new bonds. It appeared only a precise match of genetic material could merge with the creature's DNA to produce a viable cell.

She thought about it for a moment. It wasn't a parasite; it was more of a symbiotic relationship. Though what if the cells couldn't combine? What if the host DNA wasn't compatible? The very thought sent a shiver down her spine. Emmanuel Phillips' DNA was obviously not a match.

"That's it," she said. "That's it. Oh, my God—the others—Richard." She stood up quickly, but in doing so knocked over the microscope. She cursed her clumsiness and took hold of the fallen equipment.

"Damn," she cried out. She lifted her hand and saw the deep cut on the side of her right index finger caused by the broken slide. It cut right through the rubber glove and continued on to her skin. She pulled off the glove and let it drop to the counter. Her blood dripped across the Formica while she grabbed for a tissue from a nearby box.

She didn't notice that several drops landed in the ashtray that contain the powdered sample from the rec room. The crimson fluid was immediately absorbed into the blue sand. It clotted and formed a purplish glob.

Then the specimen turned black and began to pulsate.

As Margaret wrapped the tissue around her injured digit, a tiny living mass slithered to the rim of the glass ashtray and like a worm wiggled its way onto the counter. It crawled to the other blood droplets, absorbing them. Drawn towards the discarded rubber glove by a great hunger, it consumed the blood along the jagged tear.

Margaret pressed hard—the white tissue turned red. It took a few minutes until the bleeding stopped. She went to the medical kit and grabbed a bandage. She tried to open the wrapper, but the remaining rubber glove made it more difficult. Holding the compress in place with her thumb and injured forefinger, she pulled off the glove with her remaining fingers. It landed on the counter next to its damaged mate.

She managed to remove the bandage wrapper and apply the dressing to her wound. After examining her handiwork, she thought a break from the lab would do her a world of good. If she hadn't been so tired, her little accident wouldn't have happened. She glanced at the counter. To her surprise, there was no blood. The only thing out of place was the pair of rubber gloves.

She was sure she had dripped blood across the countertop. She picked up the gloves—they were clean too—not a drop of blood anywhere. Suddenly, Margaret felt a warm sensation in the webbing between her index and middle finger. It startled her for a moment and she dropped the gloves. It wasn't a painful sensation, just very strange. She examined her hand. There was nothing there.

After retrieving the rubber gloves from the floor, Margaret tossed them into the garbage can next to the desk. Turning her head to stretch her neck, the release of tension felt pretty good. Though of all the things, coffee would do her the most good right now. Even the thought alone made her feel better. Margaret started for the kitchen. Her hand shot to her mouth trying to fight off a yawn as exhaustion crept in on her.

CHAPTER TEN

The pain faded since it had returned to the one and the fear of being hurt again kept it away from those other things. They were like the one, and yet different from the one. There was no joining with them—no becoming. With them, the hunger did go away, but nothing more.

Now the hunger began to stir once more and the pain and fear were losing their hold. Resisting, it wanted to stay with the one—it felt safe with the one—but along with the cravings came other feelings—strange feelings—confusing feelings. Feelings drawing it towards something—pulling it away from the one like some giant magnet. There were brief flashes of new surroundings—images and glimpses that were not of the one. It had not left the safety of the one—it had stayed to rest and heal, but it was somewhere else as well.

The pangs of hunger grew faster. It could sense food, but there was no food—the one was not food—the one was the one. This far-off longing only drove its hunger to an unbearable point. The ache was too great—it had to follow it.

It slid down and seeped through the seams at the edge of the wall. Then guided by some force, it quickly moved in the darkness among the maze of warm pipes and cold concrete. With each passing moment, the pull became stronger and more distinct. Somehow, some way, even it didn't understand why, it drew closer to whatever was calling it.

It continued under the complex, knowing the exact path to take. It was getting ever nearer—it could sense it—it could feel it.

A small crack led it up into the light. For a split second, it pulled back, but then continued on, driven forward by something inexplicable. It pooled itself up through the tiny opening. It remembered this place. It had been here once before—another failed joining. Suddenly, it was aware of another presence—it was one of those things. It hadn't known fear, but quickly learned—it seeped back, wanting to return to the safety of the one, only to stop when it sensed a second life-force. It was that life-force that had brought it here.

Slowly, it crept across the floor towards the thing. Except for its middle section, which would rise and fall in a shallow rhythm, the creature remained motionless. The top of its body was out of view, hidden by a tall platform.

Fearful the beast would attack again, it stayed on the floor for several moments. Then clinging to a metal support rod, it quickly climbed to reach the top of the platform. There the creature was hunched forward and both its clumsy appendages were stretched out—it still didn't move.

Rolling across the hard, flat surface, it cautiously approached the sleeping creature. It had never tried to merge with this one, but there seemed a strong connection. It slid closer, touching the creature's skin. It was warm and smooth and soft. And there was something else. That presence—that force that had been calling to it was here...here within this creature and now it knew why.

Responding to its touch, a black tip wiggled and wormed upward, partially separating from the host body. It reached out for this tiny black doppelganger and not wasting another moment gently absorbed its smaller twin, joining with it and becoming whole once more. It didn't know nor understand how a piece of itself had gotten this far away or how it survived on its own, but even apart they were one being—separate, yet still connected—ever aware of each other.

Then, acting on knowledge gained from its counterpart, it rose up, poured over and covered the strange unconscious creature. It would try to join with this one; if not...it was still hungry.

~

Margaret awoke with a gasp having had the strangest dream of being smothered. She found herself in the kitchen—her head had been resting on the tabletop. It took her a moment to shake free the cobwebs enough to recall that she had been trying to make a pot of coffee when sleep swept down on her.

The brewing pot and the can of coffee were still in front of her, though none of the grounds had been transferred to the basket. She glanced at her watch. Her catnap had lasted for less than a half an hour. Still a little groggy, her weak gaze fell to the empty pot. Should she make the coffee and go back to work? Not able to stop it, she let out a huge yawn.

"That answers that," she said to herself, and stood up. Almost immediately Margaret felt dizzy and quickly grabbed the back of the chair to steady herself. She had been pushing herself too hard and deciding to call it a night and go to bed made for the best course of action. She wanted to have a clear head in the morning when she explained to the others what she had discovered. She wanted to explain her theory and why the crew of this station had disappeared. But to give the facts in any coherent manner she would need her rest. Normally she'd be too excited to sleep, but something had her dead on her feet.

She left the coffee and pot on the table. It would be waiting in the morning. Then, on the way to her room, with her footsteps echoing down the empty hall, Margaret casually scratched the back of her hand just below the index finger. She didn't notice the small red blemish on her skin.

~

The next morning a very loud knock practically threw Margaret out of bed. The knocking continued even while she stumbled to the door. She slid back the small bolt that had served as a lock. She opened to find Adam and Carol staring back with worried eyes.

"Thank God," Carol said. "We've been knocking for almost five minutes. Didn't you hear us?"

"Five minutes?" Margaret's voice was weak and raspy. "I'm sorry. I went to bed late last night. What time is it?"

"Almost eleven."

"Eleven," she said through a yawn. "I must've really been tired. Where's the lieutenant?" she asked Adam. He kept turning his head away from her. It wasn't until she looked down that she realized she was standing there in only her bra and panties. The embarrassment pulled her the rest of the way out of her sleep. She closed the door to cover herself, leaving only a crack to speak through.

Carol continued talking without missing a beat. "He's with his brother. Eric seems to be doing much better. He's talking some—just a little actually. Bruce tried to get him to eat something but he's not interested in taking any food yet."

"He'll eat when he's hungry," Margaret said. "And Susan?"

"I left her in her room," Adam said, finally speaking up. Margaret could tell he also was a little embarrassed by her overexposure.

"Do you think that wise?"

"She seems fine. Do you think she's a danger to herself?"

"Probably not," Margaret said. "Considering she locked herself away in the other storage building and survived on only baked beans. Eating nothing but baked beans, if that's not a reason to do yourself in, what is?" She could tell by the expression on their faces that the couple was not amused by her attempt at humor. "She should be okay," the woman said seriously. "Just don't leave her too long."

Adam nodded.

"Let me get dressed. I found out something last night and all of you should hear it. Get Bruce and Susan and meet me in the lab." After they agreed, she closed the door to her room.

Margaret walked over to the dresser where she had placed her clothes. On the way, she passed the full-length wall mirror, catching a glimpse of her scantily clad body. She stopped and took a step back to get a better view.

She didn't look too bad. In fact, she thought she looked pretty damn good. She had a little extra sag off the hips, but for her age, she was in good shape. She recalled the feeling of embarrassment while standing in front of Adam half-naked. Though deep down she also felt a slight twinge of excitement. It had been a long time since a man had seen so much of her. In fact, only one other man since Richard.

She never admitted it to her ex-husband, but their divorce had been quite hard on her—emotionally, anyway. The grounds were mutual—neither pointing an accusing finger; the settlement was fair and just—an easy split of join properties; no harsh or bitter words were exchanged—both acted mature and patient during the proceedings. The divorce was the one time when they got along perfectly.

Though sometimes, during weaker moments, she regretted their decision to part. And finding he was still wearing the watch she gave him for their first anniversary, he might have thought so too. Richard was a man who would never do or keep, not to mention wear, anything that reminded him of bad times. He must have had some fond memories of their time together. Maybe the ease of the divorce was their true downfall. If one of them had made a fight of it to stay together, the other would have known there still was something worth fighting for. If only they had talked more.

Now it was too late for talk. She had had so many chances over the years, but carelessly tossed them all away. Margaret had to fight back tears and turn away from the mirror, no longer able to stand the sight of her own reflection. But not looking in the mirror, she did not see the ripple of flesh moving along her right side. It was like a muscle spasm she could not feel. And as quickly as it started, the spasm stopped.

Slowly she got dressed—the weight of what-could-have-been pressed heavily on her. There was a sluggishness to her actions. Then, while slipping her shirt over her head, a sharp pain shot from her elbow to her neck. She dropped her arm to her side and the pain vanished. She pulled her pants on followed by her shoes. After running a brush through her hair, she left the room.

Walking down the hall, she entered the lab. The others were sitting around the table waiting for her, except for Bruce. He was leaning against the wall near the door.

"I understand your brother is doing better," she said sincerely.

"Calmer anyway," Manning replied. "He fades in and out, but at least when he's conscious, I can talk to him. Though he isn't saying anything that makes much sense." He glanced down the hall. "Is this going to take long, I should really get back to him."

"I shouldn't think so, but what I have to say is important to us all and it will require your focused attention."

"Then let's get on with it," he told her.

Margaret continued across the room to the table. She thought about turning on the Macintosh to run the simulations, but decided against it. They would serve only to add complexity and confusion to something in which the bottom line was quite simple—they were all in great danger.

"I've gone over it all," she started, "the notes, the samples, the computer files. I believe the organism that was excavated from the ice sheet had—has a bizarre DNA—an incomplete DNA. That's what John Blackwood modeled on his computer. The 'X's didn't represent a new bond of DNA, but a missing bond. The creature seeks out that special sequence that can complete its own DNA. It would need the right combination of bonds in the right order."

"What does that have to do with the missing people?" Carol asked.

"In the process of trying to bond to the correct DNA, it absorbs any bonds that don't match. It metabolizes them for energy."

"Absorbs, metabolizes," Adam said. "You don't have to sugarcoat it with your scientific jargon. That thing eats people."

"That's not exactly correct. I believe it would seek out organic material indiscriminately."

"What's that suppose to mean?" Carol asked.

"It's not picky about what it eats," Manning said from the doorway.

"That explains what happened to the rats I brought up," Adam told the group.

"Maybe," Margaret said, "but I think Blackwood used the rats in his experiments with the creature."

"Yes," Susan spoke up. "You're right. He did. He must have. One day I noticed two of the poor little things were missing. I asked him about it. He said they weren't very healthy and had died. He'd already removed them from their cage, though he never showed me the bodies. I never thought anymore of the whole thing after that."

"No disrespect intended," Adam said, "but now what? You have some answers, but do you have the answers we need? How do we stop it? Can we stop it?"

"I don't know," she said straight out. "I don't have a clue."

"We hurt it once," Manning said. "We can do it again. But this time we finish the job."

"How?" Carol asked. "It got away once. Maybe we can trap it instead."

"Trap it?" Susan said. "Trap it! It killed all my friends. People I lived with, saw and talked to exclusively for eighteen months. That may not sound like a lot of time to you people, but up here it seems like forever and those people were all I had." She had to take a fast breath. "I say kill it. Kill the damn thing before it kills us."

"But how?" Adam asked. He turned to Margaret. The others did too.

"Acid maybe," she said, knowing the group was counting on her for a solution. "No matter its strange DNA, it's still an organic life form. And as such should react to the same corrosive properties as our own tissue." She paused. "Unless..." She thought for a moment.

"Please, Doctor," Manning said. "We're all listening."

"Unless it has a natural buffering agent."

"I don't understand," Carol said.

"Remember the damaged hand we found when we first arrived or the condition of Emmanuel Phillips?" She saw the strain on Susan Dawson's face. "I'm sorry," Margaret said to the woman. "If this is too uncomfortable…"

Susan raised a single hand signaling it was okay for her to continue.

And Margaret did. "The damage in both cases was caused by what best could be described as digestion. Not unlike our own stomachs."

"And your point," Manning said impatiently. Obviously he wanted to get back to his brother's side and no one in the room could really blame him.

"My point," she continued, "is that our stomachs contain hydrochloric acid, but it also has a layer of mucus to act as a buffer so the stomach won't digest itself. It's highly likely that the organism has the same sort of protection around its cells."

"So you're saying the acid won't work after all," Carol spoke up.

"No, I'm saying it's a big unknown. With enough acid, even stomach tissue will dissolve. Ask anyone with an ulcer. It comes down to a matter of amounts. It's a simple problem of we might not have enough to do any real damage."

"Fine, fine," Manning said, "forget the acid. We know gunshots hurt it. We just have to find something else more effective that we have in ample supply."

"How about fire?" Susan said. They all looked at the woman, puzzlement clearly on their faces. She shrugged. "Sorry, I thought it was a good idea."

"No, not good," Manning said. "It's a great idea. We can siphon some gasoline from the plane's tank and make ourselves a half dozen or so Molotov cocktails. With a little luck, we should be able to take care of that thing."

"And burn the place down to boot," Carol said.

"We can use fire extinguishers to control the flames," Manning said. "If we're careful we can incinerate the thing, but keep this place standing."

"Though for your plan to work," Margaret said, "you must realize two important things. First, we have to find the thing again and second, someone's going to have to get close enough to throw your little toys."

"She's right on both points," Adam said. "Not to mention we will need an open area to burn it. And I don't think herding it into a dark room will work again."

"And why not?" Manning asked.

"I don't know. It's just a feeling I get. The way it's been hiding—staying out of our way—evading us—even how it escaped our attacks, first Richard's and then again last night, I get the feeling that the thing is a lot smarter than we give it credit for."

"Smart?" Manning laughed. "Smart! You can't be serious. The thing may have strong animal instincts for survival, but it being smart, I seriously doubt that. And more importantly, like any other animal, it hunts when it's hungry. We can use that to our advantage."

"Advantage?" Carol said, "what advantage? This is all becoming quite complicated."

"Simple. We wait until it's hungry. When it comes out, we burn it, we kill it." Manning looked around the room at the faces of his companions for any sign of disagreement. He saw none. "That's it then. We'll burn the little monster. Burn it back to hell."

"I have an empty gas can in the plane," Adam said, "but I'm not sure if that will be enough. Do we have anything else we can use?"

"Wasn't there a gas can where we came in?" Carol said. "Remember, it was by the ax and that...you know."

"Yes, I remember," Adam said. "With two cans, we should be fine."

Margaret stood up. The twinge of pain returned to her shoulder. "If we're going to do this thing, we better hurry."

"I'll head to the plane right now," Adam volunteered.

"Would that be prudent?" Margaret asked. "I mean, you going out by yourself. We should stay in pairs. We can cover each other's backs that way."

"She's right," Manning said. "I should go with you." He briefly glanced at the door to the hall.

"I'll stay with your brother," Carol told him as if she knew what he was thinking.

"Then let's get going," Adam said. "I have the strangest feeling this is going to be our last chance."

"You don't remember me, do you?" Susan said to Margaret, who was poring over the notebooks one more time searching for more clues, perhaps even a hint on how to destroy the creature. She wasn't too keen on the fire idea. Fire had a nasty way of getting away from you. And she didn't want to simply exchange one danger for another.

Hearing the question, she turned her head towards Susan Dawson. She gave the woman a very deep look. "No. No, I'm sorry I don't."

"That's okay. It was well over three years ago...a fundraiser in D.C. I had longer hair back then and we met for only a few minutes."

"It was at the Hamline Clinic fundraiser, wasn't it?"

"Yes, it was." A tiny smile formed on Susan's lips. "And it was John Blackwood who introduced us..." Her smile immediately disappeared and her voice trailed off.

"That's right. I don't know why I didn't recognize you."

"I'm sure you have other things on your mind. And I'm not looking my best. With all that's going on and all."

"That's understandable. Did you enjoy yourself?"

"Enjoy myself?"

"At the fundraiser."

"Honestly, it was more important to my date than it was to me. Though, I did meet my future husband at the buffet." There was another long pause. And then, "Do you mind if I ask you another question?"

"I guess that would depend on the question." Margaret smiled. "Go ahead, ask."

"Is it true you turned down the chance to be stationed here?"

"It is. Does that surprise you? Not everyone wants to be stuck on top of a giant ice cube. No offense." Her eyes moved back to the computer screen comparing the image to Blackwood's notebook sketches.

"But you are here," Susan pointed out. "You're here now."

Margaret closed the notebook and reached for another. Her shoulder felt very stiff while leaning across the desk. "True, I am." She pulled back once with the pain, but then grabbed the next book. She began to thumb through the pages. "Though, I can honestly say I wish I was someplace else."

"What do you think of our chances?" Susan asked.

"Chances for what?"

"Getting out alive."

"That's good. For a moment I thought you were asking my opinion if we were all going to die." Margaret cringed once, which did not go unnoticed by Susan.

"Are you all right?" Susan asked. "Do you need help?"

"No, just a headache. I..." Margaret winced again, but this time it was followed by a slight body tremor. Quickly the tremors became more severe and within seconds Dr. Margaret Walker began having a seizure—her entire body began to bounce in the chair.

Susan watched in horror, petrified by fear. She tried to move but couldn't. Her eyes were glued to the events unfolding before her.

Margaret's jaw clenched tight—her head kicked back—her arms locked down to her side. The violence of the seizure intensified. Her eyes opened suddenly, then turned a solid black. The front of her face began to collapse. Her nose fell inwards, followed by her eyes and sockets. Her mouth and teeth began to dissolve. The top of Margaret's head finally caved in. Soon the face of Dr. Walker disappeared completely. Her hair was gone; her head was gone. In its place was a black molten mass.

Inch by inch, Margaret's body began to melt. And from the shoulders down, her clothes emptied. Susan's eyes strained to stay in her skull as she watched Margaret's hands and fingers liquefy into a black goo. The rest of her upper torso had been completely consumed and now her legs were going. Her pant legs collapsed and the shapeless creature poured out, rolling over her shoes—the empty clothes fell in a heap under the desk.

The thing began to roll towards Susan. She let out a breathless whine and leaned too far in her chair, tipping herself over and onto the floor. The thing continued to slide her way. Susan, on hands and knees, scurried across the floor like some wild animal. With the thing very close, the woman barely managed to get to her feet.

She ran down the hall. Her terror made navigating the long corridor difficult. She bounced off the walls, ran into doors—she would stumble and fall, get up, stumble and fall again. She could hardly breathe. Then something grabbed her arm. She screamed at the top of her lungs and her fist began pounding on whatever had grabbed her.

"Stop it," a far-off voice said. "Stop it."

A loud crack echoed in the hall and a sharp sting radiated through Susan's cheek. The pain cleared her head enough for her to see it was Carol speaking while holding her hard by the arms.

"Calm down!" Carol commanded. She shook Susan. "Calm down."

"She's gone," Susan whimpered. "It got her. She's gone."

"Dr. Walker," Carol said, knowing she was the only other "she" in the place. "Show me."

Susan shook her head wildly. "No, I can't." That response was met with another sharp sting across the face. "Please, I can't." And still another sting.

"I said show me. Now!"

"Back in the lab," Susan cried. "In the lab."

Both women moved down the hall. Carol had to push Susan several times along the way. At the lab door, Susan refused to enter, but with the threat of more pain, she went in, followed by Carol. The lab was empty.

"Where?" Carol asked.

Susan pointed to the other side of the room. "Over there," she whispered. "Over there."

Slowly Carol made her way across the laboratory. She did not see the pile of clothes until she had walked halfway. Hesitantly, she tapped them with the tip of her shoe—they were completely empty. Her eyes moved quickly along the floor, the walls, even the ceiling. Where was it, she thought. It must have crept back into the darkness.

Carol went back to Susan, who stood frozen by the door.

"What do we do now?" Susan asked. "What do we do?"

Carol stared at the frightened woman, but said nothing.

"Do we have enough?" Adam yelled to Bruce over the blowing snow. The body of the plane blocked some of the wind, but not enough to stop the biting cold.

"I certainly hope so," Manning shouted back. Even with his hood up, he tried to keep his face turned away from the tiny darts of flying ice. "These cans are full. Let's head back."

"You'll get no argument from me." Adam pulled the siphoning hose from the tank and capped it off, while Manning sealed the second gas can. Both men began their trek back to the Research Station each hauling a can. Their earlier path from the station to the plane had already been half-covered by a fresh white blanket. Now, as they trudged through the drifting snow, the remnants of the old tracks were completely destroyed by the new. On the return trip, the two men did not speak.

At the station entrance, using his free hand, Adam tugged open the door and stepped inside. Once in, he set his can down and began to brush the snowflakes from his shoulders, then, after a quick headshake, he pulled down his hood. To his surprise, he found Carol standing there wearing her coat and boots.

"I was just coming to get you," she said in a desperate tone. "Dr. Walker. She's dead."

"Dead?" Lieutenant Manning said, pulling down his own hood.

"I found her clothes in the lab. They were empty, like the others."

Adam hurried to undo his coat. "Where's Susan?"

"I left her at the other end of the complex."

"You left her?" Manning asked. "Alone?"

"Well, I couldn't bring her with me. She was hysterical—on the verge of a breakdown. What would you have me do?"

Adam kept silent. He remembered how wild Susan had been when they found her hiding in the storage building. And that it took both him and Manning to control her—what chance would Carol have if the woman had gone berserk? "We should get to her," he finally said. "And the sooner the better."

All three ran from the warm room down to the lab. At such a rapid pace it didn't take them long to reach that end of the station. The men boldly rushed into the lab, while Carol stood back as if afraid to enter the room.

As Carol had told them, they found the empty clothes of Margaret Walker. They were in a heap next to the desk exactly like the many other piles they had found. Manning knelt down for a closer look. If he had any remaining doubts regarding the doctor's theories, they were most certainly gone now. "Why didn't you do something?" he asked Carol, who stood her ground on the other side of the door.

"Me? Why me? I wasn't with Dr. Walker when it...when this happened. I was with your brother. Remember?"

Manning turned away from the woman.

"Of course he does," Adam said. Suddenly, a look of bewilderment washed over his face. His head snapped sharply to the left, then to the right. "Where's Susan?"

"I don't know. I left her here."

"We need to find her," Manning said. "Maybe she can tell us something."

"She must be hiding in one of the other rooms," Adam said, "we would've passed her coming down the hall."

"I told her she'd be safe here," Carol told them. "Maybe she went back to her room."

"Okay," Manning said, "you check her quarters. I'll check the galley. Adam, you start searching the rooms down at this end. We'll search the rooms coming back. We should meet somewhere in the middle of the complex."

The others agreed with Bruce's plan and split up to hunt for Susan. The soldier headed down to the galley and entered without a single hesitation. The large room didn't have anywhere to hide. Even someone crouching under a table would still be clearly visible.

Bruce crossed the room to the kitchen. It hadn't changed since the last time—there were a couple of dirty pots in the sink, but that was all. He continued on to the pantry. That too was empty, as it should be. He made his way back to the refrigerator and pulled open the metal door.

"Oh no," he said, looking, seeing what he hoped not possible—there was no cold beer. "Damn!" He sure could use a cold beer right about now.

This minor dilemma was quickly upstaged by a sharp scream coming from the hallway. Bruce tore out of the kitchen, but before having to decide on a direction, he heard his name being called out—he was off. A very short distance down, he spotted Adam standing in the hall holding Carol. She buried her face in Adam's shoulder and sobbed.

"What's wrong?" Manning asked. "What happened?"

"We found Susan," Adam said. He nodded towards the door. "She's in there."

Manning stepped into the room. What he saw shocked him. Susan was swinging from the ceiling with a bed sheet tied around her neck. A chair tipped on its side rested on the floor directly beneath her feet. The woman's eyes were still open in a frozen stare of terror.

After a few moments, Manning realized he was just standing, gazing up at the dead woman. He turned around and left the room. "I'm going to need your help," he said to Adam. "You'll have to hold the body while I cut her down."

Adam nodded, then gently broke Carol's hold and said, "You stay here. This shouldn't take long."

Both men reentered the room. Adam's gaze fell to the floor. He couldn't bear seeing Susan hanging there again.

"We have to do this," Manning told him, in a mild tone.

Adam nodded. "I know." He finally looked up. "Why would she...?"

"Probably thought it was a better fate," Bruce said. "The deaths of her crewmates and now Dr. Walker must've finally and completely pushed her over the brink...she must've wanted an easier way out."

"Maybe, but..." Adam did not continue the thought. Instead, he picked the chair off the floor. "I'm sure you'll need this." He placed the chair so Bruce could use it to get high enough to deal with the makeshift rope. The base of the seat, when upright, was below Susan's feet about five inches or so. Manning climbed on the chair, removed a folding knife from his pocket, then cut a small slit in the sheet—the hanging weight of the body did the rest.

Adam eased the body down as the fabric tore, then carried it over to the nearby bunk where he closed its lifeless eyes and removed the remaining piece of sheet. "Something doesn't feel right about this," he told Manning. "Something seems out of place."

"It's never easy when someone dies," Bruce said, "especially by their own hand."

"No, it's something more than that. I just can't put my finger on it."

Manning walked over to the body and gently picked it up, cradling the feather-light woman in his arms. Except for the red marks around her neck, it looked exactly like Susan was simply sleeping. "I'll put her in the locker with the others," Manning said. "It's becoming our own little morgue."

"Too late," Adam said. "This entire station is a morgue."

CHAPTER ELEVEN

Bruce Manning pondered Adam Hayes's last words to him. A startling, even sobering truth—*this entire station is a morgue*. Bruce stood at the foot of his brother's bunk watching him sleep. With the exception of an occasional twitch, it was a peaceful sleep.

He had told the others that he would meet up with them in the galley after placing Susan's body in the locker, but decided to steal a moment to check on Eric. Being a soldier, he knew he had to detach himself from the woman's death—she was a casualty of war—and yes, this was war. No matter how bizarre the enemy—they would hunt it down and kill it.

The side of Bruce's neck began to itch. It began as a pinpoint tingle, but quickly grew to an irritating eruption of needle pricks. Without a thought, he reached up and scratched. When he pulled his hand back, he found it streaked with blood—his blood.

"Damn."

He gingerly patted his neck several times—a slight sting replaced the itch. He had forgotten about the scrapes he received during the struggle with Susan. They had scabbed over, but his own scratching had opened them up.

For a brief moment he thought about going to see Dr. Walker—she would fix him up. But almost immediately, the cold hard fact that Margaret was gone returned with a sharp sting—another casualty of war.

Again, he pushed his feelings aside. He could not—would not—let himself be weakened by sorrow or regret.

Bruce pulled a tissue from the box lying on the small table next to the bunk and brought it over to the room mirror. Turning his injury towards its reflection, he raised the tissue to his neck. The open sores weren't too bad—a little pressure would stop the bleeding.

From behind him, Bruce heard a short, but distinctive wheeze. He turned back to his brother at the exact same moment the man let out a loud gasp. Suddenly Eric Manning went into convulsions. Bruce rushed over to his brother and held him down by the shoulders. Eric's body arched up, but Bruce held fast. The force was almost enough to knock Bruce off the bunk. He pressed down using his entire weight for leverage.

"Eric," Bruce called out, hoping the sound of his voice would snap his brother out of the seizure. "Eric, can you hear me?"

Eric moved his lips, but there were no words—only a shallow gasp for air. Then with almost lightning speed, a thick stream of black shot out of Eric's open mouth, hitting Bruce's upper neck just below his chin. It clung tight to his flesh and began to strangle him. From Eric's eyes and nose, his ears, from his very skin, more of the mass seeped free. It covered Bruce's hands and began to run up his arms.

Within seconds, the creature engulfed Bruce Manning. The soldier could do nothing to fight back, call out or even breathe.

Not long after Lieutenant Manning had left them, Adam and Carol made their way to the galley. Adam kept a close eye on even the tiniest of shadows. The thing got along, it would now seem, plenty well in the light, but it still must prefer the comfort of darkness. He reasoned, after a "feeding" it would hide away somewhere—somewhere it could rest—somewhere it felt safe. That had to be the explanation to why they didn't encounter it all that often...a good thing to be sure...still Adam had to wonder where it hid. Knowing would make it easier to kill—to go find it rather than waiting for it to find them.

"Will we make it out of this terrible place?" Carol asked. She gazed up at him with those big eyes hoping to hear his assurances.

He didn't want to lie to her, but then again, he wasn't all too happy with the truth. The whole situation was starting to feel hopeless. What did they know about fighting this thing? When Dr. Walker was alive, it seemed they had a fighting chance. She understood the creature—well, up to a point. With her knowledge they could have set up some kind of defense. "I'll do whatever it takes," Adam finally said.

"That doesn't answer my question, does it?"

"I'm sorry, but that's the best I can do. I'm not going to fill you with false hope. Just know, whatever it takes to keep you safe, I'll do."

"Do you really think fire will kill it?"

"It's a good bet," he said. "Bullets hurt it."

By the expression on her face, Adam could practically read her mind. He knew exactly what she was about to say.

"But they didn't kill it."

"True, but I would think fire would do a lot more damage in a lot less time. It won't be able to recover as quickly. We just have to make sure it doesn't have an escape route."

"I still think we could trap it. Keep it contained. I just hate the thought of killing any creature."

"That creature has no problem with killing us, so I think we should show it the same consideration. Besides, with the speed it moves, I really doubt we could catch it. Not to mention, what would we hold it in?" He shook his head. "No, trapping is definitely out of the question."

The two entered the galley, and continued directly to the kitchen area. It occurred to them both that there were many nooks and crannies for the creature to lurk in wait—either here or in the pantry. Any of the cupboards, the storage bins, even the drawers were a potential hiding place.

"Be careful," Adam said, but the words sounded so useless he wished he could take them back. He listened for any strange sound—for any noise out of place. He glanced over at Carol. She appeared to be doing the same thing. At that moment, he could tell her "trapping" idea was the last thing on her mind.

They both ventured farther into the room.

"What exactly are we looking for?" Carol asked.

"Get the beer bottles out of the pantry and empty them in the sink."

"Empty them?"

"As much as it pains me—yes."

He watched the woman following his instructions, then said, "save one or two." He shrugged. "Don't want to be too wasteful."

Adam went over to the drawer next to the sink. He hesitated once, then opened it. From inside he pulled out an off-white cotton dishtowel. He started to rip the cloth into strips.

"How is this going to work?" Carol asked, emptying her third bottle.

"Just like in the movies," he said. That left a blank expression on her face. "Let me guess, not a big movie person."

"No, I like movies, but not ones where people burn each other up."

"It's quite simple really. We fill the bottles with gasoline, stuff a rag in the neck. When we're ready, just light the rag and throw."

"Blowing us all up in the process?"

"Not if you do it right. The bottle shatters on impact, spreading the gas, while at the same time the flame ignites it."

"Wonderful," Carol said, "simply wonderful. What sort of mind would even come up with something like this in the first place?"

"Hey, there's a lot of history in these little things."

"You can keep it." She put one of the bottles to her nose. "Do you need me to rinse them out?"

"No, they'll be fine. The gasoline won't mind a little beer. How many do you have?"

"Five," she answered. "And before you ask, there's three full bottles left."

"Good, just enough to celebrate our victory. One beer apiece, since Eric is in no condition to drink."

"Now you're optimistic?"

"Hey, when it comes to a cold beer, you bet'cha." They both let go with a tiny laugh. The statement was so absurd, they couldn't help but find it funny.

Having the empty beer bottles and rag strips ready, Adam began searching through the lower cupboards until he found a box containing a half-filled plastic spray bottle of cleaning fluid and two hardened green sponges. He dumped the bottle and sponges on the floor. "No time to be neat."

Adam loaded the box with the beer bottles and rags, picked it up and started towards the main galley door.

"Smooth as you may think you are," Carol said, following him out, "it did not escape my attention that you never answered my question… What if fire doesn't kill it? What then?"

He looked her straight in the eyes. "I don't know. I just don't know."

"I don't want to die like the others," she said bluntly.

"You are not going to die," he told her.

"We have to be realistic. It could happen. That thing could get us."

Adam nodded. "I know."

"Then if you see I'm about to get…you know. I want you to kill me. I don't want to suffer like the others."

Adam stood silent in the hallway.

"Promise me," she said. "If that time comes…"

Adam nodded.

~

Hunched over, Bruce Manning held his side. The pain was becoming more intense by the second, like tiny snakes crawling through his small intestine —pulling and pushing through the twists and turns of bowel. A sharp burning sensation moved up to his lungs—even breathing became a grueling ordeal—he almost passed out. Bruce had to stop himself from falling completely to the floor.

Heavy sweat beaded across his forehead—every inch of skin felt wet and clammy—his entire body seemed on fire. His arms and legs, no longer under his control, began to spasm. Bruce fell forward face-first, landing hard on his chin—his head bounced once, blood splattered out of his nose, then that was it. He just lay there bleeding.

When Bruce managed to open his eyes, the room appeared like a blurry kaleidoscope of color. *This is the end,* he thought. The pain surely was a prelude to death. And death would be a welcomed release. When he didn't think it would be possible to endure any more pain, the pain stopped.

The agony that had him wishing for death only moments ago had been replaced with a strange detachment. The thoughts and images that filled his mind made no sense. They were like having disjointed memories of places and events he had never experienced. He saw faces of people he had never met, and others he barely recognized: John Blackwood, Emmanuel Phillips, both before their deaths.

A flood of new emotions poured over him: anger, terror, confusion, the fear of being trapped, the fear of being hurt again. And then there was a feeling of hunger—an insatiable, uncontrollable hunger.

His view of the room changed, as if on the outside, peering through a dirty window, then being pushed down some dark corridor. He had an overpowering sense of being lost.

"You have to fight it," a voice came from across the room. "Fight it." The words were very weak, but still discernible.

Through a watery gaze, Bruce looked towards the voice. It was his brother speaking. "You can't let it win. It wants you now. You have to keep control."

"Eric," Bruce wheezed. The shock of seeing his brother sitting up had brought him back from the void. "Eric, what's happening to me?"

"You have to fight it. It wants to control you."

"Am I going to die?"

"No, I don't think so. We're different…different from the others. It won't kill you. You're not that lucky."

The scratches on the side of Bruce's neck stopped bleeding, closed and disappeared.

~

Adam, carrying the loaded box, and Carol, a half step behind him, started off towards the warm room where they had left the gasoline. They had not spoken since she had made her bizarre request. He couldn't fault her, he just didn't know if he could kill another human being, especially someone he cared for. He wouldn't have agreed, but he could tell by her eyes that it would give her, be it strange, peace of mind.

It struck him odd that she had a strange fascination about keeping the creature alive. He could understand if she were a scientist like Dr. Walker, though even Margaret never brought up the subject of catching the thing, but then again, knowing how the others felt, she might have never voiced her true opinion.

In his mind, the matter was clear—he wanted to see the thing destroyed. It was a mindless, soulless, killing machine. If it somehow got off this station, many more lives would be lost. It disturbed him knowing that John Blackwood had been in contact with someone to sell the creature. What madness—greed can cause otherwise honorable men to do such foolish and terrible things.

"Lieutenant Manning should have been back by now," Carol said, breaking the silence.

Lost in his thoughts, it took a moment for Carol's words to register. "Yes, well, his was not an easy task." What was he thinking—Manning had been gone too long—he had been too preoccupied with Carol to notice the man's lengthy absence.

"I'm worried about him," she admitted.

"He's probably just checking on his brother," he said to keep her calm.

She turned her gaze in the opposite direction. "Can we make sure?" she asked, while gently touching Adam's hand. "Please, it would only take a minute. I can't shake the feeling something else has happened. Something bad."

Adam set the box down. "Well, there's no sense lugging that around. We'll pick it up on the way back."

Carol gave him a hug. "Thank you." She ran her hand along the small of his back. She felt a lump. "What's that?" she asked.

"A gun," he said blankly. He had kept the weapon in his waistband, covered with his shirt so its presence wouldn't upset her—so much for that idea. He knew that guns wouldn't kill the creature, but it still could hurt it and that made it worth carrying. Some protection, no matter how small, was better than no protection at all.

The two started their reverse trip down the long hall, all the while Carol keeping a tight grip on Adam's hand. Up ahead they could both see the door to Bruce's quarters had been left open and light from the room poured out into the hallway.

"See," Adam said. "I told you. He's just checking on his brother." After a couple more steps, Adam called out. "Manning, we're waiting on you... everything okay?"

There was no answer.

Adam's pace quickened, moving to the open doorway—Carol stayed right on his heels. They both peered into the room. What they saw shocked them both. They found nothing but an empty bunk.

"Oh my God," Carol cried out. "It got them...it got them like Dr. Walker and the others." The woman let go of Adam and was about to bolt, but acting quickly Adam grabbed her by the arm.

"Wait," he said. "There are no clothes."

She tried to pull free.

"Listen to me," Adam said firmly, "listen to me! Their clothes aren't here. If that thing killed them we would have found piles of clothes."

Carol began to cry. "Where are they?"

Adam pulled her closer and gently rubbed her back. "I don't know. I just don't know."

"I can't stay here," Carol said between sobs. "I can't stand being in this place any longer."

"I'm sure my crew will be here any time now," Adam tried to reassure her.

"That thing...that thing will get us by then! We have to leave now."

"There's no place to go," he said, pulling her tight. "I'm sorry."

"The other building," Carol said. "We can go to the other building. It has to be safer there. Susan survived on her own. Oh, Susan...you shouldn't have brought her back here. She would still be alive." Carol sobbed more.

A hard lump formed in Adam's chest. She was right. Susan would still be alive if she hadn't been forced back to this building. She had been safe from the creature. "All right," he finally said. "We'll go to the other building." He truly believed it would only be a day, maybe even hours, before a rescue plane would arrive for them, so with any supplies they could scrounge up, they should be fine.

Carol looked up at him. "What about the lieutenant...and his brother?"

"We'll gather up what we need—some food, water. If neither of them show up by the time we're ready to go, we'll leave a few notes around the station, that way they'll know what happened and can join us...if able."

Before going back to the galley, Adam retrieved a large canvas shoulder bag from the storage closet he remembered seeing during their first search of the complex. He took the largest one he could find. Then, in the kitchen, he and Carol loaded the bag with canned goods and bottled water. She suggested some bread as well. Even though Adam assured her it would only be a day at the most, he told her to take only those items that would keep and wouldn't need to be cooked. It may not make for the most enjoyable meals, and meat was definitely off the menu, but it would keep them from starving.

"That should do," Adam said. "Anything else?"

She shook her head, but then said, "The notebooks! We should take Blackwood's notebooks with us."

"What? The notebooks? Why?"

"Proof. Proof of what's happened here. No one will believe us. I can barely believe it myself."

"We should travel light," Adam told her. "There's no need to bring a load of books with us."

"I don't mean all of them...just the one about the creature."

"It's not worth the risk. That thing is still out there."

"I should be safe if I make sure to stay in the light."

"You? Now you're talking crazy. What's come over you?"

"I'm just thinking maybe we can find something else in that notebook to help protect us."

Adam gave her a strange look. "If Dr. Walker couldn't, I don't think..."

Before Adam could finish his objection, Carol turned to leave the room. In her haste, she ran headfirst into a man's chest. She screamed and fell backwards.

With speed that even surprised him, Adam pulled the gun from his waistband. He aimed the gun straight ahead and took a tight bead down the barrel. To his shock, he was pointing the weapon at Eric Manning.

Adam rushed over to the woman. He took her arm and pulled her up. "Get behind me," he said, keeping a close eye on Eric. He wasn't sure if the man was violent, but his actions were at best unpredictable. It was better to play it safe.

The two watched Eric take a final labored step closer before collapsing. They quickly, but cautiously, moved over to his side. Carol checked his neck for a pulse.

"He's very weak," she said.

"I'm not surprised—with all the drugs pumped into him the last couple of days. It's amazing he made it this far."

"Shouldn't Bruce be with him?" Carol asked.

"Good question, but one thing at a time. Let's get him off the floor." With brute strength Adam heaved the soldier up and succeeded in getting him close enough to a table, where Carol pulled out a chair.

They both stared at the man for a moment, then Carol said, "Now what?"

"I don't think this changes much. We will all be safer in the other building."

Carol simply nodded.

"Well, we'll never make it like this," Adam told her. "I'll go get our gear. Stay here and keep an eye on him...I'll be back as soon as I can."

"Do you think..." She stopped speaking and looked over to Eric. "Do you think it will be okay to leave him here? I mean..."

"You mean, will you be safe?" Adam said. "Yes, you'll be safe. He's in no shape to...he can't even stand up on his own. Stay here. I won't be long."

After Carol reluctantly agreed, Adam headed for the galley door. Before leaving the room, he turned back once to make sure she would be fine. He smiled at her. She smiled back.

Carol could hear his footsteps get softer and softer until they had vanished altogether. She moved to the far side of the room, while still keeping an eye on Eric Manning. Adam was right, he was almost helpless. She stepped over to the cupboard area, never letting the man out of her sight. She reached for a drawer and pulled it open. From inside she grabbed a long carving knife. Then slowly she retraced her steps.

"Can you hear me?" she asked Eric.

There was no answer.

Carol took several more steps with the knife tight in her grasp.

"See, that didn't take long," Adam said, suddenly appearing in the doorway. He had on a parka and carried two others.

Surprised by the man, Carol hid the knife behind her back. "Long?" she asked.

"I wasn't gone too long," he said, marching into the galley, placing the jackets on the table and two sets of boots on the floor.

"No, you weren't. I'm glad you're back. I was getting scared."

"I told you you'd be safe enough."

She grinned. "Yes, you did."

"We should get moving," Adam told her. "There are gloves in the jacket pockets.

"What about him," Carol said, pointing to Eric with one hand, while keeping the knife concealed with the other.

"We're taking him with us," Adam said, grabbing the largest parka from the table.

"He can barely walk...do you think you can handle him?"

"Do I have a choice? He can't stay here—he'd be a sitting duck." Adam helped Eric put on the jacket. The first sleeve slipped on easy enough, but the man pulled away when the second sleeve was attempted.

"Bruce..." Eric said softly, "I couldn't help him." He tried to lean up in the chair. He didn't get very far, but it was enough for Adam to get the jacket on the rest of the way.

As Adam helped Eric, Carol dropped the knife in a nearby garbage can. She was sure he didn't see her dispose of the weapon.

Then Adam turned his attention to Carol. He had the sternest expression on his face, which she could not miss.

"What's the matter?" she asked.

"Boots and jackets weren't the only things I brought back with me." Adam's hand disappeared into his jacket pocket. "Take this," he said, pulling out something and reaching for Carol. He gently opened her hand

and tried to place in it a revolver—the revolver Dr. Walker had kept with her.

Carol pulled away. "I wouldn't take one before, what makes you think I'll take one now?"

"Because I'm asking you to." Again, he handed her the gun. "Please."

This time she took it.

"Don't let it out of your sight," he added. "You may need it."

Carol stared down at the weapon.

"Once we get to the other building we should be safe enough," Adam said. "With only one main door, it's more defensible. Later, I'll go out and leave a message inside the plane. If any of my crew comes that's the first place they'll check."

"You still think there's hope."

"Of course I do."

Hearing the confidence in his voice, she leaned forward and kissed him.

"We better get going." He helped Eric Manning to his feet. The man coughed once and Adam wondered what effect the cold would have on his condition. Though better to take a chance, than have no chance, Adam thought. If he left the man here alone, the creature would go after him.

"Leave me," Eric groaned, followed by another short cough.

"That's not going to happen," Adam said, hoisting him up and throwing one of his arms over his shoulder. The heavy parkas both men wore made it difficult, but Adam did his best to manage. "You're coming with us."

Adam had to time his steps to match Eric's, but after a few seconds, all three of them had left the galley, heading towards the exit and, hopefully, safety. Not too far down the hallway, they passed the box of empty beer bottles and rag strips Adam had placed there earlier.

"Should we bring these with us?" Carol asked.

She had her hands full already with the canvas bag of supplies and he had all he could manage with Eric Manning. "Forget them for now," Adam said. "I'll come back for them later. It's more important that I get you two to the other building."

They had made it to the cold storage room, when a loud crash came from behind them. The noise caused Carol to look back. Adam didn't hear the sound or chose to ignore it. He moved himself and Eric down the hall.

"It's coming," Eric said, forcing himself to get the words out. "I can feel it."

Carol stopped.

A dark shadow emerged from the room that had once been the cook's quarters. It pulled back once more, out of sight, hesitating. Then the shadow reappeared, and finally moved into the open view of the hall.

"It's the lieutenant," Carol shouted out.

Adam turned, pulling himself and Eric around. "Move it Manning! We're getting out of here."

Bruce staggered down the hall as though fighting each step—his face squinting several times in pain.

"It's here," Eric said. "It's here!"

"No, that's your brother," Carol told him.

"Not anymore. It controls him, like it tried to control me. But I was too strong—I could fight it. I wouldn't do what it wanted. My brother...my brother's not strong enough."

Bruce stumbled closer. "Help me," he said, reaching out with both arms. His plea surprised and startled the others.

"Don't let it come any closer," Eric said.

"Stay back, Bruce," Adam said; with his free hand he held up his gun. "Stay back or I will shoot you where you stand."

"Maybe we should try to communicate with it," Carol said.

"What?"

"We can't just kill him," she said. "I know you, Adam. You won't kill him. It's not in you."

She was right. He lowered his gun, but that didn't bring about the reaction in Bruce he thought it would. The man appeared almost angry at the show of mercy.

"No, you don't understand," Bruce said, anguished, "I can feel it trying to take over my mind. It's trying to become part of me. I hear its thoughts. They are becoming my thoughts. It's hungry all the time. Like a baby, it cries for food." He winced in pain. "Its thoughts are wild, confused. Except that it wants to feed."

"Bruce, you have to fight it," Adam said.

"It's controlling me. I can barely focus my own mind. It's angry. It's forcing me to come after you. Forgive me." Suddenly, Bruce lunged towards Adam. But before his hands could get around Adam's throat, Adam instinctively thrust the gun upward striking Bruce on the chin with the butt of the weapon, sending both it and Bruce flying backwards. Amazingly, Adam still kept a tight hold on Eric, preventing him from falling too.

Only knocked off balance, Bruce quickly regained his footing. The large gash on his chin produced a trickle of blood. As the others watched, the blood stopped and the wound immediately sealed itself.

"You can stop it, Bruce," Eric called out. "You can beat it. Be strong."

"Yes...yes. I won't let it win. I won't live this way."

"We can get you help," Carol said. "We'll find someone to fix this."

"There's only one way to help me," Bruce said. He reached down for the gun lying at his feet. "One way," he repeated. He put the tip of the barrel in his mouth.

"No, Bruce..." The gun went off before Adam could speak another word or take a single step. Carol screamed and looked away. With half his brain spread out on the wall behind him, Lieutenant Bruce Manning fell backwards, ending his struggle.

"Why did he do it?" Carol cried out. "Why?"

A moment later, she had the horrible answer. The black creature began to pour from Bruce's body. From his fatal wound, his face, his neck, even his hands—anyplace there was exposed skin the thing oozed out. It pooled into a thick moving puddle. Adam grabbed back the gun he had given Carol. He aimed carefully. He fired.

The creature recoiled slightly when hit, but it did not stop.

"It wants me back," Eric said and pushed Adam away. "You two go. Leave now. It's me it wants." The man could barely maintain his own balance.

"No, we're not giving up." Adam shot off another round. The creature stopped. A small blue pool formed where the bullet hit. "You see, it remembers. It knows pain."

Eric let out a moan, then collapsed. He was unconscious. As if sensing the man's sudden vulnerability, the creature moved towards him. And again, Adam shot at it. Though this time it didn't stop very long.

"It's not working, Adam," Carol cried. "It's not working!"

The bullets were starting to have little effect. Adam thought about the gasoline, but it was too far away to do any good—there simply wasn't time to get it. And with Eric out cold and Carol on her last nerve, he couldn't cope with them both before the creature was upon them—the situation appeared hopeless. Suddenly, he realized there was another way. Without a word, Adam shoved the gun back into Carol's hand. "Keep shooting." Then he ran into the cold storage room.

"Where are you going?" she said, squeezing off another shot. This time the black creature didn't even flinch. "Adam, it's coming closer. I can't stop it."

Adam reappeared carrying a canister of liquid nitrogen. Setting it on the floor and quickly putting on the long gloves for protection, he opened the metal casing.

Immediately upon removing the lid, white vapors formed in the air around the opening. "Stand back," he warned. Tiny bits of nitrogen splattered up. "Stand back." Adam kicked over the canister. It spilled out across the floor and down the hallway. More white vapors rose into the air.

The nitrogen rolled fast along the tiles—they cracked and peeled with the tremendous cold. The frigid liquid hit the creature, and in that second, whatever part came in contact with the clear fluid froze hard. The thing couldn't move away in time. Finally, every inch of the creature was frozen into a solid mass.

"You did it," Carol said. "I don't believe it. You stopped it. Killed it."

"I'm not so sure it's dead. Remember, the crew dug it up from the ice. Who can really say if it can ever die?"

Before Adam could say another word, something caught Carol's ear. "Wait, do you hear that?" she said. It was a strange swooshing sound coming from outside.

Adam couldn't believe it. "Yes, I do." The sound was like that of a powerful propeller, though it was no plane. "But it can't be my crew. There's no way they could get their hands on a helicopter. It must be some other outfit."

"That can't be right," Carol said. "This is still a military station. It's not like anyone can find this place. Whoever it is would have to know the exact coordinates. It must be your crew—who else? The plane's homing beacon was destroyed. There's no way anyone could lock in on our position, not to mention even knowing we were here."

"How did you know about the beacon? I didn't tell you. You would've had to have seen it smashed. But you couldn't have. Unless...unless, it was you. You destroyed the plane! Why?"

"How can you think that? Why would I?"

"And Susan Dawson. I thought there was something wrong about the way she died, I just didn't pick up on it until now. She didn't commit suicide. She was murdered."

"Listen to yourself—you're acting insane."

"Am I? When I put the chair back for Bruce, Susan's body hung over it by almost half a foot. I don't think a person killing themselves would jump up to put their head in a noose. After Dr. Walker was killed by that thing, you were alone with Susan. You killed her. It could only have been you. The question now is why?"

Carol answered with a twisted little smile. "It took some *special* arrangements to get me added to our little group. Dr. Blackwood reported his findings on the organism. I was sent to make sure he didn't change his allegiance. And if he had, I was to take the organism from him. The thing running amuck took care of half my problem and you've taken care of the rest."

Adam took a step towards her.

"Don't try!" she ordered. "I'm sorry, Adam, but you're too smart for your own good."

She pulled the trigger.

The main door opened, followed by a cold blast of air. A man wrapped up in a parka entered. Carol had the gun pointed at him as he came down the hall. The man pulled down his hood and stared at her. Then he looked down at the stilled body of Adam Hayes.

"I take it you were successful in containing the organism," he said.

"Do you really have any doubt?" Carol asked, pointing to the frozen gob.

Eric was still unconscious, but he let out a soft moan.

"You were to leave no witnesses."

"He's more than a witness. He and the organism merged. Apparently, he has the DNA pattern that the creature needs. It would be worth examining him. Though, I'm afraid he's on the verge of madness."

"All the better," the man said. "We'll need a scapegoat. Now we have one."

PART TWO

CHAPTER TWELVE

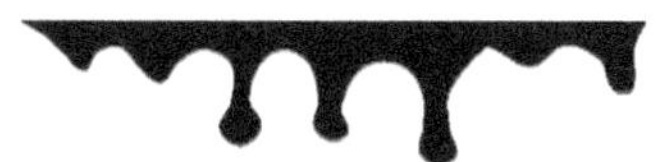

MAY 7, 2003

Brandon Dahl rubbed his eyes, awakening from his sleep. Watching the highway roll by and the soothing vibration of the tires proved to be too much for the frail youngster. He lifted his head enough to glance out the window. Like most of the trip so far, there wasn't much to see—just trees, trees and more trees. When he first got off the plane with his doctor, Allison Cook, for the final leg of their journey, he thought the trees were sort of neat. But that was over five hours ago—being stuck in a car for that amount of time, a fourteen-year-old boy easily got bored by seeing the same surroundings.

"You're up," Allison said, from behind the steering wheel. "How are you feeling?"

"Tired," Brandon replied.

"Do you have a headache? Do you need a pill?"

"No, not yet." He looked up at her with his dark sunken eyes, turning the bill of his baseball cap forward. It turned easily on his bald head, a side effect of the drugs he had to take. "I hate being sick. I hate my medicine. I'm always tired."

"I know, Brandon, but you have to keep your spirits up. There's always hope."

"That's what you all keep telling me. But sometimes I think it would be better if I die."

Allison slammed down on the brake, stopped the car and threw it into park. "I don't want you to ever say that again!" She had the most stern expression on her face. "Life is a precious gift. You should never wish it away."

"What difference does it make? My mother died over a year ago. I never knew my father. I have no family. Who would care if I died?"

"I would care."

"In a few days, I won't ever see you again. Even the hospital doesn't want me."

"Now Brandon, you know that is absolutely not true."

"I heard some of the nurses talking. The insurance money from my mother's car accident ran out, and the hospital couldn't keep me on as a charity case."

"Some people have very big mouths," she said, "and don't know what they're talking about."

"Then why are you bringing me to this new place, if the hospital didn't want to get rid of me?"

"Listen to me, neither the insurance company or the pencil pushers at St. John's had anything to do with this. We've already been over it. Dr. Hamline runs a very special home for children with certain needs."

"You mean they have cancer."

She gave a slight nod. "Some do, but not all. His research encompasses many areas."

"Why me?" Brandon asked.

"Why you what?"

"Why did he pick me for his next lab rat?"

"You won't be a lab rat. You've seen the pictures. It's a very nice house —a lot of room, a large estate. It's nothing like those sterile hospitals you're used to."

"That still doesn't explain why," he said.

"He thought you would be a good candidate for his treatments. He has had some very good results."

"But how did he find out about me? Who told him?"

"Dr. Benson, I think."

"You don't know, do you?"

"Well, no, but it had to be someone at the hospital. If not Dr. Benson, then one of the other board members—they all have so many connections.

But what does it matter? All that really counts is that he might be able to help you. Remember what I said about keeping hope? Dr. Hamline is your best hope for a longer life. I've read a lot about his work. It's very promising."

"Dr. Benson said he doesn't have a cure."

"That's true, but he's getting closer everyday. Who knows, maybe you'll be the person to help him find one. Keep in mind, whatever the reason why, he wants to help you and other children like you."

Brandon nodded. "Okay, I'll try to remember."

"And no more talk about dying." She touched his cheek. "You're a very special boy. You'll see. Things are going to change for you." She smiled and put the car back into gear. "Have faith, Brandon, have faith."

Once more, the boy nodded and they were back on their way. They didn't talk much more, after all that had been said earlier, what more was there to say? Brandon knew he would miss Allison Cook, and he decided to make sure he wouldn't do anything to make her ashamed of him.

He had liked her better than all the old men doctors at St. John's Hospital—maybe because she didn't tower over him like they did. Or maybe it was because the other doctors always looked so grumpy. She had a large smile with perfect white teeth and big bright brown eyes—he was never afraid when he saw her. When he began to lose so much weight because of his treatments, she once joked that she was too skinny too, but he told her, he didn't think she was skinny at all. In the hospital, he had only seen her with her brown hair up and it surprised him when they started their trip. It was the first time he had seen it down—it was long—well past her shoulders—it sort of reminded him of his mother. One other thing he really liked about Allison Cook—she always smelled nice.

After several more miles, Brandon spotted a sign: *Wobblewash, population 750*. Wobblewash, what a stupid name for a town. "Are we almost there?" he asked. The trees along the side of the highway were starting to thin.

"Soon," she said. "We'll have to drive through the town first. The clinic is on the other side, though I'm not exactly sure where."

Ten minutes later, they spotted the first house. It was like something out of a child's picture book, right down to the white picket fence. Allison didn't think places like this really existed. They continued the drive and the houses soon changed to buildings. Storefront windows of one building had mannequins wearing a hunting jacket and cap while sporting a rifle. There was a diner, a bank, even a movie theater. Towards the center of town there was a taller red brick building with three squad cars parked out front. Next to it, another building had a sign denoting it was the town hall. The street curved both to the right and to the left, forming a small island of grass surrounded by concrete fencing of small pillars. In the center of the grass island was a huge oak tree. It had to be at least two hundred years old.

Allison spotted a man in uniform approaching one of the squad cars. She let go with a short toot on her horn to get his attention. It worked.

She drove along the side of the squad car and rolled down her window. "Excuse me," she said.

"What can I do for you?" he said, leaning forward, glaring at Allison. He was an older man, who had a hefty bulge for a stomach. From under his hat poked out a few sprigs of sandy-brown. Both hands grasped the car over the window slit. Brandon couldn't believe the size of the man's hands. They were so rough, covered with calluses.

"Can you give me directions to Dr. Edward Hamline's clinic?"

"The Hamline Clinic?" The man tipped back his hat and scratched his head.

"Is there a problem?" Allison asked.

"No. No problem." The man stood there staring at her with puzzlement etched across his face.

"Could you give me directions?"

"You don't look sick," he blurted out. "What do you want with Dr. Hamline?"

"No, I'm not. And I don't see what business it is of yours."

He gave her an angry stare. "This here badge makes it my business. I'm the sheriff and I don't take kindly to reporters coming to my town and making all sorts of trouble, asking stupid questions about Dr. Hamline. Why do you people hound the man? He's doing nothing but good work."

"I think there's been some misunderstanding. I'm not a reporter. I'm a doctor. And I'm bringing Dr. Hamline another patient." She pointed to the passenger's side and to Brandon.

It wasn't until that moment the sheriff even bothered to check. His eyes met Brandon's eyes. The big man's dark, narrow-slit gaze almost cut through the boy. "You should have said so straight out," the sheriff scolded.

When did you give me a chance, she thought. "You're right. I should have. My mistake."

Allison watched the man during the awkward moments of silence.

"So," she finally said, trying to stay calm and sound pleasant.

"So what?"

"The directions?"

"You sure you ain't no reporter?"

"I'm sure. I have identification." She began to reach for her purse. "Would you like to see it?"

"Yes," he said. "Yes, I would." He gave her a fake smile. "If it's not too much trouble."

"Trouble? Of course not." She opened her purse, took out her AMA card and handed it to the surly man. He examined it very carefully, before handing it back to her.

"It appears in order," he said, but the unsettled glint in his eye told that he still had doubts. Then he turned and pointed down the road. "Continue on a half mile or so out of town. You'll come to a dirt road on the left-hand side. Turn there. Follow the road and there you are. Simple, huh?"

"Sure. Simple." She smiled and began to pull away from the curb.

"You have a nice day," she heard the man say when she drove off.

"Drop dead," she said, certain he couldn't hear her, but Brandon did and giggled. She was going to say something about respecting the law, but changed her mind. The guy was a jerk. And she knew Brandon was smart enough to realize you can respect the law without necessarily respecting the idiots who use it to throw their weight around.

They followed the sheriff's directions out of town. There were more of those storybook houses along the way. The town, what she had seen, seemed so peaceful. She could understand why Dr. Hamline would pick such a location for his clinic.

Down the paved road, they found the dirt road as the sheriff had said. What he didn't tell them was that you could see the main house from the turn. It was huge.

"Wow," Brandon said, rolling down his window. "Are you sure we're in the right place?"

"Yeah," Allison said. "I think so. Pretty fancy." As they drove, both of them couldn't help staring out over the grounds. Like the grand house, it too was enormous. The grass was perfectly mowed. There were several large oak trees spread out across the land. And up by the house itself was an excellent flowerbed of many different colored blooms.

Continuing up the dirt road, the house got closer and closer by the second. The distance did nothing to hide its grandeur. Allison turned along a slight bend to the front of the house. She couldn't help but notice how empty the grounds were. With such a great piece of land, she would've thought people would be out enjoying it. It was a place of sickness, of course, but she thought that a few of the patients would, at the very least, be out in wheelchairs.

Brandon also thought it was so peaceful—so quiet—so calm. It gave him the creeps. It reminded him of the ward he had to stay in during his radiation treatments. It was quiet and peaceful there too. When one of the other kids died, the whole floor became very quiet, very calm—the peacefulness of death.

Was that what this clinic really was—somewhere they bring kids to die? No, he thought, he had promised Allison he wouldn't talk about dying—but was thinking about it the same as talking about it? He wasn't sure, so decided to stop in case it was. He briefly turned his eyes towards Allison. She returned the quick glance with a smile.

"Quite a place," she said, shifting the car to park and turning off the ignition.

Somehow he could tell this place wasn't exactly what she had expected. He didn't want to say anything that might let on that he knew how she felt, so he simply said, "Yep."

While they were admiring the grand house, the front door opened. A woman with gray hair stepped out onto the porch. Brandon squinted to see her face. It was a lot younger than the gray suggested—he even thought she was sort of pretty. He remembered watching the TV commercials about premature gray hair. Normally he wouldn't have paid them any mind, but for Timmy Hudson, a boy he shared a room with once, his mother also had premature gray hair. During the short time they were together, he and Timmy became best friends. After Timmy died, every time Brandon saw the commercial, it made him think of his lost companion.

"That must be the welcome wagon," Allison said. "Guess it means we're at the right place after all."

"Let's wait and see if she calls the police—or I guess that would be the sheriff. I'm sure he'd love to throw us reporters in jail." Brandon giggled, then coughed.

"Smarty pants," Allison said. "You be on your best behavior." Her false scolding helped to lighten the mood. "I don't want to have to report back, you got thrown out on your first day."

"Does that mean no frogs at the supper table?"

"We'll see," she bantered back. Then her light expression changed to something more serious. "It's okay if you're scared," she told him. "I would be too, but I'm here with you. And I'll make sure everything is going to work out just fine."

"I know," he said. "I know you will."

Allison and Brandon got out of the car at the same moment the woman came down the steps. She drew closer and Brandon could see he was right about her being pretty. She had a very warm and inviting smile. She moved quickly to the car.

"Doctor Cook," she said, reaching out with an open hand.

"Hello." Allison returned the gesture and shook the woman's hand.

"I'm Jenny Gordon," the woman added. "I'm the administrator here."

"But I thought Dr. Hamline…"

"I'm strictly a paper pusher. I attend to admittance, paying the bills, buying food and supplies, that sort of thing. Dr. Hamline is the real brains here. I simply do and keep track of those mundane things—the standard clinic stuff."

Allison's gaze turned to the beautiful building—it was so impressive. "I would hardly call this a *standard* clinic." She would love to work in a place like this.

Jenny returned a big warm smile. "It is lovely, isn't it. Dr. Hamline wanted the surroundings to be as pleasant as possible—for the children." Then the woman turned her attention to the boy. "And you must be Brandon," she said, again extending her hand. "I'm very glad to meet you."

She had such caring eyes that Brandon felt himself relax some. "Hi," he said. It always seemed a little odd when he shook an adult's hand. Though this woman's hand was very soft and warm. "Nice to meet you too," he added. That's what you were supposed to say, he remembered.

"I'm sure you must have many questions," Jenny said to Brandon, then turned to Allison. "How about I take you both on a tour of the facility?"

Allison glanced over to the car.

"It's fine where it is for right now," Jenny said as if reading Allison's mind. "And don't worry about your bags, I'll have one of the staff bring them to your rooms. You'll both be on the same floor. Though your stay here, Dr. Cook, is temporary, I thought it best to put you close to Brandon. I'm sure, being in a strange new place, he'll feel more at ease having you close by." She smiled at Brandon. "And I'm also sure it won't take long for him to fit in and feel comfortable on his own."

With that, they started the tour of the house and grounds.

They walked along a brick path to the backyard. Once there, several heads turned—the children watched them pass by. Jenny didn't bring the two close enough for Brandon to meet any of the other children. But that was fine with him. He was never very good in big crowds. The way Jenny smiled at him, it was as though she already knew that about him.

He didn't return the smile, because he felt embarrassed. Instead, he directed his gaze to the other side of the yard. Farther away and well off the estate grounds, Brandon spotted a forest. Great, he thought, more trees.

"Oh, look," Allison said to Brandon. "Do you see the rabbit by the bird feeder?"

"There's a wide variety of wildlife that visits us from the nearby woods. Some of the other children spend hours bird watching. How about you, Brandon, do you like animals?"

He simply shrugged.

"Now that you've seen the grounds, how about we go inside?"

Entering the three-story mansion, they were shown several rooms, including the living room, a TV room, a music room, a room with several Macintosh computers with Internet access and a separate library with shelves of book after book lining each wall. And passing through a huge dining hall, they were even shown the kitchen where the cooks were preparing the evening's meal. They would be shown the sleeping quarters on the second floor a little later.

The interior of the building had detailed woodwork, vaulted ceilings in the foyer, banister staircases to the upper levels. Details restored, Jenny told them, to bring the house back to its original beauty. Even the detailed plasterwork had been restored, along with the many fireplaces throughout the house.

There were also modern enhancements. Sensor light switches, auto-opening doors, even two elevators—one for each wing of the house. Jenny explained that several of the children living at the clinic needed either braces or crutches to walk and a few were confined to wheelchairs. The changes were added to allow those children access to all that the house had to offer. Allison Cook was impressed.

"And here we have the activities room," Jenny told them while walking along the west wing, then stopping by an open door. Inside, there was a small girl sitting in a wheelchair doing a jigsaw puzzle. "Would you like to go in?"

Brandon's shy gaze moved up to Allison. She smiled and nodded.

"Okay," Brandon said.

The group entered and Brandon quickly sized up the room but said nothing.

"What activities do you have here?" Allison asked, after a minute of silence.

"Many. We have all kinds of games, cards, checkers, monopoly, chess, you name it and we probably have it. If we don't, ask for it, and we'll get it."

"And group projects?"

"Yes, we have those too." Jenny easily read the anguish in Brandon's eyes. "For those who wish to participate. We don't force anyone to do anything they don't want to do." That worked—Brandon's face eased.

"How does that sound?" Allison asked him.

"Good," was all he said.

Jenny knelt down and met Brandon eye to eye. She took his hand. "I know this whole thing is scary," she said. "But I also know you are a very brave person. You have gone through so much so far—this place is going to be a snap. And I'll be here for you. If you ever need anything or have any questions or are afraid, even if you only want to talk, you come see me. My office door will always be open to you. All right?"

He nodded.

"Now I want you to meet someone," Jenny said, standing up. "She was nervous just like you are when she first got here. Come." She took him by the hand and led him to the table with the girl in the wheelchair. "Katy," Jenny called out.

The little girl's head popped up with a smile. "Hi, Jenny. Is this the new boy? Hi, my name is Katy Redden. What's your name?"

"Brandon. Brandon Dahl."

"Do you like jigsaw puzzles?" the girl asked. Her voice was so soft Brandon barely heard the question.

"Yes," he answered.

"This one's of Warwick Castle in England." She held up the box cover. "Pretty neat isn't it. I really like castles. When I'm all better, I want to go to England and Scotland and visit them all. I hear some of them even have ghosts, just like the woods."

"Uhhm, that will be enough talk about ghosts, Katy," Jenny said with a smile. She reached over to another table and grabbed a chair. She put it next to Katy's wheelchair. "So, how about it, Brandon? Are you up to the challenge?"

"I don't know," he said softly.

"Please," Katy said, "it's a whole lot funner with two people. I'll do most of the sky. It's all blue and not that fun. You can do the castle. Please, work on it with me."

"I'll help you," Brandon said. "But you can work on the castle part too. Seeing as you like castles so much."

"I guess that's settled then," Jenny said. "How about we adults leave you guys to your puzzle?" There were no objections and Brandon was already pulling all the gray stone pieces from the box.

"Will you be all right, Brandon?" Allison asked. She was happy to see him at such ease. It had been the first time in a long while. She had to admit that it surprised her, but pleased her nevertheless.

"I'll be okay," he said, peering up for a moment from his puzzle piece quest. Then he went back to the box. It rattled as his fingers ran through the many small cardboard pieces.

"Let's go to my office," Jenny told Allison. "We'll be back in a bit," she said to the children. "You won't even miss us." She beamed a smile.

The two women left the room and started down the hall.

"When will I get to meet Dr. Hamline? I have to admit I've been looking forward to it."

"And he's been looking forward to meeting you too."

The tone in Jenny's voice was a little strange—it almost seemed snide. Allison had just met the woman, but she wasn't sure she liked the tone. Though considering the stress of the situation, it could be nothing—the slight could have been only in her mind.

"Are the medical facilities also on this floor?" Allison asked.

"They are, but in another wing. We decided it was best to have definite borders between the examination-treatment area and the living quarters. That gives the children a sense of freedom from their ailments."

"That's very considerate."

They turned down a long hall and walked about halfway.

"Here we are," Jenny said, opening the office door.

Allison entered. Her eyes opened wide. The office was huge with a décor in a very expensive taste, including a large antique oak desk with leather chair, several wall paintings and a marble bust on a tall pedestal in the far corner. It was like no office she had ever seen in any clinic. Then again, she had never been to a clinic housed in a Victorian mansion.

"Please sit," Jenny said, while walking around her desk.

Allison did so. "I'd like to thank you," she started, "for what you said to Brandon. He's a scared little boy and I know your words helped to reassure him."

"And I meant what I said. Some people think we pamper the children too much. But considering how little time some of them have left, they deserve anything we can do." She folded her hands on the desktop. "How much time does Brandon have?"

"Six months—nine at the outside. Can I be frank?"

"Feel free to speak your mind."

"It was because of the short time he has left, that the Board of Directors at St. John's Hospital allowed Dr. Hamline's request to try his treatment on Brandon. As you must know, his mother was tragically killed more than a year ago and we have no information on his father. Since all attempts to locate any other family member have failed, I've been made his temporary guardian."

"And it is because of those special circumstances," Jenny told her, "that we allowed your request to stay here until Brandon becomes accustomed to his new surroundings." She leaned back in her chair. "But I must add that I can only allow that for a short time. One week—ten days at the very most. We have strict rules. Even visitations are permitted only by appointment. You must understand, Dr. Hamline's treatments require that his patients are free from any undue stress."

"Then I can't help but wonder, if it is so against your rules, why allow it in Brandon's case?"

"In a way," Jenny explained, "you've answered your own question. In Brandon's case."

"I don't understand."

"Brandon is very special to Dr. Hamline. It was he who allowed the change in our standard routine."

"Oh? Why Brandon?" Allison recalled the boy asking that very question during the drive. It was a good question, though, until she asked it herself, Allison didn't realize how important it was.

"Of all the profiles of potential cases, Brandon Dahl fit best with Dr. Hamline's criteria."

"Which are…?"

"You will have to talk to him about that. Who knows, he might even tell you." She let out a small chuckle. "Excuse me," she said. "It's just that Dr. Hamline is so secretive about his research. He goes to such extremes."

"I'm intrigued. I hope I can meet the good doctor soon."

"Oh, you will...but in good time. He's very busy working on his treatment schedule."

"Since you brought it up. Can you tell me about Dr. Hamline's treatments?"

"No, I can't."

That caught Allison a little unprepared. "You want me to leave a boy in your care and you won't tell me what he'll be put through."

"It's not that I won't tell you—I can't tell you. I really don't know anything about the specifics. I'm not a scientist. My degree is in business, not biology or some other science. I'm sure Dr. Hamline will discuss the treatment and what he hopes to accomplish with you, since you are both the boy's doctor and guardian." She smiled again. "I'm sure, even with him being secretive with his research, he would be thrilled to speak to a colleague about his work. I'm sure it's quite fascinating, but to be honest with you, I don't understand it myself. All I know is that it helps the children."

"I've read several papers written by Dr. Hamline. All were very impressive and thought provoking. His work involves gene therapy. He's considered a leader in the field."

"Again, I'm just a working stiff. I don't understand half of what Edward...Dr. Hamline talks about."

"Half? That's more than most people would." Allison watched Jenny very closely. She had the uneasy feeling the woman was holding something back.

"Only an expression, I'm afraid. When it comes right down to the nuts and bolts, it's all over my head." Jenny reached down and opened her left bottom desk drawer from which she pulled out a folder. "I don't mean to change the subject, but I must." She put the folder on the desktop, opened it and skimmed the top page. "We received Brandon's medical records yesterday, but I'm afraid they're incomplete. The last week or so are missing."

"We sent off copies of what we had at the time. The records for the past week are in the car. Or maybe in my room by now. I'll make sure to bring them to you."

"That will be fine," Jenny said, but there seemed to be a touch of impatience in her voice.

The two women continued their talk. Jenny explained the schedule—meals, studies, leisure time, lights out, wake up times. All designed to give the children some order in their lives, a normalcy to their days. She even went as far as to explain how Dr. Hamline insisted on keeping the precise methods of his work a secret. And in doing so the exact details of Brandon's therapy would have to remain his own. During routine examinations she would be more than welcome to observe, but not during the main course of treatments. Allison couldn't say she was in total agreement with those terms, but she did understand the need for secrecy.

"I think that's about it," Jenny said, rising up from behind her large antique oak desk. "Shall we rejoin the children?"

CHAPTER THIRTEEN

Back in the activities room, Brandon and Katy worked on the puzzle. Between the two of them they managed to complete over half the picture in the short time they had been together.

"Do you like it here?" Brandon asked the small girl.

Her main focus still on the puzzle, she said, "Compared to what?" She dropped in the last piece to finish that section of Guy's Tower, though the picture only showed five of its twelve sides.

"I don't know. Do you just like being here?" Brandon dug through the box trying to find the pieces that made up the clock face on the Gatehouse. They weren't gray stone, so he missed them the first time through.

"I would rather be home," she said honestly.

"Then why aren't you?" Finding the first clock piece, he put it in place.

"Because Dr. Hamline is helping me," she said. "He says he can help me live longer."

"Has he?"

Katy shrugged. "I guess so, I'm still alive." She found a piece of sky that fit between the tower and the puzzle's straight edge. She slid it into its correct position. "There was another kid, Joey Danes, he was sick too, but Dr. Hamline couldn't help him. He did at first, but then Joey died anyway."

"Why are you talking about Joey?" a voice said behind them. Busy with the puzzle and their talk, the two children didn't notice that another boy had entered the room. He was slightly stout with very light hair and pale skin. He wore a frigid scowl. "You can't talk about him. He was my best friend."

"Oh, hi, Kevin," Katy said, looking up from the puzzle. She could tell Brandon was startled by the boy's sudden appearance, his hostile stance and angry words. "This is Brandon," she added. "He's new here. Dr. Hamline will be helping him too."

"He didn't help Joey," Kevin Reeves said. "He was my best friend, now he's dead. I don't like people talking about him."

"I didn't mean anything by it," she said.

Kevin noticed that Brandon hadn't said a word since he approached them. "What about you?" Kevin challenged.

"I didn't even know him," Brandon said.

"That's right you didn't. So don't talk about him. He thought Dr. Hamline could help him with his shots and all, but he couldn't. Dr. Hamline can't help any of us."

"Yes he can!" Katy spoke up. She now had no mind for the puzzle and returned the same angry stare Kevin had been dishing out. "He's helped me," she snapped. "He's helped me!"

"All he's done is to give you shots. So how does that help you? All it does is hurt your arm."

"You think you know everything, Kevin, but you don't know anything at all." Katy pushed herself away from the table, clearing an area about four feet. Then as the boys watched, she pulled off her footrests, getting them out of the way. Next Katy put the wheel locks in place. Finally, with the boys very surprised by her actions, she rose from her chair. It took her some time to gain her balance, but eventually she did.

"You can stand," Brandon said. "Why do you use that chair?"

"She couldn't do that before," Kevin told him. He was amazed, though this miracle was lost on Brandon. It was only a girl standing up. He didn't know that her other doctors had told her she would never walk again. At a very young age, her disease had destroyed the communication between her spinal cord and legs.

"I can do more than just stand," she told them both. Slowly she moved her right foot. It was an awkward stride, but completing it made Katy beam. Then she moved her left foot. This time the movement appeared to be much smoother. Katy slowly and carefully repeated the two-step motion, walking back to the edge of the table where she took hold. "You see, you see? Dr. Hamline has helped me. You don't know anything, Kevin. You don't know anything at all."

Unexpectedly from the doorway came the shocked voice of Jenny Gordon. "Katy, what are you doing out of your chair?" The words startled all three children, especially Katy, who lost her balance and fell to the floor. Kevin snickered at the sudden event. Jenny Gordon and Allison Cook gasped. Brandon simply watched the two adults rush over to the fallen girl.

A noise rose up from Katy. At first, it sounded like crying, but within seconds, it was obvious laughter. "Did you see me? Did you all see? I walked. By myself. No one helped me." She laughed again. That caused Kevin to laugh too. Even Brandon began to laugh, though he didn't know why. Allison gave out a soft chuckle as well as she retrieved the wheelchair and pushed it over to the little girl.

All laughed except for Jenny. She knelt down and helped Katy return to her chair. "You could've hurt yourself," the woman said.

"But I didn't," Katy said. "And I walked. You saw it. You all saw it."

"We certainly did," Jenny said, as if holding back her anger. Then turning to Allison, she smiled. "You frightened me so," she said, looking back at the girl. "All the fine work you've done. You wouldn't want to wreck it all by showing off, would you? You know Dr. Hamline told you to take it easy at first."

"Yes, Jenny," Katy said, while settling back in her chair. It was obvious the little girl had to fight back a smile. She knew she shouldn't have tried to walk yet, but now that she had, she was so happy.

"Are you sure you're all right?" Jenny asked. "You didn't hurt yourself, did you?"

"No, I'm okay. Really I am."

Right then, a small thin man with ratty brown hair and black plastic-rim glasses came through the open door. Quickly, he made his way over to the small group. "Please, excuse my interruption, Miss Gordon."

"Oh good, Ratford, did you bring our guests' bags up to their rooms?"

"As requested, ma'am. Dr. Hamline sent me to tell you that he has a brief opening in his schedule and would like to meet our new resident." His framed eyes turned towards Brandon, who took a step back—the man had such a cold stare he frightened the boy. He reminded Brandon of the twisted assistants in the old monster movies.

"Excellent news," she said, "I know Brandon and Dr. Cook are most anxious to meet Dr. Hamline."

"He'll be waiting in his office," Fritz Ratford told her.

"Thank you. We'll head down immediately." Jenny's attention fell to the children. "Katy, Kevin, you two go get cleaned up. It will be suppertime soon."

"Okay," they both said in almost perfect unison.

"But what about the puzzle?" Katy added.

"I'm sure it will be fine. Get going you two. Ratford, will you be kind enough to see that Miss Redden gets back to her room without any more excitement?"

The man nodded and positioned himself behind the girl's wheelchair.

Without any further discussion, the two children obeyed. Kevin left first, followed by Katy being pushed along by Ratford. The thin man was very careful to guide her chair through the door.

After the three of them were alone, Brandon tugged on Allison's sleeve. His wince told her exactly what he wanted. She reached in her blazer pocket and pulled out a small bottle of pills. "One or two?" she asked.

Brandon held up one finger.

"Are you sure?"

He nodded.

"If you'll follow me," Jenny told them, "we'll get Brandon some water, then I'll bring you both to Dr. Hamline's office."

A few moments and a cup full of water later, they started the trek to the east wing of the mansion. While trying to keep up with Jenny's pace as she marched down the long hall, Brandon spotted two other boys about his own age heading in the opposite direction towards the dining room. They whispered among themselves then peeked at him. Brandon quickly turned his head the other way.

Jenny made a left-hand turn down another hall. About three-quarters down, she stopped at a door. "Here you are," she said, stepping to one side.

"You're not coming in?" Allison asked.

"No, if Dr. Hamline wanted me included he would have left word." Jenny started back the way she came. "Go right in."

Allison lightly rapped on the door. There was no answer. She knocked again. Still getting no answer, she turned the knob and opened the door but a crack, enough to see inside.

The large office reminded her of so many others she had seen over the years, including her own. But besides the usual desk and chairs, bookshelves and lamps, potted plants and hanging pictures, the décor also included an examination table and a cabinet readied with basic equipment and supplies—both were usually found in an examination room. The room must serve a dual purpose, at least on a minimal level.

"Is he in there?" Brandon whispered.

She shook her head, wondering if that Ratford fellow had been incorrect in relaying his message. "Something must've come up. He's a very busy man. I'm sure he'll be here soon." The door wasn't locked and they had been expected. "Let's go inside and wait. It should only be a minute."

It was ten minutes before the door re-opened. The two had sat in almost total silence, before they heard the knob turn. Dr. Hamline came into the room. Allison stood up and extended her hand.

"Dr. Hamline, I'm glad to finally meet you." He wasn't exactly what she had pictured in her mind. While it was true she had read many of his papers, she had never seen him, not even a photograph. He was a short, balding man with a slight stoop and much older than she would have thought. He had dull eyes and he moved slowly with each step. The words in his writings were so full of energy, but they would seem foreign to this man.

He shook her hand. "Who are you?" he asked.

The question surprised and embarrassed her to almost speechlessness. She said the only thing she could. "Allison Cook. Dr. Allison Cook."

"Oh, yes," he said, as if the name barely meant something. "You used to be the boy's doctor."

"No, I still *am* Brandon's doctor," she said with a sharp tone. "For the time being. And until I determine that you can help him I *remain* his doctor."

"Of course I can help him. That's why he's here." He shuffled over to the cabinet and took a blood pressure cuff and stethoscope from the top shelf, then shuffled his way to Brandon's chair. "Roll up your sleeve," he said. Those were his first spoken words to the boy.

Brandon looked over at Allison for reassurance. She nodded to him.

Dr. Hamline wrapped the cuff around Brandon's thin arm and began to squeeze the black bulb. The cuff tightened. Dr. Hamline placed the round stethoscope end on Brandon's inner arm below the inflated cuff. He released the air and listened for a pulse. After a minute, he said, "His blood pressure's a little low. When's the last time he's eaten?"

"Lunch," Allison said, "after getting off the plane. I guess they're having supper right now in the dining room."

He glanced at his watch. "They are. You both can catch a bite after we're done here." He removed the blood pressure cuff. "Do you have a list of his current medications?"

"I do, but not with me. All his paperwork is in my room. I thought this would be an informal meeting, so I didn't bother to retrieve it."

"I would appreciate a little more cooperation in the future." He took the end of the stethoscope and wrapped his hand around the diaphragm to warm it. "Open your shirt please," he told Brandon. The boy complied. "Tell me if this is too cold," he said, gently placing the shiny end on Brandon's narrow chest. "Okay?" he asked.

Brandon nodded, but didn't say anything.

After a few seconds of listening, the doctor shifted the chestpiece an inch to the right. "Good. You have a strong-sounding heart." He lifted the scope and switched its position to Brandon's back. "Take a deep breath and hold." After a second, "Release. Good. Again, inhale. Release." He pulled back the stethoscope, letting it dangle from his neck. "Your lungs sound clear."

In the course of a half-hour, Dr. Hamline continued his examination of Brandon Dahl. He took his temperature, tested his reflexes, checked his eyes and ears. He had the boy lay on his back while he probed his abdomen. Allison Cook watched the man very carefully. He was doing things she had done hundreds of times before. She guessed he was trying to get the lay of the land, in a manner of speaking, but he could get all the information he needed from Brandon's records. That is, she thought, if she would have brought them with her.

"I would like to do some blood work," Dr. Hamline said. From the cabinet, he took out a bottle of alcohol, a cotton ball, a sterile finger prick and a collection tube. He returned to the table, opened the bottle, wetted the cotton and rubbed it on the end of Brandon's middle finger. After tossing the spent cotton in the waste can, the doctor saw the fear in the boy's eyes. "Would you prefer if Dr. Cook takes the blood?" he asked.

Again, without saying a word, Brandon nodded.

"If it will make things easier," he said, and passed the small metal prick to Allison.

Immediately Brandon's face eased. Dr. Cook had taken blood from his finger several times. He knew it would not hurt. After she was finished, Allison handed the sample to Dr. Hamline. He put the thin blood-filled tube in a small refrigerator next to the cabinet.

"We're done here," he said to Brandon. "You can button up your shirt."

Then he jotted something down on a notepad. "Do you think you can find your way to the dining hall?"

"I think so."

"Let's make sure, shall we." His fingers began to point in the air. "Go down the hall to the end, turn right and keep going. You'll find it." The boy didn't budge from his spot. "You'll be okay," the man added. "I wish to speak with Dr. Cook for a moment. She'll join you soon."

"You go eat," Allison said, "I'll see you in a bit."

"Okay," Brandon said. He left the room and closed the door behind him.

Dr. Hamline gestured for Allison to sit. "The boy seems to be in good shape considering his condition."

"Yes, he is. I..."

"You've been his primary physician?"

"Yes, I..."

"You've done a fine job."

"Thank you."

"But now he will be under my care."

"Not until I release my authority to you." She took a breath. "I don't know what I did to set you off, but ever since I've met you, you've been acting like..."

"A horse's ass?"

"Quite frankly—yes."

"Good. We understand each other. Now with that out of the way, how do you wish to proceed?"

Allison was surprised by his straightforwardness. He was obviously a man who was not afraid of exerting his will, a man who wanted and got his own way. "For the next week or so, I would like to observe you. I want to make sure Brandon is in the right hands."

"The boy is dying. Mine are the best hands he could be in."

You arrogant bastard, she thought. "Nevertheless, I'm here to ensure that fact. And if I think your research is ineffective or does any harm to Brandon I will take him out of here."

"But as I've already pointed out, he's dying."

"And he deserves to die with dignity."

"Very good. You sincerely care for the boy. You are more than just an overqualified babysitter."

"I'd like to think so." Why did she get the feeling, he was the spider and she was the fly?

"You want what's best for him?"

"I do." Here it comes, she thought.

"Then I would like to start the boy on his therapy tomorrow."

There it is—the other shoe. "So soon? Why?"

"Actually, it is you who set the schedule. If I am to convince you that my research will help him, I have to start as soon as possible."

She gave him a questioning stare.

"You set the ground rules, Dr. Cook—not I."

Allison still had the strangest feeling of being manipulated. She didn't know exactly to what end or, for that matter, why. "You're right," she said. "I did set the rules. Then tomorrow it is—under one condition."

"Which is?"

"Let Brandon have the night to get used to this place. No more examinations, no more tests, no more talk about his condition."

"That was always my intent. I have what I need from the boy—for the time being."

~

After eating his supper of a single pork chop, a baked potato, some asparagus and a glass of milk, followed by a half-slice of chocolate cake, Brandon followed Jenny up to the second floor to check out his room. What he found surprised and pleased him. He had never had a room so spacious. Not even at home before he got sick. He remembered his mother for a moment and a deep sadness rolled over him. He missed her so much. He hated to do it, but he forced the thought of her from his mind. He didn't want to start crying in front of Ms. Gordon.

Brandon knew if he focused on something else, anything else, before he realized it, that's all he was thinking about. A simple trick he used right after being told he had brain cancer and again when his mother died. Sometimes it seemed his cancer was a hard preparation for his mother's death.

Jenny told him he could do whatever he wanted for the rest of the evening. He could go watch TV, use one of the computers or even stay in his room, if that's what he wished. After she excused herself, Brandon continued to check out his room. He found some books already on the shelves, though nothing that would interest him.

He also found his suitcase. It was in the closet and empty. His clothes had already been unpacked—his shirts and pants hung up—his underwear and socks put in the dresser drawer. It gave him a creepy feeling to think of some stranger touching his underwear, but it wasn't anything he couldn't get over.

Brandon walked over to the bed and sat. He bounced up and down a couple times. It was a lot softer than the beds in the hospital. On his first few nights there, he had trouble sleeping because his mattress was so hard. Eventually he got used to it—he had no choice. Now he wondered if he would be able to sleep in such a comfortable bed.

Then from the door, "They put you in here?" Kevin said, guiding Katy and her chair into the room.

"Guess so," Brandon replied, standing up. He wondered how long they had been standing there. Were they watching him bounce on the bed? Not that it was a big deal. He just didn't want them to think he was weird.

"This is a nice room," Katy said, wheeling herself over to the window overlooking the sprawling backyard. "I always like the view. Tommy really liked it too."

"Tommy?" Brandon asked. "Who's Tommy?"

"Tommy Hover," Kevin said. "He stayed here a while back. He was a pretty good guy."

"Where did he go?"

"He, you know, he…" Katy said. She glanced over to Kevin.

"He died," Kevin said. "He was sick like us. He was doing real good for a while, but then one day he wasn't."

Katy watched a large blue jay eating from a birdfeeder as she spoke. "Jenny said, he lived six months longer than he was supposed to, so we shouldn't feel sad about his death. I know she's right, but I hate to say it." The bird let out a harsh jeer then flew off.

"But that's the way it is," Kevin said. "It's best if you realize that from the start. We are here because we're all sick. And part of being sick means that we may die."

"Kevin," she said, "don't be so cruel."

"My last foster-father told me that," the boy said—and to Kevin that made it gospel. He hung on every word the man would say. "Though…" His eyes shifted around the room. "…it's still kind of creepy."

"Creepy?" Katy said. "How?"

"I don't know. This was his room—now it's not. I walked by one day and Jenny was taking his stuff out. It was like he just disappeared."

"I still like the view," Katy said. "Even though it looks out towards the woods. And the ghosts."

"You said that before," Brandon said, remembering her words in the activities room. "What ghosts?"

"The ghosts who live in the woods," she replied matter-of-factly, as if he should've automatically known what she was talking about. "The ghosts—the ghosts."

"There's no such thing as ghosts," he said, though he found himself peering out the window at the forest.

"Sure, there are."

"Forget it," Kevin said. "She really believes that junk. One of the groundkeepers likes to tell her old stories."

"They're not stories," she said.

"Then who are they?" Kevin asked. "If there are ghosts out there, then they had to be living people at one time. You can't be a ghost, if you weren't alive."

"There's some kind of Indian burial ground out there someplace," she said, without missing a beat. "The original townspeople disturbed it and caused the ghosts to walk. They killed the ones who woke them and those people became ghosts too. That's why no one goes in the woods anymore—they don't want to end up a ghost."

No one in the room spoke for several seconds. Then Kevin said, "That's so stupid!"

"Hey, I didn't make it up," Katy insisted, "and I believe it too."

"And I believe it's stupid."

Brandon had had enough talk about ghosts. "What are you guys going to do now?" he said, hoping to change the subject.

"We were going back to the activities room to finish the jigsaw puzzle," Katy told him. "You want to come with us?"

"Sure," Brandon said half-heartedly—he still wasn't at ease in this place yet.

"We can introduce you to some of the other kids here," Kevin said. "Most of them are nice, except for Buddy Platt. He can be a real pain in the butt."

"Kevin!" Katy said. "You're not supposed to talk like that."

"Oh, big deal. I said 'butt'—butt, butt, butt. Big deal."

The other two children let out a giggle. They both delighted in the boy's rebellious talk.

"Let's get downstairs," Katy said, "before someone else finishes our puzzle."

The three new friends left the room, but before Brandon walked out, he turned back and peeked out the window. He didn't know why, but he believed what Katy said about the woods. He wasn't sure if it was only because she believed it so, or because maybe there really was something out there.

~

The long day ended for Allison Cook by reading by the light of a small lamp sitting atop the desk in the corner of her room. Earlier, she had made sure Brandon was comfortable and tucked in tight for a good night's sleep. She assured him she would be right down the hall if he needed anything. With his bravest voice, he told her he would be fine. She could sense a guarded state of glee when he spoke of his two new friends, Katy and Kevin. She reminded him of his big day tomorrow, though really doubted the need, and told him to get some rest. After final "goodnights" she headed to her quarters and began her own preparations for the next day.

"You're up late," Jenny Gordon said, standing in the open threshold to Allison's room. "May I come in?"

Allison looked up from her papers. "Please do," she said, closing the folder.

While walking in, Jenny said, "I would've thought you would be exhausted after your long trip."

"I would've thought so too, but to be honest with you I have a lot on my mind."

"You're worried about Brandon, aren't you?"

"I am. Wouldn't you if in my position?"

"I suppose," Jenny said. "But you really have nothing to worry about. Edward Hamline is the top man in his field."

"I am very much aware of Dr. Hamline's credentials. Still, this is so new to Brandon. He's all alone. Since his mother's death, he's been taken care of by strangers—myself included. And now, if I decide he can stay, I'll be putting him with strangers again."

"*If* you decide?"

"Yes—if." She studied Jenny carefully. "I've already made my position clear with Dr. Hamline and we have come to an understanding."

"I'm glad to hear that. If Dr. Hamline okayed your agreement, then it must be to his satisfaction."

"First of all, he didn't need to okay anything. And second, it was to my satisfaction, not his."

Jenny's expression quickly changed. "I didn't mean to imply..." she started. "Hey, whatever you decided, I'm sure you have what's best for Brandon in mind. You're his guardian after all."

Allison eked out an embarrassed smile. The woman obviously meant nothing by her statement and she had read much, too much, into it. Jumping on the woman the way she did was well out of line. "Yes, I am," she said, a little more at ease. "And I take my responsibility very seriously."

"I can see that. You care for the boy."

"If you mean above and beyond the job—I have to admit I do. He is a very special little boy. He's so fragile, so timid. I'm the closest thing he has to family." She felt her embarrassment melt away and turn to sadness. A boy his age should not have to go through such tragedy, such heartache.

"Here he has the best possibility for survival," Jenny said.

"I only hope you're right."

"You don't believe it, do you."

"It's not what I believe or what I don't believe. It's just... I've been going over some of the files Dr. Hamline provided me." She pulled the closed folder over to her, and reopened it. "One of the cases, a Mark Yorksten—he was under Dr. Hamline's care. He was receiving regular treatments and yet he still died."

"That's true," Jenny said, "but if you note the dates, you will see that Mark was under his care for little more than a month. When the boy arrived at the clinic, he was already near death. They flew him here in a helicopter. His own doctor gave him only days to live. But with Dr. Hamline's therapy he lived an extra month. And the quality of that time was beyond anything anyone could dream. He ran and played with the other children. If you didn't know better you would never suspect he was ever sick."

"Then what happened?"

"I'm not sure. He had a relapse. It came on him quite suddenly. If you want the exact details you'll have to speak with Dr. Hamline."

Allison turned the page. "And here's another case very similar."

"Thomas Hover?" Jenny said.

Allison confirmed the name. "Yes, that's right. Again another failure."

"You have to understand. The research being performed here comes with no guarantees. You, being a doctor yourself, should realize that. If Dr. Hamline had a cure by now, he would dispense it all over the world. He has had his share of setbacks, but the children's final days were all more fulfilling then they would have been without the attempt."

"I suppose you're right." Once again she closed the file. She could finish reading it tomorrow when she had a clearer head.

"If you're having doubts you should really speak with Dr. Hamline, not me."

"I thought a second opinion might be helpful, that's all." The real truth was that the man intimidated the hell out of her. She had admired his work for so long and their first meeting did not go over all that well. Who was she kidding? The meeting was like two fighting roosters. They kept pecking at each other trying to draw first blood.

"If you would like an unbiased point of view, how about your own?" A tiny smile formed on the woman's lips. "Earlier today you witnessed Katy getting out of her wheelchair and taking several steps."

Allison nodded, though cautious to what gilded path Jenny may be leading her down.

"When she arrived here, she could not stand, let alone walk under her own power. She suffers from Type III Spinal Muscular Atrophy. I understand the initial diagnosis was made at age two, and by age six she needed the use of a wheelchair. Poor child—her condition has deteriorated ever since."

"But she did walk," Allison said.

"A result of Dr. Hamline's treatments."

"That's amazing. I had no idea he had made such progress." Allison glanced down at the folder of unfortunate children. How frustrating it must have been to get so close then fail. She wondered if that accounted for his gruff attitude.

"But he still has so far to go," Jenny added. "His work will be of great benefit to all."

"You being the administrator, here's a question I'm sure you can answer. Who pays for all this? Running a facility of this size has to cost a pretty penny."

"Without question. But I don't know why that's important."

"It's not really all that important I know, but it would make me feel better. If it's a secret…"

"Secret? Heavens no. This clinic is partially financed by fundraisers the doctor puts on twice a year."

"And lavish affairs, I've heard—I've never attended one myself."

Allison recalled the saying—you have to have money to make money. "But you said partially. The remaining moneys come from…?"

"Private donations."

"I've heard rumors about Dr. Hamline having a secret benefactor, but I thought they were just that—rumors."

"No, not rumors and hardly a secret. Mr. Fisk prizes his privacy. Once the word gets out about someone willing to donate large sums of money for research, you would be surprised of the number of causes that come out of the woodwork. And some of the requests are quite strange. Filtering through all the proposals diverts attention from those projects he considers truly worthy."

"I would like to meet this Mr. Fisk," Allison said.

"You will. Tomorrow. He likes to meet the new patients. And I can tell you, he is particularly interested in meeting Brandon."

Right then, Allison had to fight back a small yawn. "Excuse me," she said.

"That's quite all right," Jenny said with a smile. "I should be going. We'll talk again tomorrow. And I understand Brandon will be starting his treatments."

"Dr. Hamline told you that? I didn't realize he kept you so well informed."

"I do run this place," Jenny blankly stated. She walked to the door. "Tomorrow then."

"Tomorrow," Allison answered. Jenny left the room and Allison leaned back in her chair. With that single word came so much hope, but also the chance of disappointment. And in the deep recesses of her mind, it also brought with it the fear of some lurking danger.

CHAPTER FOURTEEN

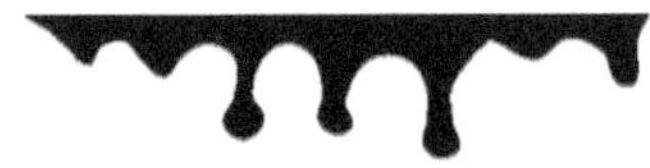

Allison knocked on Brandon's door.

Staying up late last night, reading over the case files of Dr. Hamline, had left her a little tired, but the morning sunshine pouring in through her window helped to shake it off.

She knocked again.

It was too easy to take things like sunshine for granted. Working with children such as Brandon had her remembering to enjoy the simpler things. She only wished she could do more for him—he was a sweet kid and deserved better than pain and suffering.

She knocked on Brandon's door a third time. He still didn't answer.

Allison became worried and cracked the door an inch. "Brandon?" she called out through the narrow gap. She waited a moment, then called out again. "Brandon, are you here?" She pushed open the door and peered in. Brandon, still in his pajamas, was curled up on his bed. His arms wrapped around his head, he was sobbing quietly.

She rushed over. "Brandon, Brandon, can you hear me?"

His eyes moved up to meet hers, but he could not speak. Allison pulled out the small bottle of pills from her pocket and dumped two tablets in her hand. She helped Brandon to sit up, then carefully put the pills in his mouth. She took the glass of water, still half-full, he had on the nightstand from the night before. Holding the glass to his lips, Allison told him to swallow. He did the best he could and managed to get the medicine down his throat.

She eased him down on his back and told him to try and relax. She sat with him, holding his hand, for the next fifteen minutes. Finally, Brandon's eyes opened.

"Are you feeling better?" Allison asked, releasing Brandon's hand, as he slid his legs around to the edge of the bed.

"That was a bad one," was all he said.

"It's over now," Allison assured him, gently using her fingertips to straighten his hair. "I should've gotten here sooner." For the first time, she doubted the decision of taking Brandon out of St. John's Hospital. There he had twenty-four-hour care. All he had to do was hit a call button when he needed help—not lie in agony until someone simply showed up.

"It's no big deal," Brandon told her.

Feeling a heaviness in her throat, Allison stood up. "I'll wait in the hall, while you get dressed." She reluctantly left the boy alone again. Pulling the door closed behind her, Allison heard a very soft, almost angelic, voice.

"Good morning, Dr. Cook," Katy said, wheeling herself along the hall. "Is Brandon going down to breakfast?"

"Not right now, dear. He's getting dressed."

"Can I wait for him?"

"It will be a little bit. You go down. I'll make sure he meets you at the table."

"Okay," the little girl said, with a big grin. She continued on to the far end of the hall to the elevator and disappeared inside.

Allison did see the girl do the impossible yesterday—walk. She pushed the recent doubt from her mind. Dr. Hamline must be making progress to produce such a miracle. And regardless of all other shortcomings, Brandon deserved the same chance for help—the same chance for life.

The bedroom door reopened. "You can come back in now," the boy said, dressed, but standing in his stocking feet. "I just have to put my shoes on." He marched over to the foot of his bed.

She watched and almost marveled at the boy's spunk. A short while ago he was literally incapacitated and now it was like nothing had happened. Of course, the drugs helped, but he would simply shrug the whole event off as something he had to endure.

"How did you sleep?" she asked him.

"Okay, I guess, until I woke up with my headache." He grabbed his sneakers and pulled them on—first the left foot, then the right foot. "It's sort of weird here," he said casually, while tying up his laces.

"Weird? How so?"

"Back in the hospital I had to wear those white gowns and slippers. I never got to wear tenny-shoes."

"That's what's weird? The clothes you get to wear? I thought you enjoyed dressing normally again."

"I do, but if this place is supposed to make me better, why isn't it more like the hospital we came from?"

"It is, in the ways that are important. They just do things a little different here, that's all."

"If you say so." With his shoes on and tied, he got to his feet.

"I do say so. Let's go downstairs. I'm sure they're holding your breakfast."

Brandon grabbed his baseball cap from the nightstand. With a quick flick of the wrist, he placed it on his head.

"You know you don't need to wear that here," Allison told him.

He nodded. "Yeah, I know, but I like it."

She smiled and followed the boy into the hall. They took the elevator to the first floor.

Upon arriving in the dining hall, Brandon found only a small glass of grape juice awaiting him. When asked, a server told both he and Allison that Dr. Hamline insisted that new patients refrain from eating until after their first treatment which he had scheduled for the first thing this morning. Allison told Brandon that she would also wait to eat until they both got back from the appointment. In the meantime, she told him to drink his juice.

Soon they were on their way to Dr. Hamline's office. They both were silent in their march. Allison didn't want to force Brandon to speak, so she remained quiet herself. She couldn't help wondering what was going through the little boy's mind. She knew he must be nervous, and that he wouldn't admit it to her. The walk seemed a bit longer than it had the day before. One fact that didn't escape her notice either time was that this wing was always so devoid of activity. People stayed out of this part of the mansion. She hadn't been told so, but she guessed it was an unwritten rule.

Turning the second corner, they saw Dr. Hamline standing by his office door. Had he been waiting for them or was it that he simply heard their footsteps echo down the hall? The truth was probably somewhere in between.

"Good morning," Dr. Hamline said; like their footsteps, his words echoed too. "Did you sleep well?"

Brandon looked up to Allison, then back to the doctor. "Yes, thank you."

The man led them both into his office. "That's fine," he added, "it will make things a lot easier." He walked over to the cabinet in his usual sluggish way and took from it a white gown. "Please put this on." He handed the garment directly to Brandon. "We'll give you a moment alone to change. You can leave your briefs and socks on, but remove the rest of your clothing. Tie the gown in the back. We'll be going to another room—one better equipped."

"I don't understand," Allison said. "I thought you said you had all that you needed."

"I did—last night. Now I need to take some baseline readings. It will help me judge his progress during the treatments. That's why I gave orders to have him skip breakfast this morning. I didn't want anything to affect his blood chemistry, blood pressure or body temperature." Hamline paused a second, waiting for another question or objection. When it didn't come he said, "Time is getting short. Let's leave the boy to change."

Brandon watched the door close and then did what he had been told. While he disrobed, his gaze moved in all directions around the office. Of course the room hadn't changed since yesterday, but being alone made him feel very uneasy. It took him only two minutes to change and one minute after that there was a knock. "You ready?" Allison asked, through the office door. She didn't enter until he gave the all clear.

"What did I say about getting to wear normal clothes?"

She smiled at the cute question. "It's only for a little while."

"How's our boy," Hamline asked, standing in the opened door.

"I'm ready," Brandon said in an unwavering voice. He took a deep breath and started towards the doctor.

"Very good," Hamline said, then led the two down the hall. They entered a room, which had nothing but cold, impersonal equipment. "Jump up on the second table," he told Brandon. "Lay on your back with your legs straight out."

Again, the boy followed the man's instructions exactly. The thin matting felt chilly against the back of his bare legs. He watched Dr. Hamline wheel over a device with several dials, switches, and lights. On the side, a slip of white lined paper came from a thin open slot. Then Brandon noticed all the wires attached to the opposite side. He didn't particularly like the looks of that machine. In fact, for some reason it scared him.

"I'm going to attach a few receptor electrodes to specific parts of your body," Hamline told him. "And I want to assure you that they will not hurt in the least." Hamline put some stuff on the ends of the round electrodes. "Only a little glue," he said. He gently placed the first round disk on Brandon's right temple.

"This won't make my headache come back, will it?" Brandon said.

"You've been having headaches?" Hamline asked, attaching the second sensor to the boy's left temple.

"Yes, but Dr. Cook gave me my pills."

The man stopped what he was doing. "Pills?" He turned to Allison. "You've been giving him painkillers?"

She nodded. "Codeine. Only when needed."

"Recently?"

"About an hour ago."

"And you didn't see fit to tell me?"

"I didn't think it was important," she told him.

"Everything is important. Were there any other instances when you thought fit to give Brandon painkillers since you both arrived at the clinic?"

"Yesterday," she said. Then pausing briefly, added, "Before our first visit with you."

Dr. Hamline shook his head. "Unbelievable." He let out a sigh and turned his face towards the floor. Then massaging both temples with tiny circular strokes using the middle finger and thumb of his right hand, he told her, "I would appreciate if in the future you record any medication you give the boy and let me know immediately."

"I will, you have my word."

"I don't need your word. I need your cooperation—for now, anyway."

"Will codeine effect your examination that much?"

"It's nothing I can't adjust for," the doctor admitted. "He's not the first patient I've had that needed help controlling the discomfort of their malady." He looked over to Brandon and with a weak smile said, "Hopefully soon, help of that nature will no longer be necessary." He picked up a third round disk centered with an electrode and wire.

Brandon was hooked up to the machine for about thirty minutes. Most of the time he was to remain still, but every so often Dr. Hamline asked him to lift a hand, an arm or a leg. Once, he was even told to hold his breath. All in all Brandon found the whole experience boring.

After being disconnected, a full syringe of blood was taken from his arm. Even though Dr. Hamline allowed Allison to draw it, Brandon did not enjoy that one bit. Next, they stepped out a moment so he could give a urine sample.

On returning, Dr. Hamline took a long cotton swab and swiped the inside of his mouth. Finally, and the strangest part, the man pulled a few strands of Brandon's hair out by the root with tweezers. The doctor apologized for any discomfort and very carefully placed each sample in separate containers. He treated them as if they were more precious to him than gold.

"How are you holding up?" Dr. Hamline asked.

"Good," Brandon said.

"Thatta boy. Because now comes the important part. Your first treatment." Hamline took a breath, then looked the boy square in the eye. "This will require another shot," he said. "Now, I will allow Dr. Cook to administer the injection this time, but I think it best that I do it. You'll need to get used to me, Brandon. I hope we will be together quite a while. What do you say? Do you trust me?"

Brandon's eyes shifted over to Allison, hoping for advice, but none came. He knew he had to make this decision on his own.

"You can give me the shot," Brandon told him.

"Good man."

Man, Brandon mused. No one had ever called him a man before.

"I've done this more times than I can remember," the doctor told him, preparing the needle, filling the syringe with a dark fluid from a small glass vial. "I've become quite an expert on the painless injection." He gave Brandon the shot and to Brandon's delight, Hamline had spoken the truth about it being painless.

From start to finish, the whole examination and treatment took slightly more than one hour. Dr. Hamline told Brandon he could go back and change into his street clothes. He was happy to hear that news. He changed quickly. Maybe now he could eat some breakfast—his belly felt so empty. He waited for Allison to come and get him from the office. When she didn't, he thought maybe he was supposed to return to the examination room. He crossed the hall, but stopped before entering. He heard hard voices—they were arguing about him. At times, the voices were quite loud.

"In this case, I don't care if you are the boy's doctor! I cannot divulge that information. It's the core of my research."

"I think I have the right to know."

"No, you do not! In fact, it's my right to hold back any information that would compromise the security of my work. I can only say that it will help the boy—give him the chance for a normal life."

"Fine, but let me tell you this, I do have the right to pull Brandon out of your program, if I feel it is a danger to him. And if I see any adverse side effects I will do exactly that."

Brandon heard her voice coming closer to the door. He ran back to the office and waited for the knock. It came.

"Ready to go?" Allison said, through what Brandon knew must be a forced smile.

He simply nodded.

Jenny waited outside by the main entrance, resisting the impulse to look at her wristwatch again. From that vantage point she had a clear view of the road leading up to the clinic, so constantly checking the time would not help the situation. Several minutes passed before she spotted the long black limousine take the turnoff and start up the hill. It had arrived from a direction opposite to town.

Finally, the limo pulled up and stopped in front of the mansion. A tall man, wearing a black crisp-seamed chauffeur's uniform and matching cap, stepped out of the driver's side. Jenny straightened the hem of her skirt, then hurried down to receive her visitor.

"Hello, Karl," Jenny said, wishing she had had a little more time to prepare.

"Good morning, Ms. Gordon," he replied, before moving around the front of the car and opening the back door closest to the curb.

The first thing to appear was a brown leather, two-hundred-dollar shoe. It touched down on the sidewalk. Seeing the man exiting the lavish vehicle, Jenny forced a big smile. His suit was impeccably tailored tweed. Under his coat was a vest with a small gold chain hanging out of the watch pocket. He was handsome with a strong chin, dark eyebrows, a distinguished nose and straight jet-black hair. Though his apparel sent the message of a staunch businessman, his build and bearing conveyed he would be equally comfortable rock climbing or white water rafting.

He stepped up towards Jenny. "Is everything proceeding as planned?" he asked, moving past her. She took up a position behind him.

"Yes, Charles. All is going well."

"I would hope so, considering the time and expense."

The two walked through the front door. "We will all meet in my office," Jenny said.

"Very good. They are waiting?"

She hesitated for a moment. "No," she said. "Not waiting. I was about to send for…"

Charles stopped and stared at the woman. "You know how I hate delays."

"Yes, sir. It will only be a moment. I'll go get them myself."

"Fine, I'll proceed to your office." He started to walk away, but then paused and turned back to face her. "And Jenny, don't keep me waiting any longer."

She didn't say another word. Instead, she rushed off to gather the others. She had to rectify this mistake as soon as possible.

~

Brandon had a bad case of butterflies and with each quick step down the hall they grew. He recalled his earlier feelings of apprehension and dread when he first set eyes on that needle in Dr. Hamline's hand. This was worse! And considering how he hated needles, that surprised him.

Ms. Gordon had caught up with them both, mere moments after they left Dr. Hamline's office. She appeared a little anxious, but after apologizing for the short notice, she told them there was someone very important that wanted to meet the clinic's newest patient. Brandon hadn't eaten yet, but this sudden, unexpected news had pushed his hunger pains away.

He peeked up at Allison, but turned away before she saw him. He wouldn't let on how nervous he felt—he didn't want to make her more upset than he knew she already was. He wouldn't even let on that he knew she and Dr. Hamline were arguing—arguing about him.

Brandon stayed close to Allison—she seemed to know where they were going. Still, Jenny kept looking over her shoulder making sure they kept up with her pace. Finally, the three of them stopped at a door. He read the dulled brass plate attached to its front: "Jennifer Gordon, Administrator."

"Go right in," Jenny said, standing by the door.

Brandon hesitated.

"Go ahead," Allison told him, "I'll be right behind you."

Entering the office, they found a strange man with jet-black hair sitting behind the large desk. He watched them all come in, but didn't say a single word.

Jenny directed Brandon to sit in the chair closest to the desk. He didn't want to but he knew he didn't have a choice. Allison took the chair next to him. Jenny stood out of the way by a bookcase on the other side of the room.

"Hello, Brandon," the man said, resting his arms on the desktop. "My name is Charles Fisk."

"Nice to meet you," Brandon eked out.

Fisk smiled. "Nice to meet you, too."

"I'm Allison Cook," she said, not waiting to be asked or introduced.

"Brandon's doctor," Fisk said. "You've done a fine job taking care of the boy. I only hope you find this facility up to your standards."

"With what I've seen, it already exceeds them. I understand you are a major contributor of financial support for Dr. Hamline's work."

"I do my part," he said.

"With what I've heard you're being modest." And a false modesty, she thought. Something about this man made Allison feel uneasy.

"Please," he said with another smile. "I'm here to meet the boy, not discuss my minor deeds."

Allison nodded. "Fair enough," she said.

For several seconds, Charles Fisk watched Brandon very carefully. It almost seemed like he was studying the boy—dissecting him and examining each and every piece.

Brandon tried to look up at the money-man, but he just couldn't meet his gaze. For the most part, he stared down at the floor.

Suddenly Fisk sat back in the leather chair. "How do you like it here?" he asked in a stale voice. The question seemed over rehearsed.

"It's okay," Brandon answered. "I really haven't been here long enough to know if I like it, but my room is nice."

"You like your room." Fisk aimed a short glance over to Jenny. "Is there anything else you like?"

Brandon shrugged.

"There must be something." He sat with his eyes fixed on Brandon as though the answer would be very important to him.

"I like some of the other kids," Brandon finally said, after giving it a good long thought.

"You've already made friends. Good, everyone needs a friend."

"Yes, sir."

"I'd like to be your friend too Brandon, so why don't you call me Charlie. That's a lot better than 'sir' and not so stuffy as 'Charles'. Okay?"

"Yes…Charlie."

"I understand you began your treatments today."

The very tone of Fisk's words resulted in Brandon feeling even more nervous than he did before. He didn't know what this man wanted from him, but it sure seemed like he wanted something. He was a strange man —a strange man with a lot of money.

"Yes, sir. I mean Charlie." Brandon held out the middle of his right arm displaying the tape and gauze.

"That's a beauty. It must've hurt."

"No, not really," Brandon told him.

"You must be very brave. I myself hate going to doctors. Ever since, oh, way before I was your age. I would kick and scream all the way there. Do you ever feel like that?"

"No, I don't think so." His head turned towards Allison for reassurance. She smiled at him.

"Brandon has always been a very good patient," Allison volunteered.

"That's what I like to hear," Fisk said. "It would be a shame if children wasted Dr. Hamline's time with disruptive behavior."

"I wouldn't do that," Brandon said.

"I do believe that of you, Brandon." He grinned. "It was very nice to meet you." The man extended his hand—it dwarfed Brandon's as they shook. "Jenny, will you make sure the boy gets something to eat." His full attention fell back to Brandon. "You haven't had breakfast yet, have you?"

"No, Charlie."

"Dr. Hamline has pretty strict rules about that, I know. But have no worries, the kitchen staff will fix you right up."

"His breakfast is already waiting for him," Jenny said. "You go right down." She glanced over to Allison. "The both of you."

"I was hoping to speak with Mr. Fisk a little longer," Allison said.

"I would enjoy that," Fisk replied, "but my time here is limited. I must be off. We will have other opportunities to speak, I promise you."

"I'll hold you to that," she said.

"By all means."

After Allison and Brandon left the office, "Are you sure we have the right boy?" Fisk asked Jenny.

"As sure as we can be. The records appear to bear it out. And Edward's tests will give us the definitive answer. It's only a matter of time before we know absolutely."

"Don't let me down," Fisk said.

"I haven't in the past and I won't now."

"Let's hope so," he said, slowly rising to his feet.

Late that afternoon, Brandon put on his ball cap and headed outside. He had spotted Katy and Kevin from his bedroom window. They were playing checkers. He was usually so tired by this time of day that it surprised him he had the energy to go out. From the front door, he followed the blacktop path around to the back of the house. And there he found Katy and Kevin in the exact same position he saw from his window —sitting on opposite sides of a checkerboard. But by this time the board had been cleared of all black pieces and Kevin had a spoiled frown on his face.

"How did you get so good at this game?" Kevin asked her, while fingering the only four red pieces he managed to capture. Of course, they came at great cost. He jumped one of her men and she double jumped two of his.

"I don't know." She looked up. "Hi, Brandon. Where have you been?"

"In my room mostly." He scratched his arm. It had been well over an hour since he removed the tape and gauze, but the small patch of skin still itched. "I saw Dr. Hamline this morning."

"He's a good doctor," the little girl said. She turned her wheelchair towards him. "Did he give you a shot?"

"Yes."

"I hate getting shots," Kevin said. "I'm glad I only have to take pills."

"How do you feel?" Katy said, ignoring Kevin's statement.

"Okay." Then Brandon gave it a little more thought. "I feel good. I really do." The pains he had with him all the time were a lot less. They weren't gone completely, but they weren't too bad either.

"I told you he's a good doctor," Katy said of Dr. Hamline. "Set up the pieces again," she told Kevin.

"I don't want to play you anymore," Kevin said. "You're too good for me. How about you, Brandon? You want to get beat at checkers?"

"I'll take it easy on you," Katy told Brandon, "...for the first few games."

"Yeah, and after that, watch out," Kevin said, standing up from the chair. "Sit here," he told Brandon.

"You can be black and go first," she said.

Kevin shook his head. "It won't help, believe me."

It took a minute to reset the board. Brandon took up Kevin's previous position at the table and made the first move. Immediately Katy made a counter move. She did it without even thinking.

"I thought you said you'd take it easy on me?"

"I am," she giggled.

Then from behind the three children: "Aren't you done with those checkers yet? Give someone else a turn." The voice belonged to a rough, heavyset boy with an angry scowl.

"We haven't even had an hour yet," Katy said.

"Who's that?" Brandon whispered to Kevin.

"That's Buddy Platt," he whispered back. "He's the mean kid."

"That's plenty of time for you losers," Buddy said, stepping closer to the table, expecting Katy to move back—she did not. "Give someone else a chance."

"The checkers were sitting here most of the day. You could've had them then."

"I didn't want them then. But I want them now."

"You don't even have anyone to play with," Katy challenged.

"Do too! Me and myself! And that's good enough for you."

"Go away, Buddy!" Katy yelled. "You're the meanest person I've ever known. Mean, mean, mean."

"No, if I was mean, I'd do something like this." The large boy lifted the edge of the checkerboard and tipped it over, sending the red and black pieces in all different directions. "But I'm not mean, so I wouldn't do anything like that." The boy began to laugh.

"Get out of here Buddy!" Katy shouted. "Get out of here! I'm going to tell Jenny on you. I'm going to tell."

"I don't care," he said. "I'll tell her you were hogging the games again."

"But we'll tell her too," Kevin said.

"You're her friends. Everyone knows friends lie for each other."

"Get out of here, Buddy, or I'll scratch your eyes out." Those words startled all the boys, Buddy, Brandon, even Kevin. Her tone was so harsh it frightened them all.

"Ahhh, who needs this. Bunch of babies, if you ask me." Buddy turned sharply and left the group.

"You told him," Brandon said. "Did you really mean it? Would you have scratched him?"

Katy didn't answer. Instead, she drooped in her wheelchair. Suddenly, she didn't appear very well at all.

"What's the matter?" Kevin asked.

"I don't feel so good," she said. "Would you guys mind pushing me to my room?"

"Maybe we should tell somebody," Brandon said.

"No, I'll be okay. It's that mean old Buddy. I get so upset it makes me a little sick. I'll be all better in a bit. Just bring me to my room."

All the way up to the second floor, Brandon couldn't help thinking he should tell someone about what happened. It might be important. Even when they stepped off the elevator, Brandon suggested they tell Jenny—Katy told him no. Once inside her room, the little girl made both boys promise to keep the whole thing a secret.

Reluctantly, Brandon agreed.

Lying in bed, Brandon stared up at the ceiling through the darkness. Off in the distance, he thought he could hear some kind of loud engine—a truck maybe. The mechanized sound had him thinking of what Dr. Hamline said about him having a normal life. If it were true, if he could have a normal life again, he would like to travel somewhere someday—though not by car or airplane, but by train—maybe even by boat—that would be cool.

His head resting snugly on his pillow, he turned towards the bedroom clock with its bright red glow. It was a little past one AM. He didn't feel all that tired and thought he should be exhausted considering the day he had had. Maybe the lack of sleep was because of the shot Dr. Hamline had given him. When he was having his chemotherapy at St. John's, it always wrecked his sleep, but not this bad.

Brandon worried that Allison would know he wasn't sleeping well—she could always tell. And he remembered what she told Dr. Hamline about any adverse side effects. He didn't want to give her any cause for concern or reason for stopping these new treatments.

Katy told him how the treatments were helping her and he witnessed it with his own two eyes. He wanted the same—he wanted to be well again. Allison had told him not to get his hopes too high—he wouldn't notice any change for several days, maybe weeks, but except for a soft strange ringing in his ears, one of those side effects he would keep to himself for now anyway, he already felt different—better. He wasn't sure if it was all in his head—what did the doctors call it—psychosomatic.

Brandon told himself he had to get some sleep. He tried his best to relax and put everything else out of his mind: Dr. Hamline, his treatments, even Katy. It was at that point when he first heard the strangest sound. At first, he thought it might be music, because of its beat and rhythm, which seeped through the walls with its low, soft tones. It was so soothing. He laid still with his hands folded behind his head. He closed his eyes and focused on the curious melody. But soon the sound began to fade and before long, he couldn't hear it anymore. The boy was left in total silence.

Suddenly, Brandon shot up in his bed—he had a terrifying feeling that someone else was in the room with him. He stared out into the blackness, but that was useless—anything could be hiding out there in the dark. He reached over for the lamp, fearing someone would grab his hand before he could pull the switch.

His fingers slid along the nightstand, groping for the lamp. The seconds passed and the urgency within him grew—whoever or whatever it was, was getting closer. He had to hurry. He had to get the light on.

At last he found the lamp and pulled its short metal chain. Light flooded the room, blinding him for a moment. He let out a short scream—the blindness made him vulnerable. The thing from the darkness could see him. It knew, he knew, it was there. It would surely be coming after him now.

Brandon shielded his eyes until they stopped burning—peeking out between his fingers helped lessen the pain. He looked around the entire room.

Nothing.

Brandon tucked down and pulled his blanket up past his nose. His gaze darted throughout the room, to every corner, to every nook and cranny, all the while not feeling very protected. He stayed that way—motionless—for an hour until his eyelids began to droop. Sleep began to finally overtake him. He slowly blinked once, twice, then there was only blackness.

Barely thirty minutes had passed before the boy's eyes opened. He heard someone calling his name.

"Allison?" he said groggily. He sat up, realizing that he had managed to nod off with the light still on. The single small lamp cast some long shadows across the far wall.

His head cleared second by second—the last remnants of sleep left his body. It wasn't Allison who had called out to him. It wasn't even his name he heard. It was that strange rhythm again, but it wasn't music as he first thought. And the sound wasn't within his room or anywhere else in the clinic. It came from outside.

Brandon got out of bed and hurried over to the window. In his haste, he banged into a chair, knocking it over. The loud crash made him jump. After picking up the chair, he eased closer to the window and looked out. To his shock, a face stared back at him. His heart almost skipped a beat. Then he laughed, seeing it was his own reflection. With night being the backdrop to the glass, it made an excellent mirror. He rushed over to the lamp and turned it off, then rushing back, he peered outside.

The moon shined full above the woods—those woods Katy found so fascinating with her ghosts and Indian burial grounds. Did the sound come from there? He thought about opening the window for a better listen, but when his fingers wrapped around both handles, he changed his mind.

He let go of the brassware and stood silent—his eyes not straying from the dark grove. A minute passed, he heard nothing. A second minute passed—a third—a fourth, still nothing. Brandon let out a sigh as if he hadn't been breathing all that time. He turned around and headed back to his bed, only to stop cold in his tracks. This time the strange sound was unmistakably a construct of words—mumbled words—words he couldn't make out, but words nevertheless. Slowly he returned to the window and stared out into the night. He thought if he tried hard enough, he might be able to see something through the trees, but they were simply too far away.

Again, the words came—clearer, but in a whisper. He couldn't believe what he heard—until they repeated themselves—this time louder and sharper—this time sending an uncontrollable shiver down his spine. They were two simple words.

Help me.

Brandon wanted to scream out. He wanted to run and get Allison. He had to tell someone. He had to get help.

He took a quick step, but then suddenly, stopped. What if no one believed him? Or worse yet, what if it was all in his imagination—a hallucination. A terrible side effect of his new medicine—something Allison feared. She would force Dr. Hamline to stop giving it to him. He would never be better.

Though, what if someone really was calling for help? If he could hear it, certainly other people could hear it too. But why would anyone be in the forest at this time of night?

A very strange thought entered his head. Maybe he was still asleep and dreaming. It wouldn't matter if he went and got Allison if it was only a dream. And to prove it, all he had to do was to wake up. He would find himself nestled in his warm, soft bed.

Help me, the words echoed.

This was no dream.

CHAPTER FIFTEEN

Brandon couldn't believe his luck. Pancakes and linked pork sausages for breakfast. That was his favorite. He took the sausages and wrapped them with the pancakes.

"Why did you do that?" Kevin asked him. He had been down to the table five minutes before Brandon, but they had agreed the previous day to wait for each other before eating.

"Pigs in a blanket," Brandon said.

"What?"

"Pigs in a blanket. That's what it's called: pigs in a blanket. The sausage is the pig and the pancake is the blanket. It's good. Try it."

"I'll pass." Kevin raised his orange juice glass to his lips and took a big swallow. He had mentioned earlier that he wished they still had some grape juice leftover from yesterday.

"Really. It's good. Give it a try."

Kevin carefully studied Brandon, suspicious he was being set up for a joke. "All right," he said with a cautious tone, "I'll try it." Taking one sausage, he rolled it up in a pancake, covered it with maple syrup, then cut off a piece and popped it in his mouth. He chewed. "Hey, this is pretty good."

"I told you so."

Brandon kept looking up from his plate—his eyes focusing on the dining room door. Every time the door opened, his head shot up. He would hide his disappointment when it wasn't the person he hoped it would be.

"What are you doing?" Kevin asked, finally noticing Brandon's strange behavior.

"Just watching for Katy. She's late for breakfast."

"She's eating in her room today."

"Her room?"

"She's still not feeling very good, so they brought her food up to her."

"Did somebody call her parents?"

Kevin looked up from the table. "She doesn't have any parents," he said, surprised by the question. "None of us do."

The shock clearly showed on Brandon's face. He never gave it any thought that, like him, the other kids here at the clinic were orphans too. "Everyone?"

"Yep. I never knew my parents. I was in foster homes most of my life. The last people I stayed with were great. But when I got real sick they brought me here. Now, I'm doing pretty good."

"What happened to Katy's parents?"

"I don't know. She never told me. And I didn't think she wanted me to ask." Kevin took another bite from his pigs in a blanket. "Who taught you this?" he asked.

"My mother," Brandon said softly.

"Oh," Kevin said.

"Kevin, how long have you been here?"

"Three months and a week," he told Brandon. "Why?"

Brandon shrugged. "And you're doing better?"

"For now. When I came here, I had pneumonia. They had to wheel me into this place. I couldn't even sit up without help. I almost died."

"That's why you're here…pneumonia?"

"No, not because of that. My real mother had HIV and I got it from her when I was born. Dr. Hamline gives me pills, but they cause anemia—I get tired real easy—sometimes I even get dizzy."

"How did your foster parents know to bring you here?"

"They didn't. I guess they were all worried about the bills and everything. Then somebody paid them—paid them all. A little while after that they talked to me about the clinic. I didn't want to come…at first."

"What changed your mind?"

"Well, I knew my foster parents couldn't afford the medical expenses and such, so that meant I couldn't stay with them anymore. I figured a clinic wouldn't be any worse than another foster home."

"I suppose."

"How about you?" Kevin asked. "How'd you get here?"

"Same as you. Somebody paid all the bills and arranged for me to be treated by Dr. Hamline. Isn't that weird?"

"Nah," Kevin said, putting a tiny bit more maple syrup on his pancake-wrapped sausage. "Some people just like helping out sick kids. Makes them feel all good inside."

Brandon nodded. "Hey, you want to go for a walk later?"

"Can't. I'm supposed to see Dr. Hamline later on. But I don't know exactly when. I can't go anyplace." Kevin took the last bite of food. "Where would we go anyway?"

"Just around," Brandon said. He thought about telling Kevin about last night, but at the last moment changed his mind.

It was close to noon and Brandon sat in the library, his nose buried deep in a copy of *The Adventures of Tom Sawyer*. No one could have measured his joy when he found the book on the third shelf just right of the sliding double doors. This was his most favorite book. He especially liked the part about Tom and Huckleberry Finn rafting down the Mississippi River. He loved reading about the two friends always going on grand adventures together.

The door skidding along its tracks broke the boy's concentration, though it didn't upset him. He had been waiting patiently. "Hi Allison," he said, putting the book aside and sitting up straight.

"Sorry, I couldn't get away any sooner," Allison said, coming over the threshold.

"That's okay," he said with a big smile.

"My, aren't you the happy one."

"Just excited."

"Excited? About what?"

"I was hoping we could go for a walk. You know, go exploring."

Allison tilted her head slightly to one side. "I don't know. I have a lot of things to go over."

"Please," he begged. "It will be fun—like Tom and Huck." He held up the book.

"You and your stories. They really spark that imagination of yours."

"No, that's not the reason. I got the idea way before I even found the book."

"I'm not sure I can get away," Allison told him. She saw the sudden sadness welling in his eyes. "But I can always make the time. Where do you want to go?"

"I thought going down by the woods would be sort of fun." He tried not to look too eager. If you looked too eager about something, adults seemed not to want to do it without knowing why. Brandon wasn't ready to tell anyone just yet—not even Allison.

"A walk in the woods? I don't know about that."

"We don't have to go in the woods. It's just I've never been that close to a group of trees like that before."

"Okay, if it's that important to you." She glanced at her wristwatch. "Give me a little time to change my clothes. Maybe I can get the kitchen staff to pack us a lunch. If you want you could ask one of your new friends if they would like to come with us. I'm sure I can get permission from Jenny to bring them."

Brandon shook his head. "Kevin is seeing Dr. Hamline and Katy doesn't feel well."

"She doesn't," Allison said sounding surprised, but quickly changed her tone. "Maybe if you have fun, we can bring them next time."

Brandon nodded.

"How about I meet you at the front door in about fifteen minutes," she added. The sunshine pouring through the library windows was so appealing, so inviting. "I think we both could use a little change of scenery and some time in the fresh air will certainly do me good." She turned to leave. "Don't forget—fifteen minutes."

"I won't," he said. Brandon stood up and returned the book to the same spot on the shelf where he found it. The woods and those calls for help weighed heavy on his mind. He wondered if he would find anything.

"You have a lot of energy today," Allison said to Brandon while they walked along the road. She carried a small woven picnic basket in her right hand. After changing into a pair of blue jeans and a loose-fitting button-up shirt, she had pulled her hair back into a loose ponytail—she welcomed the change.

"I'll slow down," he said, from his position several feet ahead of her. He had been walking at a very determined pace.

"No, that's okay. I can keep up." She shifted the basket to her left hand. "How are you feeling?" she asked.

"Good."

"You're certainly acting well."

The way she said those words, her very tone, made Brandon worry she had something else she wished to say. She couldn't have known the real reason why he wanted to leave the clinic. He hadn't told anyone about what had happened last night—about the calls for help.

"You never told me," she started, "what you think about Dr. Hamline?"

"What about him?"

"Do you like him?"

"He's all right, I guess. I like you a lot more."

"Well, thank you. I like you too."

"And you're a lot prettier than he is," Brandon said, though he didn't look at her and he said it so matter-of-factly.

"Where did that come from?" she asked.

He shrugged. "I don't know, but it's the truth."

She could definitely see a change in Brandon's manner and attitude. He was more up—happier—maybe "bubblier" was a better word. He had more energy, that was for certain. But this transformation couldn't be a result of his treatments—they only began the day before. Nothing, no matter how cutting-edge, works that fast.

Maybe the new surroundings, she thought. Getting out of that sterile hospital must be doing wonders for his spirit. And he had made a couple of new friends, which was what a boy his age should be doing. She started to understand why Dr. Hamline ran his clinic in such an environment. A good mental attitude does promote good health. Of course, it wasn't a cure-all by any means, but it had to help—especially for children with terminal diseases.

The road began to curve back towards the woods—the treetops became visible over a small rise. Soon Allison and Brandon stood before a field of perfect green with old-growth pine trees forming a distant black wall. Without a word, Brandon started to cross the grassy piece of land. Allison didn't see any "no trespassing" signs so she figured it should be okay. She followed behind her charge, having very little choice, it seemed.

With a little effort, Allison managed to catch up to the boy. "A very pretty landscape," she said, after taking a breath. "Almost reminds me of a painting."

"I've never seen so much grass in my whole life," Brandon said. "My mother had to work all the time—we never got to get out of the city."

"You must have gone to a park sometime."

"Yeah, it even had a small lake, but it's not the same thing. It was always so crowded. And once in a while the police had to shoo away a bum. There's no one here but us."

"That's life in a small town," she told him. "And being outside town limits makes it even more isolated."

The two kept walking and started over the crest of the hill. The first thing they saw was a small statue. That's an odd sort of thing to have in the middle of nowhere, Allison thought. And when the walked down the hill, they saw another, and another, and still another.

It took mere seconds for them both to realize that those statues were in fact gravestones. They had wandered into the town cemetery, which explained the lack of people. Allison stopped and got the lay of the land. From the rise, she followed the road with her eyes, and sure enough, farther ahead, it turned and twisted back through a couple of stone pillars with an overhanging sign.

"I don't think we should..." she began to say, but when she turned, Brandon had already made a beeline for the tall pines. A large clearing of untouched land separated the graveyard and the trees, so she supposed that area would be fine for a picnic. Once again, she started after him.

"How about here?" she asked, but got no answer. "Brandon?"

He was so fascinated by the dense grove, it took a moment for her words to register and for the boy to turn her way.

"How about here?" she repeated.

"It looks like a good spot," he said.

"Don't go too far," she added. "I'll have lunch ready in a minute." She wasn't sure if he heard her or not. After spreading out the blanket and unpacking the food, Allison opened the thermos of milk—it was still plenty cold. Sitting comfortably, she glanced over at Brandon. He was standing at the edge of the forest, just staring into the trees. She was about to call him back when a dark shadow draped over her body.

Her head snapped around. Whatever it was that stood between her and the sun did not completely block all the bright rays. She had to lift her hand to shield her eyes enough to tell the dark mass was a person. "Who's there? Who are you?"

"That's my question," a distinctly male voice said. The man stepped to the side, out of the blinding sunlight. The first thing Allison noticed was his badge, though this man wasn't the sheriff. Where the sheriff was old and had a potbelly, this man was young and fit. He had a full, but well-trimmed, beard and mustache of dark brown, and bright matching eyes.

"My name's Allison Cook, Dr. Allison Cook," she told the lawman.

"Are you with Dr. Hamline's clinic?" he asked, with a very suspicious glare.

"Yes, I am. Well, sort of. On a very temporary basis. And you are?"

"Deputy Kean, ma'am."

"Nice to meet you. I've already met your sheriff on my drive in."

"That's Sheriff Muldoon, ma'am. He mentioned the incident."

"I'd hardly call it an 'incident'. I asked for directions." She recalled the sheriff's cranky manner. Sizing up this man, she wondered if it came with the job.

"You're here by yourself?" he asked.

"No, I have a patient with me. We're out for some fresh air."

"Patient?" The man raised a surprised brow.

"Brandon," she called out. But when she looked, he was gone. Shock had her call out again. "Brandon." This time the boy appeared from behind one of the thick tree trunks. She felt a sudden rush of relief. "Come back now," she said.

Allison glanced at the deputy and found him smiling. "What is it about boys and trees?" she asked.

When the deputy saw her looking at him, he cleared his throat and simply said, "My brother and I were the same way." His smile straightened. "Do you often hold picnics near graveyards, Dr. Cook?"

"We didn't know there was a cemetery here until we arrived. I figured it was far enough away that it wouldn't be a problem. We could move."

Just then, Brandon made his way to the blanket.

"No," the deputy said. "If it doesn't bother you, I don't have a problem with it."

"Brandon," Allison said, "this is Deputy Kean."

"Hello," Brandon said, extending his hand.

The innocent gesture seemed to impress the man, but quickly his stern face returned. "Hello," he said, shaking the small boy's hand. "You like exploring?"

"Sure, I guess."

"Just be careful," the deputy said. "Those woods are deep. I'm sorry to have bothered you," he told Allison. "When I spotted someone out here, I had to investigate."

"I understand. You're doing your job."

"I should get back to my other duties," Deputy Kean said. "You two have a nice rest of the day."

"Thank you," Allison said. And with that, the man walked away. Then it dawned on her. He told her, seeing someone on the grounds, he had to investigate. What was the deputy doing patrolling a cemetery? Maybe he was merely visiting the grave of a loved one, she thought.

The rest of the afternoon was lovely and both she and Brandon had a wonderful time, but Allison could read a distraction in the boy's eyes. He had been full of enthusiasm when they first arrived—now it had been replaced slightly with disappointment. She tried to ask him about it, but decided not to push the issue.

"Are you ready to head back?" she asked.

"Okay," he answered, a hint of sadness in his voice.

It took them a moment to gather up their things and start back to the clinic.

When Allison had her back to him, Brandon stared back to the woods. *Why didn't you answer?* he thought. *I know you're there. Why didn't you answer?*

~

Kevin sat on the edge of his bed while Brandon told him about hearing the voice. The burden became too great and Brandon had to tell someone. Kevin didn't say a single word—he just listened. The expression on his young face was a cross between shock and disbelief. At first Kevin let out a little laugh, thinking Brandon was joking, but after a few minutes the laughter stopped.

"But how could you hear it from your window?" Kevin said. "It's so far away."

"I don't know." Someone walked by the open door and Brandon stopped talking. He waited until the hall was clear again. "But it came from the woods. I know it did. I just know it."

"Maybe you should tell someone. You can tell Jenny."

Brandon shook his head. "No, she'll think there's something wrong with me. And she might tell Allison."

Kevin nodded as if he agreed, but Brandon wasn't sure he really did.

He didn't want to tell his friend what he overheard Allison say to Dr. Hamline about stopping the treatments, fearing telling might somehow make it happen.

It had been difficult to tell Kevin about the previous night. His first thought was to talk to Katy about the voice—she would believe him, after all, she's the one who told him about the woods. But they had given her a shot to help her sleep.

He had entered the girl's room after knocking and could tell by the nurse's surprise that he wasn't whom she expected to see coming through the door. The woman immediately rose up from the chair next to Katy's bed, dropping her magazine to the floor. She shooed him into the hallway where she told him Katy would be asleep for hours.

Now he ended up in Kevin's room with a plan. "I'm going to go back," he said. "I know I heard a voice. Someone called for help."

"Maybe it was one of those ghosts Katy's always talking about." Kevin couldn't hold back his laugh this time.

"Shut up," Brandon said. "Did you know there was a graveyard next to the woods, smarty pants?"

"Sure," Kevin said. "That's where they buried my friend Joey. And Tommy's buried there too. You know, the kid who had your room before you."

That revelation stunned Brandon. "Why didn't you tell me?"

"Why should I? It's no big deal. A lot of kids are buried there. The ones who were too sick for Dr. Hamline to help."

"I'm going back there—tonight," Brandon said. "After dark." Those cries for help were so clear in his mind. He knew it didn't make any sense, but they were so very clear. "And I want you to come with me."

"Come with you?" Kevin asked.

"Yes, if it happens again I want someone else to hear it too. Or are you afraid?"

"Afraid of what?"

"Afraid I'm right. That I did hear a voice calling."

"Okay, I'll come with you." A small smile formed on Kevin's lips. "It should be fun anyway. Sneaking out, I mean. And if we don't hear anything, you have to tell Katy there's no such thing as ghosts."

"Whatever you say," Brandon told him. "Now we have to figure a way out of here."

"No we don't," Kevin said displaying another impish grin. "I already know a way. I've snuck out at night before."

CHAPTER SIXTEEN

Climbing the stairs after dinner, Brandon wondered how Kevin would manage to get them both out of the mansion. He kept asking, but Kevin would only say, "You'll see, you'll see."

In the meantime, Brandon had decided to go back to his room for a while. He wasn't tired—he just wanted to be alone. He started down the hall. At the far end, he saw a nurse come out of Katy's room. "I'll be right back," she said and closed the door while balancing a barely-touched supper tray.

Brandon walked right past her. It was a different nurse than earlier that day. He stepped into the doorway of his room, but went no farther. From there, he secretly watched the woman waiting for the elevator. When she finally disappeared from his view, he left his room and ran to Katy's door.

He knocked lightly.

"Come in," Katy said.

He poked his head in the door. "It's me."

"Brandon, what are you doing here?"

"Can I come in?"

"Okay, but only for a minute. The nurse will be back soon. We'll both be in trouble if she finds you here." The girl smiled. "Thanks for coming to visit me," she added.

"How are you doing? I tried to come earlier, but you were sleeping."

"I'm doing okay, I guess. Dr. Hamline gave me another shot and it made me feel a little better." She shrugged. "My stomach still hurts. I can't really eat anything."

"Why wouldn't they let me come see you?" Brandon asked.

"I don't know. It's just the rules. I don't like it either. I get so bored sitting here. They took my chair away so I wouldn't sneak out."

"Sneak out? Who said anything about sneaking out?"

"Out of my room," she told him.

"Oh," Brandon said with a smile. He wanted to tell Katy all about hearing the voice and how he and Kevin were going to slip out tonight, but at the last moment thought it better if she didn't know yet. "I should get going," he told her. He felt bad that there was nothing more he could do or say to help her feel better. "There's a new puzzle in the activities room. I'll make sure no one does it until you can help too."

"Okay," Katy said, then coughed. She gave Brandon a weak wave. He waved back and started towards the door. Suddenly, the door began to open.

"Hide," Katy whispered.

Brandon dashed over to the other side of the bed, ducking out of view just as the nurse returned.

"I think I sent the tray away too soon," Katy said to the woman before she stepped a foot into the room. "I'm still a little thirsty. Could I please have a glass of water?"

The nurse nodded and left again.

"Now hurry," Katy told Brandon.

He leaped up and exited the room. "I'll come back later," he said before closing the door.

"Bye," the tiny girl said.

Dr. Allison Cook left the Hamline Clinic and drove down the long hill towards town. She turned onto the road that would eventually cut directly through the heart of Wobblewash. Only a single car passed her on the road and it was heading away from town. Out of boredom, she tried the radio, but couldn't find any station to her liking.

Ten minutes later, she crossed the border into town and immediately all eyes were on her. From front yards and porches, from sidewalks and behind picket fences, heads would turn, no matter it be a man, woman or child, young or old, they all watched her drive by. Regardless of the rude stares, she wanted to see the town, and it gave her the opportunity to pick up a few personal items.

The picture-book houses quickly disappeared and were replaced with the shops and stores of Main Street. Allison pulled over to the first available meter. After getting out of her car, she was about to stick a coin in the slot when she read a small sticker that said parking was free after four o'clock. She smiled and put her money away—one of the quaint benefits of a small town.

Starting down the street, she browsed several of the shop windows, most of which displayed a closed sign. She continued on to the drugstore, only to find it was closed too—one of the quaint drawbacks of a small town.

Suddenly, from further down the street Allison heard the roar of laughter. Out of the door of the only open business, a tavern, came three gruff men. They all had the same style of dress—blue jeans and red flannel shirts. Their laughing broke up somewhat when they spotted her on the sidewalk. After a bit of whispering among themselves, they began coming towards her, though the smell of alcohol arrived before they did. Allison thought for a second about turning around and walking back to her car, but before she had the chance…

"Hey, pretty lady," the biggest of the three men said—he literally dwarfed the other two. "Never seen you before."

"Sure enough," the second man said, scratching the rough black stubble on his chin. "We would remember a piece of work like you." His eyes wandered up and down her body. "A fine piece of work indeed."

"Please, excuse me," Allison said, moving past the men.

"She don't appear too friendly, does she, Bobby?" said a third, rather thin man wearing out-of-date horned-rim glasses.

"No, she don't, Ray," the big man said. "No, she don't. What do you think we should do to make her more friendly?"

"How about dropping dead," Allison said.

All three howled with laughter.

"She's got a real mouth on her," Bobby said. "Just like your ex-wife, hey Curt?"

"Yeah, but her body's a whole lot better."

"Maybe if we ask real nice," Ray said, "she'll give us a little peek."

Allison definitely didn't like the way that sounded. She had left her pepper spray in the glove compartment of the car—forgetting that there were creeps everywhere—even in picturesque little towns. Curt reached for her hair. "I wouldn't, if I were you," Allison said, taking a step back.

"Oh? You should learn to play nice, little lady." Bobby grabbed her arm. Then, at great surprise to the others, the big man let out a tremendous moan. Allison removed her knee from the man's groin. He dropped to the ground.

She thought that would be that—taking out the largest guy usually solves the problem—she was wrong.

Curt stepped around to Allison's other side. She stood trapped between two men, with the third rapidly recovering from the low blow.

"We know how to deal with women like you," Curt said. "We're going to teach you a lesson about coming to our town and disrespecting us."

"And it's going to be a good time," Ray snickered, "...a good time...for us." He reached out for her, but that was only a distraction. Curt grabbed Allison from behind, pinning both arms at the elbow. She tried stomping on his feet, but he shifted them too quickly. He laughed with each step. Obviously he had a lot of practice dodging that defense.

"I get first feel," Bobby coughed out. He got to his feet, but stood with a slight hunch. He extended a cupped hand and chuckled, moving closer to her breast.

"Freeze!" a strong voice ordered.

To Allison's surprise, the man did exactly that—he didn't budge an inch.

"Evening, Deputy Kean," Bobby said without even turning around.

Allison's gaze moved over to the lawman. Neither her nor her attackers had heard his cruiser pull up. Now the bearded man she had met at, of all places, the cemetery, stood pointing a gun in her direction.

"Let go of the lady," the deputy commanded.

Unlike Bobby, Curt ignored the order. "This ain't none of your business," he said instead.

"How do you figure that?" Deputy Kean said, still staring down the sight of his gun.

"This ain't no concern of any outsider," he replied.

"If that's your only reason, I'm going to have to disagree. Now, let the woman go or I'll drop you where you stand." After a very brief pause, "You know I'll do it, Curt."

The man finally released Allison's arms.

"Now back up...slowly," Kean ordered.

Allison felt a great relief when he took that first step back. Curt couldn't have been the brightest bulb—she would've been the perfect shield. The deputy wouldn't have shot with her between him and the gun. Though seeing the stern scowl on Deputy Kean's face, she suddenly wasn't so sure.

"Now Bobby, Ray, you two get over by Curt."

Without any questions, the two followed the deputy's orders. Allison took this opportunity to put a little more distance between herself and those men.

"You two," Kean told Curt and Bobby, "lie on your stomachs."

Only Bobby complied with the order.

"You can't be serious," Curt said.

"It's not open to discussion," Kean replied.

"And if I don't?"

"Then I'll shoot you. Starting with your knees and working my way up until you comply."

That seemed to convince the man, but before Curt was completely flat on the ground, Kean gave him another command. "I want your head by your pal Bobby's feet."

"What the hell for?"

"Just do it."

The man mumbled something, but did what he was told. With the gun still pointed squarely on the men, Kean pulled out his handcuffs. Using his one free hand, he skillfully grabbed Curt's right hand and slapped on the metal cuff. Then took the other cuff and put it around Bobby's ankle.

"You crazy son-of-a-bitch," Curt snapped. "Why'd you do that?"

"Just making sure you two can't run off on me while I call for another car."

"What about me?" Ray asked, with a very shaky voice. The man was a simple coward without the support of his cronies.

"If you run, I'll have to chase you down. And I *will* catch you. I know you won't like that."

Allison could tell that the threat worked like a charm. The man plopped his butt down next to his oddly joined friends. At first, she thought the way the deputy bound the men was a little sadistic, but then realized how truly ingenious it was.

The man named Bobby outweighed his tethered chum by a good sixty pounds. Curt had no chance of carrying him in an attempt to getaway. And with Curt cuffed to Bobby's ankle, he would have to hang upside down while Bobby held him up by the legs—not exactly a feasible way to escape. And even if it were possible, Curt, the apparent leader of the three, would not subject himself to such an indignity. So as it turned out, the deputy had a very imaginative way of handling the situation.

With everything under control, Deputy Kean approached Allison. "Are you okay?" he asked.

"Yes. Thank you." She glanced back at the men. "Nice work."

"All part of the service."

"She was asking for it," Curt shouted. "Hey, baby, come on over, I still have one free hand."

"Shut your mouth," Deputy Kean yelled back. "The lady doesn't want to listen to your crap."

"Hey, I'm exercising my first amendment right to free speech." He cackled a laugh. Bobby joined in with a horselaugh of his own.

Allison eased closer to the squad car. "It's all right," she said. "I've heard worse things."

He smiled at her through his beard, then leaned in the open squad car window for the radio microphone. He held down the call button. "Base," he said.

"Base here," a voice crackled.

"I need Jimmy out here with another cruiser. I have some garbage that needs to be hauled away."

After a second, "Didn't quite get…you broke up. Please…your message." There was a loud blast of static.

"Damn radio," he said. "I should really get it replaced." He opened the cruiser door and slid across the seat. Quickly he unscrewed the radio from its mountings. He took a small folding knife from his shirt pocket and pried opened the casing. "Third time this week." Using the smallest blade, he adjusted some of the connections. "That should do it." He returned the radio to its usual spot and pressed down the button again. "Base?"

"That's better," the voice said with less interference. "What's up?"

"Have Jimmy bring another cruiser to the front of Peterson's Drug Store. We're going to have some visitors tonight."

"Peterson's Drug Store, you got it. Base out."

"Out," Deputy Kean said, then returned the microphone to its clip.

"You seem pretty handy," Allison said.

"You talkin' about the radio or dealing with thugs?"

"Both."

"One's my job, the other's a hobby."

"I'd like to thank you again," she said.

"No need really."

"Do you need me to fill out a complaint?"

"It would help. I witnessed most of it firsthand and that's enough for a short stay in a cell, but without a complaint, I can't file charges."

She nodded. "All right. I remember seeing the station when I first arrived in town. It's down that way, isn't it?"

"How about you follow me back? I'll be taking big Bobby in my car. Best to separate those boys."

"Follow you? That would be the easiest way, I suppose."

"Give me a couple of minutes to finish things here," he said, "and we'll be off."

"Take whatever time you need," she said, starting down the street to where she had parked. She looked back at the deputy just as another squad car pulled up. The tall skinny deputy who got out had to be Jimmy. Allison got in her car, started it up and waited.

~

The sun finished setting and darkness crept over Darcrest Cemetery. Irwin McGraff, the groundskeeper, was hurrying to his favorite spot next to a large rock that had cracked in two under its own weight. His flashlight cut the night and guided him on his way, though he had always thought he could make it without any help.

On nights like this when he had the need, he could practically smell his way to the spot. If Agnes weren't so pigheaded about the whole thing, he wouldn't have to sneak around. It was a real shame that a man couldn't do what he wanted in his own house. Who paid the bills after all? He did, but that argument never held any water with his nagging wife.

His light finally hit the big broken rock. He smiled then squatted down and pushed his hand into the wide crack. He had to extend his reach farther than he thought he would have to, until finally he felt something against his fingertips. He grabbed hold and pulled out the paper bag. Brushing off a small amount of dirt, he slid the bag down the neck of the whiskey bottle. Irwin unscrewed the cap and took a heavy swallow. After he drank, he let go with a happy sigh.

He was about to take a second swallow when a noise from the woods stopped him. It must have been a deer. How he wished he had his rifle. Deer were out of season, but that never stopped him before. Being far from town, he could easily get away with poaching a doe or two. Like last year, he dropped one at sixty yards, then hid the carcass in his truck. When he got home, he simply told Agnes he sideswiped it out on Old Simpson Road. She would never get close enough to the dead animal to see the bullet hole. And with all the dents in the truck already, she could never tell he was lying.

Before Irwin could continue his fantasy of acquiring a year's supply of venison, he heard the noise again. This time it was much closer. It couldn't be a deer after all. The sound was too close to the ground to be a large animal. The notion of a raccoon crossed his mind. It certainly sounded heavy enough. Though a raccoon would most certainly have seen his light and stayed away.

But the sound was definitely coming towards him and coming fast. He had heard stories of raccoons going mad with rabies and attacking the first thing they see. He figured it best not to take a chance. He had his bottle, so what was the point of sticking around anyway?

Irwin started to take a step when something shot out from the brush. In the blink of an eye, it coiled around his ankles, tripping him to the ground. He hit hard, breaking his whiskey bottle on impact. Whatever it was slid up his legs with the sensation of a thousand mosquitoes, all biting and drawing blood at the same time. He tried to fight, but soon his struggle stopped.

An odd sensation forced its way into Irwin's mind—a single overpowering desire: hunger—an uncontrollable hunger.

A sharp knock brought Brandon out of a light sleep. He sat up in bed. Through his bedroom window, he saw it had already turned dark outside.

The knock repeated.

Brandon hurried across the room and opened the door. He found Kevin standing in the hall, peeking over his shoulder.

"You still want to sneak out?" Kevin whispered.

"It was my idea," Brandon replied in the same hushed tone.

"Okay then. Meet me in the TV room right next to the dining room. Be there in a half-hour. Don't be late. We'll only have a couple of minutes."

"A couple of minutes for what?"

"You'll see," again was all Kevin would say while disappearing down the dark hall.

Brandon closed the door and started back to his bed. He didn't bother to turn the lights on. The moon glowing through the window was just enough to guide his way.

He sat on the edge of his bed and could feel the tight grip of sleep tugging at him. Brandon wanted to lie down, but knew that would be a big mistake. It would be too easy to fall back to sleep now and he feared that this time it would be for much more than a half-hour. By Kevin's words, he could not afford to be even a minute late.

The image of Katy lying in her bed popped into his mind. He began to regret his decision about not telling her what he and Kevin were planning. At the time, he didn't say anything because he didn't want her to worry. She didn't look at all well—telling her about their night visit to the woods might make things worse. He hoped she would be okay, though down deep, and he couldn't explain why, he knew different. Brandon hated thinking such a dreadful thought and tried with all his might to push it away, but he couldn't—and that made him sad. Katy was the closest thing to a friend he had, even more so than Kevin. If he could he would easily exchange the two and have Katy come with him instead, but her wheelchair and now her sickness made that impossible. It wasn't that he didn't like Kevin, he did—very much so. Katy just had a gentleness about her—a kindness. She made him feel welcome the moment they met, which turned to an instant friendship.

Help me.

Those words tore Brandon from his thoughts. He rushed over to the window and stared out at the woods. Brandon stood motionless for a moment. Along with the words, there was something more—a strange feeling. He couldn't describe it and he hadn't felt it before—it was something new.

Help me.

The words took on a more dire tone—an almost painful tone. He tried to concentrate on hearing the voice, but as quickly as it started, it stopped. Pressing his face closer to the glass, he could make out the shadowy form of the trees. To his shock and amazement, he also saw a bright orange ball bouncing back and forth at great speed throughout the tall growth. He watched for several moments until he realized what he was looking at. It was a light. Someone was walking by the edge of the woods with a flashlight or lantern.

Brandon's first thought was to go find Kevin—he even went to his bedroom door and pulled it open. But before stepping into the hall, he stopped himself. He had no idea where Kevin would be—maybe the TV room, but with twenty-five minutes remaining before their agreed time it seemed doubtful. Having no other choice, Brandon shut the door and returned to the window.

Could he have imagined it, he wondered. Maybe it was only moonlight bouncing off something shiny. No, he told himself, an ordinary reflection couldn't speed about by itself. He gazed out for any other movement, but detected none. He waited for over five minutes—still nothing. He had no doubt of what he had seen—the question then became who or what made that light—and what about the voice—that pain-filled voice.

Another five minutes had passed. There was neither light nor sound as if something had happened to switch them both off. He slipped back over to the edge of his bed. He sat. All he could do now was wait. The clock on the nightstand told him he still had fifteen minutes to go—a long fifteen minutes.

CHAPTER SEVENTEEN

"And what is the girl's current condition?" Fisk asked directly to Edward Hamline. He pulled a cigar from his inside jacket pocket and snipped off the end with a stainless steel cutter. Then he followed that action by pulling out a silver lighter. He lit the cigar.

Edward waited to answer the question until Charles Fisk blew out a heavy bellow of smoke. "I'm afraid the diagnosis is not good. She is starting to experience cellular decay."

"I thought you had that problem solved," Jenny Gordon said.

"And you based your conclusion on what?"

"It's been a while since you started her treatments."

"I've been able to slow the adverse effects, not eliminate them."

"You led us to believe…" Jenny snapped.

"You believed what you wanted to believe," Hamline snapped back.

"This bickering is getting us nowhere," Fisk said, taking another pull on his cigar.

Fisk had called this meeting and all three met at his estate. They sat in a large study, which was furnished with only the finest and most expensive trappings. The walls were covered with all manner of what Fisk liked to call his trophies. He had the usual deer and bear heads, but next to them were plaques and citations of humanitarian achievements.

Jenny Gordon and Edward Hamline arrived in separate cars. First, because it was easier to slip out at different times. Second, it wouldn't look too good for them to be seen together in the same car at that time of night. Third, they didn't like each other.

Edward rose from his chair and began to pace. Sucking in a deep breath, he shuffled across the floor, his arms flung in the air. "There are many complications to be overcome. More than I ever imagined."

"You've had years," Jenny said. "And what progress have you made?"

"He's gotten further than any one else," Fisk said, coming to the man's defense. Edward stopped dead in his tracks, but before he could speak, Fisk said, "Still, I would have expected more."

"You know what I'm faced with," Edward said. "I have advanced my research to a point beyond anything else in the field of genetic therapy."

"But keep in mind," Jenny said, "the basis for your research and the efforts that it took to get your material. If it wasn't for..."

"Enough," Fisk shouted, slapping his hand on the desktop. "Can we end this arguing and get on to more important matters? I don't want to hear you two squabble. I want progress."

"I am close," Edward said. "Soon I should have the right combination of amino acids to counter the destructive effects while keeping the healing properties intact."

"What about the boy?" Fisk asked.

"It's too soon to tell."

"But you said..." Jenny interrupted.

Edward immediately spoke up, cutting her off. "I said he would have a high probability of the right genetic pattern, but I never guaranteed an exact match. There are too many variables."

"That doesn't do me any good," Fisk said. "I want answers. Do you hear me, I want answers!"

Brandon stood by his door listening for the slightest sound. Lights out was twenty minutes ago—everyone should be in their rooms. He cracked the door and peeked out. His eyes confirmed what his ears had already told him—the way was clear.

He crept out into the empty hall. The normal illumination had been turned down to a third of its daytime levels. Carefully he pulled his door closed, but the bolt clicking into place seemed to echo like thunder. Releasing the knob, Brandon realized he had been holding his breath.

Exhaling, Brandon started down the hall. He tried to walk lightly, but cringed with each step. Even in tennis shoes, each step produced a muffled clatter. Fearing all the doors would open, his heart skipped a beat when the rattle of a doorknob came from behind him. He had to make a split second decision—either stay or run.

Within seconds, he was down and around the corner to the stairs. Fearing his pace had attracted others, he paused a moment to catch his breath and to make sure no one had followed. Except for him, the hall was empty. A half-second later, he continued on to the first floor.

Following Kevin's instructions, Brandon hurried on his way to the TV room next to the dining hall. He couldn't stop himself from constantly looking over his shoulder. He didn't realize how creepy it would be sneaking around the mansion at night. Suddenly, from up ahead, he heard the sound of footsteps. Thinking fast, he ducked into the nearest room. The last thing he wanted was to run smack into someone coming around the corner.

Staying very still, while peeking through the thin gap left between the door and its frame, Brandon saw that the footsteps had belonged to Fritz Ratford—and the man was heading straight for his hiding place. Within an instant, several scenarios raced through Brandon's mind—none of them good. Luckily, Ratford stopped two doors short of his position. Ratford turned his head both ways, then stepped into the room. A bright light filled the hallway, but was quickly snuffed out when the man closed the door behind him. Brandon waited a moment, then eased his own door open. He took a deep breath and hurried off.

With a fast heavy beat still in his chest, Brandon entered the TV room. The light had been left on and he thought Kevin must be waiting for him. However, his friend was nowhere in sight.

Several more minutes passed. He began to worry that Kevin wouldn't show up. Did he get caught or was this whole thing just a practical joke? Whatever the reason, he would still be sneaking out tonight—with or without Kevin.

More steps caught Brandon's ear. He feared it might be Ratford coming back, so he scooted down along the side of the couch. He eased some when he saw Kevin standing in the doorway. The boy didn't enter, but instead glanced down the hall to make sure he had not been followed, then he waved Brandon over.

"You ready?" Kevin asked.

"Isn't it a little too late to back out now?"

"Yeah, but I thought I'd ask anyway."

"Now tell me your plan," Brandon said.

Kevin gestured for Brandon to follow him to the dining room entrance, from there they continued to the far end of the room and to the white kitchen door. Kevin peeked in the square thick-glass window above its center. The kitchen was clear. He pushed open the door. "Through here," he said.

Brandon couldn't believe his bad luck. He had just stepped into the kitchen when the cook, Mrs. Pit, returned and found Kevin. "My lordy, you gave me such a start," she said.

Without the slightest hesitation, Kevin took the heads-on approach to the situation. "Hello," he said boldly to the woman. He released the door, letting it swing back freely.

Brandon didn't dare look through the small window, but he could hear the woman's angry voice. He imagined the hard scowl on her face. "What are you doing down here this time of night?" she scolded. "You should be in bed." Her tone was so sharp, so harsh.

Fearing she would yell at him too, Brandon stayed safe behind the white door. He thought her wrath would be double for him since he had managed to make it all the way into her kitchen. Kevin didn't answer her question right away and it seemed like a very long time before either of them spoke again. This was going to end his trip to the woods, Brandon thought. No doubt the woman would call Jenny Gordon and turn the two of them over to her. He hadn't seen Mrs. Pit many times, but the times he had, she always appeared so strict.

"I just wanted a glass of milk," Kevin said. "I'm thirsty."

"Milk?" she said. "You know the rules. Nothing to eat after bedtime."

"But I don't want anything to eat. I just want some milk."

"Milk is food," she told him, "and no food after bedtime."

"Please," Kevin said, trying his best to sound convincing.

"I don't make the rules, but I do follow them."

"But I'm very thirsty."

"Then have some water," she said, "but from your bathroom sink. I have to lock up the kitchen for the night. Some of us have families waiting. I've already used up too much time on you. Now go back to your room."

"It will only take a minute," Kevin said.

She stared at the boy. "I'll give you one chance. If you go back to your room right now, I won't tell Ms. Gordon that you were down here after lights out. I think that's more than fair. Don't you?"

"Yes, ma'am."

"Then get going, before I change my mind."

"I'm going," Kevin told her.

Those words shocked Brandon, still hiding behind the door. He was about to say something, but stopped himself.

"Goodnight," Kevin said.

The woman just continued staring at him. "Get going," she said.

Brandon could make out Kevin's departing footsteps. He didn't have time to make any sort of decision before the kitchen door opened. But it opened only enough for a pudgy-fingered hand to slip in and turn the light switch to off, plunging the kitchen into darkness—the only light coming from the window.

The next sound horrified Brandon. It was the sound of a key sliding into the lock, followed by a slight grind, and then a loud click. The door shook once as Mrs. Pit tested to make sure it was secure.

Brandon finally peeked through the glass, only to see Mrs. Pit waddling across to the dining room entrance. Once there, she reached over and turned off that wall switch as well. All light vanished. He didn't know if he should shout for help. The penalty at this point would be a lot worse than it would have been if he had revealed himself earlier.

He had to think—what should he do? He couldn't stay there all night. How would he explain himself in the morning? If he pounded with all his strength maybe someone would hear him. He could tell his rescuer he had gotten locked in by mistake. But most certainly, Mrs. Pit would hear about it, then there would be even bigger trouble.

A sudden knocking caught the boy off guard and he took a step backwards. He stared towards the sound, but saw nothing but an absolute blackness.

"Brandon?" a voice said from the other side of the door. It was Kevin.

"I'm locked in," Brandon said.

"No, you're not," Kevin told him. "This is working out fine. Just reach up and turn the knob."

"What knob? I can't see anything."

"You know, the knob for the lock. Just turn it."

Brandon's hands fumbled along the door until he felt a protruding piece of smooth metal. He took a firm hold and turned. To his relief, it sounded exactly like the click he heard when the door locked.

Kevin pushed the door from his side. "See, I knew it would work."

"How does this get us outside?" Brandon asked. "We can't see anything."

"Simple." Without warning, Kevin's face lit up. "Boo," he said, then laughed. "Here, take this." He handed Brandon a flashlight.

"Where'd you get it?"

"I told you this wasn't the first time I've snuck out."

Brandon switched on his light. "I know, but how?"

Kevin locked the kitchen door behind them. "Come with me." He led Brandon to a door at the far end of the kitchen and opened it. The stairs behind that door led down. "The basement," Kevin said with a smile. "And our way out."

With the flashlights to guide them, the boys went down the stairs. Brandon didn't like the idea of going into the basement. They always smelled so musty and were full of spiders. But when he took the final step and shined the light around, he saw it wasn't like that at all. It was clean and neat. The shelves were full of canned goods and dried foodstuffs, along with many other unmarked boxes. Obviously, someone had converted the basement to a dry, clean storage area.

Without saying a word, Brandon followed Kevin across the short subterranean room to a set of concrete steps that led up to a pair of cellar doors.

"You wondered how we would get out." Kevin climbed the steps, slid back an iron bolt and pushed open the doors. "Here's how," he said.

Going up himself, Brandon saw the clear, starry skies. Kevin had made good on his promise—they were out of the clinic—they were at the back of the mansion. Brandon looked up at his bedroom window, then out to the woods.

"Let's hurry," Kevin said, "before somebody sees our lights."

They ran across the grounds, keeping their lights low. It was a warm, perfect night. Being out of the city and in an empty field, Brandon never realized how quiet the world could be. All he heard was the sound of an occasional cricket. The night seemed darker too. There was a very slight breeze and it brought with it the smell of wildflowers. For a moment, Brandon forgot himself and stopped to take it all in.

"What are you doing?" Kevin whispered from several feet away. "Do you want to get caught?" As he spoke, it seemed as if he began to rise up and walk through midair. "Come on," he urged.

Brandon took several steps closer. It was then when he saw the fencing. Like Kevin, he climbed over the top. After landing on the hard ground, he spotted several stone markers and realized he was on the other side of the graveyard.

"We're not going through there, are we?" He never imagined he would be sneaking through a cemetery in the dead of night. The very thought sent a shiver through his body.

"Why not? It's the fastest way to the woods. You're not scared are you?"

"Maybe a little," Brandon said honestly. "It gives me the creeps."

Kevin let out a small snicker. "There's nothing to be afraid of. Zombies and vampires are only in the movies. Come on." Kevin started the march again. Despite his fear, Brandon followed behind.

It was strange, Brandon thought. He was scared, but also excited. Being out here gave him a sense of freedom he never knew before. He was taking matters into his own hands. He didn't run to anyone for help. Sure, Kevin did help him out of the clinic, but that wasn't the same thing. He had a mystery that needed solving, and he would meet the challenge head on. For the first time in his life, he felt in control of his own destiny.

The two boys marched past many more headstones. The farther they went, the less the monuments bothered Brandon. He kept his mind focused on the task at hand and listened for the voice. He didn't hear anything but somehow sensed he was right on target.

"How about it?" Kevin asked, keeping his light aimed a good four feet in front of them. "Any voices?"

"No," Brandon said, "not yet."

"We still have a little ways to go. Maybe when we get closer."

The boys walked over the small rise and the night surrounded them. If it weren't for the beams from their flashlights, they would have been totally engulfed. The moon high overhead glared down on them with its blank stare. The distant trees stood like twisted soldiers guarding some terrible secret.

Soon Brandon and Kevin came to the very edge of the cemetery—the woods threw up a natural barrier. Even though this piece of land had no headstones, it still looked like a graveyard.

"How about now?" Kevin said. "Anything?"

Brandon stood still for a second. He concentrated—concentrated hard. After a minute or so, he shook his head. "No, nothing." He stared into the woods again. They seemed even darker than the night. Their blackness was completely devoid of any and all light. Not even the moonlight could penetrate the heavy growth.

"Come on," Kevin said. "We've come all this way."

"I can't force it. It just happens." At this point Brandon was starting to have his own doubts. He had no real proof that the sound came from these woods. In fact, he had no proof that he even heard the cries for help in the first place. "I don't know what's wrong."

"Maybe it doesn't work with other people around," Kevin said. He looked deep into the woods, then shined his flashlight between two trees. The darkness seemed to absorb the beam.

Brandon shrugged. "I don't know. Maybe, I guess. I was always alone when it happened."

After several more minutes of staring into the woods. "Maybe we should go in," Kevin said.

"Why?"

"Maybe it will help. You don't hear the voices all the time do you?"

"No, but..."

"Well then maybe whoever or whatever is still too far away. If we go in maybe we'll hear something."

"I don't know if that's a good idea. What if we get lost? It's pretty dark in there."

"We won't get lost. And we have flashlights, don't we? Besides, we can see the lights from the clinic from here, so if we walk so we keep them in view through the trees, we should be okay."

"I suppose," Brandon said reluctantly, but waited for Kevin to take the first step. He had a real strange feeling about this whole thing. He didn't know why, but he could sense something was coming towards them.

"Let's go in," Kevin said, cautiously approaching the first tree.

But before the boys could enter the woods, a sharp rustle rose in the air. It was low at first, but the sound grew louder and closer. They stood still, shining their flashlights into the blackness. They saw nothing, but the sound kept coming.

"Do you hear that?" Brandon said wanting to make sure that the sound was real, not just something in his imagination.

"Yeah, I do." Kevin darted his flashlight back and forth, up and down, side to side. The sound seemed to be swirling around. It was one place, then jumped to another. Kevin's light always fell a step behind. "Maybe it's a bear or something," he said.

"I don't think so." There was another loud crash. "Are there bears in these woods?"

"Could be."

"What should we do?" Brandon asked.

"Maybe we should leave."

Both boys turned and were about to run, but something blocked their way. It was an old man. He grabbed his head and began to scream. Brandon and Kevin started to back away.

The man screamed again.

This time Kevin took off running.

Brandon was about to follow when he heard something that stopped him.

"Help me," the old man said. "Help me, Brandon, help me."

"Who are you?"

Before the man could answer, he let out a final awful cry. Then as Brandon watched with young eyes, the man's features began to disappear. His entire head started to collapse and melt. His shirt started to fall in on itself. And within seconds, the old man's clothes dropped to the ground —empty.

Brandon shined his light down on the crumpled pile. Something black was oozing out.

"Come on, Brandon!" Kevin yelled from halfway across the graveyard.

Brandon started to run. From behind him came those words.

Help me.

Brandon stopped for a moment.

"Come on, Brandon," Kevin yelled again. "Run!"

Brandon took another step.

Help me, Brandon.

The boy couldn't shake the image of that old man dissolving to nothing —he turned to nothing, but a pile of empty clothes. And the screams—the screams. Brandon ran towards Kevin, ignoring the pleas.

Help me, Brandon.

The words became weaker the farther he got from the woods.

Allison Cook drove back to the clinic after a four-hour stay at the Wobblewash Sheriff's Station. Once she left town that stretch of road became void of any streetlights. And with only her high beams to cut a path through the darkness, the night seemed especially black.

It felt good to be leaving town. The whole experience left a bad taste in her mouth. Though, she had to be careful not to judge the entire town solely on the basis of a few creeps like those three who tried to attack her, or the grumpy, nosy sheriff. Even her first meeting with Deputy Kean wasn't the most pleasant, but she had to admit he had more than made up for the coldness displayed at the cemetery.

After the incident with Curt and the others, she followed the deputy to a red brick building. Once there, it was a short trip up a set of concrete steps, through a glass black-stenciled door and into the main lobby. Allison remembered the look on the sheriff's face when he saw her walk in. It was enough to tell her he was not happy—not happy at all. Immediately, the portly man called Deputy Kean into his office. She tried not to watch them through the office window, but the man kept flailing his arms. When Kean returned, he told her he had been put on another call and that a different deputy would be with her soon to take her statement. Allison couldn't help but notice the hard glint when he glanced back at the office. Before leaving, he found her a chair and a hot cup of coffee.

During her wait, she overheard the sheriff speaking to one of his men. She heard only bits and pieces, but what she heard was something like, "outsider causing trouble" and "maybe she'll get bored and go." Her own pigheadedness stopped that from happening. Finally, when Deputy Kean returned from his "assigned" call and saw she was still there, he went ahead and filed her complaint himself—even over the angry stares of Sheriff Muldoon.

Allison slammed on her brakes, screeching across the blacktop to an abrupt halt. Lost in her thoughts, she had driven past the turnoff to the clinic. Shifting into reverse and backing up, she corrected the mistake and made the turn. Going up the hill, she saw the lights of the mansion—mostly on the first floor, only two on the second and none on the third.

She parked her car and went inside. For a brief moment, she thought about going up and checking on Brandon, but glancing at her watch figured the boy would already be in bed sound asleep. She would see him tomorrow. Allison smiled. If asked, she would have to admit she had good feelings about Brandon and his adjustment to the new people and surroundings. He was fitting in well, especially with some of the other children. In her experiences with Brandon, she knew he wasn't one to easily make friends—she was glad to see that had changed.

She took the stairs up to the second floor, where several nurses rushed past her. Surprised, she asked one of them what had happened.

"One of the patients is having troubles."

"Who?" Allison asked.

"I'm sorry, I can't give out that information. You shouldn't be here. Visitors aren't allowed on this floor."

"I'm not a visitor, I'm a doc…" Allison didn't even have time to finish when the woman dashed off.

Allison began a dash of her own. She started towards Brandon's room —her thoughts at the worst. She shouldn't have gone out tonight. The decision to give Brandon some time to himself may prove to have been the wrong one.

She was only five feet from his door when a nurse rushed out from a different room. She felt both happiness and shame at her relief that it wasn't Brandon getting all this attention. Again the door opened and another nurse stepped out.

"There's nothing more to be done," a male voice said as the woman pulled the door closed. "You and the others are no longer needed. Please pass that on."

Allison recognized the voice of Dr. Hamline. She walked up to the door and gently knocked. She had to knock a second time.

"I told you, you wouldn't be needed," Hamline said, opening the door. His eyes widened. She was the last person he expected to find standing there.

"May I be of assistance?" she asked.

He stepped into the hall, pulling the door closed behind him. "No," he said. "It's all over. She couldn't hold on any longer."

"Katy?" she asked.

Hamline nodded, then let out a deep sigh. "She showed so much promise. It's a shame really. Of all my subjects to date." He shook his head.

"She's not just a 'subject'," Allison snapped. "She was a little girl."

"Of course she was. And I did as much for her as I could. She lived months longer than she should have. Not to mention the quality of life." He glanced down the hall both ways. "This is not the time nor the place to discuss this. If you have something to say, come to my office tomorrow. If you would please excuse me, I have things to attend to." He reopened the door to Katy's room.

"When will you be contacting her parents?" Allison asked before the door closed.

"That won't be necessary, Dr. Cook. Both her parents are dead. We are the only family she has."

The door closed.

Allison had a real bad feeling about this, though she wasn't sure why. Was it still guilt that she felt happy Brandon was okay? Or was it something else? She had blown up at Dr. Hamline for no real reason. What he said about Katy was correct. He had helped her. He gave her a better life. Free from pain and suffering, a nice house, good and healthy food, even friends. She could only have wished that for Brandon and Dr. Hamline had made that come true. The only question Allison Cook worried about was the price. What was the true cost for Dr. Edward Hamline's generosity?

~

"You can't tell anyone about this," Kevin said. "Or say anything about how we got out."

Both boys sat up in Kevin's room for the last half-hour. He had turned on the one small light on his desk—it wouldn't shine under the door. Being up well past their normal bedtime, if any of the staff saw the light, they would most surely investigate. To make things worse, there was definitely something going on. Several of the staff had been rushing around. They both had to be very careful not to get caught now. They had entered the house the same way they left. Getting off the first floor was a snap. Navigating the second floor proved to be the real challenge.

"I have to tell someone. Maybe Allison, she'll understand."

"Are you crazy?" Kevin asked. "Do you want to get kicked out of this place?"

Brandon shook his head. "No."

"That's what they'll do if anyone finds out."

Brandon started to feel the pull of slumber and thought it was about time he left for his own room. He had had enough adventure and right now just wanted some sleep.

Kevin moved across the room and placed his flashlights back in their hiding place under some papers in the bottom desk drawer. Then he returned to the bed.

He looked at Brandon. "Is there something you're not telling me? Did you know that old man?"

"No," Brandon said. "How could I?"

"I hope he doesn't know who we are. If he tells anyone we were out there..."

"He won't tell," Brandon said.

"How can you be so certain?"

Brandon sat there silent. He tried to push the images from his mind. He didn't want to remember them anymore.

"Did he say anything?" Kevin asked. "Was he the one calling to you?"

"I'm not exactly sure. He did call out to me—called me by name. But his voice sounded so different than the one I heard in my room."

"Of course it would sound different close up."

"I don't think it was him exactly.

"Well, what did he say?"

"Nothing. He didn't say anything." The man just called out his name, but for some reason that terrified Brandon. How did he know my name, he thought all the way back to the clinic. He thought and thought all the way back—how did he know?

"You mean he just stood there watching you." Kevin stared at him. It was obvious Brandon was leaving something out.

"No," Brandon said, not wanting to talk anymore. He just wanted to go back to his room. Inside he could feel his stomach twisting into knots. He didn't want to even think about it.

"Tell me what happened," Kevin said.

"I don't know."

"Didn't I come with you?" Kevin asked. "Didn't I show you how to get out? If it weren't for me, you would never have gotten to the woods in the first place. You owe me."

"All right. All right. I'll tell you." There was a short pause and then Brandon said, "He melted." Brandon could see the stunned look on Kevin's face. "He dissolved. One moment he was there, another moment he wasn't."

"You're making that up."

"I'm not. And there's more. After he was...you know...gone, some black stuff came out of his clothes."

"What was it?"

"How would I know?" Brandon snapped. "How would I know?"

Kevin watched Brandon very carefully. "Hey, how do I know you're really telling me the truth?"

"Because I am, that's how."

"People don't melt," Kevin said. "Tell me what really happened."

"I did," Brandon said. "I did. Why don't you believe me?" He kept pleading with his friend that he was telling him the truth. "I wouldn't lie to you. I wouldn't lie. I swear it happened just like I said."

CHAPTER EIGHTEEN

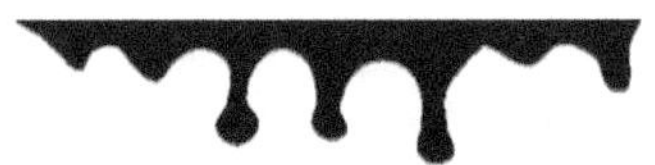

At the breakfast table, the gangly man, Fritz Ratford, approached Brandon and Kevin as they scarfed down their plates of scrambled eggs and bacon. He told them to go to Jenny Gordon's office after eating. Both boys looked at each other, but said nothing.

Finally, Brandon asked, "why?"

The man gave him a crooked, but cold grin. "I'm sure Ms. Gordon has her reasons."

"But..."

"Just go to her office. She's expecting you...soon."

The two ate much slower. The longer they stayed put, the better things would be for them. Ratford did say, "after they eat," after all.

After the serving dishes and milk pitcher had been cleared from the table, the boys had no choice but to follow Ratford's instructions. They marched down the long hall barely talking to each other.

At the office door Brandon whispered, "Do you think she knows about last night?"

"How would I know," Kevin said. "Knock already."

"No, you knock."

Kevin shook his head.

After a moment, Brandon was the one to finally knock.

"Come in," came from the other side. It was Jenny's voice. Brandon hoped their delay in the dining room would have sent her on other tasks—

it hadn't. He took the knob in hand and turned. Neither boy entered. They simply stood at the threshold, being too afraid to go in.

"Don't dally, boys," Jenny said, seeing their hesitation. "Come in." She stood up and met them halfway. Once she started walking, they started walking too, but at a much slower pace.

She touched both boys on the shoulder. "Come," she repeated, guiding them along. "Sit here." She stopped at the large stuffed couch. All this time the boys didn't say a word.

After she had them sitting, Jenny walked back around her desk and sat herself. She watched the boys for a minute. "This is always difficult for me," she started. "A task I hate to do, but one I must." She took in a breath and placed her palms down on the desktop. "Last night," she added, but then stopped.

Brandon and Kevin looked at each other.

"She knows," Brandon whispered.

"I have some sad news," Jenny told them. "I'm afraid Katy Redden is no longer with us."

Both boys' attention snapped forward.

"She died last night. She went very peacefully." Jenny's words were sharp and clear to make sure there was no misunderstanding. "I know the three of you were close. I'm sorry to be the one to tell you this."

"But I thought she was getting better," Kevin said. "She was even walking. I saw her. You saw her. Why did she die?"

"I don't know why, Kevin, except she was very sick. It's all very sad and I know I will miss her as much as you two will."

Brandon wanted to say something. He had snuck into Katy's room yesterday after supper. She looked okay then. He wanted to tell them that, but he was afraid he would get in trouble for sneaking in while the nurse was out for a few minutes. So he just stayed quiet and listened to the woman talk. He looked over at Kevin, who looked back at him with an angry stare.

"You two were her friends and I want you to know that you made her remaining time here very happy. You two should be very proud of yourselves."

Neither of the boys responded to the woman's comment.

"Can I go now?" Kevin asked.

Jenny gave the boy a sad smile. "Yes. Yes, you can go."

Both boys got up from the couch.

"Brandon, will you please stay a moment."

"All right," he said. He glanced over at Kevin. His friend continued on his way out, not once looking back. When Kevin disappeared through the open door, Brandon moved closer to the desk with short timid steps. "Yes, ma'am?"

"We're going to hold services for Katy later this afternoon, so your appointment with Dr. Hamline will be put off until afterwards. It really won't be much later. Maybe an hour or so."

Brandon nodded.

"I would understand if you would rather not go to Katy's burial."

"No, I want to go. I went to my mother's funeral. It was sad, but I knew she would've wanted me there. I know Katy would want the same thing."

"That's grown up of you, Brandon. Very brave. But then I know that of you, you are a very brave boy."

"Not really," Brandon said. "I'm not brave."

"I disagree. Dr. Hamline tells me you never complain. Not even about your shots."

"It's no big deal."

"It would be to me." She grinned. "Don't tell anyone, but I can't stand needles."

"Honest?"

"I hate them. Ever since I was a little girl."

Brandon shrugged. "I don't like them either. I just got used to them, that's all."

"I think there's more to it than that," Jenny told him.

"May I go now?" Brandon asked.

"Sure. Just don't forget about the change in your appointment with Dr. Hamline. You're very important to him and his work."

"I won't forget, ma'am."

Down in the east wing, Dr. Allison Cook sat opposite to Dr. Edward Hamline. She came to his office wanting an explanation—in fact, she demanded an explanation. A little girl had died and she wanted to know why. Why did her treatments fail? What were the adverse effects? She would ask hard questions and get hard answers.

"Frankly, Dr. Cook, it's none of your business." He sat back in his chair looking at Allison over his huge mahogany desk. "You are here as an observer and an observer only. Your observations are limited to and include only those things that affect Brandon Dahl."

"The death of Katy does affect Brandon," she replied. From the first day she met this man there was something about him she didn't like. That dislike could easily be turned to hate and at this point it wouldn't take much.

"How so?" Hamline asked.

"He and Katy had become friends."

"And that's fine. I encourage such things. Friendships are a vital part of normal life. And I feel a normal life promotes well-being. That's one of the reasons I treat children around the same age. The chances of bonds building are much greater." He slid up in his chair and rested his arms on the desk. "That withstanding, the unfortunate death of Katy Redden, her body's rejection of my treatment, is none of your concern. You have no right to any of my files or research. If you have a problem with that—if you find it unacceptable, then I suggest you take Brandon Dahl and leave."

That statement surprised her. Allison couldn't tell if he was bluffing or not. She couldn't read the man, which made it harder to trust him. She knew what trouble he went through to get Brandon here. Was he really willing to throw away the time and effort already spent?

"Take him," Hamline continued, "return him to your hospital, put him in your white sterile bed and wait for him to die."

"That was uncalled for, Dr. Hamline," she said shocked.

"But it's the truth, Dr. Cook. I am the boy's best chance for life. My treatment is his best hope. And I can honestly say, his last hope."

"You egotistical son-of-a-bitch," she started.

"You may be right about that," he said cutting her off. "But it does not alter the facts. Katy's own doctor could only prescribe painkillers to ease the time before her inevitable death. I pulled a lot of strings, put my reputation on the line to get her to my clinic. It is true she died. Of that, I can't tell you how sorry I am. But her last days were much happier than the alternative. You said it yourself—she and Brandon were friends. Do you truly understand the significance? Three months ago, she couldn't even recognize her friends."

"Nice speech," Allison said, after allowing the man to finish. "But let me tell you what I think. You don't care about these children any more than you would lab rats. And the only reason you feel sorry over the death of Katy is that you lost another guinea pig."

"Are you through?"

"I think I've said enough—for now."

"Fine. Now with that out of the way," he said emotionlessly. His phone rang. "Please, excuse me."

Allison rose from her chair and turned to leave. She barely took a step when...

"Could you wait a moment, Dr. Cook?"

She stopped and thought to herself, *now what?* After turning back, she saw Dr. Hamline signaling her to sit again.

"All right then," the man said to whoever had called. "Make sure everything is in order... Very good." Hamline returned the handset to its cradle. "I have some news for you," he told Allison. "And since you do worry, this may affect the boy."

"And that is?"

"Katy's funeral will be this afternoon at two o'clock."

"Today? So soon? How could you have arranged it so quickly?"

"I have an understanding with the local mortuary. They take special care with the internment of our children. They understand the need to have this trauma dealt with as soon as possible, so the children can adjust."

"Adjust? Adjust to what?"

"To the loss, Dr. Cook. These children all know they are going to die. And until my methods are perfected they will continue to do so. A sad-but-true fact. Someday I hope to be able to say different, but for now..."

"What does this have to do with Brandon?" she asked.

"You said it yourself. They were friends. He has expressed his wishes to attend the services."

"Brandon knows about Katy? I was hoping to get a chance to..."

Hamline raised a hand. "That won't be necessary. We have a procedure in place and Ms. Gordon is very apt in carrying it out. It's part of her job. But back to the boy—I think it will not cause undue harm if Brandon does attend."

"Oh, I see, he has your permission."

"No, Dr. Cook. He has *your* permission—or not. It's entirely up to you." He looked her dead square in the eyes—his cold black pupils cut through her. "We are done here." Allison was being dismissed like a lowly servant would be.

She didn't like that—she didn't like that one bit. But at least she didn't have to look at him any longer. His face began to disgust her—that arrogant smirk. She left the office without another word.

With each step her anger grew. She hadn't learned a thing. Now, she thought, she would have to take more radical steps to find out what was really going on here. Edward Hamline was hiding something and she planned to learn what it was.

~

The clouds kept strolling past the sun, contrasting the day between bright and shadow. They were white giants that threatened no rain and the breeze kept them in flight through the remaining blue sky. Brandon stood next to Allison. She held the boy's hand.

It had been a short ceremony and at the end, a tall skinny man wearing a coal-black suit with starched white cuffs walked past the priest and signaled for the casket, containing Katy's body, to be lowered into the ground. The thin man had a very drawn face with tight skin pressed to his skull. He smiled at Brandon with a toothy grin. That frightened the boy. It almost seemed as if the man wanted to say, "You're next."

With a wave of his skeleton-like hand, four large men pulled up on wide leather straps. The thin man slipped three planks out from under the coffin. He performed the task with such grace and ease, that it almost seemed a sacred duty. The four men in unison slacked the straps and the casket began to sink out of sight.

The priest opened his bible once more and began to read another passage of scripture. Words Brandon didn't hear. His focus was already split. Partially on Katy, and partially on the events of last night. His eyes constantly wandered across the graveyard to the woods. There was a loud, "Amen." The word snapped Brandon back to his surroundings. The group, made mostly up of the clinic staff, started to disband.

Brandon stood still for a moment just staring at the hole that held Katy's body. When the others began to walk away from the gravesite, he looked up at Allison. She smiled and gave his hand a gentle squeeze.

Suddenly, from behind them, "She must have been a lovely child," a man said.

When Brandon turned towards the voice, he gasped. It was the skeleton man. Brandon took a step back, not saying a word. What could he say? Or do? If anything, he wanted to run.

"Yes, she was," Allison said.

"I'm afraid I don't know you." The man extended a gaunt hand. "I know all the doctors and nurses at Dr. Hamline's clinic."

"I'm Dr. Cook. I'm not on staff. I'm a…a visitor."

"Then it's a real pleasure to meet you. My name is Morris Latt, local undertaker."

"Nice to meet you, Mr. Latt."

"Kind words, considering the situation."

Over by the gravesite, one of the men shouted, "Should we start fillin' now?"

Allison couldn't help looking over. So did Morris. The burly man yelled something about needing to get back to town.

Morris let out a slight sigh. "I'm sorry," he said. "But my regular groundskeeper didn't show up for work today. I have to do with the help I could get. Not very professional, I'm afraid."

While Brandon watched the two adults, he had to force back a tear. Katy was dead and everyone, even Allison, acted like nothing had happened, that nothing had changed. His friend was gone. A friend he had just seen the night before. Now he would never see her again.

"I hope you find your stay a pleasant one," Morris said grinning, showing his slightly yellowed teeth.

"Thank you," Allison said. "We should be going now." She forced a return smile at the thin man. "Good afternoon," she added.

"Afternoon," he replied. He bowed slightly, then turned away.

That was odd, she thought, watching the man shuffle off. Her eyes moved down to Brandon. "You okay?" she asked him. "You have such a far-off look."

"Just thinking," he wheezed out, not wanting to talk. If he spoke too much, he would start to cry and he didn't want her to see him cry.

"It will be okay," Allison promised. "I know it hurts, but I also know it will get better."

They began to walk. Brandon kept his head down, watching the grass pass under his feet. Then, without a word, Allison stopped. The boy wasn't aware of Jenny Gordon's presence until looking up. She had a beaming smile—the same one he remembered from his first day at the clinic.

"Would you like to ride in the car with me and Dr. Hamline?" she asked, kneeling down to meet his gaze. "Would you like that?"

At first, Brandon remained silent, but then asked, "Can Allison come with us?"

The expression on the woman's face was one of surprise and for a split second disappointment, maybe even anger. But as always the smile popped back. "Of course she can," Jenny said, rising to her feet. "Of course."

The two women locked eyes. If Brandon were older, he would be able to tell that the unspoken words were not pleasant.

"Unfortunately," Allison said, "we came in my car. I can't just abandon it."

"That is a shame," Jenny said. "But still, I'm sure you have no objections to Brandon riding back with us."

"It's up to him."

They started to walk once more and Brandon held tightly to Allison's hand. Every other step or so he would look up at her—she was watching Jenny very carefully, though he didn't know why.

The three made it over to a silver Mercedes Benz. The driver's window rolled down with an electric hum. Dr. Hamline leaned forward. "Hello Brandon," he said.

"I'm trying to convince him to ride back with us," Jenny told the man.

"That would be fine," Edward Hamline said, looking at his watch. "I would've been calling you down for your treatment soon anyway. This should save us some time."

"Well, there you have it," Jenny said. "I guess we have a decision."

Allison looked down at Brandon. "You go with them. I'll see you later."

Again, Brandon didn't speak. Instead, after Jenny opened the rear door, he jumped in. Jenny smiled at Allison and followed the boy inside the expensive car. Hamline's window rolled up and the engine fired.

Allison turned and made her way back to her own car. She got in, and from behind the steering wheel, watched the silver car disappear around the bend. She turned the key, shifted into gear and stepped on the gas. For a moment, she thought about catching up to Dr. Hamline and the others, but realized there would be no point.

She hadn't driven very far when something else caught her eye—something in her rearview mirror. Flashing lights.

"Great," she said aloud, then signaled and pulled over. Staring in her mirror, she watched Deputy Kean step out of his cruiser. She had mixed feelings about seeing him again—she wouldn't deny the strange pleasure that accompanied his sudden appearance, but on the other hand, being stopped by the law was never a good thing.

As he approached, Allison rolled down her window. "You can't tell me I was speeding," she said, when he got to the car.

"No," he answered. "Nothing like that. I just have a few questions for you."

"For me? Why me?"

"Because I'm hoping you have some answers."

"I don't know what information I would have."

"You attended the funeral services for the Redden girl."

"Is that your question?"

"Not quite," he told her. "The cemetery's groundskeeper didn't show up for work today."

"Yes, I know."

"You do? How, may I ask?" He pulled out a small black notepad from his shirt pocket.

"Morris Latt mentioned it after the funeral."

"You know Morris Latt?" he asked making a note, then returning his eyes to Allison.

"Not really. I met him just today. He introduced himself to me. Though to be very honest I don't know why."

"Really? He introduced himself to you?"

"Tall, skinny man. Sort of scary looking?"

"Yeah that's him," Kean said.

"Deputy, may I ask what this is all about? Is there a problem?"

"I'm not sure yet. I'm simply gathering information."

"You still haven't explained why you're asking me these questions."

"You were the last person known to be by the woods."

"The woods?" She stared at him. "What do the woods have to do with anything?"

"The groundskeeper, Irwin McGraff—we found his clothes out there. They were in a pile just outside the tree line."

"That's odd. Why would he leave his clothes?"

"That's the real question," Kean said. "And I'd ask him if I could find him. His wife reported him missing." The man's expression suddenly changed. "Have you seen or noticed anything strange around the clinic?"

"The clinic? I..."

Before she could finish her sentence, a second cruiser pulled up. It stopped alongside her car. It was Jimmy. "Sheriff's been calling for you," he told Deputy Kean. "He's plenty mad. Why didn't you answer your radio?"

"Must be out again. You know that electronic piece of garbage."

Jimmy nodded. "I suppose, but he told me to, and I quote, 'drag his ass back here' and that's what I intend to do."

"All right, I'm finished here." Kean looked back at Allison. "Just a warning this time, ma'am. Be careful." He tipped his hat and started back to his own squad car. "Radio ahead and tell 'em we're on our way in," he called out to Jimmy.

"You got it," Jimmy said.

Deputy Kean jumped into his cruiser just as the radio crackled to life. He quickly pulled the door shut and looked over to Jimmy, who was busy speaking into his own hand mic. Kean turned down the volume, but left enough to still hear.

"Sheriff, come in. Jimmy here."

"Jimmy, did you find that sorry s.o.b.?"

"Yes, sir, Sheriff. Out on Edgerton Road—near the cemetery. He's having radio trouble again. We're both coming in now."

"What the hell is he doing out there? Get your sorry asses back here now."

Deputy Kean switched off his radio, then reached to the back of the box and pulled out a small red wire.

CHAPTER NINETEEN

From the second-floor window of her temporary quarters, Allison Cook watched several of the children chase down butterflies. She wished Brandon would have joined them on such a beautiful day, but instead he was in the activities room working on a jigsaw puzzle—his simple way of mourning Katy. It would do no harm so she thought it best to let him be for now.

"Excuse me, Dr. Cook," a young woman dressed in white and wearing wire-rimmed glasses said from the open doorway.

"Yes," Allison replied turning around. "Can I help you?"

The woman gave out a tiny snort. "Oh no, nothing like that. I just came to tell you, you have a phone call waiting at the main reception area."

"For me? Are you sure?"

"Yes, ma'am."

"Who is it?" The list of possibilities flashed through her mind. A long list of two—her mother or Emily Stark, her department head at St. John's Hospital. But why would either of them be calling her here?

"He didn't say," the woman told her.

"He?"

"That much I could tell on my own."

"Thank you," Allison said. She left her room and headed down the hall. The woman in white didn't follow Allison down to the phone—she just delivered the message and left.

Allison made her way to the front desk. "I was told there was a call for me."

Without saying a single word, an older woman pried herself away from her computer screen, picked up the receiver and handed it to Allison. She then pushed a flashing red button.

"This is Dr. Cook," she said, still wondering who would be calling.

"Dr. Cook, this is Jason Kean."

There was a strange tone to the man's voice. She opened her mouth to ask him the reason for the call, when…

"Please, do not say my name. It's important that no one knows I'm speaking to you."

"All right." Allison smiled at the woman behind the desk, trying to hide her surprise. All of a sudden she felt very paranoid.

The deputy continued speaking. "I'm taking a big risk, but I need your help."

"My, that is interesting. Please go on."

"Can I trust you, Dr. Cook? Can I trust you?"

"Yes, yes," she grinned as if talking to an old friend. "I think that's a very reasonable request. Though I can't tie up this line—I'm sure the receptionist doesn't want to hear me prattling on so."

"Can we meet somewhere?" Jason asked.

"Well of course. That sounds perfect. What do you have in mind?"

"It will have to be somewhere secluded. We can't take the chance on being seen together."

"I understand completely," she said with another smile for the receptionist. "Situations like that are best to be avoided."

"On the other side of town, about five miles out on the main road, there's a run-down barn. It's all that's left of an old farm. Do you think you can find it?"

"I'm sure that's possible."

"Can you meet me in an hour?"

"So quickly?"

"It's important we meet as soon as possible."

"Very well then—I'll see to it. Goodbye." Allison handed the phone back to the woman and watched to make sure it had been hung up.

"Thank you," Allison said and started back to her room. It would be too obvious if she left right then. And by what the deputy said, it would be best if her actions drew little or no suspicions—she needed a plausible excuse to leave the mansion.

~

The sharp ping of the microwave signaled Morris Latt to push the stop button on his VCR remote control. He rose from his brown La-Z-Boy reclining rocking chair and hurried to the kitchen. Once there, he removed a hot bag of popcorn from the machine. The steam that shot up when he pulled open the bag stung his fingers. He dropped the bag on top of the microwave and shook his thin hand.

After letting his snack cool down for a minute, he poured the white popped kernels into a large plastic bowl. He tasted it and shook his head. Not enough salt, he thought, they never make these bags with enough salt. He grabbed the shaker from the table, and began sprinkling more salt over the popcorn with great authority. It took him three tries before it tasted just right.

Satisfied and with bowl in hand, Morris rushed back to his chair. But why did he feel the need to hurry, he wondered. He had watched this movie several times before on lonely nights, and it would always be there when he was ready just like it had been so many other times. Though he could never admit to anyone that he watched this kind of movie—he had a reputation to uphold. If anyone else knew of his passion, they would surely start making jokes behind his back. He was even forced to buy the movies he craved through the mail. He couldn't buy them in town—with Wobblewash being so small the word would spread like wildfire.

He pressed the play button. He could feel the anticipation building. Of all the movies in his collection, this one was the best. The others did fill a need, but not like this one. This movie made him feel the way he did as a young man. And nowadays, he needed that feeling even more. Working on the bodies of the dead made the experiences for the feelings of life more important, especially since he had no one to share that life. Maybe if he did he wouldn't need his movies. Many, many years ago, before he took the assistant job at the mortuary, he did date some of the plainer girls in town, some were downright ugly, but he being an overly skinny teen, he couldn't be too choosy. But after he took the job of cleaning the bodies, getting them ready for embalming, all the girls stayed away from him. Now, all he had were his movies.

The videotape came back on and the room was immediately filled with a loud wail from the TV speakers. The screen filled with the action of several moving bodies. His eyes lit up with glee knowing what would come next. Lou Costello had just found the secret room where Dracula had hidden the Frankenstein Monster. Morris let out a loud laugh and at the same time took a handful of popcorn.

He had all the *Abbott and Costello* movies, but *Abbott and Costello Meet Frankenstein* was the best. The other movies like *Abbott and Costello meet the Mummy* or *Abbott and Costello meet Dr. Jekyll and Mr. Hyde* were all excellent films, but how can anything beat the comical duo in the same movie with the Monster, Dracula and the Wolfman? Though thinking about it *Abbott and Costello go to Mars* was also a very fine work. But he always wondered why it was "go to Mars." The two comedians ended up on Venus —not Mars.

Morris put that philosophical question out of his mind until later. He let go with another deep chuckle watching the bumbling pair fumble their way through the spooky house. He sat and laughed, ate popcorn, laughed, ate popcorn—the next thirty minutes were a joy he lived for. Totally enthralled with the cinematic events unfolding before him, he didn't see nor hear the shadow creep up to the back of his chair.

Once more, he laughed out loud, but suddenly began gasping for air. Something had wrapped tightly around his throat. His skinny fingers pulled and grabbed at whatever was cutting off his breath. His struggle did not last long.

Morris Latt's dead eyes stared out at the flashing screen of the TV. Bud Abbott and Lou Costello were being chased by Frankenstein's monster—that had always been Morris' favorite part.

~

Allison glanced down at the odometer. She had driven twelve miles—three of which were already past town limits. Her quest had taken her through the center of town. Luckily, the way had very few onlookers. She remembered from her last visit that they rolled up the sidewalks pretty early in Wobblewash. It must be the best, maybe only, route, she supposed. If Deputy Kean wanted her to take a more discreet roadway, she was sure he would have told her.

She continued driving, all the while mulling over the excuse used for her sudden departure. She told the woman at the front desk that she had forgotten her asthma medicine and if anyone needed her, she would be in town picking up a new supply. Allison figured the best way of sneaking out was to do so in plain sight. Not hiding the fact about leaving, who would suspect the reason was a total fabrication?

Another mile down the road, she spotted the old barn in the distance. The gray structure loomed high in the middle of nowhere and nothing. Allison got closer and she could make out patches of blistering red paint dotting the sides of the dry timbers.

She turned off onto a small entrance road. The car bounced hitting a couple of large ruts. The gate had been left open, but her car was the only one there. She drove up as far as she could and stopped by the barn door. She peered out the passenger window. Was this the right place? Only one way to know for sure.

Allison stepped out of the car and immediately surveyed the area. The high grass told her that no one had been here in quite a while. By the looks of the barn, she could even think in terms of years. Then the barn door opened slowly with a very loud, almost painful groan from three large rusty hinges.

"In here," Allison heard a voice say.

She hesitated.

"Hurry please."

Allison rushed into the barn. Deputy Kean pulled the door closed behind her, producing another metal-on-metal scream.

"Thank you for coming," he said stepping towards her.

"What's this all about?" Allison asked, folding her arms in front of her body. She knew it was a gesture of being closed, but she didn't care. "Why did you call me out here?"

"I have to know first, can I trust you?" He watched her eyes carefully to pick up any signs of deception.

"I'd like to think so," Allison said with a smile, which seemed to go unnoticed. The man stood silent. "Look, you called me. Remember? You must feel you can trust me—at least on some level. What is it you want from me?"

"First of all, you're right. And secondly, what I'm about to tell you must stay between us—for now anyway. Promise me that."

"You have my word," Allison said. "Now, what is this all about?"

Jason moved several steps away and turned his back to her. "I believe the children at the clinic are in danger."

"Which children?"

"All of them."

Those words shocked her. Though, not in the way she would have thought. Instead of thinking of all the children, her thoughts were only for Brandon. Being a doctor that fact disturbed her. All she could say was, "How?"

"I believe Dr. Hamline is using them for his experiments."

"Of course he is," she said. He called me here for that, she thought. He didn't seem like a man to fall victim to small town paranoia.

"No, you don't understand. What he's doing is evil. He's subjecting those children to unnecessary danger. He's killing them."

"How do you know this?"

"I can't explain. I can only ask you for help."

"What can I do?"

"Being a doctor, you can ask questions, make certain inquiries without attracting too much attention. You know, professional curiosity."

"That doesn't explain why you want my help."

Jason took a deep breath. "You are in a position to go places and ask questions I cannot. It would be risky for me to be seen looking into this. I need someone on the inside."

"Risky? How?"

"Again, I can't explain." He turned back to face her. "You'll have to take my word for it."

She looked at him—there was something about this man. "All right—for now. Though I have trouble believing you can't find someone else to help you. I'm an outsider. With your resources, I'm sure you could..."

"I might be able to find someone, but..." His eyes stared past her almost as if he was about to make a painful decision.

"Then I ask you again, why me?"

"The boy, Brandon, you care about him."

"Yes, I do."

"That's why I asked you to help. I figured if you care for Brandon, you would help the others too."

"Is Brandon in danger?"

"No, not yet."

"And I'm not going to wait until he is. I'll take him away tonight."

"No, you mustn't do that. He's critical to their plans. If you take him away, you *will* be putting him in danger."

"Critical? How so?"

"I guess that's two things you'll have to trust me on. It is best that I keep that to myself—for the time being."

"You're asking a lot."

"Yes, I am," he said. "But I have no choice. I need your help."

"Okay, what do you want me to do?"

"For starters, you need to speak with Morris Latt."

"The undertaker?" she asked, the surprise clearly reflecting in her eyes.

"Yes. Without thinking, he said something about the condition of the girl's...Katy's body. He realized his mistake and tried to backpedal, but it was too late, though I acted like I didn't pick up on what he had said. He was very nervous about the whole thing. I think with the right questions, asked by the right person, he might crack."

"And that person is me?" she said.

Suddenly, a loud crackle came from the far side of the barn. "So, that's why I couldn't see you when I pulled up." Allison saw the roof of the squad car through a broken window situated opposite of the barn door, which was also the farthest point away from the road.

"Deputy Kean," a staticky voice said. "Deputy Kean come in please."

"I see your radio is working again," she said.

"Amazing, isn't it."

The man left the barn, followed closely behind by Allison. He walked around to his squad car, grabbed the radio mic and said, "Yeah, Kean here."

"We have a 10-70 by Reed's Creek."

"Can you repeat that?"

"A 10-70 by Reed's Creek."

"Did you contact Dave Johnson and his crew?" Jason asked. His face lost all color.

"They're on their way now."

"All right. I'll meet them there. Out."

"10-4, I'll pass that on. Base out."

The man stood by his cruiser for a moment staring at the microphone in his hand. Then he leaned in and returned it to its clip. He stood up and turned towards Allison.

"What's wrong?" she asked. "I can see it in your eyes."

"I think we're too late."

"Late?"

"That call was a report of a fire. A fire at Morris Latt's place."

"Oh my God," she said, feeling herself tremble. "Could it be just a coincidence?"

"Could be, but I doubt it."

"You have to do something."

"Without proof? With only my suspicions? That and fifty cents will buy me a cup of coffee." The deputy shook his head.

"You can go to the sheriff."

The man stood silent.

"He's in on it, isn't he. That's why you wanted to meet me in secret. So he or anyone else wouldn't find out about your investigation into Dr. Hamline."

"I think it's time we leave."

"Wait a minute. This doesn't end it. I have an idea. Are you willing to hear me out?"

"I'm listening," Deputy Jason Kean told her.

In the activities room, Brandon sat quietly at a table fitting together the final few pieces of his jigsaw puzzle. The picture was of another castle—Katy would've liked this one. Without thinking, the boy rubbed his arm on the exact spot where Dr. Hamline had given him the injection. It always itched after getting his shot.

The moment's distraction had him glancing up and out a nearby window. Outside he saw a small cluster of clouds rolling by, blotting out a bit of the setting sun. He couldn't see the woods from that side of the mansion, but still felt them beckoning him. After what happened last night, he tried with all his might to ignore those feelings. And that horrible image, he tried to banish it from his mind, but found it next to impossible—that man...that old man melted right before his eyes. He pushed away the thought and returned his attention to the puzzle.

He had been alone since his appointment with the good doctor. He had worked on the puzzle right through suppertime. Neither Allison nor Jenny came to get him, which suited him just fine—he wasn't at all hungry and he didn't feel like being around people—not even Kevin, his best friend.

Before his sickness, Brandon didn't have many friends—none really. The other kids on the block thought he was weird. More than once they would circle him and push him back and forth between them in a sadistic game of catch. He remembered how his mother would wipe his tears when he ran home crying.

But now his mother was gone and he had no one. Of course, there was Allison, but she would be leaving him too in the next couple of days. That thought made him very sad. He had put it out of his mind to the point where he had almost forgotten it. She would leave him, like his mother, like his father, like everyone did.

Though, he supposed his father didn't really count. He never knew him, and his mother never talked about him. Brandon would bring him up, but she would always change the subject. Distracting a small boy was a simple task—ice cream usually did the trick. When he grew a little older, he simply stopped asking.

Then he got sick. The doctors said he wouldn't live for more than a year or two. Brandon remembered hearing his mother crying late at night. He never told her he could hear her from his room and he always pretended he believed her when she told him he would get better.

Brandon recalled the day his mother died in a car accident on the way to see him in the hospital. He was lying in bed with all those tubes in his arm when Dr. Cook came in. She struggled, but finally gave him the news with small tears welled in her eyes. That night he prayed to God that he would die too, so he could be with his mother again—and maybe even with his father, though he didn't know that for sure. But his prayers went unanswered and he couldn't understand why.

Brandon reached across the table for the last two puzzle pieces—treetops. He always did the trees last.

Suddenly, the puzzle seemed to explode and some force knocked him backwards off his chair. The room seemed to spin as he rose to his feet and a loud laugh seemed to follow him up. It took a few seconds for Brandon to realize he was no longer alone.

His eyes focused on Buddy Platt, who still had a handful of puzzle. The large boy continued to laugh. He slowly opened his hand and let the pieces trickle to the floor.

"You and your stupid puzzles," he said. "Now that your little girlfriend is dead, you guys can't hog them anymore."

"Shut up," Brandon said. "Just shut your mouth!"

"Oh, listen to the big baby." Buddy shoved the remaining puzzle pieces off the table. They shot across the room, several of them pelting Brandon.

"Stop that!" Brandon yelled.

"What are you going to do about it?"

Nothing—he could do nothing—and both he and Buddy knew it. He had no chance against such a big lug. Brandon tried to move past the bully, but the boy simply pushed him back—and laughed.

"Let me go," Brandon said.

"Or what?"

A terrible feeling of being trapped shot through Brandon—an overwhelming desire to be set free. He wanted to run. He wanted to get away.

An anger began to boil within him—an anger directed squarely towards Buddy for keeping him trapped in this room. "Let me go now," Brandon snarled. He had never felt such anger before. Without any consideration of the consequences, he screamed out and charged the larger boy.

Brutally and viciously Buddy struck Brandon, hitting him square in the mouth with a tight fist. The large boy laughed again when Brandon dropped to his knees. But within seconds, Brandon got up—blood dripping from his broken lip. He stared at Buddy with cold eyes.

"So, you want another," Buddy said, cocking his fist back. He was about to strike when he saw something unbelievable. Brandon's lip stopped bleeding and the large gash began to close. Within seconds, the wound had completely and totally disappeared. "You're...you're some kind of freak!"

~

The sirens screamed out Deputy Kean's arrival. Driving up, he spotted two men handling a fire hose, already trying, but in vain, to douse the blaze—the house appeared to be a total loss. The pressure from the water truck's tank was not enough to control the flames. They engulfed the entire structure, turning it to a mass of oranges and yellows, blacks and grays. The heavy smoke poured up into the sky, which must have been visible for miles.

Jason stopped the squad car and got out. Immediately he felt the heat. It surprised him by its intensity. Several men ran by him pulling a second large hose. Apparently, they had managed to hook it up to a town water feed.

The men struggled with the hose—it snagged on the brush and undergrowth. Because of the time wasted hunting for the pipeline under all the heavy foliage, the fire quickly grew out of control, making the task of saving the house impossible. The only thing now was to stop the flames from spreading to the nearby woods. With the shortage of rain this year, it had the forest more susceptible to destruction by fire.

Dave Johnson, the fire chief, walked over to the deputy. The man had a slight limp, received several years ago, when the second floor of the Collins place collapsed on top of him. His suit protected him from the flames, but the main support beam had crushed his leg.

"Anyone in there?" Jason asked before the man spoke a word, even though he had the unsettling feeling he already knew the answer.

Dave removed his helmet and rubbed his forehead with his sleeve. "Don't know for sure, but it's a good bet. Morris left work at four-thirty today and knowing him, he probably came straight home." The man glanced over at the burning structure. "We won't know for sure until it's all out."

"Any ideas what could've started it?"

"Not yet," Dave said. "We'll have to wait until things cool down. But by the way it's going up, it could have been a gas explosion."

"I don't think so," Jason said. "Morris Latt didn't have gas. They couldn't run any piping through the cemetery; he was strictly wired for electricity."

"Like I said, we won't know until it cools down."

"Nothing against you or your men, Dave, but I want an investigator down here from the county seat."

"Why?"

Jason had to think of a reason quickly—the truth would be too dangerous. "Insurance fraud," he said. "There's a lot of money in that these days."

"Insurance fraud? But Morris Latt didn't have any family that we know of."

"I thought I heard he had a brother up north. Let's check it out to be sure."

"Whatever you say, Deputy."

The fire chief walked away and Jason stood staring at the burning house. It would eventually burn to the ground. He had a sinking feeling in his gut that this was no accident. Somebody wanted Morris Latt dead, and he had a pretty good idea who, but he had no proof—not a shred. And evidence had a nasty habit of getting "misplaced" at the Wobblewash Sheriff's Department. Only with an outside investigator did he have a chance of obtaining any proof of foul play.

Jason Kean glanced down at his watch. It was almost time.

CHAPTER TWENTY

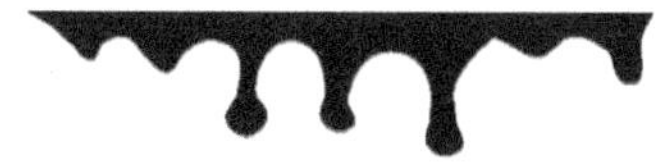

"What can I do for you?" Dr. Hamline asked, staring across the desk at Allison with that look of superiority. She really hated his smugness; if it wasn't for the fact that she needed to be here at this particular point in time, she would have tried to stay clear of the man. That not being the case, she put on her best smile.

"I would like to speak to you about Brandon." That was a valid-sounding reason to be here.

"Is everything all right?"

"You tell me," Allison said.

"I'm sorry. I don't understand."

"The reason I came without Brandon was to ask you directly, are your treatments helping him? If the answer is no, I don't want him to lose hope."

"You mean you want to keep the truth from him."

"No, I want to spare his feelings. So I ask you again, are your treatments helping him?"

"It has been a very short time since they started, but yes, I believe so. Of course, I must remind you to be cautiously optimistic, it is still very early."

The phone on his desk began to ring.

"Excuse me," he said, picking up the handset.

Right on time, she thought.

"Yes..." The expression on his face was obviously one of surprise. "He is? What does he want...? All right, if he insists—put him on." After a few seconds, "Hello Deputy, what can I do for you?" The look on the man's face quickly changed. "Damn!" He listened a few more seconds. "Are you sure it's my car?" Another pause. "Yes, all right. I'll be right up." Dr. Hamline slammed down the receiver. Then he remembered he wasn't alone. His grimace eased. "You'll have to forgive me, but something has come up that requires a few minutes of my time." He stood up. "If you wish we can take this up tomorrow."

"If you're not going to be long, I'll be more than happy to wait."

"I don't know..."

"Please, Doctor, my time here is growing short—I need to make my final decision. With your tight schedule, I'm not sure we would have another opportunity to talk."

"Suit yourself," Edward said, slightly annoyed. "I should be back very soon—I hope." Without another word, he left the room with Allison sitting there alone.

She waited a moment, then got up and walked over to the door. Listening carefully, she heard the far off echo of Dr. Hamline's footsteps. Once Allison felt confident he was well on his way, she began her search. She had to move fast—she wouldn't have much time. And her immediate problem was she didn't know exactly what she was looking for or where to look for it. She started with the file cabinet. All the drawers were filled with what had to be years and years of research. She would need a couple of days to go through it all. Obviously, that was out of the question.

Allison grabbed a folder out at random, hoping to get lucky. She found a heavily worded report on some blood specimens, including a breakdown of their components. It was similar to many other blood reports she had seen before, but the depth was unbelievable—even breaking the blood cell down to the nuclei. She closed the folder and placed it back where she had taken it from. She took another folder, but found the same thing. They might have been a little excessive in their analysis, but hardly anything telling or incriminating. She moved down to a different drawer. The files there were a breakdown of tissue samples to the genetic level. She did notice something strange, the files weren't in order by name, or any ID number, but instead they were in order by genetic code sequence. She opened several of the folders. Inside each, Allison discovered a genetic testing card with a code that matched the folder label. Again this was strange, but nothing that could help her.

Time was running out. She had to think. If whatever she was looking for wasn't in the file cabinet, where would it be? She turned towards the large mahogany desk—it seemed worth a try. Rushing over, she began pulling drawers.

Drawer by drawer, she found nothing unusual—only those typical things one would find in a desk. Then she reached for the lowest handle on the right-hand side. She gave it a pull, but it didn't give. Unlike the other drawers, this one was locked. Bingo, she thought, why lock a drawer unless you have something inside to hide?

The only question at that moment was how to get it opened. She examined the lock. It was an old desk, which was in her favor. The locking mechanism was very simplistic—just a barrel with a single pin that would turn when struck by a specific point on the key. She looked around the desktop and found the perfect pick—a thin tipped letter opener. Taking her tool she inserted it into the keyhole and tried to turn it. Nothing happened. It always seemed so easy on the TV.

Tilting the tool at a sharper angle, she tried again. This time the barrel did turn, but way too easily. She needed a position somewhere in between. On her third try, the sound of a click made her smile, but she reminded herself that this meant nothing. He might just be hiding a box of cigars or maybe even a bottle of booze.

Pulling the drawer open, she discovered more files. These however were labeled—labeled with names: Thomas Hover, Joseph Danes and others she didn't recognize. All folders had a date, in red, next to the name. The name on the sixth folder was Kathryn Redden—"Katy," Allison said out loud. And the red date—yesterday—the date of her death.

The last folder, marked with name only: Brandon Dahl, had her forgetting about all the others. For a moment she thought about taking the file and leaving, but quickly dismissed the idea. This file would surely be missed. She would have to rely on her memory. Opening it, she began to read.

The first page was data from Brandon's initial examination—what Dr. Hamline called his baseline. The second page was Brandon's admissions form—not a duplicate, but the original. She recognized her own handwriting. A strange thing to have in a medical file. She moved on to the third and fourth pages, but again these weren't medical records, but personal data.

What she read next caught her totally off guard. She held in her hand a copy of the court order changing Brandon's name. His real name had been

Brandon Manning and according to the papers, his mother had both their names changed when he was only three years old. Because it was changed at such a young age, Allison realized that Brandon didn't know he had been born under a different name—his mother had obviously never told him.

But why, Allison wondered. *Why change names? Change identities?* Again, she found her answer in the folder. This time her surprise turned to shock. She pulled out an official-looking document stamped with the seal of the U.S. Army. In her experience, that was never a good sign. And it begged the question, how would a private researcher, like Edward Hamline, get his hands on military information?

Allison flipped over the coversheet. *Odd,* she thought, seeing a date of January 30th, 1991 in the top right corner. *What could a twelve-year-old document have to do with Brandon?* She read on. Within a few short moments, both a sadness and an anger swept over her. That poor little boy had been lied to all his life. Though this information was so disturbing, she doubted if she could even tell him.

Brandon's father, Second Lieutenant Eric Manning, was committed to a mental hospital for the criminally insane. He had killed the entire crew of the Antarctic research station where he had been posted. For reasons unknown, he had mutilated several of the bodies and presumably buried them at some isolated location in the ice and snow, with the exception of three bodies he had hidden in a climate-controlled storage locker. When a rescue team was sent to find out why the crew lost contact with its main base, that team was also killed. When a second rescue team was dispatched, one equipped with weapons, only Eric Manning was found alive. The only bodies found of the original rescue team were that of Adam Hayes, a civilian pilot, and a first lieutenant, Bruce Manning, Eric Manning's older brother—both had been shot to death. In his delusional state, Second Lieutenant Eric Manning claimed that the personnel had been attacked and killed by some kind of creature.

Allison turned to the next page. The date on top of that sheet was almost two years later. She read it and gasped. It said that Eric Manning assaulted a security guard during an escape and his current whereabouts were unknown.

Holding back the truth bordered on cruel, but this sadly explained why Brandon was never told about his father—it explained the name change—it explained it all. An eerie silence had Allison looking up at the office door. She paused a moment, fearing it would open.

When that did not happen, the woman let out a breath and returned the document to the folder. Suddenly she noticed something on the bottom edge. She flipped back through the pages. On each sheet was the same thing—a printed date and time. This information must have been faxed to the doctor. But again that made no sense. The fax date was only two months ago and only a couple of days before Dr. Hamline had contacted St. John's Hospital regarding Brandon.

The final item in the folder puzzled Allison more than any other—it too was a faxed copy—a copy of a death certificate. She turned it to read the name: *Nancy Dahl*—Brandon's mother. The bottom date was written the same as the others along with "Page 4". This whole thing was getting more confusing by the minute. Who would have the power, the connections to gather such information and pass it on to Edward Hamline? And again, that nagging question: Why?

~

A small house sat far back from the road. It stood alone on a piece of old farmland that had long since been parceled into several lots. The glow from the windows did nothing to hold back the night.

Inside, two people, barely more than strangers, secretly met to judge the success or failure of their actions.

"I hope you had enough time," Jason Kean said.

"Yes, I did." Allison gave the man a curious smirk. "Dr. Hamline didn't tell me what you said when you called. Would you mind filling me in?"

He simply shrugged. "I just told him someone broke into his car. And whoever it was smashed out the front driver's side window."

"How did you manage that?" she asked.

"Nightsticks are for more than making a fashion statement. When he saw the glass spread out across his front seat, I figured you would have the time you needed. And just to make sure, I had him go over the car's contents to see if anything had been stolen."

"Very clever," she told him, "though a bit devious."

"Hey, you needed time—I got you time. Was it worth it?"

"I think so, but I now have more questions than answers."

"How so?" Jason asked.

"The information I found wasn't medical. He had papers about Brandon—papers he shouldn't have—information about his mother and father. Why he would have them or why he would even care is the real question."

"Brandon's mother?" Jason said. "What information would Hamline have about Brandon's mother?"

"Her death certificate for one thing."

Jason became very silent.

"And a court order for another. I'm guessing she must have been frightened of her husband—enough so that she had both their names changed."

A cold stare came over his face. "Frightened? Why would you say that?"

"It seems Brandon's father—a man named Eric Manning—was a soldier who went insane and killed a research team several years ago. After being locked up for two years, he escaped. She must have feared he would come after them—possibly to harm her or Brandon."

"No, that's not true," Jason blurted out. "I mean, it can't be." He ran his finger through the hair above his ear and scratched his head. "Look, I'm sorry. I'm a little edgy, I'm afraid—my sleep's been off a bit lately."

"I am a doctor—I could prescribe you something."

He smiled and raised a hand. "No, that's okay. I'll be fine. Tell me, did you find any connection between Eric Manning and Dr. Hamline's research?"

Allison shook her head. "Nothing obvious. Should I have?"

"I don't know," Jason said. "I thought maybe if he had that information, there might be a connection." After several seconds of uneasy silence, he added, "You want coffee or something?"

"Do you have any beer?" she asked.

He let out another smile. "Sure thing." He disappeared into the kitchen. Allison couldn't help looking around the room. It was very neat and organized. Most of the men she knew were such slobs. Moments later, Jason returned holding a glass and two bottles.

"I won't need a glass," she said, taking a bottle and twisting off the cap. She took a long swallow, then glanced at the bottle. "That's good."

"I wouldn't have thought you to be a drinker."

"I'm not really, but once in a while." She took another sip. "I like your place," she added.

"It will do," he said. "Rent's cheap. It's quiet—out of the way." Then he took a drink from his own bottle.

"May I ask you a personal question?"

Jason pulled the bottle away from his lips and swallowed. "Sure," he said, "though I won't promise an answer—depends on how personal."

Allison returned a slight grin. "Remember the other night when you saved me from those...those...men."

"You mean Curt Sutten and his buddies? Yeah, I remember. What about it?"

"One of those *gentlemen* called you an 'outsider'. What did he mean?"

"Just that," he said. "Some of the townspeople don't take kindly to strangers—no matter how long they've been in town—or even what job they have."

"I noticed. So you're not from here originally."

"Nope, like you I'm a stranger in a strange land."

"Oh, you've read Robert Heinlein."

"One of my favorite books."

"How did you end up here in Wobblewash?"

"I traveled around for a while and finally found this place. I was getting short on money and the rest, as they say, is history."

"No family?"

"No—not anymore anyway. Someday I'll change that."

"You must like it here?"

"Most of the time, except for times like tonight."

"You mean the fire. Were you friends with the man who died?"

"I'm not sure Morris Latt had any friends. He was a greedy little S.O.B. But that aside he didn't deserve to die like that."

"You don't think it was an accident, do you."

"Not in the least. Morris knew something and somebody wanted to make sure he didn't tell anyone else."

"Then there was a connection with Dr. Hamline?"

"I think so, but I have no real proof. Too many pieces are missing. Even with what you found, I have no more than I did before."

That was a strange thing to say, Allison thought. "What's our next move?" she asked.

"*Our* next move? I don't think it's a good idea that you get in any deeper. I don't want you ending up like Morris Latt."

"I'm already in it deep. I know too much to be left out now. The only way to protect myself is to help you find out what's really going on. Besides, there's another person involved. Brandon. I have to know what kind of danger he is in."

"He's safe for the time being."

"And you know that for sure? I still haven't ruled out just taking him away."

"We've been over that," Jason said. "They need him. And there's no telling what they will do if you try to take the boy from them."

"Tell me how you know this," she said.

"I can't. You've trusted me so far. Please—just a little longer."

Because of the sincere tone in his voice, she felt she had no choice. "All right—for now." Allison stood up. "I should be going. I don't want to draw too much attention to myself."

Jason did not disagree. "I'll walk you out."

Crossing the room, Allison asked, "How will I get hold of you if I need to?"

"Call the station. Tell them you're my sister from back east. When I get the message I'll call you back."

"Let me guess, you'll be my brother from back east."

"You catch on quick," he told her.

"And you, sir, are just too good at this sneaky spy stuff."

When they reached the door, the two stopped and looked at each other. "Be careful," Jason said. Then he opened the door for her.

"Thanks for the beer," she said.

"Next one's on you."

"You got it."

Allison walked to her car. She turned back and waved. When he returned her wave, she couldn't help thinking there was something sad about the man, something she couldn't quite put her finger on. Even so, she did trust him—he truly wanted to help both her and Brandon.

She got in and started the engine. The road was dark and devoid of any life. A good thing, she figured. It was probably best if she wasn't seen coming from the deputy's house.

The next morning, while Brandon finished dressing, he happened to catch his own reflection in the mirror. Surprised, he stopped and took a second look—his hair was growing back. He reached up and gently touched the stubble, fearing it was just a trick of light. He smiled, feeling the roughness against his fingertips. It was true—he had hair again.

Happily leaving his baseball cap behind, Brandon headed down to breakfast. On his way, he stopped by Kevin's room. He knocked once, but no one answered. He didn't bother knocking a second time thinking his friend must have already gone to eat.

Reaching the dining hall, he saw he had been right—Kevin sat at his usual spot leaning over a full plate. Brandon grabbed a tray. For food, he took a bowl of dry cereal, a glass of milk and a banana. When the server asked if he wanted eggs or waffles, Brandon declined, saying he wasn't that hungry.

Brandon walked over to the table and stood across from Kevin. "Hi," he said.

Kevin remained silent.

"Can I sit here?" Brandon asked.

"I don't care," Kevin replied.

Brandon took the seat and poured a small amount of milk into his bowl. He picked up his spoon and began to eat. For no reason, he had the weirdest feeling someone was watching him. He turned his head towards the back of the room. In the far corner sat Buddy Platt, alone as always. When the boy saw Brandon looking his way, he suddenly stared down at his food. Brandon still didn't understand what happened yesterday. Buddy hit him, then called him a freak and ran out of the room half scared to death. Bullies were never really tough, they're just cowards—and when it came to Buddy, his punches didn't even hurt.

Brandon took a spoonful of cereal. After about the third bite, he realized Kevin hadn't looked up once. He swallowed and said, "Those waffles any good?"

Kevin shrugged. "They're okay."

"Are you mad at me?" Brandon asked. He didn't really need to, it was quite obvious, but he decided to anyway.

"I don't know. Just don't talk to me."

"What did I do?"

"I wasted my time with you," he said, finally raising his head. "I should have been with Katy. Now she's dead. She was my friend."

"She was my friend too," Brandon said. "And I didn't know how sick she was. She looked okay when I saw her."

"You saw her?" Kevin asked. "When?"

"Before we went out. I sneaked into her room. The nurse almost found me."

"You got past her! I always thought that was impossible. When Tommy got sick, I must have tried five times to get by her. You're lucky you didn't get caught."

"I didn't care about that," Brandon said. "I wanted to make sure Katy was okay. She looked fine, but I guess I was wrong. I miss her."

"Me too," Kevin said. "Sorry I haven't talked to you since…you know…we found out. And sorry I didn't believe you about what happened by the woods. I heard some of the staff talking about how old man McGraff disappeared and they only found his clothes. It was him, wasn't it?"

"I think so."

"What do we do now?" Kevin asked.

"Maybe we should tell someone."

The boy seemed shocked by those words. "We can't do that!" Kevin had to force his voice down. He saw the food server staring his way. "We'd be in big trouble. Besides, no one would believe a couple of kids."

"Yeah, I guess you're right," Brandon said, and took another spoonful of cereal. He didn't want to get his friend in any trouble, so that left only one option. He would have to get some proof—he would go back to the woods—he would go back to the woods alone.

Just off Highway Exit 125 a rest stop had been constructed for the benefit of weary travelers. A large swatch had been cut out of the nearby forest and several picnic tables sat surrounded on three sides by tall, green trees —the perfect spot for a family outing. It was not very well known, but those who took a break from their long drive and were fortunate to discover it, often came back.

The Forbsons had stopped on the first leg of their journey back home from a family reunion. Patty Forbson had packed a picnic lunch of all their favorites—ham and cheese for her husband, Jack; bologna with mustard for Mikey; peanut butter and grape jelly for little Annie. That with a thermos of milk for the children, coffee for the adults, a Tupperware bowl full of potato salad, lime Jell-O with marshmallows and fruit chunks, carrot strips and chocolate cake for dessert, the feast was set.

"Can we play some Frisbee before we go?" Annie asked her father, between bites of her sandwich.

He arched his back to stretch out a kink. "Maybe your brother will play with you."

"Dad," the boy said, sitting at the far end of the table. "Do I have to? She's not very good."

"I'm as good as you," Annie said. "You just like to throw it over my head."

"You should play with your sister," Patty told her son. "It's going to be a long ride, you should both get some exercise."

"But Mom," Mikey whined.

"You'll play with your sister, young man, and that's final."

"Yes, ma'am."

After eating her cake, Annie ran to the car for the Frisbee. She came back and saw her father lying flat on an outspread blanket with his eyes closed and hands tucked under his head.

"Let's play Frisbee now, Mikey," she said.

He peeked over at his sleeping father. "No way, creep."

"Play with your sister," Jack told his son—not bothering himself to open his eyes.

"Okay, but I'm not going to have any fun." He trudged several feet away from the picnic table. He started to throw.

"I'm not ready yet," Annie cried out, running a good distance away. She stopped about ten feet from the trees. "Okay," she yelled.

After only three minutes of tossing the Frisbee, it was obvious Mikey didn't want to play anymore. He threw extra hard.

Annie reached up high. She stretched until she could stretch no more, but still the white plastic disc flew high over her head. "You did that on purpose," she called out.

"I told you you weren't any good at this," he laughed.

"You go get it," Annie told her brother.

"Why should I," Mikey replied. "It wasn't me who missed it."

"You threw it too high."

"Says you. But if you don't want to play anymore that's fine with me."

Annie looked into the woods. The Frisbee had landed a good six feet past the first tree. "Okay, I'll get it," Annie said. She crept over to the edge of the forest. "If I get a tick on me, you're going to be in big trouble."

"Yeah, yeah. Big trouble."

Annie took a hesitant first step between the trees. While sticks and leaves crunched beneath her tiny feet, she hoped she wasn't smooshing any gross bugs. After several more cautious steps, she reached down for the toy, but something stopped her.

From not too far ahead, the child heard a sharp rustling sound. She thought about turning to run, but her curiosity got the best of her. She eased towards a nearby thicket, slowly inching her way closer and closer.

Something was definitely moving under the heavy growth, but she couldn't make out what.

She leaned forward to get a better look and gently pushed a patch of branch and leaf out of the way. Annie's eyes shot open when she saw it move. Then she saw another, and another, still another.

The tiny girl wanted to call out for her family but that would scare them off—a whole nest of baby bunnies. The mother was lying on her side carefully watching over her brood. Annie had never been this close to wild rabbits before. They were so cute!

Then the mother rabbit's ears shot up. Her nose began to twitch, smelling the air. She didn't appear to be frightened, but nevertheless gathered up her young and started to scoot them along. The rabbit family began to move and Annie followed. She couldn't keep her eyes off the tiny balls of fur. They all had such big feet compared to the rest of their bodies.

It wasn't long before Annie had ventured far into the forest, suddenly finding herself surrounded on all sides by the tall dark trees. She looked back at the fresh-cut path she had made on her walk and happily knew she could backtrack at anytime with no problems. Unfortunately taking her eyes off the rabbits, even for that second, they had quickly disappeared.

Annie stood perfectly still, not budging an inch until finally hearing the rabbits rustling around under a leafy bush nestled behind some tall grass. She sneaked towards the sound and gently pushed the grass to one side. This must be the rabbits' home, she thought. Annie had to squint to see through the darkness under the bush, but what she saw this time was not rabbits.

The little girl screamed and fell back in terror. Something like a snake shot up past her. Whatever it was was black and slimy. At first, it appeared to be a pool of crude oil floating atop the dirt, but then it sprung high and dropped down next to her.

Within a blink of an eye, the black thing began to slither up the little girl's leg. It felt so cold Annie shivered.

"Please, don't hurt me," she said. "Please, don't hurt me." The girl began to cry. The thing crept up her shin to her knee. "Please, please." The tears streamed down her face.

The black creature stopped, hesitated, then finally slid off. It crawled away, retreating into the underbrush, disappearing from view. The crackle of dead leaves was all it left in its wake.

Annie sobbed. The rustling grew fainter and fainter. It took several seconds for the girl to feel the hand on her shoulder. Through soaked eyes, she looked up to see her father standing over her.

"What are you doing in the woods?" he asked. "You could've gotten lost." Seeing the tears running down his daughter's cheeks, he picked her up. "It's all right now, I've got you."

"It talked to me, Daddy. It talked to me."

"What did, sweetie?"

"I don't know, but I heard it talk. It's...it's very mad, Daddy, but not at me."

CHAPTER TWENTY-ONE

Dwayne Dormy sat stunned and in utter confusion, cradling the last swallow of coffee at the bottom of a dingy white mug. One nagging question he kept asking himself: what was he supposed to do now? He had no clue how to run the mortuary alone. He was only an assistant in preparing the bodies. He knew nothing of the business side of things nor did he have the skills to meet with clients—he didn't do very well with the living. With the dead, on the other hand, he felt at ease—they never talked back to him or complained when he was a little clumsy.

He had always been awkward, even as a child. His fumbles around people made him the butt of jokes and ridicule. Once, being short-handed during a service, Morris Latt needed him to help lower the body into the ground. Unfortunately, he lowered his corner much too fast for the others and ended up tipping the casket sideways into the hole. Morris never let him help again. Eventually, Dwayne found his place—with the dead. Sure, he would drop a tool during the preparations, but that was the extent of it. He was more relaxed around the corpses and in his mind they always laughed at his jokes.

The recent events had everything turned upside-down. He wasn't even sure who would get the mortuary with Morris gone. His boss didn't have any family, and he was Morris's closest friend, though that wasn't saying very much at all. It would all probably end up in the courts with the only winners being the lawyers.

Dwayne stood up, leaving his mug on the desktop. He left the office and started down the hall. Mrs. Beatrice Swanson was waiting for him. The woman had to have tipped the scales at over two-thirty-five. She had been his fourth grade teacher. He remembered how she would yell at him to take his seat, or to sit up in his chair, or not to talk out of turn. And she wouldn't stand for any back talk. To do so meant a wooden ruler across the knuckles. She always got the last word. Dwayne laughed on his way to the Preparations Room. It was now *his* turn to get the last word.

A satisfying smirk accompanied him as he continued down the long hall, totally unaware of the shadow lurking by the open doorway of one of the chapel rooms. When he passed, the shadow bolted out and hit him on the back of the head. Dwayne hit the floor face first and for him there was only darkness.

Skulking down the hall, the shadow returned to the office from where Dwayne had just come. The intruder moved with such speed and grace, knowing exactly where to go. Inside, it opened the file cabinet and began going through all the records. The sought file was not there. It wasn't in the house—an exhaustive search proved that. So it must be hidden somewhere else in this building, if not in this office.

If the file couldn't be found, then there may have to be another fire. But it was hoped it wouldn't come to that, this was a much bigger structure and it was doubted flames could bring it all to the ground. Not to mention the questions caused by another dead body, though if planned out carefully Dwayne Dormy could take the fall. Angry with his boss, he killed the man and burnt it all down, house, mortuary, all of it. And then, as fate would have it, his own wickedness trapped him. Killing Dwayne wasn't the issue—so many others had to be taken out of the way—one more wouldn't matter.

The shadow moved over to the desk and tugged open the top drawer. The wooden tray flew off its guide bars, falling to the floor, spilling the contents out into open sight. All six drawers were searched in this quick and sloppy manner. Nothing!

Then it was over to the bookcase. The shadow began pulling books off, letting them drop. The larger books were rifled through for any hidden papers. Again nothing! Looking around the room for another hiding place something odd was revealed. One of the desk drawers had been knocked on its side by a heavy book landing inside causing it to pivot on another drawer resting underneath. Taped to the bottom of the tipped drawer was a large manila envelope. Rushing over, and tearing it off, the envelope was opened. Inside was the missing file. Grabbing all the files to hide the theft of one, the shadow quickly left the office. Too much time had already been spent in this miserable place.

~

Allison Cook knocked only once, before a strange face suddenly appeared in the small window. She let out a short gasp and took a half step back, but then quickly calmed herself realizing Deputy Kean wouldn't answer the door himself—he would most likely stay out of sight until she arrived.

He had telephoned using the "brother from out east" signal. She answered the call cheerfully and with a big smile, knowing eyes were always on her. The deputy told her to come to the mortuary. Something had happened that might be of interest to her, but he wouldn't get into it over the phone.

The mortuary, being on the far end of the cemetery, would be a brief walk and "needing some fresh air" proved the perfect excuse to leave the clinic. She had followed Kean's instructions and went around to the side door. Even though the chances of being seen were slim, approaching the building on the blind side made for a more prudent course of action. A small concrete path led up to the gray metal door.

Allison heard the sharp snap of a sliding bolt, then the door opened slowly. "Can I help you?" a short, but stocky man with nervous eyes asked her.

"I'm looking for Deputy Kean. He said he would be here." The man stared at her blankly. It wasn't until that point that she hoped she had understood Jason correctly and had come to the right place.

She opened her mouth to repeat what she had just said, when the man spoke up, "This way."

Walked down the hall with the man, Allison noticed that he kept rubbing the back of his head. Finally he stopped by a door and pointed. "He's in there."

She walked alone into the office. "What happened here?" Her eyes tried to take in the whole mess. "A tornado?"

"Looks like it, doesn't it," Jason said. "According to Dwayne, the only thing missing are the client files."

"Which ones?"

"Whoever did this didn't leave a single one behind."

"Why would someone break in and steal all the files?"

"Maybe to hide which ones they really wanted."

Allison nodded. "Seems to be the case. How many of Edward Hamline's patients do you think are buried at this cemetery?"

"No idea," Jason said, "but we can sure find out. Dwayne, could you come in here please?"

A half-second later the stocky man entered. By the speed, he must have been waiting just outside the door.

"Dwayne Dormy," Jason said, "this is Dr. Cook. She'll be helping me with the investigation. She has a few questions for you."

The man's gaze moved over to Allison.

"Of the children who died at the clinic, how many are buried in your cemetery?"

"All of them," he said, sounding surprised by the question. "None of them had any family, so Dr. Hamline always paid for the services himself. He is a very generous man."

"What condition were the bodies in when they arrived? Did they ever have strange marks?"

"I wouldn't know," Dwayne said, with a tone of disappointment.

"But you prepare the bodies, don't you?" Jason asked.

"Yes, normally, but not them. Morris always took care of the clinic children himself. They were the only clients he would deal with."

"You never saw the bodies?" Allison asked.

"No, ma'am, never. Is that important?"

"Only if someone was trying to hide something," she said.

"And by the condition of this office and the missing files," Jason added, "that seems just about right."

"We've got to find out for sure. And I can only think of one way to do that." Allison was silent for a moment. "I need to examine the body of Katy Redden."

"That means exhuming the body," Dwayne said. "You'll need a court order for that."

"He's right," Jason said. "And that will take a few days."

"We can't wait that long," Allison said. Then Jason gave her a nod that he had things under control.

"And that's even if Sheriff Muldoon lets me file one. But by the way he's been acting lately, I rather doubt it."

"Well, then that's that," Dwayne said.

"Too bad really," Jason told him. "We'll never find out what's really going on. The only one with the slightest amount of information is you,

Dwayne. I suppose it will only be a matter of time before whoever trashed this office will be coming after you."

"What do you mean 'a matter of time'?"

"Think about it. Someone kills Morris Latt, then breaks in here. They were trying to destroy any and all evidence. It won't be long until they start thinking you might know something."

"But I don't," Dwayne said, his voice a little shaky.

"They don't know that. And when I file my report on the break-in, it will become part of the public record. I'm sure that will cause heads to turn. Though, of course, it's possible they already have their suspicions and are just waiting for things to cool down a bit. They could be coming for you at any time. If I could find out who did all this, I could stop them before they get to you. But that doesn't seem too likely. Even if I managed to sneak it past Sheriff Muldoon, which I doubt anyway, you know Judge Hanson—he's mighty cautious on these matters. He likes to take his time —consider all the facts." Deputy Kean shook his head. "Yep, only a matter of time."

Allison forced back a grin while she listened to the man's banter.

"Hmmm, they did murder Morris in his very own home," Jason continued. "I hope you're a light sleeper, Dwayne." The deputy turned towards the doctor. "I think we're done here, we should get going."

"All right," Allison said. The two took only a couple of steps, when…

"Please wait," Dwayne spoke up.

Ten minutes later, the three were standing at the gravesite of Katy Redden with shovels in hand.

"We must hurry," Dwayne said. He began to roll up the sod patches. And in two minutes, the first shovel of dirt was thrown on a large canvas tarp.

Allison watched as the two men re-dug the large hole. The work took another thirty minutes. Every so often, Dwayne Dormy would poke his head out of the hole. Presumably to make sure their deed went unnoticed.

Finally came the dull thud of shovels hitting the top of the casket. Both men brushed the remaining dirt off the smooth top.

"We'll never get this out by ourselves," Dwayne said.

"That was never the plan," Jason replied. "We just need a look inside." Jason cleared away more dirt along its side, then felt for the securing latches. Dwayne jumped out of the hole. He said it was to give the deputy more maneuvering room. Jason doubted that was the real reason, but it did give him the room he needed.

"Ready?" he asked, grasping the coffin lid.

She nodded.

Jason took hold of the handle, but applying the slightest pressure, it broke off in his hand. "It seems Morris was taking a few short cuts with his clientele," he said, while trying again by sliding his fingers into the gap between the lid and the base of the under grade casket. He lifted, breaking the other latch with ease.

"Oh my God," Dwayne muttered. His head snapped to one side and he threw up his lunch.

Inside the coffin was a body barely recognizable as anything human. Over half of it was gone—eaten away. The rest was a mass of blistered flesh hanging loosely upon what bleached bone fragments remained. The torso, emptied of all organs, attached to the shoulders and hips on only one side. Both arms were missing and most of the right leg—so were the jaw and throat, exposing the spinal column leading to the base of the skull.

Jason leaned in closer.

"Be careful not to touch anything," Allison said, surprised at the man's seeming indifference. During her residency at the Mother of Mercy Hospital Emergency Room in Chicago IL, she had seen many destroyed bodies from the result of car crashes, point blank shotgun wounds, fires, even knife fights. Dealing with such trauma on a nightly basis, Allison had developed a thick skin. But what gave this man his shield to the grotesque condition of that which was once a sweet little girl? It was almost as if he found exactly what he expected.

"The body almost appears to have been dissolved by acid," Allison added. "A method sometimes used to destroy diseased or contaminated tissue, but Katy had nothing contagious. Was the body in this state when it first arrived at the mortuary?"

"Don't asked me," Dwayne wheezed out, now on his hands and knees. "Like I told you, Morris handled the clinic kids himself. I never saw any of them. And if they're all like this, I'm glad I didn't." The man began to heave again.

"Have you seen enough?" Jason asked Allison.

"Unfortunately. You can close it up." She glanced over at Dwayne, still on all fours with a pool of vomit below his head.

Jason climbed out of the hole at the same moment Allison grabbed one of the shovels. "I'll give you a hand," she said.

In less time then it took to dig the hole, they filled it up again. With the sod rolled back, the site had practically been returned to its previous condition. In a couple of days, it would appear undisturbed all together.

"I want you both to leave now," Dwayne Dormy said, still slightly green. His popping eyes and curled lips told them he would be throwing up again at any moment.

Allison and Jason started back towards the building. Jason was very quiet for the first few minutes, then said, "Remember our conversation about Irwin McGraff—the cemetery groundskeeper who went missing?"

"Yes, I do."

"What I didn't tell you was that his clothes were found empty and intact. Down to his underwear still in his pants."

Allison nodded. "I heard vague rumors at the clinic, but I don't see…"

"The two are connected. The condition of Katy's body and McGraff's empty clothes."

"How?"

"You said the girl's body looked like it had been dissolved. What if that's what happened to Irwin McGraff? What if his entire body had somehow been dissolved?"

Allison gave him a strange stare. "How did you come to that conclusion?"

"Because there's something else you don't know. About three months ago, a group of campers found another set of clothes, but they weren't exactly empty—there was a leg from the knee down still in the pants, sock and shoe. The rest of the body was missing. With the lack of a better explanation, Sheriff Muldoon ordered it filed as a mountain lion attack. Now seeing Katy's body—well, the tissue damage is exactly the same."

"What are you saying? That Edward Hamline's treatments have been used outside the clinic?

"No, I'm not saying that…I'm not saying that at all—I just thought you should have all the facts."

~

The only thing Brandon hated more than the darkness and the silence was being alone in the darkness and the silence. But he hadn't dared to use the light switch at the top of the stairs. If anyone opened the door, it would most certainly alert them to his presence.

Armed with only a flashlight borrowed from Kevin, he cautiously walked across the concrete floor. On the far side, the fading beam of light hit a new stack of boxes—several more had been added since the last time.

He couldn't explain his strange need to return to the basement—he tried to resist, but the pull was just too strong. At this time of day, the task required a bit of sneakiness and good timing. He had to wait and watch for the kitchen to clear before he could go through. The staff usually took a break during the time between lunch clean up and supper preparation. It took over thirty minutes before the room had emptied.

It was a little chilly and Brandon's hand shook slightly as he followed his light to the steps that lead to the outside. The beam climbed each stair in his place, finally hitting the pair of cellar doors. Brandon knew full well that during the day this route to the woods was useless with the other kids playing in the backyard of the mansion. Besides, why sneak out through the cellar doors—during the daytime he could go outside to play like the others—no one would stop him. It was getting off the grounds that required a bit of cageyness. The best time would be after supper—the backyard would be empty. He'd eat quickly, then make some excuse about going back to his room feeling tired. The rest would be easy after that.

"Hello?" Brandon said softly, suddenly no longer feeling alone. He turned and scanned the room with his flashlight. "Is anyone there?"

A whisper answered his call—a whisper that sent a shiver down the boy's spine.

Brandon.

"Who's there?" Brandon hurried his light around the room. "Kevin? Is that you?"

Help me, Brandon.

"Cut it out, Kevin."

Help me, the whisper continued.

The words became clearer in his mind and Brandon knew it wasn't Kevin playing a joke. It was the voice that had been calling him from the woods. But now it wasn't coming from the woods—the voice—the voice was in this room.

"Where...where are you?"

Help me.

Brandon took a step forward letting the hollowing whispers guide his way. He couldn't help being a little frightened—whoever had been calling to him was now down here in the basement with him. Keeping his light focused straight ahead, he saw only a large crate snugged tight against the brick wall. One of its top planks had been pried up.

Help me, Brandon. Already, the words began to weaken.

He walked across the basement, not letting himself be controlled by his fear. He inched his way closer never taking his eyes off the large wooden box. Did the voice come from inside?

Hel-l-p... The final whisper faded to nothing.

Brandon slipped his fingers under the loose board and lifted it off. Cautiously, he peeked into the crate. Even using his flashlight, he had to strain to see through the darkness inside. There was something at the very bottom. He couldn't quite make it out, so he pulled off a second plank.

In the farthest corner of the crate, he saw a gray, almost blanket-like material—something laid hidden underneath. Slowly he reached in and took hold. He tugged hard. When the cloth gave way, a loud clatter erupted. Brandon jumped back, away from the noise. After a few seconds to gather his nerve, he eased forward and again shined his light into the crate. He saw what had made the noise—a stack of brown plastic food trays—now spread out across the bottom of the crate. That was all.

Stepping back, he was sure the whispers came from this spot. He waited and listened for any sound—another whisper, a half-word, he didn't care—any sound—any sound at all—but nothing came. And he had no place else to go. He had reached the end of the basement. He stood staring at his own light bouncing off the brick wall.

After what seemed to be a long time alone, Brandon snuck back upstairs. He peeked through a small gap he had made between the door and its frame. Taking a deep breath, he moved quickly out of the kitchen the same way he had entered—unobserved.

After a few moments, his paced slowed. He trudged through the halls, beginning to feel very tired. His treatments at St. John's Hospital always made him feel tired, though he hoped Dr. Hamline's treatments would be different. But he would rather get tired, than have one of his headaches.

He decided to return to his room—maybe lie down for a couple of minutes.

When he woke up two hours later, it was by the sound of a soft knocking.

"Come in," he said.

Allison entered the room. She saw him rubbing his eyes.

"Were you sleeping?" she asked. "How are you feeling?" She walked over and touched his forehead with the back of her hand.

"I'm okay," Brandon said. His voice seemed to catch in his throat.

"I thought maybe you would like to talk," she said.

"About what?"

"Well, about Katy for one thing. And maybe how you're feeling right now. You must be feeling bad about her dying. She was your friend."

"I miss her," Brandon said. He knew it had been only a short time since he first met Katy, but they had grown very close. She was always nice to him. Not like those other kids at his old school before he got sick—they picked on him and called him names. Katy never said a bad thing about him.

Allison took his hand and gave it a gentle squeeze. He squeezed back. The strength of the boy's grip surprised her—maybe even shocked her. She hid it by giving him a smile. "I'm sure you do. It's always hard to lose someone. I know it hurts, but remember, she's in a better place now."

"Do you think she's with my mother?"

Allison smiled again. "I'm sure they are together."

"Good, they can keep each other company."

"I'm sure they will." She rubbed the top of his head. "Feeling better?"

"Yeah…but…"

"Go ahead. I'm listening."

"There is something else," Brandon said. "I've been…" He stopped and turned his head away from her. After a few seconds of silence, he looked back.

"It's all right," she said gently, "you can tell me."

"I've been hearing…something."

"Has someone been saying bad things to you?"

"Not exactly. I hear a voice."

"What kind of voice?"

"Just a voice. It calls out to me. It keeps asking me for help."

"For help? How long has this been going on?"

"A couple of days."

"Why didn't you tell me sooner?"

Brandon shrugged. "I don't know. Just scared, I guess."

"I don't think it's anything to be scared about. There has to be a logical explanation. Where did you hear this voice?"

"Usually when I stand by my window." He pointed. "Right there."

She stood up and told him to follow her. "Right here?" she asked.

He nodded.

Allison knelt down and searched along the baseboard. "I thought so. Look." She pulled the nightstand forward. On the floor was the metal faceplate of an air vent. "I think someone's been playing a joke on you."

"How?"

"I bet one of the other children was yelling through a vent in one of the other rooms. My brother used to do the same thing to me when we were kids. One night I tried to convince my father my room was haunted. You should have seen my brother laugh."

"But it sounded so real," Brandon told her.

"I'm sure it did. Next time you hear the voice put your ear to the vent. I'll bet you'll hear it coming from there."

"There was another place too," he said softly—his eyes moved to the floor.

"Keep going. Where else?"

"In the basement."

"Basement? When were you in the basement?"

"A little while ago," he said. "Before I fell asleep."

The entire kitchen staff turned and stared at Allison when she suddenly appeared asking how to get to the basement. Not pleased to have a stranger in her kitchen, Mrs. Pit scowled before pointing to a corner door. Allison thanked the woman and thought it best to move on quickly. She hurried across the floor and could almost feel eyes, like pinpricks, on the back of her neck. She opened the door, flicked on the light switch and scooted down the stairs.

Reaching the bottom step, she stopped and looked out over the sub-level of the mansion. Brandon was right—"it wasn't yucky like most basements." His description, however, was lacking in several details, but she figured that was due to his method of sleuthing by flashlight. She didn't buy his excuse that he was just exploring, but decided not to push the issue.

Like the rest of the mansion, the basement had also been remodeled. It was a good use of space to create a storage area for canned and dry goods —there was even a potato bin. The naturally cool temperature made for the perfect environment.

Allison stepped down onto the concrete floor. Off to the far left, she spotted another door. That had to be it. She walked over, but froze for a moment before entering. Feeling a little silly at her hesitation, she gripped the knob firmly and turned. A stream of light cut forward into the darkness. She found what she had been looking for—the furnace room. She groped along the edge of the wall until she found another switch. Seconds later the room filled with more light. Besides the furnace, which had been shut down during the warmer season, there were two large capacity water heaters going at full bore.

She moved in closer to examine the main heating vent that led to the upper levels. The sealed sheet-metal duct would make it impossible for anyone to yell up a message of any sort, be it a cry for help or a simple hello. Even if it were possible, the whole house would hear it, not just Brandon. If someone was trying to scare the boy, they were not doing it from here.

She left the furnace room and headed to the other side of the basement where Brandon confessed to hearing his mysterious voice. She couldn't help wondering who would want to scare a sick child. As jokes go, it bordered on sadistic.

This section of the basement was exactly how Brandon had described it—full of boxes and crates. Plenty of places for someone to hide and pretend to call for help. But something didn't appear quite right. She looked over to the brick wall, and then back at the rest of the basement.

The west end of the basement had the furnace and water-heater room. The center section had been converted to a shelved storage area for easy access from the kitchen. The east end contained stacks of boxes and crates. With the dining area and kitchen above her almost at the dead center of the mansion, that would make the staircase leading down to the basement a good midpoint marker for the house. But the two halves weren't equal. This side of the basement was much shorter than it should be. She examined the brickwork closely. It took a sharp eye to notice the difference and she moved several crates out of the way to make sure, but she was right. A large patch of bricks were slightly different from the others in the wall—newer—not as faded. Great care had been taken to fill a large hole—even the mortar between them hadn't crumbled with age. It must have been done during the remodeling, she thought.

Allison looked back at the door to the furnace room. Its position mirrored that of the brick patchwork. At one time, the basement must have run the entire length of the mansion. Now it would only extend about halfway into the east wing—the east wing—Doctor Hamline's wing. But why? What was behind this wall?

Deciding she had seen enough, Allison climbed the steps and re-entered the kitchen, fully expecting more stares. Instead, she found the kitchen crew busy serving supper to the children and the staff. Mrs. Pit did give her a quick glance, but immediately returned to the task at hand.

Allison went out into the dining hall, but had to sidestep to the left to get out of the way of a server carrying two full pitchers of milk. After letting the man pass, she headed straight to the door leading to the main corridor. It was not a clean getaway.

"Dr. Cook," a familiar voice said, before she reached the exit.

Allison took a deep breath, turned and forced a smile. "Hello, Dr. Hamline."

"Join me for a bit of dinner?" he asked.

"Oh, thank you, but I was just going to check up on Brandon."

"No need for that." Edward pointed to a back table. "He's over there with his friend Kevin."

"So he is. It's good that he's made a friend." Not the lamest thing to say, she figured, but it was close.

"Yes, as you know I like to encourage such things. It helps with the treatments."

Treatments, Allison thought, I've seen the results of your treatments. She wanted to come right out and say those words to his face. Rather, she just smiled again, and said, "Of course you do."

"So, how about that dinner?"

"To be honest, I'm not very hungry right now…maybe I'll grab something a little later."

"Suit yourself," the man said, then shuffled off in his usual manner.

She watched Hamline for a moment, then looked over at Brandon. If she was going to act, she would have to act now—it was time to learn Edward Hamline's secret.

CHAPTER TWENTY-TWO

Allison hurried down the long hall of the east wing. She kept glancing back over her shoulder. Having absolutely no idea of how much time she would have or need, she could only pray Edward Hamline was a slow eater. If she got caught, there would be no valid explanation—no plausible excuse—and the consequences would be dire. It wouldn't simply be a matter of being tossed out of the clinic on her ear or even the possibility of arrest—the charge of industrial espionage had a nice ring to it. No, someone had killed Morris Latt to hide the truth—to protect some foul secret—and she could easily share his fate.

Reaching the end of the hall, Allison stood facing the door to Hamline's office debating if she should really go in. It wasn't too late to change her mind—to turn back like nothing had happened, but she had to have another look at Edward's files. Something about them kept nagging at her. They did contain reports on the blood work of his patients and she remembered them being very detailed and complex, and yet they weren't exactly what she would call research. And Brandon's file seemed to have nothing to do with research of any kind. They couldn't be the only files—there had to be others. Starting with Edward's office seemed to be her best bet, but if that didn't pay off, with the many rooms in this wing, they could be anywhere—if in fact he even kept his research files in this part of the mansion.

Looking up and down the hall, Allison mentally counted the remaining doors, contemplating the other possibilities and most likely locations for her next try. It was then when she noticed something she hadn't before. The office door seemed to be farther away from the end wall than it should be. Curious, she paced off the distance, which turned out to measure somewhere around twenty-five, maybe twenty-six, feet from door to wall.

She then went into the office and tried to pace off the same distance. The results were interesting, though somehow not surprising. She returned to the hall and tried again—without a doubt, the length was just over twenty-five feet. Allison tapped on the wall—it sounded a dull empty thud. She took a step back. The surface had no seams or splits, not even a scratch of any kind—it was flawless. Allison began to fear that her imagination had run amuck—the whole thing seemed so farfetched. Oh well, she thought, she'd already come this far.

And with that, she rushed back to the office and paced it off once more to be sure. The room measured slightly under twenty feet meaning it had been shortened by six feet or so—an excellent piece of work indeed. Allison stared at the wall, but the wallpaper was perfect—not a visible seam anywhere. And the only things on the wall were two wildlife prints in black lacquer frames and a large recessed bookcase.

She moved to the bookcase for a closer look. It all appeared quite normal—just medical books and journals sitting on shelves. Following a hunch, she tapped on the back panel—that too produced an empty thud. She carefully examined every inch of the bookcase and found a small latch hidden under the fourth shelf. She released it. The whole bookcase moved. There was some resistance, but she pulled it forward, swinging it out on large hinges. So much for her imagination running amuck.

Behind the bookcase a light snapped on, illuminating a deep stairwell, but a ninety-degree bend made it impossible to see the bottom. Cautiously she stepped in—the bookcase swung closed behind her. For a brief moment, she thought about turning right around and leaving, but her curiosity drove her forward—she had to know what Edward Hamline was hiding. Finally starting down, she took each step slowly and kept close to the wall, not knowing what would be around the corner. Suddenly, halfway down, the light snapped off, leaving her standing in the dark.

"Isn't that just great," Allison said, realizing the light must have been on a timer and that she had wasted the time pussyfooting around. She began groping her way along, praying she wouldn't fall and break her neck. In the blackness, she successfully managed to maneuver around the corner, though it was an eerie feeling not knowing from that point on how far the stairs would go.

After seven of the longest steps Allison ever thought imaginable, she came upon a wall. Blindly, she reached out to find the passage forward. It didn't take her long to realize she was at a dead end. She ran her hand along the surface until it struck something metallic. It wasn't a dead end after all—it was a door. She took a breath, turned the handle, then pushed. The light snapped on again, stinging her eyes. She didn't know which was worse—being blinded by the dark or being blinded by the light.

Her eyes adjusted quickly and she found herself standing in that section of the basement that had been sealed off—she found herself standing at the mouth of one of the best-equipped research laboratories she had ever seen. Though impressive, it wasn't the instrumentation that caught her attention and interest, but rather, on a shelf, she saw several stuffed folders and a set of black notebooks. She moved quickly to examine the bundles of paper. Rifling through the stack, she had reached her goal—these were Dr. Hamline's true research notes.

Allison then grabbed the first notebook. Opening it, she found handwritten text. But what surprised her was the date in the top right-hand corner: January 16, 1991. Edward Hamline hadn't written this notebook—the name on the inside cover was Jonathan Blackwood and the book was more of a journal than a scientific work. She had barely thumbed through half the pages when a noise made her turn back towards the lab door—someone was coming down the stairs.

She returned the journal to its exact spot before rushing back to close the door and then look around for a hiding place. The only possible place to hide was a small storage closet. She ran across the room, and pulled open the sliding doors, hoping there would be enough room inside. The doors barely settled back on their frame when she heard the lab door open and then close again.

The darkness of the closet made her nervous that she might accidentally knock something over giving herself away. With a gentle hand, she reached out through the blackness. The space was snug but clear enough that she could move without worry.

Then a sound made her heart beat fast. It was the sound of footsteps coming towards her. They came in such a determined pace and straight for the closet. Whoever it was must have seen her enter the upper office and was now searching for her. With the lack of other hiding places, it was not a difficult choice.

Out of fear, Allison took in a deep breath. The footsteps grew closer and closer. She thought she would cry out. In her mind, she could already see her own surrender. "I'm here, I'm here," she imagined herself sobbing. "You've found me, you've found me." What would they do with her? If it was the same person who killed Morris Latt, they would surely kill her too. They would know she was on to them.

Before another thought crossed her mind, the door shot open. Allison jumped to one side, pressing her body tight against the closet wall, trying to stay out of sight. She felt like an animal hiding from a predator hunting for his supper.

A hand reached into the closet and grabbed something from the third shelf. She couldn't take her eyes off the hand pulling back a pair of long heavy gloves. Then to her relief, the door started to close and she heard the footsteps moving away. A sliver of light cut into the darkness. The closet door hadn't closed completely.

She eased over to the light and put her eye up to the crack. The hand had belonged to Dr. Hamline. She watched him walk back across the room. He stopped at a wall phone, picked up the handset and punched out several numbers.

"This is Hamline," he said to whoever answered on the other end. "I need you to cancel my appointments for tomorrow." He paused. "Yes, even Brandon Dahl… I don't care! It's my call—I said cancel them!" He slammed down the receiver.

He pulled on the long gloves while at the same time walking over to a strange metal canister. She watched with curiosity as the man undid the latches and lifted off its lid. White vapor immediately rose up from the canister. Allison recognized the effect of liquid nitrogen hitting warm air.

With a pair of heavy metal tongs, Dr. Hamline reached in and pulled out an inner gray cylinder. It had a looped handle, which he used to pry it up, while steadying it with the fingertips of his free hand. A heavy frost formed on the metal casing. He carried it over to a center-island counter and placed the bottom end into a round inch-deep cavity cut into the surface. He secured it in place with clamps that locked into notches on the metal skin.

Next and with some effort he undid the latches of the looped top with his gloved hand. Once free, he popped off the top, which produced more white vapors. Hamline placed the top in a metal basin. Then from a drawer under the counter, he pulled out a strange device. It appeared to be another lid, but instead of a loop, it had two red rubber-coated grips. On the end he lowered into the cylinder were a pair of sharp pinchers.

With the new lid secured in place by the latches, Dr. Hamline squeezed the grips together. By the strain on his face, the task must have taken a lot of effort. After closing the grips, he reversed the latches then lifted off the lid and held the pinchers over a glass beaker. He pressed a small side button and the pinchers opened, dropping their contents.

Allison tried to see what had been put into the beaker, but it was too far away.

Edward had just secured the looped top back onto the cylinder when suddenly the door to the lab opened. Jenny Gordon walked in.

"What are you doing here?" Dr. Hamline asked.

"After your phone call, I thought it time we had this long overdue chat." She stood glaring at the man for several seconds. "Do you think it wise to cancel your appointments?"

"It can't be helped. I have too much work to do. With the recent setbacks I need to rethink the entire formula."

"Fisk is not happy with your progress, Edward," she said, bluntly. "He feels that you are not using all the resources to their fullest."

"I'm doing the best I can."

"He doesn't agree with that assessment and neither do I. You have only one child receiving the specimen."

Edward looked down at the glass beaker. "Because that is more than sufficient. I can learn what I need from him."

"Fisk wants you to continue your work with the other children."

"We agreed on one or two at a time. If too many die at once it will cause too much suspicion."

"I don't understand your problem. Brandon Dahl is one—simply pick another. His friend Kevin Reeves, maybe. Fisk paid a lot of money to get him here—now it's time he becomes useful. Just move him out of your conventional treatment group to your progressive group. It will make no difference to him."

"But it will make a difference to me. Nothing I do seems to work. You remember what happened to Katy Redden. I can't go through that again—I won't go through that again. I can't keep doing that to children."

"My, my, is the doctor developing a conscience?" She gave him a smirk.

"Maybe I have. And it's about time."

"We found you the boy, now you have to live up to your end."

"No, it's over. Find someone else. I quit!"

"Is that your final word on the subject?" Jenny asked him.

"Yes, my final word."

"Very well." Jenny pulled out a gun and without a word or even a blink, shot the man in the chest. Seeing this Allison flinched at the sound of the blast. She put her hand to her mouth to force back a scream. She could only watch while Jenny moved closer to the body, took another careful aim and shot Edward Hamline once more in the head. The woman gave out a satisfied smirk before heading out of the room.

Finally alone, Allison exhaled—she didn't even realize that she had been holding her breath. After a moment, she opened the closet door and rushed over to Edward's stilled body. By the hole in his head, there was no need to check for a pulse.

She moved closer to the island work-counter—and the gray metal cylinder. There were no markings to tell what was inside. Her focus immediately shifted to the beaker. On the bottom edge there was a black droplet almost an inch long. She was about to pick up the beaker when the black stuff moved—it moved on its own.

"It's alive," she said.

A hand touched her shoulder.

She screamed and turned.

"It's me," Jason Kean said. "I heard the shots from upstairs. Are you all right?"

"Yes, but I can't say the same for Dr. Hamline."

"I can see that."

"Jenny Gordon—you must have passed her on the stairs."

Jason shook his head. "No, I didn't pass anyone."

"We have to stop her," Allison said abruptly. "Before she gets to Brandon. We have to stop her!"

"You go—I'll call this in. You get Brandon and drive him to my house. You'll both be safe there."

She nodded and ran to the door. Jason moved over to the telephone and picked up the handset to make the call. But once Allison disappeared up the stairs, he put the phone back down.

Jason walked over to the cylinder. He gently touched the loop, but pulled back from the cold metal. He looked around and saw the heavy gloves still worn by Edward Hamline. He knelt down and pulled them off the dead man.

With the gloves for protection, Jason pulled off the lid. Inside was a black frozen mass, which looked like simple hard tar.

"I prayed I'd never see you again." He released the clamps and carefully lifted the cylinder from the counter.

~

Allison hurried up to Brandon's room. She knocked and waited. Since the dining room was the last place she saw him, it had been the first place she looked. But one of the servers told her he had already left, complaining about feeling tired.

The woman's hand shook—still she knocked again. She tried to remain calm, but it wasn't every day she witnessed a murder. After a few moments, there was still no answer. He must be sleeping, she thought. Allison knocked once more.

"He's not there," a voice said.

She turned to find Kevin standing in the hall watching her. "Where is he?" she asked. The boy said nothing. Instead, he turned his attention to the floor. "Please, Kevin, it's important."

"I don't want to get him in any trouble," Kevin told her while still watching his feet.

"I don't want him in trouble either. That's why it's important I find him. Do you know where he is?"

Finally, but reluctantly, he nodded. "He went to the woods." Kevin looked up at her. "He says a voice keeps calling him from there."

A sudden rush of guilt poured over her. Because she had doubted him about hearing voices, he must have gone off to prove it. If only she had believed him, he would be here now. She had to go after him.

Allison left the clinic, cut through the backyard and climbed over the fence exactly as Kevin told her he and Brandon had done the other night. She had no reason to think Brandon would take a different route. The moment her feet hit the ground, she began to run across the cemetery. Her eyes squinted—the woods were so far away. She still couldn't see him—she prayed she wasn't too late.

The closer she got to the woods, the better her view became. Finally, she spotted him standing, staring into the trees.

"Brandon," she called out. "Stay where you are." The boy didn't budge. Still she wasn't sure that he had heard her. Allison repeated her call. "Stay where you are, Brandon. Don't go in the woods."

"They hurt people," Brandon said. "They hurt Katy."

"I know, Brandon, I know. And I'm going to stop them. I promise."

Cautiously, slowly, she reached out to the boy, afraid he would bolt into the woods at any moment. If Jason was right about the previous attacks, she had to stop him from doing that at all costs. "Come over to me," she said. "It could be dangerous."

"The voice told me. The voice told me how they hurt people. I have to find it."

"Come with me and we'll find help. We'll find someone to tell, I promise."

"You shouldn't make promises you can't keep." Both Allison and Brandon looked up and over to Jenny Gordon. She had followed them up to the edge of the woods.

Allison and Brandon could only stare at the gun in Jenny's hand. With the smile on her face, it was as if she had wanted them at this spot all along.

"You know, don't you," Allison said.

"That there's something in these woods?" Jenny said. "Something that feeds on people? Yes, I've always suspected. I can only assume that it left the bodies of those test subjects after they were buried. Who would've imagined that the pieces would find each other and rejoin?"

"It knows you," Brandon said. "It remembers you."

"It should, I helped in its capture and brought it back from Antarctica over twelve years ago. I always thought it was intelligent, even back then."

"It's all over," Allison said. "You will never hurt any more children."

"Hurt them? You have it all wrong. The organism has the ability to heal—heal all injuries, all diseases. When the side effects are all worked out…"

"You mean rejection, don't you?"

"If you like, but with Brandon's genetic code, a formula can be developed to give the organism the matching DNA it needs while at the same time healing the host in which it is injected."

"Why do this in secret?" Allison said. "You could help so many people."

Jenny laughed. "I know you dug up Katy Redden's grave. You saw the results. Do you think anyone would allow open research with such side effects—the test subjects literally get consumed from within?" She shook her head. "No, a treatment would never be developed. Millions—maybe billions of dollars would be lost. Imagine what people would pay for an absolute cure—or a treatment to add years, even decades to their lives."

"Money!" Allison yelled. "This was all about money."

"Not was—is—is about money. After I see to it that you are—how can I put this delicately—eaten, I will take Brandon and we will start again somewhere else."

"Why Brandon? Won't he end up like Katy and the others?"

"Look at him. Don't you see how much stronger he is? The organism is in him now, bonding with his DNA—healing him. Just like it did with his father. He's very special—one in a million. Only members of his immediate family would be such a match."

"Eric Manning?"

Those words even surprised Jenny. "Very good," she said. "I see I've underestimated you. Well, knowing that will do you no good. It changes nothing."

"You killed them and blamed Lieutenant Manning—you killed the crew in Antarctica."

"No, not all of them. The organism did most of the work for me."

"And now you have to subject a little boy to your experiments."

"If his father hadn't managed to escape years ago, we would still be using his DNA for a template. During our search, we uncovered the death records of his wife—and the location of his son. All quite by accident really. And after finding out about the boy's condition it was a very simple matter getting him to our clinic." Jenny glanced over at Brandon. The hate in his eyes caused her to chuckle. "The one side effect neither Dr. Hamline nor I could anticipate was that he would be able to communicate with the organism once it merged with him."

"You can't possibly think you'll get away with this—other people know what's going on at that clinic of yours."

"I've changed my identity before, I can change it again. And if anyone does happen to stick their nose where it doesn't belong, it's easy enough to take care of."

"Like Morris Latt?"

"He was a fool. He should've taken his money and kept his mouth shut. And if you think Deputy Kean will cause trouble, don't believe it. Sheriff Muldoon will be sending him out on patrol tomorrow—a patrol he won't be coming back from."

"I wouldn't count on that," a voice said from behind her.

Without a thought, Jenny fired her gun, not at the Deputy, but just inches from Allison's feet. "Stop where you are or I will shoot her right now." She didn't even bother to look his way. "I mean what I say."

"I know you do."

"Move around where I can see you," Jenny ordered.

The deputy complied, stepping into view.

"Well, this certainly makes things easier."

"Does it?" Jason said.

"I don't know what it is, but I've never liked you. I'll be glad to see you dead."

A rustling in the woods cut her off.

"I think our guest has arrived." She cocked the gun and aimed it directly at Allison. "Don't try anything stupid, kid. You tell the creature to do the wrong thing and the good doctor is dead, followed by the deputy—and then even you, if necessary."

The black blob glided through the sticks and leaves of the forest floor like some giant snake. It slithered towards the group. Jenny Gordon took one quick step back watching the creature draw closer and smirking as it approached Allison. Suddenly it stopped. Brandon knelt down, reaching out for the organism. The very instant he touched it, it was absorbed into his skin.

"What are you doing?" Jenny shouted.

"I will not kill for you," Brandon said, standing up. The voice was his, but not the words. "Killing innocents is wrong. You are bad. You cannot hold us any longer. We will be one once more. The other is here—the other is here."

"Yes," Jason Kean said. "I am here." Then from his hands a dark mass formed. Within seconds, a black pool of living mass tore itself free from the man. The same thing happened to Brandon. The two pools merged and fused together.

"It's whole again," Jason said. "After all these years."

"It can't be," Jenny said. "How could you do that? The creature should have killed you. It's not possible."

"You're not the only one who can change their identity," the man said. "You robbed me of my life, robbed me of my family—I'm going to make sure you pay."

"Very clever—hiding in the open. I knew there was something about you. But that doesn't change anything. I will kill you, then take your son. The organism should be easy enough to catch again. With the right bait, that is."

"You don't understand," Eric Manning said. "It's not mindless. It understands now. It won't kill for you anymore."

"Maybe it won't, but I certainly will." Jenny held up the gun, taking aim. "Say hello to your brother for me, Lieutenant." Her finger began to ease back on the trigger.

Before she could fire, the black creature shot up from the ground and covered the woman. The gun went off, but her aim was spoiled. The bullet only grazed Eric's shoulder.

The creature engulfed the woman quickly. During a brief struggle, the outline of her face in a frozen scream could be made out in the heavy black skin. Then without a sound the mass of black collapsed to the ground. There was nothing left of Jenny Gordon or Carol Chambers or whatever her real name was. The black creature slid towards the others causing Allison to take a step back.

"It's all right," Brandon said. "It won't hurt you. It won't hurt anyone again."

The creature stretched out a piece of itself like a long finger and touched Brandon's hand. Moments later, it released its hold and retreated back into the woods.

"It said, 'thank you'."

~

After returning to the clinic, the state police were called in. With the body of Edward Hamline to corroborate their story, and his papers detailing the experiments done on the children, things moved rather quickly.

Within the hour, many of the graves were already being dug up for inspection. Sheriff Muldoon had been implicated by a ledger book found in Jenny's office safe, listing every date and dollar amount. It also made the connection between her and Morris Latt—an investigation into Jenny Gordon's past was underway.

Out on the porch of the grand house, while the sun began to set, a man and boy stood together, trying to sort things out.

"Are you really my father?" Brandon asked, staring up at the man with wonder. He had tried so many times to remember his father's face, it was hard to believe he was seeing it now for real.

"Yes, I am." He looked at the boy with sad eyes. "I...I only hope..."

"No need to hope," Allison said, coming out of the front door. "I've been through all the records. There's more than enough evidence to clear you of all charges. And if that's not enough, both Brandon and I can testify on your behalf. Jenny Gordon admitted everything to us. And with Ex-

Sheriff Muldoon telling what he knows..." She smiled at him. "You'll be a free man."

"It's been a long time since I've had a normal life."

"How did you get this far?" Allison asked.

"After I broke out of the hospital I went searching for the organism. I figured I could prove myself sane if I could find 'the monster' and the people who had it. I knew samples of my blood were being shipped somewhere, so I just followed the trail. It took quite a while and several dead ends, but eventually it led me here. And when I heard about the children in Hamline's clinic and his miracle treatments, I knew I was in the right place."

"You took a big chance that Jenny Gordon might recognize you."

"Well, the beard and ten years helped. And I spent as little time as I could being around her. I even sent Jimmy up on any calls when possible. Basically I stayed out of her way. I also counted on the idea that they wouldn't be looking for me in their own backyard. That and a little luck."

"Thankfully, it's over now," Allison said.

"And I'll be happy when I shave this beard off—it itches."

"I don't know," she said with a smile, "I think it suits you." She paused for a moment, then asked, "What about the creature?"

"It won't be a danger to anyone else," Eric said. "When it was first discovered in the Antarctic, it was like an infant. It understood nothing but its own hunger and its need to survive. When it merged with me those many years ago, I almost did go mad. It was like a baby trying to control the mind and body of an adult. Can you imagine the confusion of an infant finding itself with the thoughts and feelings of a full-grown man?"

"But it understands now?" Allison asked.

"As with all living things, it grew and matured. When the pieces tried to fuse with the children, it began to become more and more aware of the concepts of right and wrong. And it learned killing was wrong. It only did so to stay alive. The hunger was just too great for it. It's not evil—it was simply following its natural instinct for survival. It deeply regrets all the damage it has done."

"What will it do now? Where will it go?"

"The woods are immense. It should be safe there. It will feed on smaller forest animals for food."

"Why did it pick the woods in the first place?" Allison asked.

"Simple. It was scared and needed a place to hide—a place to wait. Pieces of its body were literally being torn apart. You have to understand, it's a life form so different from our own. Even when pieces were cut off, they were still connected on some level. They would seek each other out to rejoin. What one piece felt, all felt. Even frozen, the main mass had a sense of consciousness. It felt the pains of hunger too, but its greatest need was to be whole again. With a small piece bonding with Brandon it found it could communicate with him."

"It kept asking me for help," Brandon said, "but I didn't know what to do—at first."

"I'm just happy you're safe," Allison said. "Both of you. And you two should have a wonderful life. There's no sign of cancer anywhere in Brandon's system. Dr. Hamline was right about the creature's healing properties. It's a tragedy he and the others had to pervert it for their own greed. No one at St. John's is ever going to believe this."

"You don't have to leave, do you?" Brandon asked Allison.

"Do you?" Eric also asked. "You can always stay with us."

"I might just take you up on that offer."

The sound of a horn made them all turn their heads.

In front of the building, a long black limo pulled up. Charles Fisk got out and walked over to the group. "Well, Deputy, you gonna stick around? The town's going to need a new sheriff. Who would have thought that Muldoon would get mixed up in this whole sordid business? And I hate thinking how my money was used to do such terrible things."

"Of course," Eric said, flatly.

Fisk extended his hand. "Whatever you decide, the best of luck to you."

Eric did not shake the man's hand.

Fisk returned to his limousine. And while watching it pull away, Lieutenant Eric Manning couldn't help thinking that there was indeed a monster still on the loose.

ABOUT THE AUTHOR

Keith Ferrario enjoys horror movies, writing, and traveling. When it comes to writing, Keith's greatest influence for stories and writing style is the old black-and-white monster movies he still enjoys to this day. His love of horror goes back as far as he can remember. As a boy, watching *Shock Theater* and *Creature Features* on late Friday nights, he became a fan of Boris Karloff, Lon Chaney Jr, and Vincent Price. Shows like *Dark Shadows, The Outer Limits,* and *Kolchak: The Night Stalker* and comics like *Tales from the Crypt* and *The Vault of Horror* pushed him farther down this dark path.

Also by Keith Ferrario
Dark Carnival
Deadly Friend
Messiah

For more information:
www.keithferrario.com
keith@keithferrario.com
Twitter: @KeithFerrario

www.ingramcontent.com/pod-product-compliance
Lightning Source LLC
LaVergne TN
LVHW091031080826
845145LV00002B/447

* 9 7 8 1 9 3 8 9 9 0 2 9 8 *